Gunner Girls and

Gunner Girls and Fighter Boys

Mary Gibson

W F HOWES LTD

This large print edition published in 2016 by
W F Howes Ltd
Unit 5, St George's House, Rearsby Business Park,
Gaddesby Lane, Rearsby, Leicester LE7 4YH

1 3 5 7 9 10 8 6 4 2

First published in the United Kingdom in 2016
by Head of Zeus Ltd

A CIP catalogue record for this book is available
from the British Library

ISBN 978 1 51003 461 7

Typeset by Palimpsest Book Production Limited,

Print   in
by TJ In   rnwall

*Dedicated to the memory of my parents
Mary and Bill Gibson, whose service in the ATS
and RAF during the Second World War
was my inspiration.*

CHAPTER 1

HOME BIRD

3 September–December 1939

Heat burned May's cheeks and stung her eyes so fiercely that water trickled from their corners. She jerked away from the searing blast, and the wailing continued.

'Everyone's running to the shelters! Come on, May, we've got to go!' her sister Peggy's terrified voice came from the open kitchen door.

May slid the beef into the hot oven and slammed the door. She knew she should leave the dinner, turn off the oven and run, but though the siren's howl was like a cold knife slicing her heart, it opened a deep vein of defiance in May. If she could only carry on with the weekly Sunday dinner ritual, she told herself, then nothing could harm her home or loved ones. The keening note, rising in intensity, held all the essence of fear, the seeds of panic and the promise of loss that her eighteen-year-old self strained to resist. Momentarily, strength and youth drained from her limbs. But she held tight to the oven door, drawing courage from its domestic familiarity.

1

'I can't go to the shelter. I've got to put the dinner on!' May said, her face flushed with heat from the oven and irritation with the Germans. 'Typical! They have to choose a Sunday dinner time to start dropping their bloody bombs!'

She spun back to the oven, checking the temperature, while her sister strained to look up at the sky from the kitchen window.

'Where's George? He'll get caught in it, and Mum and Dad! May, what the bloody hell are you doing? Come on!' Peggy pleaded, her face an odd mixture of panic and bewilderment.

Just at that moment, their brother burst in, his face flushed, eyes wide with excitement.

'She won't come to the shelter, Jack. Tell her,' Peggy said.

'May! Didn't you hear on the wireless? We're at war! Leave the soddin' dinner and get to the shelter now!' His voice sounded unusually tight in his throat.

She stood her ground, back to the oven, as if shielding the heart of her home. 'No, I'm waiting here for Mum and Dad, and then we're having dinner.'

'The dinner'll be no good to us if we're all dead!'

When she didn't move, he grabbed her arm. 'Come on, do as you're told!'

She twisted out of his grasp. 'Do as I'm told? Who put you in charge? You're not in the bloody army yet, Sergeant Major!'

She registered the shock on his face. Normally

2

she indulged her brother's every wish, as they all did, but her defiance towards the Germans seemed to have infected her normal peace-loving nature with a belligerence that matched Jack's own.

'Well, I will be soon,' he said lamely.

Just then May heard a voice calling her name. She slipped past Jack and dashed up the passage to find Flo, their next-door neighbour, peering anxiously in through the open front door.

'You all right in there, love? Did your dad finish your shelter? If not, we've got room for two littl'uns in ours.'

'Thanks, Flo, he finished it yesterday.'

Flo retreated into her own house and May peered out at the street. Peggy had been right. The whole world was in motion. All their neighbours in Southwark Park Road without Anderson shelters were streaming out of their houses, hurrying to the nearest public shelter. Suddenly May felt herself grabbed from behind. Before she could resist, Jack twisted her round. Grasping both shoulders, he propelled her along the passage, through their house to the back door and out into the garden. Trampling freshly dug, soft earth, she stumbled forward as he forced her head low enough to enter the dim, curving interior of the Anderson shelter. Whether or not anyone had put him in charge, Jack was undoubtedly stronger than May. Peggy was already settled inside as Jack slammed the heavy door shut, confining them all to the dark, damp womb of corrugated iron. She gave Jack an ineffectual thump on the arm and took a deep breath of dank air. A sheen of sweat covered her face and she found her legs were trembling, mostly with anger at being manhandled by her brother. But as she squeezed herself on to a wooden bunk next to Peggy, she realized she'd forgotten all about the dinner.

'Oh no, I've left the oven on!' she said, getting up.

'Leave it!' Jack growled, pulling her back on to the bunk. 'You're not going nowhere.'

She knew he was only being protective, but she hated it when he turned bossy like this. She had a feeling he was going to love this war.

'We could be in here for hours!' He was stronger but she was swifter, and before he could stop her, she dashed back into the house. She wouldn't let a good bit of beef burn to a crisp for anyone, not her brother and certainly not Herr bloody Hitler.

And after all that, the first air-raid warning of the war turned out to be a false alarm. No planes darkened the skies; no bombs fell. It had been like the flick of a whip, a sharp warning of what was to come. After half an hour, spent mostly trying to quieten Peggy's fears about their parents' and her husband George's whereabouts, May was back in the kitchen, and soon the oven was piping hot, ready and waiting for the roast beef.

'See! If I'd listened to you, it would have been dry as Old Harry by now!' she said to Jack, who was looking over her shoulder, waiting to steal a roast potato. She pushed him out of the kitchen.

4

'They're not done yet. You'll just have to wait. And don't blame me, blame Hitler.'

When her mother and father finally walked through the door, accompanied by Peggy's husband George, May was laying the table. One look at Mrs Lloyd's white face told her the usual leisurely Sunday drink at the Blue Anchor had been anything but relaxing.

'Oh, me poor kids, and I wasn't here!' Mrs Lloyd said, crushing May to her and looking round at her other children. 'Are you all right? I can't believe I'm up the pub, just when the war's finally started!'

'I can,' her father said, and winked at May as he took off his jacket and cap.

Her mother gave him a sidelong look.

'Well, if it was up to May, we could've all been blown to pieces, so long as you still got your Sunday dinner!' said Peggy, who had rushed to George's side and was now helping him off with his overcoat and hat.

'I'll give it to her, if she ran the railways they'd always be on time.' Her father smiled at May. 'Keep calm and carry on. They don't have to tell our May that, do they, love?' he said, giving her an appreciative peck on the cheek.

In that moment May was glad she'd resisted being bullied out of her weekly task of cooking the Sunday roast. She'd taken on the job because it seemed the least she could do for her hard-working mother. And though she might pretend otherwise, May secretly loved it when Jack crept in to steal a roast potato before they all sat down to eat: Mum and Dad, Peggy and George, her brother Jack. The white cloth on the kitchen table, the steam from the scullery, the smell of the meat sizzling in the roasting tin. It was a tradition, home. And she was proud that the small matter of a German bomb had not prevented her from dishing up the Sunday roast.

'Well, next time, not so much of the brave Jack Lairy,' her mother said sharply. 'If we're not here, you just get yourself straight in the shelter!'

'Beef turned out lovely, though,' May said, noticing her father's small smile as she placed the joint carefully in the centre of the table.

Peggy linked her arm through George's as they walked home from her mother's house. 'I was worried about you.'

'Hold up, Peg, we're not runnin' a race, are we?'

Twelve years her senior, George Flint suffered from bouts of breathlessness. Today he was bad. She'd learned to hold herself back when walking with him, but sometimes she forgot.

'Sorry, love.' She slackened her pace.

'Well, if we'd been having Sunday dinner in our own home like most people do, I wouldn't have been traipsing up to Southwark Park Road during an air raid, would I?'

'Mum loves having us. I thought you liked her spoiling you?'

6

In spite of the age difference and his dubious occupation, George had always been a favourite with her parents. Wide'oh, as he was more commonly known, was the local bookie and though this was his primary source of income, he was involved in other unspecified 'businesses', which meant he was never without a wad of cash in his pocket. Yet it wasn't so much his money that her parents approved of as his unconcealed, extravagant adoration of Peggy. This was the first time George had baulked at her mother's insistence on having them there for Sunday dinner. She counted three of George's laboured breaths before he replied.

'Gawd's sake, Peg, you're a twenty-four-year-old married woman. It's time your mother understood that. Anyway, I don't want no one spoiling me but my wife.' He put a hand over hers and pulled her closer. 'I think we should knock it on the head, going round there *every* Sunday.'

The suggestion was no doubt reasonable, but it filled Peggy with unease. The regular Sunday gathering was a comforting anchor not just to her family, but to the girl she'd been before she married. Perhaps it was because her nerves were still jangling from the fright of the raid, but she wasn't as careful in her reply as she normally would have been.

'Oh, you know what Mum's like. She'd rather have us there than eating dinner on our own indoors. If we had a family it'd be different, I suppose.'

She felt George stiffen. 'You back on that? There's more to marriage than kids, you know.'

'I know that, George. Don't get upset with me.'

She could have kicked herself. This was a subject she normally steered clear of; it was guaranteed to turn George's habitual cheery expression to stone. She looked up at him, trying to gauge his mood. His trilby hat shadowed his eyes, but his mouth was set in a way she knew meant a miserable evening ahead unless she could distract him.

'Talking of marriage, I reckon our Jack and Joycie will be next. You were having a good old chat today. Has he said anything to you about it?'

'No, he never said nothing, only that he needed some cash for something – might be an engagement ring?'

'He never asked you for the money?'

'You know I don't mind helping out. Anyway, he's going to do a few little jobs for me.'

Now it was Peggy's turn to stiffen. She knew her brother's weaknesses. As the only boy, their mother had spoiled him and, in a house where money was tight, she'd always made sure that Jack had the best. If she only had a shilling left in her purse, it would be spent on Jack. She and her sister were just as bad. May might have occasional tussles with him, but neither of them could deny Jack anything.

'What sort of jobs?'

'Oh, this and that down the lock-up. Nothing you need worry about.'

8

His smile dared her to ask more. But their tacit agreement was that she delved as little as possible into how George came by his money.

'Don't you get him into trouble, George. It'd kill Mum and Dad.'

Now they'd reached the entrance to their block of flats on the Purbrook Estate. George disengaged his arm from hers and leaned against the entrance arch. He paused to catch his breath, beads of sweat dotting his forehead.

'Chrissake, Peg, grow up.' His breath rattled in his chest. 'Jack's been doing bits and pieces for me ever since you and me got married. Where d'ye think he gets the money for his expensive suits? Not from unloading oranges down Butler's Wharf!'

She hadn't known, but perhaps she'd never wanted to. 'George! You know Mum and Dad wouldn't like it.'

'Don't tell 'em then.'

Her mother always boasted to friends that George would do anything for Peggy and her family. And it was true, he was generous, but only in the ways he chose. Peggy gave up trying to sway him and turned towards the stone staircase. When he didn't follow she looked back.

'Got some business with Ronnie. I'll see you later.'

'What time will you be home?'

But he was already walking away, and it was a stupid question anyway. George's business was best conducted after dark and she had grown used to spending most of her evenings alone. He might love her, he certainly wanted to be seen with her, called her his princess, yet sometimes she wondered if he actually liked her company. Why he was making such a fuss about spending Sunday dinner at home with her she couldn't fathom.

She paused a moment, listening, as his harsh, rattling wheeze faded away and he disappeared into Tower Bridge Road. She wouldn't say anything about Jack. Her parents might turn a blind eye to George's thieving, but involving their son would be a different matter. If George put Jack in danger they would never forgive him, and neither would she.

May had rarely seen her mother cry, but in the two months since that first false alarm Mrs Lloyd did little else. It had come as a surprise to May, people's reactions to the war. Those she thought would be weak often turned out to be the strongest. And now it was shocking to see her capable mother in such distress. Carrie Lloyd had always been the lynchpin of the family, but now May's throat tightened at the thought that her mother might not be as strong as she'd always appeared. Mrs Lloyd believed they would either be gassed in their beds or overrun by Germans any day. Her mother's fear seemed to permeate the very walls of the old house in Southwark Park Road, but it wasn't primarily fear for herself or even her daughters – it was for

Jack. May saw her mother jump every time a letter dropped through the letterbox. Jack hadn't yet got his call-up papers, but he would soon, and then May feared Mrs Lloyd's world really would fall apart.

It was Saturday evening and her mother had taken herself upstairs for 'a nap', which meant she'd been crying and didn't want her red eyes to give her away. May was in the kitchen with Jack.

'You should get your nose out of that book and go out a bit more,' Jack said as he stood in front of the kitchen sink, carefully swiping the long blade of the razor up under his chin. Four years her senior, he felt himself entitled to pronounce upon her life.

She was sitting in the corner, and he had perhaps noticed that her book was not holding her. In fact she'd been mesmerized by the razor ploughing its way through the white lather on her brother's chin. She looked up and met his clear blue eyes in the small mirror tacked above the sink. It was true that as the world grew grumpier and sadder around May, she'd felt herself yearning for a glimpse of light-heartedness.

'And you should watch you don't cut yourself getting that bum fluff off.'

'Keep your hair on. I was only thinking of you! There's always Garner's girls up the Red Cow, and they've got this new piano player – he's pretty good. You can come with me and Norman tonight, if you want.'

Garner's was the leather factory where May worked, and she would probably know a couple of the girls drinking at the Red Cow tonight. She hesitated, feeling guilty for snapping at him.

'Thanks, but . . . you know me and pubs.'

But her shyness had nothing to do with pubs. She'd always been the quietest of their large family, with nothing remarkable to make her stand out apart from a useless bookishness, which they found puzzling rather than praiseworthy. She preferred to watch family life from the side-lines. Peggy, the princess, and Jack, the golden boy, always took centre stage in their family dramas. And though May had learned to make herself indispensable around the home, she had also learned to be a great hider. It seemed to her that she'd spent her childhood searching out hidey-holes, spending hours, sometimes whole days, immersed in her own world, perhaps with a book from Spa Road Library, or engaged in imaginary games.

Jack raised his eyes as he wiped soap off his neck and proceeded to slick back his hair with Brylcreem, till the golden curls were tamed and darkened.

'It's only Norman! He don't bite!'

Norman Carter was Jack's best friend and he was nice enough, but whenever he came to the house he insisted on teasing her till she blushed. As if on cue there was a knock at the front door, which she ignored. 'Your hair looks better without that stuff on it.'

'Joycie don't mind it.' He chuckled. 'Go and get that, will you, sis?'

'No!'

He pulled on his clean shirt and smiled. 'I'm getting ready!'

Reluctantly she put down the book and went to answer the door. Norman smelled of Brylcreem and cigarettes. He was a gangly, skinny young man and his wide-lapelled, new brown suit was too big in the shoulders. His long chin bore the signs of an inexpert close shave. He gave her a crooked-toothed grin.

'Hello, gorgeous, got yourself a chap yet? I'm free.'

A blush began to creep up from her neck, and she was glad of the dimly lit passage.

'Jack's in the kitchen.' She let Norman pass her, but didn't follow. She went into the front room and waited, listening to the two boys laughing. She wished she'd brought her book. But then Jack stuck his head through the door.

'Take no notice of him. You coming?'

She shook her head. 'Next time perhaps.'

The front door slammed as the boys went off for their night at the pub and May watched them walk past the front window. Norman suffered by comparison, for Jack had filled out since joining his father at the docks and his new suit jacket sat snugly across his shoulders. His confidence had grown along with his muscles and as he strode off, hands in pockets, leaning forward, eager for the night ahead, May realized that her brother was no longer a boy.

She went back to the kitchen to retrieve her book, annoyed with herself that she could be shy around an idiot like Norman Carter. She flung the book on to the kitchen table just as her mother came in.

'Oi, oi, what's going on? Has Jack been teasing you?'

'Jack? No, Mum!'

The truth was her big brother, with his winning smile and affectionate ways, had only ever been her champion. It wasn't his fault that he was the only boy she could be herself with.

'You busy tonight?'

'I'm washing my hair.'

'When you're done, you can help me sew them new blackout curtains. Your eyes are better than mine. I can't see the stitches in this light.'

It was always the way. If she made herself visible, there was sure to be a job for her to do. Mother's helper, that was her. And although she loved her home, she sometimes longed to be more than just 'the quiet one' in the midst of so many other clamouring voices.

Her mother was right about her keen eyesight, though. Ironic, really, as there was a time when she'd been quite blind. A case of childhood measles had left her with ulcers behind her eyes. It had been a strange, frightening time, sunk in an unseeing world for almost three months, the most unsettling period of her life – to see nothing in a world where she was so seen, on show to every pair of curious eyes that cared to stop and stare and yet not to know she was being stared at. Perhaps that was the cause of her shyness, and why, ever after, she'd chosen to make herself invisible whenever possible.

May sighed. 'All right, you start cutting up the material and then my eagle eyes are all yours!'

She left her mother to get on with it while she washed her long fair hair in the big enamel sink in the kitchen. It took many jugs of water before the soap was fully rinsed. Her parents, in the back room, must have forgotten she was still there, and May's ears pricked up as she heard them talking about Jack.

'I can't help it, Albert, I'm so worried about him. What if he gets called up?'

'Well, it's not happened yet, has it? And you can't wrap him in cotton wool, Carrie. I'm more worried about where he's getting his money from. He gets less hours than me at the docks, but I ain't got no money for new suits like he has.'

She could tell that her father had his pipe clenched tight between his teeth.

'Don't tell me that. If he's nicking stuff from the docks, he'll go inside,' Mrs Lloyd said. 'Still, at least he'd be safe in there.'

There followed sounds of muffled sobs and May knew her mother's tears had returned. She decided it was time to make her presence known. Her parents fell silent as she came in and kneeled in front of the fire. Mrs Lloyd brushed away her tears, took the towel from her and began gently rubbing May's long fair hair.

'At least I'll be able to keep me daughters with me,' she whispered.

Her father smiled fondly and said, 'Just look at my golden-haired girl, ain't she beautiful, Carrie? I feel like that miller in *Rumpelstiltskin*.'

'Me, beautiful?' May gave a small snort, uncomfortable with compliments, even coming from her father.

'What you blushing for? It's true!'

'It's the fire – I'm hot.'

She stood up quickly and caught sight of herself in the mirror above the fireplace. Beautiful? She couldn't see it, but perhaps someone might one day think her pretty enough, with her wide blue eyes and high cheekbones. She was slim and straight-backed, and Peggy was always telling May she had a good figure. '*And* you'll never need to worry about getting fat!' Peggy had joked. 'You do everything at a run!'

'Come on then, Mum, let's get these blackout curtains done,' she said.

She gave her mother a quick kiss, and thought of Jack, walking through the cold November night in search of a good time and who knew what else.

'Look at the state of yer!'

Jack attempted to pull Norman's jacket up on to his shoulders. 'No wonder you can't get no girls to look at you!'

16

Norman shoved Jack off. 'I'm only interested in one girl . . . your sister!'

Jack looked genuinely shocked. 'Our May? I thought you were joking! No, mate, you're on a loser there. May's a home bird. If even I can't get her to come out to the pub, you've got no chance!'

Norman gave his crooked-toothed grin. 'I think she likes me.'

'You really interested then?'

'Why not?'

Jack shrugged. 'She's me little sister. I still think she's about twelve, I suppose.'

Norman sniggered. 'Jack, you ain't looked lately – she's not twelve no more!'

They had reached the John Bull pub when Jack stopped.

'Hold up, Norm, I've just got to pop in here, have a word with me brother-in-law – family business.' Jack winked at Norman. 'You wait here.'

When Jack emerged from the pub with a blast of warm, smoke-filled air he waved a handful of notes under Norman's nose.

'Gawd, Jack, how much you got there?'

Jack laughed. 'Five quid. Not bad for a couple of nights' work.'

'What d'you have to do?'

'Only the same as down the docks, just a different employer. I turn up tonight at Wide'oh's lock-up, move a load of tea chests from one lorry to another, then go home to bed. So instead of ending up at Lipton's tonight, that finest Darjeeling goes

17

straight in your old mum's teapot! Wide'oh says it's just cutting out the middle man.'

Norman's long face took on a worried look. 'But you could get in bad trouble, Jack.'

Jack sighed. He went on as if talking to a child. 'Everyone's at it. Your mum gets cheap tea under the counter, don't she?'

Norman nodded.

'Well, I just work for the supplier, mate!'

By the time they reached the Red Cow, the piano player was in full swing and the Garner's girls had made a little space in the small interior to practise their dance steps.

'Don't suppose we'll be doing any dancing tonight. I've got Joycie now and you're saving yourself for our May, ain't you, Norm?' Jack said mischievously.

May spent her days at Garner's, one of a cluster of leather factories situated in an area known as The Grange. Once the site of Bermondsey Abbey's farm, all trace of its bucolic past was long gone. The air was no longer filled with the sweet smell of apple orchards. Instead the triangle of land exuded the many noxious tanning fumes, familiar to Bermondsey people. May, like all the other Garner's girls, had long ago grown accustomed to the smells, but what she could not get used to was the tedium of her days spent sitting at a bench, trimming softened leather hides, or hanging them on stretchers to dry.

On one particularly dull December day, she and her two closest workmates, Emmy Harris and Dolly Dixon, had been put to work in the dying room. One by one, May and Emmy lifted the wet dyed skins, hung one corner over a large hook and stretched the hide to another hook. It took two of them as the sodden hides were heavy with evil-smelling dye, and it was back-breaking work. As she turned to fetch another hide, one of the hooks caught on May's long golden hair, yanking her back and entangling her.

'Help me, Em!'

'You and your bloody hair. You should get one of those nets,' Emmy complained as she tried to disentangle May.

'What's the hold-up?'

Eddie Barber, the young foreman, strolled over from his bench. He was more relaxed than the older foremen, who'd usually been fixtures at the factory for years.

'She's caught her hair,' Dolly said with a mischievous look. 'She needs a man to sort her out, Eddie.'

Eddie grinned back and stood in front of May. One hand taking the weight of the hide, he encircled her with his other arm and unhooked the last lock of hair.

'What do I get for setting you free then?' he asked.

May felt herself blushing a deeper scarlet than the dyed leather hide. It didn't help that Dolly was miming a kiss behind Eddie's back. She cursed her hair and vowed to change the girlish style at the earliest opportunity.

'You could do worse,' Dolly said once Eddie was back at his bench.

May picked up a corner of another hide and slapped it into Dolly's hand. 'Don't! He'll hear you!'

She'd worked at Garner's since leaving school at fourteen, four years earlier, and mostly she'd been content to do her work and go home. While Emmy was funny and Dolly brash, May's diffidence hindered her as surely as the long hair tangling in the drying hooks. But for some reason, the two girls had taken her under their worldly-wise wings and had made it their mission to set her up with a nice chap. It was largely out of kindness, but sometimes May knew they used her innocence as a foil to their bravado. Their latest target was Bill Gilbie, a young leather worker, who'd also taken on fire-watching and ARP duties at the factory.

'Well, if you don't want Eddie, I suppose I could let you have my Bill!' Dolly said with a sigh and Emmy shot back, 'Your Bill? He's never looked twice at you, Dol.'

Dolly pulled a face. 'Just where you're wrong 'cause we had a nice chat at the Red Cow the other night.' She looked at May. 'He plays the piano there most nights.' She gave a mock swoon. 'He's got lovely hands!'

As Dolly pretended the workbench was a piano, the object of their discussion opened the dying-room door.

'All down the basement!' Bill called out, so the whole floor could hear.

She heard Emmy and Dolly stifling their giggles. But May couldn't help but notice his hands, one of which lay flat against the swing door. Strong, rather tanned from the leather work, his long tapered fingers were definitely those of a piano player. Bill wore a leather jerkin and an armband, identifying him as a fire warden. In the three months since war had been declared, every raid had been either a drill or a false alarm, so the girls took their time laying down the hides. Emmy and Dolly deliberately dragged their feet.

'What you all hot and bothered for?' Dolly asked Bill. 'You'd think there was a war on!'

'One day it'll be a real one and then you'll move yourself!' he said. Pushing back a strand of dark hair that had fallen across his forehead, he hurried off to clear the lower floors. May, who could do nothing slowly, even when she tried, was well ahead of the rest of the girls as they shuffled down the stone staircase to the basement. She caught up with Bill, who shot her a quick smile, and she realized that his hands weren't the only lovely thing about him.

'At least someone's taking it seriously!' he said.

They arrived in the basement together and Bill took off his jerkin, tossing it over a chair by a battered old piano that the bosses had installed as a morale booster. Bill beckoned her over.

'First to arrive gets first choice.'

He clasped together his long fingers and gave an exaggerated stretch before seating himself at the piano. 'Any requests, madam?' he said.

She thought for a minute. 'Do you know "Happy Days and Lonely Nights"?'

'Only too well,' he said, looking down with a wry smile, so that for a moment she wondered if he'd broken up with a sweetheart. But as the shelter began to fill, he struck up the opening chords and soon a chorus of voices was joining in. '*You broke my heart a million ways, when you took my happy days, and left me lonely nights!*' They belted it out and Bill didn't seem to be shedding any tears, so May dismissed the idea. She noticed that he appeared more relaxed now he was sitting at the piano. Seemingly he could play any tune by ear: 'Old Bull and Bush' or 'We'll Meet Again' – whatever the request, he picked the tune up in no time – and when the all-clear sounded they were reluctant to leave.

'Bill, are you *sure* it's safe for us to go upstairs?' Dolly asked. It wasn't just that she was flirting. The game was to string out the practice for as long as possible, anything to avoid the piles of hides stacked up waiting to be hung.

Bill raised his eyes. 'I've done my bit getting you down here, *and* entertaining you. I reckon you can get yourself back up whenever you like!' He shot May a parting look and bounded up the stairs two at a time.

'He likes you,' Emmy whispered and May let out a groan.

Although she resented her friends' constant matchmaking, at the end of the day rather than rushing home as she usually did, she took her time in the cloakroom getting ready to leave Garner's, and when Emmy asked her to come to the Red Cow with them on Saturday she surprised herself by agreeing.

May was checking her hair in the mirror above the fireplace when her father paused over his pipe 'Blimey. You going out?'

May blushed and her mother shot him a warning look, so that he quickly turned back to his paper.

'You look nice,' Jack said. 'Wait till I get ready and I'll walk you down.'

'No, no, I'm all right. I'm only meeting some girls from work,' May said, escaping into the passage before she attracted any more attention. As she pulled her coat from the hook she heard her mother say, 'Well, that's a turn up!'

The Red Cow at the corner of The Grange was Emmy and Dolly's favourite haunt. When May pushed open the corner door she was met by a blackout curtain. She waited there, unseen for an instant, and it crossed her mind to turn round and go home. But then she heard Emmy's unmistakable throaty laugh, and she pulled aside the curtain.

She scanned the room and caught sight of the piano. There was no one sitting at it, and May felt an instant of disappointment before realizing the real reason she'd agreed to come here with the girls.

Dolly spotted her and beckoned her over. They were laughing, Emmy explained, about the last air-raid drill.

'Did you see Bill's face when he was trying to round us up?' Emmy laughed.

'Oh, I don't know, I quite like him when he looks stern,' Dolly said.

'And you, Miss Goody-Two-Shoes,' Emmy prodded May, 'don't rush to get down the basement so quick next time! We're trying to string it out. All the time we're on the drill we're not hanging hides!'

'But I'll tell you something for nothing,' said Dolly. 'I've seen the way that Bill looks at you, May . . .' She nodded her head sagely.

'Don't be daft, Dolly. I've not said two words to him!'

Yet later that night when Bill took his place at the piano, she saw him glance her way, and during his break he made a point of coming over to them. He'd obviously forgiven Emmy and Dolly for their earlier teasing. He sat at their table, drinking his pint and chatting easily to her friends, but May noticed that more often than not his ocean-blue eyes were fixed on her.

'"Happy Days"?' he asked her, before returning to the piano.

She suspected that Saturday nights at the Red Cow would become a regular thing from now on.

★   ★   ★

24

May might be spreading her wings, but at heart she was still a home bird and as the phoney war limped on towards Christmas she found herself increasingly drawn into her mother's worries about Jack.

One night towards Christmas, she and Mrs Lloyd had spent the evening trying to make a Christmas pudding with a laughable amount of dried fruit and nuts. They'd made five puddings last year to give away, but this year there was barely enough for one. After snipping dates with scissors as small as they could and chopping almonds to a pale dust, grating a small lump of suet and a single orange peel, they were ready to give the mixture its magic stir. May made her own wish and then watched as her mother shut her eyes tight to make hers. With her expression unguarded, May saw for the first time how these early months of the war had changed her mother. She already looked defeated and when she opened her eyes, May saw they were brimming.

'Was your wish for Jack?' she asked softly, taking the wooden spoon from her mother's hand.

'I'm worried sick, love. I think he's getting himself in with a bad bunch. He comes in all hours, and where's he getting the money to take Joycie out? Over the West End and gawd knows where.' Her mother rubbed her forehead and sat down. 'Sometimes I don't know which I'm more worried about, him going in the army or the villains he's mixing with.'

'Villains? Mum, you're getting in a state over nothing. Jack's either out with Joycie, or it's Norman he's with . . . and he's harmless enough.' She put an arm round her mother. 'It's just the war that's got us all up the wall.'

'I'm sorry, love, I shouldn't be putting it on your shoulders. Your brother's old enough to look after himself.'

Mrs Lloyd pushed herself up from the chair just as Jack walked in.

'Mum! Come 'ere!' It was Jack's custom to greet his mother with a bear hug, and not release her till she begged to be let go. It amused him no end, and May knew no matter how much her mother slapped him away, she loved it too. But now, Mrs Lloyd had no energy to resist and Jack pulled away first.

'What's the matter?' He looked to May for an answer, but she shook her head.

'Just tired, son. I'm off to bed.'

Kissing him on the forehead, Mrs Lloyd walked heavily upstairs to her bedroom.

'Blimey, what's the matter with her?' Jack asked, his ebullience all gone.

May found herself irritated at Jack's incomprehension. 'Don't you know? She's worried about you!'

'Me? Why? Because I'll be getting called up?'

May sighed. 'That, and . . . she thinks you're nicking stuff from the docks.'

'Oh.' He was silent for a moment.

26

'So, does that mean you are?'

A cloud passed over his normal sunny features. 'No! 'Course not.' He hesitated. 'But . . . promise not to say nothing?'

May nodded. 'I've been helping George out a bit.'

May couldn't think why it hadn't occurred to her before. Perhaps because a villain in the family seemed like no villain at all. It was easier to think of them as coming from somewhere else.

'They won't like it.'

'I know but, May, I can't get by on casual work at the docks.'

May wanted to say that lots of other men did, but she knew that her brother's idea of 'getting by' didn't always refer to essentials.

Jack's face had turned sulky. 'Bloody hell, I was in such a good mood an'all. But now it's spoiled the surprise.'

'What?'

'Well, I was going to tell Mum and Dad first, but . . .' he said, spinning it out.

'Tell me!'

Suddenly he broke into a broad smile, his chest puffing out ever so slightly.

'Me and Joycie got engaged!'

'Jack!' She ran to kiss him and then she thumped his chest.

'That makes two things you never told me about!' May was used to being Jack's first port of call, whenever he was either in trouble or confused.

She didn't like the idea of him keeping secrets from her. But her irritation with him disappeared the instant she saw how happy he was.

'I only asked her today and she said yes!' The brightness of his golden hair, which he pushed back from his forehead, was matched only by the radiance of his face. She'd heard that sometimes when people were deeply happy, their faces shone, and his really was shining. And though part of her was sad to be losing her brother, she couldn't do anything other than share his joy.

'Oh, Jack, I'm really happy for you! Mum'll be so pleased. It's just what she needs.'

But then a cloud dimmed his brightness.

'What?'

'Well, the reason I asked Joycie now is because I reckon I'll get my call-up papers soon.'

'But you don't know that.'

'Oh, sis, it'll happen sooner or later. Some of the fellers at work have already enlisted.'

'Well, you're not going to!'

For some reason this made him laugh. 'If little sis says I can't, then who am I to argue?'

She shoved his shoulder, laughing, but then turning serious, she said, 'Just tell her the good news, eh? Leave out the rest.'

CHAPTER 2

BABES IN THE RUINS

January–September 1940

The New Year had swirled in with snow and a biting wind. Everything in the world was colder, bleaker, and the darkness of the blackout seemed to cast its shadows into the days. When May looked back on that first Christmas of the war she realized it was to be their last truly happy gathering together as a family. She remembered a moment when, glancing up at the mirror above the fireplace, she had seen them all reflected as if in a photograph, raising their glasses of beer to toast Jack's engagement. The flickering fire in the grate had flared and in spite of its heat, May had felt a sudden chill, which seemed prescient tonight as she lay on her bed listening to the angry voices rising up through the floorboards from the kitchen below.

'I'm telling you, son, you're riding for a fall! Do you know how long they'll put you away if the dock police catch up with you? It won't be a piddling few months, I'll tell you that!'

Her normally placid father rarely raised his voice

in anger. If he did, it usually involved Jack, and May always hated it.

'I don't know what you're talking about, Dad. I've got nothing to do with that racket!' Jack's voice was defensive, almost dismissive.

Their shouting and their anger set her heart racing and she crept downstairs to peer through the half-open kitchen door. Her mother sat white-faced, looking neither at her husband nor her son, her eyes fixed on the table in front of her.

'Now that's a bare-faced lie. I hear things at the docks. How d'you think I feel when my son's name gets mentioned when they're talking about lorry loads of stuff going missing?'

Jack jumped out of his chair. 'I think you should stick up for your bloody son, that's what I think!' He stood close to his father, shouting into his face.

'Oh, you do? Well, how do you explain this then? Your mother found it under your bed.'

Mr Lloyd snatched a black tin from the kitchen mantlepiece and pulled the lid off. As he did so, more ten bob notes than May had ever seen fluttered down on to the kitchen lino.

'You've got no fucking business taking that, it's for me and Joycie!' Jack's voice cracked with anger.

'Don't you talk to me like that!' her father roared.

May burst through the kitchen door. 'Dad, don't!'

She could never bear to see Jack hurt. Ever since she was a child, it had always been the same, and

May was the peacemaker. Her father turned away at the sight of her, addressing his son. 'And you've got no business taking what's not yours.'

But Jack was angrier than May had ever seen him, and he wasn't ready to back down.

'You're a fuckin' hypocrite, you know that? You'll take anything Wide'oh gives you, no questions asked!'

Jack looked at May, as if for help. She could see his dilemma. This was the closest he could come to admitting the source of his money, without giving up George. And she could see the injustice of it. He wasn't guilty of the crime her father was accusing him of but the one he *had* committed, they were all party to.

Into the shocked silence came an insistent sound. They all three turned as one to look at Mrs Lloyd. She was crying.

Jack swiped up the sheaf of banknotes from the floor, stormed out of the kitchen and slammed the front door, setting the thin walls shaking. Her father retreated to the scullery, where she heard him getting ready for his ARP duties. She was left to comfort her mother.

'He'll catch his death out there, it's bitter.' Her mother wiped tears from her cheek. 'He's got no coat on.'

She stroked her mother's hand, noticing age spots that seemed to have appeared overnight. 'He don't feel the cold,' May said.

★　　★　　★

But the chill in the house was palpable for weeks after, with her father stubbornly refusing to speak to Jack and May ineffectually trying to force a truce between them. Finally, she approached Peggy. She'd persuaded her sister to go to the Trocette Cinema in Tower Bridge Road, to see a matinée of *Gone with the Wind*. It was their second viewing, but May loved the film and besides she felt as if Peggy had been distant of late. She and George had stopped coming every week for Sunday lunch, and May knew it upset her mother. But today May wanted to talk about Jack.

As they walked back towards the Purbrook Estate, May asked her, 'Peg, did you know our Jack's been doing jobs for George?'

Peggy looked surprised and, to May's astonishment, guilty.

'You *did* know! Peg, what are you thinking of. Don't you know how much trouble it's causing at home? Not that they know it's George he's getting the money from . . .'

Peggy wouldn't look at her. 'Jack's got a mind of his own. Anyway, George says it's only temporary, so Jack can put a bit of money together to get married.'

May snorted. 'Oh, that'll be nice, a wedding in Brixton prison. Peg, he's not a villain, not like your . . .' She just stopped herself. 'I didn't mean that. It's just he's not cut out for it. He's not careful. He splashes those notes about – I've seen him up the Red Cow – and he'll be the one to come unstuck.'

'Sorry, May, I can't stop to chat. I've got to get George's dinner on the table before he comes home.' Peggy gave May a quick kiss on the cheek and dashed off. With her headscarf on, and the bag over her elbow, May thought she looked the picture of a respectable wife going home to her husband. It was just a pity her husband wasn't respectable. As she walked slowly back to Southwark Park Road, May reflected on marriage and wondered if it always made you a coward, for what she'd seen in her sister's face was fear.

She had done her best and failed in her self-appointed role of peacemaker, so that when spring came and Jack's call-up papers finally did arrive, for May, it was almost a relief. At least in the army he'd be out of Wide'oh's way. But her feeling of relief lasted only until the day Jack was to report for duty.

As her mother handed Jack some wrapped sand-wiches and chocolate for his journey, there were no tears, but her tight-lipped bravery was almost harder for May to bear.

Her father shook Jack's hand. 'Good luck, son,' he said, all their bitter words forgotten as they stood to wave him off down the street.

It seemed that parting had been the only peace-maker Jack and her father would heed. And so her brother left for the war, and afterwards she went upstairs to her bedroom and shed the tears that had been forbidden while he'd still been there. A part of their family had been torn away, and it was as if someone had ripped pages from a favourite book. It just wasn't the same any more without Jack. Part of them was missing.

Emmy pointed out a mobile billboard, mounted on four wheels. It showed Ginger Rogers, the Hollywood star, putting her peachy skin down to Lux soap, and alongside it a street photographer was touting for custom. It was a bright September Saturday afternoon, almost a year to the day since the outbreak of war. May and her two friends were leaving the leather factory and had been discussing the latest shortages, the most pressing of which was shampoo.

'Let's get our photo done!' Emmy said. 'We need cheering up.'

May put her hand to her hair, which she knew was her greatest vanity.

'I can't, Em, my hair's not been washed for a week!'

'Well, neither's mine,' Emmy said.

'Come on, girls!' the photographer called to them. 'Get your photo taken with Ginger! Send it to your sweethearts in the forces.'

And though May was only too aware she had no sweetheart to send a photograph to, she agreed, guessing it was the nearest she'd ever get to Hollywood glamour. After checking their make-up and assuring each other their hair was fine, the friends linked arms to pose in front of the bill-board. Then Emmy got a fit of the giggles, her throaty laugh so infectious it threatened to ruin their sophisticated pose.

'We're meant to be looking glamorous, not like schoolgirls!' Dolly scolded and May bit the inside of her cheek, trying not to squint into the sun. She tilted her chin and attempted a sophisticated smile.

The following Saturday afternoon after work the friends went to the photographer's to pick up their photographs. Eager to see the results, they stopped to open the envelope in the street.

'Look at you, May!' Emmy laughed. 'You really do look like Ginger Rogers!'

Golden afternoon sunshine bounced off the shiny print as May tilted it for a better view.

'Do you think so? No, it's just my hair.' May now wore her hair shorter, rolled under in a Ginger Rogers pageboy. But it wasn't just that. The face staring back at her from the photo looked older than her own image of herself. Perhaps it was the touch of make-up as well as the new hairstyle; perhaps it was the wartime diet which had finally rid her face of all trace of puppy fat, accentuating her high cheekbones. The hand colourist had made her large blue eyes a shade too dark, but their expression seemed that of a bolder person than herself. And that surprised her.

Then Dolly groaned. 'Oh bloody hell, look at that ladder in my stocking – Ginger wouldn't stand for that!' And they all laughed.

After they parted and she neared Southwark Park Road, she heard the heart-lurching wail of the sirens. Normally she would have ignored it as she had a hundred times in the past year of 'phoney war'. But this time it was followed by the throbbing drone of aeroplane engines, lots of them. She froze and looked heavenward, to see skeins of black aircraft, strung out across the sky, all along the line of the Thames. Like menacing migratory birds, staining the innocent blue heavens with endless arrows of destruction, they all pointed in one direction: the docks.

One part of Southwark Park Road was known as the Blue, after an earlier incarnation as Blue Anchor Lane. It was one of Bermondsey's main shopping streets, and she had just reached the first shops when the world exploded around her. A thunderous booming from ack-ack guns in Southwark Park shook the ground beneath her feet, followed by a red-hot rain of razor-sharp shrapnel. Propelled by cold terror, May ran. She shot from shop doorway to doorway, as an explosion like a muffled volcano was followed by the high tinkling of shattering glass. The blast seemed to have turned off the sun. All its former brightness was veiled now by great blooms of ashen smoke, billowing up from the first targets. She had always been fond of the sunsets in Bermondsey, and often at this time in the early evening, looking westward, beyond the crowded buildings, the sky would be all burnished reds and golds. But now it was in the east that the ruddy light glowed. Surrey Docks, with its tons of stacked timber, was on fire, and the inferno lit the sky with more brilliance than the setting sun.

Her mind a blank with fear, all she could think of was getting home, so she was tempted to ignore the advice on the nagging posters and simply make a run for it. But some instinct checked her flight and instead she looked around for shelter. The railway arch ahead, known as the John Bull Arch, after the pub that stood next to it, was only a little way ahead. The pavements on either side of the road running under the arch had been bricked up at each end to form a public shelter. If she could only reach there, she would be safe. As she approached it, a shrieking incendiary bomb passed close enough to sear her cheek and she darted to one side, making a dash for the Home and Colonial stores. But in spite of the sandbags protecting it, the long front window shattered into a crazy pattern, before tumbling in a thousand shards at her feet. She was frozen to the spot, conscious only that she was covered in razor-sharp glass needles. As she hesitated a figure shot out, grabbing her by the coat collar.

'Get inside! We're under the counter!'

'What are you doing here?'

For the person who'd yanked her through the door was Bill Gilbie.

'Buying bacon for me mum . . . and trying to stay alive!' he said, crouching low as he helped her back behind the shop counter. The shopkeeper and two assistants made room for her and she kneeled beside Bill as the whines and crashes of the bombs increased around them. But the pounding of their own ack-ack guns in nearby Southwark Park was even worse. Each thunderclap from the exploding shells reverberated through her body, so that her own heartbeat was hammering to the rhythm of the guns. Bill must have felt her uncontrollable trembling, for he slipped his arm round her shoulders, steadying her against each successive blast. Finally, she stuck her fingers in her ears to block out the din, but though the sound was muffled, she still felt the shop's foundations shaking with every round. She closed her eyes to make herself invisible, just as she had when as a child she'd retreated to one of her hidey-holes. But an insistent stabbing pain in her knees demanded her attention, and she looked down to see that she had been kneeling in a pile of broken glass.

Bill noticed too. He brushed away the glass and laid his jacket down.

'Here, sit on this!' he shouted, for it was impossible to be heard above ear-splitting whines and crashes. Pain seemed to have banished her habitual shyness and, almost glad of something small and manageable to focus on, she spent the next ten minutes watching as he painstakingly prized out slivers of glass from her knees with his deft, piano player's fingers. He gently wiped each trickle of blood away with a handkerchief only to reveal yet another shining needle of pain. When at last he was satisfied the wounds were clean, he ripped the hanky in half and bandaged each knee.

'Better?' he asked.

She nodded. 'Where d'you learn that?'

He smiled. 'ARP training – you're my first casualty!'

After what seemed like hours crouching beneath the counter, the barrage finally ceased, and the aerial timpani died away, to be replaced by the roar and crackle of fires and the clanging of fire-engine bells. While the shopkeeper began the task of clearing up, she and Bill emerged through the splintered remains of the door.

Now out in the open, May felt suddenly shy. Bill broke the silence.

'How come you were so late getting home from work?' he asked. 'Didn't you finish at twelve today?'

'Me and the girls went to pick up our photos.'

'Let's have a look,' he said.

'What, now?'

He nodded, and though her only thought was to get home, she fished into her bag and pulled out the photo.

'What do you think?'

'I think Ginger's not a patch on you.' He laughed and then, looking more closely, added, 'But they've made your eyes too dark. Yours are light blue.'

She took the print, pleased, not so much by the compliment as that he had noticed the colour of her eyes.

'Do you think they'll come back?'

Bill looked skyward. 'I think this is just the beginning. They'll be back tonight.'

'Really?'

He nodded. 'I don't think you should come out to the pub tonight, May. It's too dangerous.'

He registered her disappointment and added with a laugh, 'The entertainment won't be there anyway. I'll be on fire-watching duty, up on Garner's roof all night. Come on, I'll see you home.'

She shook her head at his offer. 'I'll be fine now, Bill. They look like they need your help more than me,' she said, looking towards a group of ARPs who'd begun searching through the rubble for survivors. His gaze followed hers.

'You're probably right, if you're sure you'll be OK?'

'Yes, yes, I'll be fine.'

She turned away and when she was sure she was out of Bill's sight broke into a sprint. Passing more damaged shops, she found herself praying all the way that she still had a home to return to.

As she approached her house, her breath coming in short gasps, she saw a few fires still burning, then rounding a bend she came to a halt, gasping with relief to see her home standing undamaged. But it was a short-lived relief, for as Bill Gilbie had predicted, later that night the bombers came again. May and her family crammed into the little Anderson shelter, this time with no complaints about its dampness or the water pooling on the floor around them. All night they were battered and pummelled by ceaseless explosions in an endless rain of sound and fury. But in the early hours exhaustion claimed her and she slept until her mother shook her awake into a silent dawn. Her first thought was of Bill Gilbie, standing on Garner's rooftop through it all.

That bombing raid had been her first taste of real fear, and from then on she looked back, almost with nostalgia, to those early months of the war when she'd viewed air raids as entertainments to break up a deadly dull day at Garner's. All her days now promised to be deadly, and never dull. Her mother had called her 'brave Jack Lairy' during that first false alarm, almost a year ago, but now she knew it hadn't been bravery at all, just fearlessness, born of ignorance.

For weeks and months on end, day and night, her home was pounded out of all recognition. Life became something that happened between air raids, and then it became something that happened during them as well. For now, at work, when the threat was all too real and the sirens sounded, they did not rush down to the basement. If they had done, the factory would have come to a halt. Instead, they waited for Bill Gilbie and the other spotters on the roof to give them the signal, and only when the planes were almost overhead did they retreat to the basement.

Autumn of 1940 announced itself with its first

golds, but the seasons seemed irrelevant, the only measure of time being the number of nights that the bombers had come. One morning, after a sleepless night in the Anderson shelter, she emerged into a muted world of pale ashes and russet brick-dust. It was as if the surrounding buildings had been ground down by a giant millstone. The covering on the pavement was like snow and sand mixed together. Deeper at the kerbsides, it rose in puffs as she walked to the leather factory in The Grange. The air in the bombed streets hung thick with a sickening smell, which she didn't want to put a name to, though its putrid signature was familiar to her from the tannery. Hides steeping in the vile-smelling mixture of faeces and urine were bad enough, but nothing could prepare her for this stench, wafting up from the crushed shells of neighbours' houses, from the pubs, shops and factories that formed her daily landscape. The odour had all the intimacy of death, and she knew its cause as surely as she knew the friendly face of Flo next door, who waved to her through her broken window, or Johnny Capp, who stood outside the ruined front of his grocery shop. He beckoned to her as she passed.

'Here, what do you think of this, May?' He held a dripping paintbrush over a can and she noticed a faint trembling in his hand, almost as if the brush were too heavy for him. May read the freshly painted sign he had propped in front of the gaping hole: *MORE OPEN THAN USUAL!*

She laughed. 'How are the family, all right?'

'Yes, love, and yours?'

She nodded.

'Thank gawd. We're the lucky ones, eh?'

But after last night's raid, many of her friends and neighbours were not, as they lay still undiscovered beneath pyramids of brick and stone punctuating the streets.

Business as Usual? It wasn't the first such sign May saw on her walk to work. She pulled her coat closely around her and shivered. How could death and destruction ever result in 'business as usual'? But here she was, going to work – as usual. The consistency of the dust changed beneath her feet; now she was crunching broken glass. There were hundreds of dagger-like shards, crushed to crystals under the booted feet of firemen and ARPs, rushing in concentrated groups to put out fires still blazing. She dodged out of the drifting spray from one of their hoses, and stepping over a rivulet running in the gutter, she rounded the corner into The Grange, where she stopped short.

A whole corner of the leather factory was open to the sky, part of a side wall completely blown off. Benches hung in mid-air; dressed hides flapped from shattered wooden bins, some torn into ragged strips. And floating on the air were the wind-blown dye samples; small scraps of dark green morocco, burgundy kid and old-gold calf, fluttering around her, like leather leaves in a hellish burning autumn. The dye room, by the looks of things, was still on fire, and a group of firemen aimed bucking water jets into multi-coloured flames leaping from its windows. Each flame took on the hue of one of the carefully cooked leather dyes. All the secret formulas! May knew they had been closely guarded for hundreds of years by succeeding foremen. What if they had all gone up in smoke? She stood open-mouthed as vats of dyes ignited, sending flames of petrol blue and vermillion shooting into the air. Saffron yellow and violet joined the mix, painting the grey, dust-smudged world with a rainbow of fire.

The flames burst up with renewed incandescence, and in spite of the heat coming off the blaze, she stood mesmerized, unable to move either forward or back. This was her workplace, the site of her daily grind, hated and yet secure, reviled and yet familiar. Now it was being transformed into all its chemical elements before her eyes. It felt as if her world was disintegrating. She thought she heard an impossible cry, coming from beyond the flames, and took one step forward, when a shout alerted her and a strong pair of hands tugged her back.

'Watch out! It's going!'

A tumbling, charred and smoking beam bounced inches from where she'd been standing and now she whirled round to see that Bill Gilbie was once again her rescuer.

'May?' he said. 'Come on, there's nothing for us to do here.'

He took her arm, leading her back across the street where groups of other workers had gathered, out of the way of the firemen, the flames and the falling timber.

Emmy sought her out through the crowd of onlookers, and she stood with her workmates, but no one spoke. A shocked numbness seemed to have infected them all. Though there was no work to go to, and nothing any of them could do to help, they stood in indecisive little groups, huddled together as if for comfort. They watched till the shooting flames lost their stained-glass brilliance and the sky faded first to smudged water-colours and then to a grey blanket, covering the sopping mass of ashes, dull molten glass and charred animal hides.

May jumped as she felt a hand rest gently on her arm.

'Don't think we'll be doing any work today, do you?'

She turned round to find Bill at her side.

'No, don't suppose we will.'

Suddenly he reached up to rub away a streak of soot from her cheek with his thumb. Realizing what he'd done, he blushed and she felt embarrassed. The normal social barriers seemed to have tumbled down along with the buildings around them.

'Sorry, you've got soot all over your face,' he apologized.

'I must look a state. Is it gone?' she asked.

He nodded and went on. 'I was helping the fire wardens earlier – we got a few people out.'

'Were there many inside?' She tried to calculate how many would have been at work, during the night shift.

'Fair few, mostly in the shelter, but that took a hit. I was up on the roof, fire-watching, when they came.'

'Did everyone get out?'

'They're still looking,' he said, glancing anxiously towards the dust-shrouded debris, where volunteers combed the ruins and firemen were still putting out scattered embers.

'What do we do now?' she asked, feeling as if she needed permission to leave.

'Come for a walk?' He turned to her with a weary smile. 'If we've got a day off, we might as well make the most of it.'

'Wouldn't you rather go home and get some kip? You've been up half the night!'

She felt a sharp nudge in her back, and looked round quickly to see Emmy, mouthing, 'Go on!'

She turned back to Bill, blushing, and he shrugged. 'I don't think I could sleep a wink, not after the night I've had.'

More to avoid the dumb shows from Emmy, May agreed, and they set off together, wandering the streets of Bermondsey, surveying the bomb damage as they went. Their route took them from the factory towards Grange Walk, where, as they passed an ancient narrow house, Bill pointed to some metal protrusions high up on the front wall.

'See those? They're the hinges from the old Bermondsey Abbey gate.'

May looked up. 'Makes you wonder, doesn't it? Something as small as a hinge, all that's left of it . . . there won't be much more left of our Bermondsey after all this is over.'

It was a melancholy thought, and they tramped on in silence. After a while, Bill said, 'It reminds me of that rhyme "London Bridge is falling down". Perhaps it's never been any different – it's always falling down, and we'll always have to build it up again.'

'Well, the bombs made a good job of the first bit last night,' May said with a wry smile.

For as they headed towards Tower Bridge Road, there was virtually no street left undamaged. They passed bombed-out families straggling in anxious little bands towards the rest shelters, others sifting through the rubble of their homes, rescuing precious family belongings. There were entire streets of houses with front walls ripped off, sometimes with the interiors still intact, wallpaper and furniture exposed to view. In one house, a bed hung precariously from a ruined top floor, ready to topple. As they stopped to put a name to an unrecognizable street or a missing building, she discovered that Bill Gilbie was easy to talk to: he seemed genuinely interested in her. Before long he had found out her unremarkable life history. It was more than any other boy had, and her usual shyness retreated enough for her to ask him about himself.

'Where were you working before Garner's?' she asked.

'I was at the Blue Anchor works.'

She wrinkled her nose. The Blue Anchor was notorious as one of the smelliest of the local tanneries, with its exotic mix of sealskins, snakeskins and alligators.

'When you first came to Garner's, I thought you worked in the office.'

He chuckled. 'What made you think that?'

'I thought you looked a bit like a college boy, that's all.'

She'd noticed that he always came to work in a smart jacket and tie, even though they were replaced by rolled-up shirtsleeves and a leather apron once he was there. Hard physical labour had given him a strong frame, but for May it was his intelligent eyes and broad forehead, with the habitual strand falling across it, that made her think of him that way.

'College boy, eh? Till you saw me lugging hides about! No, I've always been in factories, ever since I left school.'

He gave her the rather wry smile she'd noticed once before when she thought he might have been disappointed in love.

'I did get a scholarship, wanted to go, but Mum and Dad couldn't afford the tram fare to Goldsmiths,' he said, and she realized she was right about the smile. It was just his way of masking disappointment.

48

'Oh, Bill, that's such a shame.'

'That's life,' he said, pushing back his hair.

May hesitated. 'Well, I didn't even bother to take the exam. Mum and Dad didn't see the point for a girl. And they needed my wages coming in. But Garner's is not so bad. At least I've got my own money. It gives you a bit of independence.'

It was her stock response on the subject, even though it was untrue. The majority of her wages went to her mother and May got to keep three shillings, more than some of her friends were allowed, but still never enough for independence. Any lingering sadness that the family's need of her wage had curtailed her future she kept securely shut away. She tried never to let her parents get a hint of her true feelings. Why burden them with guilt, when there was nothing they could do about it?

'But sometimes I think it would've been nice to have the choice,' she added in a rush of honesty.

'Me too!' he said. 'But I don't blame Mum and Dad.' He was obviously as eager as she to protect his parents from the judgement of strangers.

Nearing Tower Bridge, they turned right, into the maze of riverside streets around Shad Thames. Smoke rising from Butler's Wharf and the warehouses fronting the Thames evidenced that they had been targeted, and the acrid smell of charred timber caught in May's throat. Here and there, they could glimpse the river, where once a slab-sided warehouse had obscured the view. And in one street, some very old houses that had begun to crumble a century earlier had finally met their nemesis. Though still standing, they seemed to be disintegrating from the bottom up. One in particular caught May's attention, as a curiously shaped shaft of sunlight cut through the dust-filled air above it, to illuminate the tall, thin frontage with two distinct wings of light. Squashed between a pub and a warehouse, the house was leaning forward at an acute angle. But as she stared at the odd wings of light, glinting off the surviving windows, a small avalanche of bricks added to the mound at the bottom of the house. May jumped.

'Looks like the roof's about to fall off now!' Bill said as a handful of old slate tiles slid with a crash to the pavement, sending up a fresh cloud of rubble dust to veil the shaft of light.

'Best get back to the main road.' He took her elbow, but as they turned to go she heard a high-pitched sound, coming from the old house. They looked at each other.

'Cat?' Bill put his head to one side and they both listened. Again came the high wail.

'Oh, it's pitiful,' she said

He seemed to hesitate, then shook his head, without her having to voice her thought. 'It's too dangerous, May. It'd be stupid to go in there for a cat!'

Again, an almost accusing cry rose from the ruined building, this time ending in a choking sound. May put her finger to her lips. 'Shhh . . . listen! That doesn't sound like a cat!'

'You stay here.'

'No. I'm coming too.'

'OK, but tread where I tread.'

She followed in his footsteps as he picked his way carefully over the pile of tumbled bricks, which had fallen from the front wall, leaving an opening into the ground floor of the house. They peered over the rubble and a cry forced itself from May's lips. Bill reached back to steady her, clutching her hand as they inched forward. But May's foot slipped and they froze as the whole rubble pile shifted. They gripped each other's hands till it had settled, and they were able to look again through the opening.

It was a scene of domestic serenity. A woman sat in a rocking chair, holding an infant in her arms. Her face was full of a calm contentment but she was obviously dead. Yet with all the determined strength of a baby's will, the screaming child was demonstrating that it was still very much alive.

For an instant May stiffened, an irrational sense of the woman's privacy holding her back. This was her home – how could they just walk into her home, uninvited. Maybe it was because the mother looked as if she were sleeping, had just nodded off by the fire after nursing her baby, perhaps waiting for her husband to come home. But the bombs had already invaded her home and there was no privacy in death.

'We'll have to go in . . . for the baby, Bill.' Her voice shook and Bill squeezed her hand more tightly. Then, letting go, he inched carefully down the rubble mound and into the woman's front room. May followed cautiously, but stumbled to her knees, setting the whole scree moving, tumbling her into the front room of the house.

Bill froze. 'Careful, May! Are you all right?'

'Yes, don't worry about me!' She gingerly got to her feet and stood watching as he gently prised the woman's arms away. She heard him say 'Sorry' softly as he lifted her baby and handed the child to May. A current of trembling life shot through her as soon as the child was in her arms. Its cries sent a shudder through her own body, its insistent blue lips parting to let out screams of rage and fear.

'Quick, Bill, we need to get it warm. It could've been there all night. Poor little thing.'

But as they began the precarious climb back out of the ruined house an agonized groaning came from the old timbers holding up the roof. She scrabbled for a foothold and, with the baby held in the crook of one arm, scrambled to the top of the pile of rubble. Bill clambered up behind her and grabbing her round the waist shouted, 'Jump!'

CHAPTER 3

JOHN BULL ARCH

September–December 1940

They launched themselves from the top of the mound. Staggering forward with the momentum of their leap, it was a minute before she looked back, to see the old house, which had resisted centuries of neglect and decay, now succumb. It met its end with a slow crash and a long sigh, almost like the exhalation of a last breath. All May could think of was the poor young mother, whose home had become her tomb.

She held the child as tightly as she dared, trying to give it her own warmth, but the baby, sensing she was not its mother, could not be comforted. She looked around for help. There was no one in sight. They stood listening to shouts and bells clanging further down Shad Thames.

'The rescue teams must have moved on,' Bill said. 'Wait, let's think. Tower Bridge nick's near here. We should take the baby there.'

He began walking rapidly and May hurried to keep up with him.

'Hang on a minute, Bill. This is the wrong way. You're going towards the river.'

Bill looked doubtful, but she knew she was right. Her father called it her homing-pigeon instinct.

They began half-running back the other way. Bill gave her his coat to wrap around the child, and looking back at the remains of the old narrow house, she called out a promise to the dead woman. 'We'll look after your baby.'

She felt warmth returning to the child in her arms. 'Oh, Bill, that poor woman, and she looked so peaceful. How could she be dead, when she didn't have a scratch on her?'

'Probably the shock of the blast, but her body must have shielded the baby.'

May gave the child her thumb knuckle to chew on. It worked for a time; the poor thing thought it was getting sustenance. But soon the aching hunger returned, and by the time they were mounting the steps of the police station its screams were piercing and the sergeant looked up sharply as Bill approached the desk, quickly explaining what had happened. Either the sergeant was a father himself or he had nerves of steel, for he was able to ignore the baby's ear-splitting cries while he went through the official procedure of taking down Bill's name and address and the location of the bombed house. May paced in front of the desk, rocking the baby, changing its position in her arms, in a futile attempt to stop it crying.

'I'll get the Auxiliary Ambulance depot on the

blower. They'll have someone nearby can deal with the little mite . . . and its poor mother too.'

The sergeant picked up the telephone and when Bill returned to her side, she said, 'Bill do you mind if we stay, just until we know the baby's safe?'

He nodded, looking down at the screaming bundle in her arms, and she continued rocking it while sitting beside him on a hard wooden bench.

But finally the child came to the end of its strength. The screams turned to deeply inhaled sobs, as its lower lip trembled and its eyes closed. The silence, after such turmoil, seemed so deep. May rested her hand on its little chest, feeling with relief the regular rise and fall as sleep claimed it.

They sat waiting while the wounded and lost, the innocent and guilty filed past them, all docketed and ticketed regardless of circumstance by the efficient desk sergeant.

'I wonder if it's a boy or a girl?' May whispered.

'Check.'

May looked. 'A boy,' she said, patting the sopping nappy. 'I wish we could do more for him.'

Bill covered her hand with his own and said gently, 'We've done a lot, May. We saved his life.'

It wasn't long before a woman ambulance driver pushed through the swing doors. She came to them and looked down at the baby in May's arms. May cradled him more tightly, reluctant now to let him go. No doubt the ambulance driver had seen it all before. She gently removed Bill's jacket and produced a soft white blanket. 'Here,' she said, 'wouldn't he be better off in this?

May nodded, tasting salt from tears she'd been unaware of. 'We promised his mother we'd look after him, didn't we, Bill?'

And the woman nodded. 'You have done. We'll do the rest, dear, and find his father if we can.' She put out her arms. 'Here, let me take him. I expect he's hungry?'

Once out of the station, May was surprised to see the sun still shining. She had no idea of the time; it was as if the drama had played out in slow motion. It must have been late afternoon and only now did she realize she was hungry. With an unspoken understanding, they turned towards the river; it didn't seem right to May, just to go home. They came to a café in the shadow of Tower Bridge.

'Shall we go in for a drink, and a bite to eat?' Bill asked, and she agreed, not realizing how tired she was until they sat with drinks and a plate of sandwiches between them.

Although they'd worked together for over a year, and she'd seen him most weeks at the Red Cow, there was still much that she didn't know about him. He told her that he lived with his parents and two younger brothers in Grange House flats, near the tannery. His father drove a horse and cart, working out of the local railway depot, and his mother worked part time, cleaning the offices at Pearce Duff's custard factory.

She told him about her own family and he asked if her brother was serving.

'Jack's in the army. I do miss him – even though he used to torment the life out of me!' she confessed, smiling at the memory. 'But it's worse on Mum. I dread to think what it'll do to her if he gets posted overseas. And it's terrible for Joycie, his fiancée . . . they'd not been engaged long when he got called up.'

Bill nodded. 'It's hard for the people left behind; not that I've got a sweetheart to worry about now.'

Dolly had often tried to find out if Bill was 'taken'. Eventually she'd concluded he was single, more because it suited her than for any other reason. May wasn't convinced, but she would never have asked – now it seemed impolite not to.

'Now? Did you have one before?'

There was a moment's silence, and then came the wry smile.

'Once, yes. Her name was Iris. But it didn't work out, probably both too young.'

'I'm sorry, Bill.'

He shook his head. 'It's for the best. War's so much harder when you have to leave someone you love behind.'

He fixed her with his sea-blue eyes and for an impossible moment she thought she saw herself reflected in their depths.

'And you, May? Is there anyone?'

The question flustered her and she broke off from his gaze.

'Me? No, no one special,' she said, and squirmed inwardly. No one special! As if she were juggling a dozen fellers.

When she looked up again, he was smiling.

'So,' she said, trying to cover her embarrassment, 'have you thought what service you'll go into?'

'I haven't had my call-up papers yet, but I'll try for the RAF, if they'll have me. It's going to be up to us young ones,' Bill said. 'We might as well get stuck in and get this war over with as soon as we can, so we can all get back to living.'

Those eyes, bright with anticipation, seemed to be looking into a future as unpredictable as the baby's they'd just saved, and as he settled back into his seat she wondered if his fearlessness, like hers had once been, was founded on ignorance of all that the future might hold.

A purple dusk had settled over the Thames as they left the café and decided to walk across Tower Bridge towards the north side. They stood on the gap between the two arms of the bridge, and May felt as though she had one foot in the past and one in the future. It was no good wishing for the world to be as it once was. Looking downriver towards Surrey Docks, she could see the pall of smoke that hung above the smouldering timber yards, and isolated flashes of flame shooting high into the air as firemen struggled to save the still blazing docks. Barges were in flames on the river, and they spotted one, loose of its moorings, floating mid-stream and staining the river red. But it wasn't until the true sunset enamelled the western sky upriver, with turquoise and pink and gold, that they finally turned for home.

The following day, May went to see if the factory had opened in spite of the bomb damage. She found workmen shoring up damaged walls and the front gate cordoned off. Uncertain what to do, she glanced over at Grange House, the block of flats where Bill Gilbie lived, and quickly scanned the windows, wondering which was his and whether he would turn up for work today. Instead, the familiar figure of Eddie Barber, the young foreman, came into view. But his normally jovial face was strained and his eyes were firmly fixed on the dust-strewn ground in front of the factory gate.

'Eddie!' she called.

He jerked his head up, and lifted a hand in greeting.

'Hello, May, you're a good 'un, turning up for work,' he said, stuffing his hands into his pockets, eyes still fixed on the rubble at his feet.

'Well, I thought some of it might be open.'

'Nah,' he said, shaking his head. 'Too dangerous. But God knows what I'll do when it does.'

'Surely there's nothing that can't be fixed and we can get back to work?'

'I should think so, but that's not what I'm worried about. I've lost the bleedin' dye book,' he said, anxiety creasing his forehead. 'All the dye

59

formulas . . . gone. I should've taken it home with me. Daresay I'm for the high jump when the managers find out.' As he spoke he rubbed grit from his eyes. The repair crew's bashing and hammering had raised a thick cloud of brick dust.

'Oh gawd, I forgot!' May said, and diving into her bag, she produced a small, black leather book, pages a little singed, but still intact and crammed with various handwritings. In all the excitement of rescuing the baby, she had forgotten the other thing she'd managed to pluck from the ruined streets.

'I found it yesterday, right up near Tower Bridge – the blast must've blown it all the way to the river!'

'The dye book! You're an angel! Here, give us a kiss!'

She didn't feel she had any choice in the matter and found herself squashed in Eddie's unwanted embrace – just as Bill Gilbie strode into view.

'What's going on here then?' Bill smiled, she thought a little awkwardly, as she extracted herself.

'I was just saying she's an angel, Bill. Look what she found – thought I'd lost it for good!'

Bill nodded, understanding dawning. 'She's an angel all right; somebody else's angel yesterday,' he said softly, a tender expression on his face.

He walked with her to the end of The Grange, but was hurrying to the ARP station to report for more fire-watching duties, and she stood watching him as he disappeared round the corner into

Grange Road. She decided to go to Dix's Place, to let her friend know there'd be no work at Garner's today. And Emmy insisted on enjoying a day off, with Dolly joining them. May had to admit she was glad of a rest from hanging the stinking hides. But with the factory still closed for repairs, they were told to report to the Labour Exchange and spent the subsequent days going from factory to factory, accompanied by Dolly, looking for temporary work. It was on the way back from a day at Atkinson's cosmetic factory that Emmy pointed to the poster urging young women to volunteer for the ATS.

'We should join up!' she suggested suddenly.

'I'd rather die,' May said. She hated any hint of conflict, it was the reason she always tried to be the peacemaker in their family. The last thing she could imagine herself as was an army girl.

'Well, you might just do that,' Emmy said, stopping beneath the poster to light a cigarette, 'if a bomb's got your name on it . . .'

The other girls lit up too and May drew on her cigarette. Looking up at the glamorous woman in the ATS peaked cap and brass-buttoned jacket, she shook her head.

'Don't be taken in by that! Jack's fiancée, Joycie, has joined up and she told me they give you these massive khaki knickers – they call 'em passion killers – and pink, boned corsets just like Mum wears! Apparently, it's all designed to ruin your love life.'

'What would you know about a love life?' Dolly nudged her. 'Never had a chap in your life!'

'Leave her alone, Dolly,' said Emmy, frowning at her friend. 'And anyway, knickers or not, I think it'd be a lot better in the ATS than hanging about here, with no work nor nothing, just waiting to be blown up!'

'No, not me,' May insisted, shaking her head determinedly. 'If I have to do war work, I'd rather go in a factory in Bermondsey. Atkinson's are starting war work soon, plane parts, I heard. I'll do that if I have to, take my chances with the raids. At least I'll die with my family round me!' She stubbed out the cigarette with finality and walked on.

By December, a bitter winter had begun to bite. Pinched faces in the streets and short tempers in the home told the tale of the past three months, when German planes had dropped their bombs on Bermondsey most days and every night. Flights of enemy aircraft blackened the sky, following the silver ribbon of the Thames, targeting Surrey Docks and the main railway line up to London Bridge, and all the factories along the way.

May was making paper chains for Christmas, pasting together odd links of coloured paper, with a strong mix of flour paste and determined cheerfulness. Her mother was adamant that there *would* be a Christmas this year, even if they had to eat their Christmas dinner in the shelter.

When the sirens interrupted them, May managed to gather up the handicrafts, along with the book she'd been reading. She was nearing the end of *Gone with the Wind* and couldn't be parted from it. Though she and Peggy had seen the film earlier that year, May found she liked the book more. Losing herself in the story of another war, in another place, made her feel less beleaguered and alone, Scarlett's lot seeming so much worse than her own.

With only two of them stuffed snugly into the shelter, they had plenty of room for a change. Her father was out on ARP duties and her brother, home on leave, had gone for a night out with Norman. At least tonight they'd have a bunk each, and May stretched out, angling the torch over her book. But her mother couldn't settle. She fidgeted and fussed, checking the time every ten minutes.

'Don't worry, Mum, Jack's not stupid. He'll go under one of the arches if they're caught out.'

But they both knew that wasn't true and that he would walk through the bombs, especially if the evening had been a boozy one. It wouldn't be the first occasion Jack had got caught out in an air raid and ignored the sirens. Their whole lives had been hijacked by the daily bombings, and her brother had quickly dropped his early cautiousness where raids were concerned, deciding that a party definitely took precedence over an air raid. In any case, this was his embarkation leave, the last before he left to go overseas, and he'd been hell bent on enjoying every minute of it. He'd visited Joycie at her ATS camp in Hull and now was making the most of his two precious days at home, before leaving for Southampton.

There was little sleep to be had that night for May, for her mother's fretting over Jack hadn't abated. Since he'd joined up her worries centred less around Jack becoming a crook and more about him staying alive, not just for tonight, but once he was overseas. When her mother finally dropped off to sleep, May lay awake listening to the deafening screams of bombs passing over the shelter. Every nerve was shredded as each explosion rocked the little structure like a boat in a storm.

'Come on, Norm, hurry up. Drinks are on Wide'oh tonight!' Jack tugged at his friend's arm and swayed a little as the cool night air hit him.

They'd started their round of farewell drinks early, in the John Bull pub, but the whiskey had run out and Jack was determined not to curtail the celebrations on his last night before going overseas. Earlier that day George had invited him to the illegal drinking club he ran out of his lock-up. Jack knew the way like the back of his hand. He led his friend through pitch-black streets, weaving their way down to the river. They were both in civvies and the night was cold, so Jack hurried his friend along, even though Norman wanted to stop at every pub on the way. 'No! We're going to Wide'ohs!' Jack protested. 'He'll never run out of booze, believe me. I've unloaded enough of the stuff for him . . . endless supply!'

They came to an alleyway leading off Bermondsey Wall, just wide enough for a lorry. At the end of it was a cobbled courtyard where they found the back entrance to a warehouse. George had the lower floor. It served as a stockroom for contraband, his office, bolt-hole and a lucrative outlet for the black-market booze he acquired. With no licensing laws to interfere with trading and no middle man to cream off his profits, the place was a goldmine.

George came up to them and laid a heavy arm on Jack's shoulder. 'What y'avin', son, you can't go off to war dry!'

Jack looked proudly at Norman, aware his connection to Wide'oh gave him some kudos. Norman grinned.

They found their way to a barrel table in the corner of the warehouse that served as a bar. It was packed with servicemen and businessmen in suits, as well as working men, all rubbing shoulders in the dense smoke-filled cavern. The search for alcohol in an increasingly sober world was the only common denominator and George was doing good business tonight.

'How's your Joycie?' George asked, pushing a bottle of Scotch towards Jack.

'She's lovely,' Jack replied, smiling vacantly and digging into his pocket for a photo. The drink and the cold had somehow turned his fingers to blunt instruments, but eventually he pushed the photo over to George.

'ATS. Still looks smashing, even in uniform.' Jack looked proudly at the image of his fiancée.

'You got time to do a little job for me tonight, Jack?' George bent down to fill up Jack's glass.

Jack waved his hand vaguely. 'Noooo! Sorry, Wide'oh, can't. Joycie made me promise when I went in the army – no more bent jobs for me.'

'Promised Joycie?' George gave a wheezy laugh. 'You shouldn't put up with that. Nip it in the bud, son, let her know who's boss!' He straightened up stiffly. 'Anyway, if you change your mind just let me know.' With that George went off to speak to another customer.

'Joycie got you under the thumb then?' Norman asked.

'Not likely!' Jack protested and then looked sharply at his friend. 'Did you ever ask my little sis out?'

'I reckon she's seeing someone on the quiet,' Norman said, sucking whiskey through his crooked teeth.

'You mean she said no!' Jack tipped back on his chair and roared with laughter.

Norman dropped his long chin to his chest and pushed the chair back. Stumbling forward, he mumbled, 'Going for a jimmy riddle.'

Jack was left alone and George wandered back over.

'Need a top-up?' He poured more Scotch for Jack and leaned in to whisper. 'Can you do me that favour? It's nothing much, just delivering a packet to a mate of mine, needs to get there tonight, but I can't do it – me breathing's playing up.' And he thumped his chest with a balled fist. 'It's on your way home . . .'

'Oh, all right, can't do no harm.' Jack shrugged.

George produced a small flat parcel and a hand-printed address from his pocket.

'Any time tonight. But don't get too pissed and lose it!' George slipped a ten bob note into Jack's top pocket. 'Get yerself some fags on the boat. Good luck, son,' he said, walking off.

Jack looked down at the photo of Joycie. 'Sorry, darl,' he said, 'just one more job.' When Norman came back Jack topped his glass up and toasted Joycie and May and whoever else came to mind, and when the bottle was empty, suddenly mindful of his early train the next day, pulled Norman to his feet. 'Better go, mate.'

Norman slammed down his glass, covering the photo of Joycie still sitting on the barrel top. They pushed their way through the noisy crowd and didn't hear George calling out. 'Jack, you've forgotten Joycie!' He was waving the photo at their retreating figures.

When they neared Norman's home in Longley Street Jack stopped.

'I think I'm going the wrong way,' he said, twisting round in a full circle.

'Well, I'm going this way,' Norman said. He grabbed Jack's hand and shook it vigorously. 'Good luck, mate.'

'You too, Norm.'

As Jack walked away from his friend, he squinted at the address George had given him. He couldn't see it in the pitch-dark of the blackout. Luckily, he'd read it at the lock-up: Bombay Street, a side turning off the Blue, not too far from their house in Southwark Park Road. Jack made his zigzag way along the Blue until he came to Bombay Street. It ran along the railway arches, which housed the usual lock-ups and garages. The blackness was even more intense here; no reflected light penetrated the shadow of the brick viaduct. He walked the length of it, inspecting each arch, but was unable to find the right one.

Suddenly a rising wail split the night.

'Shut up, moaning Minnie!' he shouted at the siren. The part of his brain that wasn't drunk urged him to take care – after all he had a fiancée to think about now. But he'd promised George and if he didn't deliver the packet tonight he'd have no time in the morning. He shrugged up his coat collar and carried on, ignoring the siren's warning. It didn't help that he couldn't walk in a straight line, and he collided with a carelessly placed tin dustbin halfway along the street. The bin clattered to the ground and, stumbling forward, Jack fell heavily to his knees.

'Shit!' he hissed as George's packet flew out of

his hand. He swept his hands in blind arcs over the slick road.

'Sod it, where's the packet? Where's the bloody packet?' he asked the impenetrable blackness. 'George'll kill me!'

Jack was still on his knees when he looked up to the sky, almost as if for help. He saw the German bomber, clearly caught in one of the dancing searchlight beams, tilted his head back for a better view and the whole world exploded around him.

When the all-clear sounded in a bleak dawn, May found she'd been gripping the wooden bunk-edge so tightly that her hands had fixed into rigid claws. Her mother was first out of the shelter.

'Let me get out of here and see if me boy's all right. If he's slept in that house all night, he'll get the sharp end of my tongue!'

'Careful, Mum!' May caught her as she stumbled over a huge lump of shrapnel. But she shrugged May off in her eagerness to get into the house.

As she emerged from the shelter, May saw how lucky they'd been. The blackened shell of the house opposite showed how close the bombs had come to them, but the only damage to her home was an incendiary bomb through the roof.

'It's still burning!' Her father poked his head out of an upstairs window. He'd obviously returned from dealing with other people's fires all night, only to be confronted with one in his own bedroom.

'Is Jack up there?' her mother called in a voice tight with anxiety.

'No. Get the stirrup pump, May!'

Her father had made sure they all knew the drill. She carted the pump and bucket of water upstairs, coughing and choking as phosphorous invaded her lungs. May's father began pumping the stirrup, while she crept across the floor, spraying a jet of water into the burning bedroom. They were congratulating each other on a job well done, when they heard someone shouting outside. 'John Bull Arch has been hit!'

The John Bull Arch was the eleven-track railway viaduct which was their nearest public shelter. An iron gridwork of girders spanning Southwark Park Road, the pedestrian walkways beneath the brick arches were long enough to hold rows of bunks with room for more than a hundred people. May prayed that it hadn't been a direct hit.

Hastily dousing their own fire, she and her father hurried down to the end of the street to see if there was anything they could do to help. But already the area around the bombed arch was swarming with tin-hatted volunteers. Besides, the road was blocked off. Flo and her husband were already there.

'Not many got out alive,' Flo said, in a hushed tone. 'Pitiful, pitiful, what they're bringing out.' And the woman bent her head, blowing her nose with a soot-stained handkerchief.

'Oh gawd forgive 'em, May.'

She shook her head, and the heavy-set woman's shoulders heaved as her husband took her hand. 'Come away, love, there's nothing we can do here.'

May and her father accompanied them in silence, back to their own damaged houses. The ack-ack guns in the park, which May glimpsed through the trees, were silent as well and she found herself wishing they'd been more effective. If only that one plane, whose bomb had hit the arch, hadn't got through. She didn't wish any German mother's son dead – though the prevailing mood prevented her from ever voicing such a heresy – yet today, she would have traded one German boy for all those innocents crushed beneath the arch. That's what war did to you. She was learning.

May and her mother busied themselves cleaning up the fire-damaged bedroom and then helped Flo, whose house had come off worse than theirs. But as the day progressed and still Jack didn't come home, her mother's strength began to falter. Later, as the details of the bombing of the arch emerged and they found out that the bomb had gone straight through the railway line into the shelter below, killing almost everyone, she saw her mother quail. May had once seen a wall sucked out by a bomb blast. It bent, buckled, then sprang back into place. Now her mother's whole body did the same. Outwardly she appeared steady and solid, but May had seen her dissolve.

When Jack didn't return home that day May began to fear the worst. Either he'd been caught in the raid or thought better of going overseas and deserted, though she couldn't see Jack ever going AWOL. Her father called May aside; his ashen face filled her with fear.

'It don't look good, love. They can't tell me anything at the incident enquiry point. I think we'll have to start looking ourselves. Your mother's in no fit state . . . will you come with me?'

'Of course I will, Dad,' she said, eager to do anything rather than sit at home with her mother and worry. She grabbed her coat and once out in the street suggested they go and speak to Norman. He was having his breakfast. He gave an involuntary grin at the sight of May, but their worried expressions wiped it from his face.

'Were you with Jack Sunday night?' her father asked.

''Course,' said Norman, looking puzzled. 'It was his last night home. Something happened . . . already?'

'No, Norman. Well, we don't know, but it's not to do with the army.' She fought to stop her voice from shaking. 'Jack didn't come home last night.'

'Didn't come home? What, you mean he went straight to catch his train?'

'No, we checked. They said he never reported in. Well, we know that – his uniform's still at home.'

'When did you see him last?' her father asked.

'Christ.' Norman tapped his forehead. 'I can't bloody remember. We'd had a skinful . . . let me think. Oh God, what time did I leave him?'

'Was it before the raid?' May interrupted.

Norman screwed up his face as he mined his alcohol-clouded memory of Sunday night.

'Yes, I remember now, I'd been in about half an hour and the sirens started up.'

May and her father exchanged looks.

'Then Jack should have been home before the raid. It's what, a ten minute walk from here?' her father said.

Norman suddenly looked sheepish.

'Don't worry about getting him in trouble, Norman, not now,' May urged.

'He was plastered. I should've seen him home. I'm sorry.' He looked at her with such an anguished expression that she had to reassure him.

'It's not your fault.' She put a hand on his arm.

They left with Norman promising to let them know if he remembered any more details of that Sunday night, but May didn't hold out much hope.

'Why wouldn't he come straight home?' her father said, once outside.

May shook her head. 'Who knows, Dad. He could've fallen down dead drunk somewhere.'

'Well, if he was in hospital, I think we'd have heard by now. May, I think we should go to the police.' But at the police station, they had no news of Jack. They directed them to a nearby yard, where rows of bodies, wrapped in tarpaulin, filled the fenced-in space. Bile rose in May's throat and tears pricked her eyes. Each little mound, a shattered family. She gripped her father's arm tightly as a

WVS helper, with a grey face and tired eyes, listened to Jack's description. She was as gentle and tactful as she could be in the face of their imminent grief, but the unspoken truth was that, by this stage, if a victim hadn't been identified, it simply meant that there was very little left of them.

'We daren't go back to your mother with no news,' her father said, his body rigid with anxiety. 'We'd better go to Guy's ourselves.'

So, with her arm through his, sometimes feeling the whole of his weight upon her, sometimes having to rely on his strength, they made the long walk to Guy's Hospital. No buses or cars were running. The unusual quiet added a ghostliness to streets lined with blackened ribs of buildings and roads rippling with torn-up tramlines. At Guy's they were directed to a basement casualty centre. Here, many of the wounded from John Bull Arch were being cared for. A busy staff nurse took down details, and after consulting a clipboard, went away to check each of the many beds crammed into the white-tiled room. After a short while, she came back with the news that none of the casualties from the arch matched Jack's description.

'You could try the other hospitals – it might be he was sent elsewhere. I know St Olave's took some of the injured.' Her tone was almost too sympathetic and May felt the nurse was merely applying another dressing, a tourniquet for their fear. She couldn't blame her; the woman obviously had more than enough live victims to worry about, without having to worry about the dead.

But Jack was not at St Olave's, and on the way home May said, 'Dad, do you think someone ought to let Joycie know?'

Her father swallowed hard and nodded. 'I'll do it.'

But after another night with still no word of Jack, May could see the anxiety was draining the life out of her parents. Desperate to talk, May went to visit her elder sister Peggy. These days Peggy was apt to leave too much to May when it came to family problems, but now she needed help with keeping her parents' spirits up. It was too easy for Peggy to put her head in the sand, pretend all this wasn't happening. It irked that Peggy seemed to have abdicated all sense of responsibility to her husband, who, May's mother said, treated Peggy like a princess.

Peggy's council flat, on the new Purbrook Estate, was small but pristine: George had provided his 'princess' with a home like a palace. The curtains and furniture were new, nothing like their own hotch-potch of inherited items. There was running hot water and even a bathroom. Bermondsey Council had been systematically demolishing the old slum streets, but when May's mother's chance had come to move into a new flat, nothing would persuade her to leave their old Victorian house. 'I don't want to live up in the air,' she'd protested. 'That's for the birds. I'm staying put!'

Now, sitting in her sister's tidy little kitchen, drinking tea from her good china cups, May explained why she'd come.

'Peg, you've got to come over and help me with Mum. She's just sitting there, staring into space. And Dad's wearing himself out. He's been tramping the streets all hours, going from hospital to hospital. I can't be with her twenty-four hours a day.'

'I'll do what I can, love – none of us can get on with our lives, not till we know what's happened to him . . . for definite. I'll come back with you now, if you like.'

Her sister slipped her coat on and glanced quickly in the mirror. She was an attractive woman, but since marrying George her look had become far more sedate, almost old-fashioned. Once she'd loved to wear make-up and fashionable clothes, but now she looked almost middle-aged and her wardrobe, though of the best quality, was muted and plain. Perhaps that's what happened when you got married, but May couldn't help blaming George for the change and she was sad that the glamorous older sister, who she'd always admired, had faded as she settled into domestic life.

It was pointless waiting for a bus – so many roads were impassable because of bomb damage or unexploded bombs. So they walked to Southwark Park Road, taking the back streets and bypassing the bombed arch. On the way they caught sight of George, touting for bets, and he gave them a wave.

'George says business is booming,' Peggy said, waving back. 'Do you know, he told me they're even betting on who'll get bombed out next.'

May shook her head. 'That's disgusting.'

'Some people will bet on anything and George says if he didn't take the bets, someone else would.'

May was about to voice her disagreement, when they heard a scuffling behind them. They turned to see Flo's grandson, Terry, dashing up at full pelt.

'Coppers! Wide'oh's doin' a runner!' he puffed. The local kids acted as lookouts for George, who was forever being hounded down by the local police for his illegal bookmaking.

They whirled round to see a row of front doors all flung open at the same time. A chorus of 'Wide'oh, in 'ere!' came from several houses and George disappeared through the nearest one. No sooner had the door slammed behind him than a constable hurtled round the corner, blowing his whistle. Children, most of whom were George's runners, scattered as he stopped short, looking around for his quarry. Peggy hissed at May, 'Keep walking!' They quickened their steps, while May glanced at a worried-looking Peggy.

'I keep telling him to knock it on the head. He's in no state to be legging it over the rooftops any more, not with his breathing.'

George, afflicted as he was with a bad wheeze, was sometimes unable to finish a sentence without stopping for a few gasps. It gave him a very odd, clipped way of speaking, as if he resented wasting his breath on unnecessary words. Not being the fittest of men, he usually enlisted plenty of help from the punters. Anyone who heard the policeman's whistle would fling open their doors, so that George could duck inside and nip over the garden fences, to emerge out of another house at the end of the street. If there were no gardens, he'd use the rooftops. It seemed likely he'd evade the police once more.

When they arrived home, Flo was there keeping Mrs Lloyd company. She met them in the passage. 'Your mum's up in the bedroom, been crying all morning. Shall I get her?'

'Thanks, Flo. Can you tell her Peggy's here?'

Just then they heard a crash from the backyard and May rushed to the kitchen, in time to see George bursting through the back door. He flopped down on a chair, chest heaving, sweat pouring from his red face. Fanning himself with his brown trilby, he gasped, 'Too old . . . this lark.' A wheezing rattle ended in a coughing fit and May ran to the sink to get him water.

'For gawd's sake, George, you'll kill yourself one day!' Peggy said, loosening his tie.

'Don't fuss! Just need . . . catch me breath. Ta, darl,' he said, taking the cup from May. 'Where's your mum?'

But the noise of George's arrival had already reached Mrs Lloyd, who came downstairs, white-faced, with red-rimmed eyes and flattened hair.

'What was all the commotion?' she asked, after Flo had said her goodbyes.

'Just my husband, flinging himself over the garden wall!'

Mrs Lloyd frowned. 'You ought to be more careful, George, they'll catch you one o' these days!'

'Can't afford . . . get caught, your daughter, costs me . . . fortune!' he wheezed, banging his chest. 'Listen, had an idea about Jack, got on to a mate o' mine. Tracked this down.' George drew breath and dug into his inside pocket. Along with a number of crumpled betting slips, and a dog-eared black accounts book in which he meticulously recorded all his shady profits, he brought out an identity card. 'Someone was tryin' to flog it.'

May took the identity card. 'It's Jack's!'

Her mother let out a small cry and took the card, staring at it as though she could extract Jack's whereabouts from its mere presence in her hand.

'But this is good news, Mum! He might be lying unconscious in hospital somewhere, and they wouldn't know who he was.' May felt hope surging through her, but her mother's face didn't show any relief.

'He'd have to be in a terrible state not to be able to tell 'em his own name,' was all Mrs Lloyd said.

After George had got his breath back a little, he explained that his mate had 'persuaded' the black marketeer to reveal that the card came from a ring targeting bombed-out houses and bomb victims. This particular card, he said, had been stolen, along with a wallet, from the body of a young man found lying in a street not far from John Bull Arch.

George looked at the silent white-faced women surrounding him in the kitchen, a puzzled look on his face.

'Bastard, I know . . . don't worry about him. My mate said he give 'im a right pasting.'

May was the one to voice the unasked question on all their lips. 'But, George, did he tell you if Jack was still alive?'

'Didn't I say? 'Course alive!'

May stifled a cry and grabbed hold of Peggy. 'Alive! Thank God!'

'You could've told us that in the first place, George!' Peggy said.

Mrs Lloyd slumped forward, gripping the identity card even tighter. 'Oh Jesus, me poor boy's alive.' And covering her face with her hand, she let fall tears of relief.

'Well, alive *then*,' George said, silencing Peggy with a glare. 'I've put the feelers out, got people looking Kent way,' he added, looking vaguely aware that his revelation was not getting him the praise he felt it deserved.

George's 'contacts' were many and there wasn't an institution in the South-east without some sort of under-the-counter trading going on that he wasn't involved in, even hospitals. If anyone could track down Jack, May was sure it would be George. He gave a self-satisfied smile as he was rewarded with a kiss from Peggy and a cup of tea from her mother, who was even cheered enough to use the family's butter and sugar ration to set about making George some fairy cakes, which, an hour later, he generously shared with them.

On the third day, May kneeled beside her bed in the early morning light. Her Catholic upbringing, with its straitjacket of confessions and its burdens of guilt had so often felt like an inconvenience, but now May groped for her faith, calling on God and all his angels and every saint that she could remember, promising that if Jack would only return to them alive, she would go and do her bit. Whatever it was, she didn't care. Even if it meant facing her own worst nightmare – leaving her home. She would do whatever was asked of her, if it would help end the insanity, where young men were blown up on their way home from a party and babies left wailing in their dead mother's arms. But as she rose from her knees, peering through the sash window at a pale, frost-bitten dawn, a feeling – half dread, half excitement – stirred in her, as she strained to see where that vow might lead her. Just at that moment she spotted George. He was bundled up against the cold in a camel coat and scarf, hustling along Southwark Park Road like a chugging steam train, breath pluming behind him. If he was coming at this hour he had news, and May's heart expanded with the certainty that her prayers had been answered, that it would be good news. She flung on her dressing gown and ran downstairs to let George in.

His lips were blue and ice cold on her cheek as he kissed her. He took off his hat and May looked at him expectantly.

'Where's Mum and Dad?' he asked.

'Still in bed. I'll get them.'

May crept into her parents' room and saw her mother lying awake, a handkerchief screwed into a tight ball in her hand.

May crossed the lino, cold to her bare feet, and leaned over to shake her father. He sat up with a start. 'George's here,' she said softly. 'I think he's got news.'

As she helped Mrs Lloyd into her dressing gown, she felt her mother's whole body shaking. May knew it wasn't from the cold and she put her arm round her, holding her tightly all the way down the stairs and into the kitchen.

'Have you found him?' Mr Lloyd asked.

George nodded, still breathing heavily from his brisk walk. 'Farnborough Hospital. Been unconscious . . .'

'Oh!' The cry forced itself from her mother's lips and May felt her buckle. 'Thank God, I knew he'd answer me prayers!' And May echoed the thanks in her own heart. Her future seemed instantly clear; she would fulfil her secret promise. But the clarity lasted barely a minute. For George was flapping his hands at them, reaching for words in his laboured, infuriating way. He raised his breathy voice above her mother's tears of joy.

'Carrie, Carrie . . . He didn't have a bit of identification on him, no wallet, nothing . . . hospital's been trying to contact you,' he managed to stutter out. His face twisted into something very like guilt before creasing into sobs. George's voice sank to a husky whisper. 'He never woke up – Jack's dead.'

CHAPTER 4

A BLACK CHRISTMAS

December 1940

The news of Jack's death was like the overnight frost which crusted rooftops and crackled over the ruined trees lining Bermondsey's streets. May had gone to sleep with hope warming her heart, but that morning it had turned to ice. Theirs had become a house of tears. They all huddled together in the little kitchen, each with their own grief and regrets – her mother, father and Peggy, hugging each other, forming a sort of phalanx, shielding themselves from the unbearable fact of Jack's death. The tears seemed to meld them into one agonized creature as they sat round the kitchen table. May sat with one arm round her distraught mother, and the other round her sister. Her father's hand closed over her own, as he sat rigid, focusing only on reining in his tears. It was then that she felt something else emerging from the numb grief, something quite alien. Anger, a cold rage, that her beautiful brother should have been robbed of his life so senselessly. She knew he was only one of thousands, millions probably before this evil war had run its course. But perhaps that was the nature of loss; it was only ever real when it was yours.

It was May who answered the door to Joycie when she arrived next day.

'They've given me compassionate leave.'

Her wraithlike face was another hammer blow to May's heart. She stood on the doorstep, hesitating, before May wrapped her arms round her and drew Joycie in. May led her to the kitchen and the young woman almost collapsed into the grief-stricken circle. She had the same questions they all had. Why hadn't he come straight home, how could someone have robbed him while he lay injured, and if they'd found him sooner would he have lived? But May knew that she hadn't really come for answers; she had come to be near Jack. His family was all that was left of him and it struck May then as intensely sad that this was the closest she would ever be to her intended sister-in-law.

As the days passed and their early tears had been shed, they each retreated to whatever privacy they could find. But when every room contained someone mirroring her grief, May took to wandering the park, circling and circling the big guns. They became her anchor in a sea of mourning. She fixed on them, drawing strength from those symbols of her own futile vow, that she would 'do her bit' if Jack was found alive. Her vow hadn't worked. But that didn't mean she wasn't going to keep it. There was a moment when it struck her that Jack might have died, not because of a German bomb, but simply because he was young and reckless. He had chosen to walk home through the raid, daring the bombs to curtail his youth. But no, that thought was too hard to bear. A German bomb was the only reason he was dead, and she was determined to make his death mean something. So she took another vow and this time she swore to be the one behind the gun. This war had become hers.

Everyone said that her flat was like a little palace, and compared to the houses she'd grown up in, it was, Peggy thought as she wiped steam from the bathroom mirror. Running hot water *and* a bathroom! It was an unimagined luxury in the years she'd been growing up. They'd lived in two rooms in Cherry Garden Street, she and her brother sharing their parents' bedroom until May came along and the family grew too big. Then they'd moved to Southwark Park Road, where a bath was a grey tin affair brought in from the backyard and filled by the bucketful from the copper.

She stared at her reflection, slapping at her cheeks to bring some colour to their sallowness. She hardly recognized herself these days. Opening the bathroom cabinet, she took out a pot of moisturizer, one of a lorry load appropriated from Atkinson's cosmetics factory by an associate of George. The rest had been sold on the black market, except for a boxful under the bed, destined as Christmas presents for the women in her family whose skin would from now on be permanently peach-like. At least they would have reason to bless George Flint, even if she didn't. She brushed her abundant fair hair till it shone and then rolled it into the confining net that George preferred.

Everyone loved George. Wide'oh, the cheery local wide boy, with a ready wit and permanent wad of money. Generous to his family and loyal to his friends, it had been easy to convince herself that he was not vicious, not like some of the other villains. And when he'd singled her out four years ago, she'd been young and inexperienced enough to be flattered. She'd married him because he made her feel special. She'd never shone at school, like her clever younger sister May, but people said she was pretty and her slim, tall figure had turned heads as soon as she'd started work.

She crossed the narrow passage into their bedroom. It had an empty feel, despite being crammed with heavy oak furniture: a curved dressing table, with a silver-backed hairbrush set; a double bed with sweeping carved headboard; two wardrobes with brass keys, all chosen by George, who said they'd fallen off the back of a lorry en route to Heal's in Tottenham Court Road. But whenever the sun broke through the net curtains, striping the patterned carpet with bars of light, she felt heavy with sadness. Perhaps the truth of her bedroom was too plainly visible in the light of the sun. At dusk or when dimly lit by the two bedside lamps, she could fool herself that all married women felt the way she did. Empty. Perhaps that was why she was one of the few who never complained about the blackout.

She drew in a long breath, sat down at the dressing table, and opened her old make-up box. A block of crumbling rouge, a half-used tub of face powder, a stub of red lipstick, all frozen in time. For at a certain point, she couldn't remember when, George had made it clear he preferred her without make-up.

He had a way of letting her know what he wanted, without saying a word. His cheery expression vanished and his silence became almost palpable. Whatever her own preferences, she often found herself suggesting the very thing she knew he wanted. There was no doubt in her mind that he loved her; it was just that she wished he'd show it in other ways, the ways that had filled her romantic girlish dreams.

Romance she could dream about, but sex she was entirely ignorant of. She'd even resorted to asking an older friend in a roundabout way, what she could expect when she married. The woman had looked at her pityingly.

'You mean how's yer father? Well, it's like tomato soup, Peg,' the woman had said. 'It's nice for a change, but you wouldn't want it every day, would you?'

From which cryptic piece of advice Peggy had

assumed she would be constantly fending off George's advances. But she quickly learned that wouldn't be the case. For them, sex was an infrequent, cold coupling, which left George fighting for his breath and herself feeling nothing but a yearning sense of failure.

His generosity meant that she had a beautiful home, with the latest cooker and kitchenette, but she would have traded all the appliances in the place for an ounce of passion. But she shouldn't blame George; after all, he wasn't a well man.

She went to her wardrobe, full of the good-quality clothes he'd paid for. No visits to the Old Clo' market for Peggy Flint. She pulled the grey, soft angora twinset off the hanger and tossed a heathery tweed skirt on to the bed. She wasn't ungrateful, really she wasn't. It was just that she'd chosen none of these clothes for herself. But what she had chosen was Wide'oh, and as her mother had once reminded her, 'There's women would give their right arm for a bloke like that – you should think yourself lucky.' George had always been a favourite of Mum's.

Her mother was right. At least she didn't have to cover up black eyes like some of the women round here, and in the early days she supposed she'd found his ways sweet. He would come home very late at night, often waking her up to show her his latest trophy. Once it was a vacuum cleaner.

'Bet there's not another one like it on the Purbrook!' he'd said proudly. 'It's brand new – just have to rub the label off, in case.' And when she'd been unenthusiastic he'd gone quiet, turning his back on her, and she had kissed him, making a joke, saying she would invite the neighbours in tomorrow to witness its maiden voyage.

She picked up the lipstick stub and lightly brushed it across her lips, dabbing it, till it had almost disappeared. She heard the front door bang shut and with a guilty jump, dropped the lipstick. She heard his wheezy breath coming from the front room.

'Princess? Come and have a butcher's at this!'

She slipped on her dressing gown and went into the living room to see what he'd brought home this time. It was a clock, made of cream Bakelite, with a bronze figure of a naked woman on the pedestal. Peggy thought it was hideous.

'We've already got a clock,' she said. It was one of the few things in the home she'd chosen herself.

'Don't you like it?' he said eagerly. 'It's an original, not another one like it – come from Bond Street. Brand new!'

'Yes . . . but I like the clock we've got.'

'You can give the old one to your mother,' George said.

And suddenly she felt tired. There seemed no point in making a fuss about the clock. She turned and went back into the bedroom.

'Hurry up and get ready, George,' she called back from the bedroom. 'You know what Mum's like about the Christmas dinner being on time.'

This Christmas, more than any other, it would be up to them to make sure Mum was happy, though how that would be possible, God only knew. She was being so brave, insisting they went on with Christmas. Christmas! Who cared with her brother in the frozen ground?

It was snowing as they walked from the Purbrook Estate to Southwark Park Road. The trees in the park were heavy with a deep icing that slid in pats on to the rimed grass. The ack-ack guns, now covered in tarpaulin, were like snow-humped beasts, and Peggy shivered at the sight of them. Even last night, the German bombers had not let up. Christmas Eve – and instead of church bells, those big guns had pealed their deadly carols.

When they reached her parents' front door, George had to stop to catch his breath, which plumed in the cold. As her father showed them in, George forced a smile and wheezed 'Here comes Father Christmas!', pulling out a bottle of sherry and another of whiskey from his inside pockets.

'Where d'you get the good stuff like this!' Her father inspected the bottles and George winked. 'Come from the Brick!' The Bricklayer's Arms was a vast railway goods depot just off the Old Kent Road.

'They say there's no way into them sealed carriages,' her father said, uncorking the sherry.

'Well, there ain't, but who says you got to always use the bloody doors!'

And George imitated the crawling motion required to get under a goods van prior to bashing a hole in its floor.

Her father poured the sherry without comment and Peggy placed the Christmas cake she'd made on to the sideboard. George had found a source of sugar at the docks.

'It must be the only iced cake in Bermondsey,' said her mother.

'Well, it needs to be, Dad told me you've invited half the street!'

'Only Flo and some of her family that got bombed out. If it wasn't for George, we'd be giving them bread and drippin' for Christmas dinner. Them chickens you got us have turned out lovely, George,' she said, planting a kiss on his cheek.

As George basked in her mother's favouritism, Peggy sought out her sister.

'You've made a lovely job of the tree!' Peggy said, glancing nervously at May. Since their brother's death it was as if she and her sister had developed a secret sign language of looks and expressions, each one designed to reveal just how well or badly their mother was doing that day.

'Are you taking the mick?' May replied, while her look and a small shake of the head, told Peggy that in spite of her make-up and cheerful expression, their mother might not last the day without breaking. The tree wasn't a proper Christmas tree – they simply weren't to be had. But they had found a large fallen branch in Southwark

Park, covered it in tinsel and hung it with old glass baubles.

As always, they sat down at one o'clock sharp. But once her mother took off her apron and sat down, her work done, she took on a vague, haunted look as if she were barely present. Peggy looked at all the pink, smiling faces: grateful Flo and her homeless relatives; May trying to interest her mother in some chicken and passing potatoes to her father; her old Granny Byron, wizard-like in a gold cone-shaped party hat; her father pouring out the sherry and lastly George. Candle ends had been lit and light danced off the red and green baubles, while homemade paper chains festooned the ceiling. Yet, in all this colour, she was conscious only of her grey twinset; in all the warmth, surrounded by family and friends, with more Christmas fare than could be expected these days, Peggy felt only scarcity. With her husband the source of all abundance in this little community, how could her heart feel so severely rationed? Perhaps they were all feeling the same way. But she knew that she wished herself elsewhere. Serving dinner to refugees from a mobile canteen; making aeroplanes in Birmingham; sorting clothes in a WVS depot; anywhere but here, the wife of the cornucopia, George Flint. When the toast was raised, her father bravely said the words. 'It can't be a Merry Christmas,' and he gulped, 'but our Jack loved a party, and so here's to our beautiful boy, who brightened our lives.' And they all raised

their glasses. 'To Jack!' and 'To absent friends.'
Peggy was left wondering how she too might
become one of the absent ones.

That Christmas night, after they got home, she
pulled the blackout curtains and in the darkness
of their bedroom she broached the subject that
had been on her mind all through dinner and
the wireless broadcast of the King's speech and the
party games during the evening.

'George,' she said, slipping into bed beside him.
'I think I should go back to work.'

After a moment's silence, broken only by the
crackling hiss of his breathing, he said, 'What you
talking about? You don't need to work! I'm making
money hand over fist since the war.'

She had expected opposition. 'But I feel guilty,
you know, doing nothing. Even May's talking
about joining up. They need women doing war
work.'

It was a long shot, appealing to George's patri-
otism, which seemed to begin and end with his
family.

'My wife's not working in no bloody factory,'
George said, ignoring the obvious fact that she'd
been working at Atkinson's when he'd met her,
and the only reason she'd left was because the
firm wouldn't allow a married woman to carry on
working there. Peggy pushed on.

'But it's not really *proper* factory work. Atkinson's
are asking for experienced women to go back,
and I wouldn't be packing face powder. I'd be

making plane parts for the war effort! Besides, it's driving me crazy here, George, I've got sod all to do all day!'

Peggy could hear her own voice rising. She hated confrontation, which she knew was the cause of half her problems. It seemed strange that a woman too meek to stand up to her own husband should feel so drawn to making weapons. But the truth was, she wanted to feel useful, more than ever since Jack's death.

'Sorry I've made it so easy for you,' George's voice was heavy with sarcasm, 'what with the vacuum and the gas cooker! You're an ungrateful cow – you've got everything. I make sure of that and you're never satisfied.' George didn't have the breath to shout, but his hoarse whisper cut through her and it was about now that she normally would have caved in.

'What about voluntary work, surely that's not beneath your wife. There's aristocracy helping out in the WVS canteens these days; even the royal family are volunteering.'

'Leave it, Peg, I'm not having you spend your days sorting through smelly piles of second-hand clothes. Anyway, you'd soon get fed up of that lark.'

Peggy had played her best hand, the royal connection. She'd felt sure that appealing to George's sense that she was somehow a queen amongst women might have clinched it.

'That's not all they do. I saw an advert in the paper asking for volunteers to look after kids while their mums are doing war work. I think I'd be good at that, George.'

He had no answer. It had touched too closely upon the one thing that George, it seemed, could not provide.

On Boxing Day, the family came to Peggy's. May arrived early to help her prepare the dinner.

'Is everything all right, Peg?' May asked. 'With you and George, I mean?'

Peggy looked up sharply and put down the potato she was peeling 'Is it that obvious? I asked George if I could do war work, but he won't have it.'

'Why not? You've got plenty of time on your hands.'

'Yeah, too much. But you know what he's like, wants to keep me wrapped up in cotton wool.' Peggy gave an involuntary shudder, as though trying to shrug off the cocoon of George's affection.

'I know what it's like, not being able to do anything.' May lowered her voice. 'I'm going to have a tussle of my own soon enough.'

'Who with?' Peggy matched her whisper.

'Mum and Dad.'

CHAPTER 5

PREDICTING THE FUTURE

January–February 1941

'Do you know why they call 'em the scrubbers?' Her normally placid father was pulling at his collar. 'Well, it ain't cos they spend all their time scrubbing floors! You're not going in the ATS and that's that.'

'But, Dad, soon they'll be calling up single women. I've got to do *something*!'

'What's wrong with Atkinson's, or Peek's, making plane parts? You always said you didn't want to leave us!'

She couldn't bear her father's hurt expression. He sat beside the fireplace, smoking his pipe, fiddling with the matches that were always balanced on one arm of his chair, as was his habit when agitated. Draping her arm round his rigid shoulders, she kissed his cheek.

'Oh, Dad, of course I don't want to leave you, but even if I sign up for war work, don't mean I won't be posted away. Anyway, I've changed my mind since . . . well now, I want to do more.'

'Is it because of our Jack?' Her father looked up quickly. He was sharp, where May was concerned. She could hide from others, but not her father. He was the person who had most noticed her as she flitted through her childhood, like a grey bird, in the shadows of her siblings.

May sat on a stool at her father's feet, resting against his legs.

'It's true. What happened to Jack, it did bring it home, Dad. I don't want to lose the rest of my family like that, not without a fight. I'm terrified of going away. You know me, the old homing pigeon.' She looked up to see him smiling at the remembrance of his pet name for her as a child. When her busy mother would sit her on the doorstep and say, 'Don't move!', May could always be relied upon to stay put all day. While the other Lloyd children might wander off into the streets, May never strayed. Even now, as a young woman, she would walk in at the end of her day at the factory, demanding as she opened the front door: 'What sort of bird am I?' And her father would reply, 'The sort that always comes home!'

'Just wait a bit, love. Your mum needs you now more than ever. She can barely get herself out the bed of a morning. Gawd knows what she'd do if you weren't here. And besides, you're too young to leave home yet.'

But at nineteen, they both knew that the government disagreed. His work-toughened hand reached for hers; in his strong grip was all the powerful attraction of home, familiarity, safety. And he was right about her mother needing May more than ever. Perhaps it *would* be enough just to make planes or bombs; perhaps someone like herself was better suited to the shadows of war. But suddenly, like a call to arms, the howl of the siren burst into their domestic haven, tearing like a hungry wolf through their home.

'Shelter!' ordered her dad, but she was already running for the back door, snatching up the box of policies in one hand and the hot-water bottles in the other.

Her mother had gathered up coats and blankets, and was already flying to the Anderson shelter. As her father banged its door shut behind them, they heard the sinister plaint of the bombers. A sustained hum, reverberating ever louder, till the vibrations seemed to set her teeth buzzing. The first whizz and thunderous crash made them jump up from the bunks as one, but there was nowhere else to run to. This little tin hut was their only protection, and after a while they settled into an uneasy stillness. Eventually, her father trimmed the lamp and took up where he'd left off.

'If you think this is loud, wait till you get near one of them ack-ack guns – then you'll know all about noise!'

On cue, the deep boom of their own guns in Southwark Park started up, ear-splitting, bone-rattling, insistent. May could only imagine what they would sound like when you were standing next to them.

Then her mother weighed in.

'They'll eat you alive, them ATS girls. They're the sort that know their way around, pubs and fellers – you're not like that, May. They'll eat you alive . . .'

May groaned and pulled the blanket round her shoulders against the freezing cold. It was going to be a long night.

But the arguments went on through the bitter winter weeks, and though there was a part of her that still desperately wanted to be talked out of it, May stuck to her guns. Those December days spent touring hospitals and morgues, searching for Jack, had lit a slow fuse in May, and now her courage lay like an unexploded bomb, dormant, cordoned off, as her parents tried desperately to disable it.

There came a day in February which made her even more determined to do something other than trim scraps of leather for soldier's gloves and airmen's flying jackets. She, Emmy and Dolly were back at Garner's, now partially reopened since the worst of the bomb damage had been shored up. As she neared the factory she spotted Emmy, but immediately she knew something was wrong. Her friend's natural cheerfulness had never once failed her in all the months of bombing, but today her eyes were dark-ringed and red-lidded, her face sombre.

'Em, did you get hit?'

Emmy lived in Dix's Place, near the leather factory. It had only narrowly escaped when Garner's was bombed, but it was a fact that certain areas seemed to be targeted over and over, usually factories doing war work, or buildings near railway lines and the docks.

Emmy shook her head. 'Not us . . .' The girl's face crumpled.

'Oh, Em, what's happened?'

Emmy shook her head, choking back tears. 'No, I'm all right, love. It's just I've heard a terrible thing this morning. Stainer Street Arch . . . it's been hit. Some of me mum's family was sheltering there.'

'Oh, Em, no!' May felt a creeping cold. She shivered, as in a second, she was transported back to the horror of the John Bull Arch bombing.

'The bomb's gone straight through the railway line, into the shelter. Mum's in such a state.'

May wrapped her arms round her friend, as her whole body shook with suppressed sobs, for it had become an unwritten code that grief must somehow be quiet, when there was so much of it around. May knew from bitter experience that she could offer no words to comfort Emmy. Appealing to hope seemed pointless, for no one could promise that tomorrow would be any better.

There was a sombre air hanging over the leather factory that day, as Emmy was not the only one to have lost family in the bombed arch. It emerged that the five-ton steel doors at either end of the arch had been blasted inwards, crushing those they were meant to protect. The water main had burst, drowning those who hadn't already been crushed. There were always people who seemed to delight in describing details of the daily horrors and, by the end of the day, May felt sick with the visions of what had happened in the arch. As she walked home that evening, she stopped to gaze at the ack-ack guns, positioned on the large oval playing field in Southwark Park. Once filled with the sounds of laughing children, playing impromptu games of British Bulldog and cricket, it now echoed to the thundering of big guns, and the metallic rain of shrapnel. May often liked to take a detour through the park on her way home. After a day enduring the stink of the tannery, the smell of grass and trees was a holiday for her senses. Though winter had frozen all the growing things, and much of the park was now given over to allotments, she still enjoyed the space and fresh air. It was a solace she needed today more than ever. She turned in through the gates, walking slowly towards the gun emplacements. The area around them was cordoned off, but as she skirted the field, she found herself overtaken by an ATS girl, hurrying along the path. She was dressed in a heavy khaki overcoat, and had her soft peaked cap pulled down to keep out the chill.

'All right for some, ambling along!' the young woman said with a grin.

'Sorry!' May stood aside, blushing, feeling instantly guilty at her civilian status, though the girl had only been joking. May quickened her pace, falling in beside her.

'Heavy night last night,' the girl said.

'Worse than most,' May said, thinking of Emmy's family.

'We're doing our best!' the ATS girl said.

'I know, we can hear them!' May smiled. 'What's it like on the guns?'

The girl looked puzzled. 'Oh no, us girls aren't allowed near the guns! I'm a clerk in the stores. I'm just delivering stuff to the command post.'

'Oh,' May said, feeling vaguely disappointed.

'Why? Are you thinking of joining up?'

May hesitated, feeling that somehow to voice her intention would make the reality inevitable. She nodded. 'I could do munitions or plane parts . . . factory work's what I've always done. It's just, something happened . . . that's made me want to do more.'

'I know what you mean. I was a teacher, reserved occupation. When my school went to the country I could've gone, but I wanted to be as near the front line as I could get.' There was a pause. 'My fiancé's posted abroad, you see, and it feels like I'm helping him.'

They had reached the gun placement, fenced off and surrounded by walls of sandbags. 'Turns out they needed clerks and secretaries, but if you're anything like me, you'd rather be behind one of those.'

May looked at the long, dull barrels, silent now, but poised to burst into life.

'I'm not sure I'm brave enough . . . but I think I would too,' May said, surprising herself.

The girl leaned in confidentially. 'I daresay I shouldn't be telling you this, careless talk and all that, but there's a rumour going round that they're going to need us women on the guns before too long. With so many men overseas, the batteries are undermanned.' She paused, putting a hand on May's arm. 'Listen, I've got to dash, or I'll be on a charge. If you're not sure about it, my advice is to talk to someone who knows you better than you know yourself. Sometimes we just don't know what we're capable of.' The young woman squeezed her arm. 'None of us are brave . . . but we're all a lot tougher than we think we are!' She trotted off. May watched as the ATS girl paused to look up at the guns, then suddenly turned back to May, mimed a shooting action and winked.

May waved and walked away. As the evening light turned red-gold through the old horse-chestnut trees surrounding the playing field, she decided it was time to visit Granny Byron.

And so, the following Saturday afternoon after work, May walked with Emmy Harris back to Dix's Place. Her grandmother lived there, in the same block as Emmy. The three-storey buildings, facing each other across the courtyard, had seen better days. Each soot-blackened block contained flats, with a shared staircase and toilet on the landings. The courtyard below was packed with children. Two girls were turning a long skipping rope, which stretched from one block to the other. An excited group waited eagerly to leap the rope, skipping to an old chant that May remembered from her own childhood. When they reached the Harris's flat on the ground floor, they found Emmy's mother on hands and knees, ferociously scrubbing the front step, as if she could scour away her troubles with those chapped, raw hands.

'Hello, Mrs Harris, how are you?' May asked. Looking up, the woman dropped the scrubbing brush into the tin bucket, sitting back on her haunches. May could tell that she'd been crying.

'Not too bad, love. We've got the funeral next week – did Em tell you?'

May nodded. 'Mum's offered to help with the wake. She's saving our sugar and butter rations to make fairy cakes.'

'Thank her for me, love. People have been so kind.' Emmy's mother wiped wet hands on her apron. 'Your nan's lent us the money for the funeral, you know.'

May didn't know how her grandmother had become the local moneylender, but as bank accounts were a rarity for the residents of Dix's Place, anyone in need of a loan for a wedding or funeral, new furniture or a new suit would go to 'Granny Byron's' for help. Everyone called her Granny Byron, not just May.

'I'm on me way to see her now.'

Emmy added, 'She's getting her fortune told. Wants to know if she should join the ATS.'

'Well, I can tell you that for nothink – *neither* of you are old enough. You've had no experience of life!'

May looked at Emmy, who raised her eyes. 'We're not kids, Mum!'

'Well, it's not safe. They can send you overseas, you know, and I don't want to lose any more of me family.'

May knew that Emmy was involved in a similar struggle to her own, and she seemed to be having just as little success.

May left them still arguing on the doorstep, and walked to her grandmother's ground-floor flat at the end of the block. It had never been her favourite place. Usually she had to pick her way round a line of women sitting on chairs in the passage, waiting to have their fortunes told. Granny Byron was of Romany descent, and as well as being the local moneylender, she would make an extra few bob telling people's fortunes, reading their palms or the tea leaves. May had always hated running the gauntlet of these strangers whenever she visited her grandmother, and found herself hoping she'd find her alone today. Granny Byron answered her knock with a look of surprise.

'May! I wasn't expecting you! Thought you was a customer. Come in, darlin'.'

Her grandmother was a striking woman. May wasn't sure of her age, but she always seemed

106

ancient, a relic from the previous century. Her grey-flecked, raven hair was pulled back into a tight bun, with old-fashioned ringlets at the temples, and from her ears dangled golden-hooped earrings. May had heard she was a handsome woman when young, but now her leathery face had been tanned by years of standing out in all weathers at her stall in the Old Clo' market. The tanning effect had been augmented by her constant use of tobacco and snuff, so that now her cheeks creased like a walnut whenever she smiled. But her eyes, her most striking feature, black as deep pools, seemed to see everything. The story was that she'd been born in a horse-drawn caravan. Sometimes May wondered how they could be of the same blood. May was as fair as her grand-mother was dark, and whereas May was firmly attached to her home – with her roots deep as the trees that lined Bermondsey's streets – Granny Byron had moved house countless times, seem-ingly unable to settle. May's mother was of the opinion that May must surely take after her father's side of the family, generations of whom had lived in the same riverside area of Bermondsey.

'Are you expecting someone, Nan?' May asked, kissing her grandmother and bending down to pet her grandmother's little dog, Troubles, who stood on two legs until May took his paws.

'Hello, Troubles! And what kind have you been in lately?' she asked, as the little dog yapped a strong denial.

She followed her grandmother into the small kitchen, dominated by a gleaming black-leaded range.

'I was expecting Mrs Green, from over the way, wants to know if her Tom's all right – she ain't heard nothing in months. But I've always got time for you, love. Cup o' rosie?'

May nodded. 'Nan, I wanted to talk to you about something.'

'Your mother told me.'

'I haven't said what it is yet!'

'No need. It's ever since Jack. I know what's going on. You're scared witless of going in the bleedin' army. But someone threatens you and your'n, and the worm turns. That's the only thing'd get *you* out of Bermondsey.' Her grandmother turned her dark, fathomless eyes on her. 'I know you better 'an you know yourself.'

May felt uncomfortable and looked away quickly. 'And how would you know all that? Don't tell me . . . you've *seen* it in the leaves!'

'Do you want my advice or not, you cheeky cow?'

'Sorry, Nan. You're right. I'm frightened to go and I'm frightened to stay.' She slumped back in her chair. 'Oh, I'll never cope away from home. I'm all up the wall.'

'Well, love, I don't want to contradict your mother, but it's my opinion you'll never be able to live with yourself if you don't go, whatever your reasons might be.'

'Really?' May hadn't seen this coming. 'Well, can you see if I'll be all right if I *do* go?'

Granny Byron nodded. 'Let's get the kittle on.' She went to boil water on the range; when the tea was brewed, so strong it was black, and they'd drunk it down, she took May's cup, swirling the dregs around.

'Ahh,' she said, peering at the tea leaves. 'Don't tell me you've not got a bit of the Romany in you. Whether you know it or not, I reckon you can survive anywhere, sweetheart. You've just got to believe in yourself.'

May couldn't credit that she'd inherited any gypsy blood at all. But she was grateful for the encouragement and listened intently as her grandmother went on.

'And there's always this to consider: if you stay here, you could just as easily get bombed out, then you won't have no home to go to anyway, will you? You might as well do what you can to protect it.' Granny Byron sniffed.

'I suppose you're right. But what about the future – can you see where I'll be in a year or two's time, Nan?'

Her grandmother sat back and picked up her old snuffbox, sniffing up a pinch and sneezing loudly. It was an outdated habit, which May hated, along with the old clay pipe that she insisted on smoking, and the peculiarly old-fashioned way she pronounced certain words. May had spent her childhood correcting 'kittle' to 'kettle' to no avail.

'Ugh, Nan, when you givin' up that habit, it's disgusting!' she complained.

Granny Byron frowned. 'I can't do a reading without me snuff. What I see, darlin', is this: a place with a *lot* of rain, pissin' it down . . . and you'll cross water, and I see fire, plenty of fire in the sky, and yes, love . . . there you are dressed in brown. And I see a feller . . . no, two, both in blue uniform.'

'Two fellers? Navy or RAF? Am I going to marry one?' May interrupted. But her grandmother frowned. She would only give a reading, never interpretations.

'I couldn't say, but here's your heart . . . ahhh.' The old woman held the cup at an angle to catch the light, then hesitated. 'Well, that's no surprise. It's all hidden.'

Her grandmother looked into her eyes, as if searching them for what she could not find in the leaves, then she nodded. 'But that only means it's hidden from yourself, love. One day, you'll see it plain.'

May found all of it infuriatingly vague. What was the use of pointing out to her the things she couldn't see. It was all a load of old codswallop and she didn't know why she'd bothered coming. But she had one more question that she couldn't resist asking.

'If I do go away, will I be coming home again?' she asked, hands clenched tight beneath the table.

Her grandmother put down the cup. 'Only if you want to, love.'

The reading was over and May wasn't at all convinced she'd been told everything that was written in the leaves. For whenever Granny Byron saw bad things in the future, the only one she would reveal them to was Troubles. May had once asked her why she'd given the sweet little dog such an unfortunate name.

'Because I tells *him* all the troubles *they've* got coming, when I dursn't tell them! And then I tells him me own, 'cause no other bastard's interested. And d'ye know what? That little dog don't get a bit downhearted! No. He's the only one fit to hear 'em.'

Perhaps seeing her disappointment, Granny Byron took hold of her hand.

'Listen here, gel. You can do more than you think. You've just got to toughen up a bit, be more like your old nan!'

Her grandmother had certainly had a hard life, with her husband, whose parents had had delusions of grandeur and had given him the unusual first name of Lord, missing in prison on and off for most of her married life. She had brought up her children largely alone, which is what she was at the moment. Lord's latest crime had been for petty theft, but he'd been given twice the normal sentence.

'Have you heard when Grandad's getting out?' May asked.

'Cocky old sod, done himself, didn't he? Got an extra six months.'

'What happened?'

'Well, the judge says to him, "What's your name?" And your granddad says, all very polite, "Lord Byron, your honour." "Oh, *Lord* Byron!" says the judge. "Is that by name or by title?" "Please yer fuckin' self," he says! "Please yer fuckin' self" – to the beak! Bang goes the gavel. "Take him down! Six months extra for contempt."'

Shaking her head, her grandmother set the golden earrings swinging and May had to laugh at her incorrigible old tea leaf of a grandfather.

'You make sure you don't end up with a wrong 'un like him, May, that's all I say.'

'Well, there's no one ever been interested in me, Nan, so I don't think there's much chance of that.'

'Don't you be so sure.' She tapped May's heart with a gnarled finger. 'I've seen *two* in the leaves!'

Just then there was a knock on the door and it was Mrs Green, come to find out if her husband were dead or alive. May hoped the woman would get more concrete proof than she had, for she wasn't sure whether her grandmother's words had helped her at all. As she left Dix's Place, she felt as if she were walking forward into the night without a compass or a star to guide her.

CHAPTER 6

DOING TIME

February 1941

That painful first Christmas without Jack had passed, but the bitterly cold weather persisted into early 1941. It wasn't until February that Peggy discovered George had lied to her about the hideous Bakelite clock. It turned out it wasn't unique at all. She discovered this when there came a knock on the door at about eight o'clock. She wasn't expecting any of her family and George was out. Much of her husband's business was conducted at night, in the pub, or in warehouses and barges down by the river. The comings and goings of contraband were best executed in the dark and the blackout helped rather than hindered George's business. Often he would come home in the early hours of the morning smelling of river fog and she knew he'd been helping to unload a boat full of cigarettes or whiskey. He always paid for it the next day, with a cough that had him doubled over, gasping for breath, but she'd given up asking him to leave the river work to others.

She inched aside the blackout curtain that screened the front door. She was always so careful, but perhaps she was showing a light. The air-raid warden, Stan, who lived on the top landing, was a stickler for picking up every last chink. She opened the door a crack, letting a yellow curl of fog creep in. It was an opaque night; she hoped the weather had dissuaded the German bombers and she was glad not to be spending the night in the public shelter down in the courtyard. The sight of a policeman standing at her door could mean only one thing. She shivered. There'd been no air-raid warning, but sometimes a lone plane got through without being detected.

'Who's been hit?' she asked.

'Can I come in, Mrs Flint? It's about your husband.'

Panic seized her and without thinking she flung aside the blackout curtain. As the policeman stepped inside, she heard Stan shout from the courtyard, 'Put that light out!'

She was trembling from head to foot as the policeman quickly ducked through into the passage. Peggy felt for the wall, her legs buckling as the policeman caught her elbow. But she pulled herself up and led him into her living room. He sat in one of her brown leather armchairs, his helmet balanced on his knee as he looked around.

'You've got a very nice home, Mrs Flint.' He smiled. He was only young, certainly younger than herself. As she perched on the edge of the chair opposite she saw him glance up at the mantlepiece.

'I'm afraid your husband won't be coming home tonight.'

'Oh no, I knew it, what's happened to him?' She stared at the constable, without seeing him. Instead a vision of George, broken and bloody beneath a ton of rubble, played like a newsreel to the pounding of her own heart.

'Don't worry, Mrs Flint. He's not hurt.'

'Oh thank God.' She let out the breath she'd been holding. 'I know there's been no raid, but you hear of so many accidents in the blackout.'

'He's not hurt, but I'm sorry to tell you he is in bad trouble. He's been arrested and we're holding him overnight at Tower Bridge Police Station.'

She'd always known George's luck would run out, but somehow the war had deflected her attention. Surrounded by so many dangers, as they all were, just going about their daily lives, George's occupational hazards had somehow been obscured. She'd felt that the police ought to be looking the other way, up at the night sky or searching out fifth columnists, rather than poking around in George Flint's lock-up.

'What's he done?' she asked.

'He was caught transferring stolen goods into a van from a lock-up near Bermondsey Wall. The items came from a warehouse in Shoreditch, we believe.'

The constable looked over at the mantlepiece

again. 'Clocks, hundreds of them. Matter of fact, they're not unlike the one you've got up there, Mrs Flint,' he said, pointing to the cream Bakelite monstrosity, with the nude woman on its pedestal.

After the policeman had left and she was on her own, Peggy put her old clock back on the mantle-piece. The young constable had taken the other one away. She sat down, listening to the seconds ticking, trying on her solitary state as though it were a new dress. She feared for George, imagining him in a damp prison cell, and yet she knew him – after a week, he'd probably be controlling the supply of prison blankets. He would be all right. But would she? As if to answer her question, the keening of the air-raid sirens drew her attention back to the war.

She pulled on her coat, picked up her knitting and torch, lifted the gas mask from the hook, and after checking every light was off, hurried down to the public shelter at the bottom of the flats. By the time she got there it was full to bursting. She would have to try for the nearest railway arch shelter. She started running. Since the John Bull and Stainer Street bombings, she'd been wary of sheltering beneath the arches, but there simply weren't enough public shelters, and sometimes there was no choice. People staked out their places early on in the evenings, not even waiting for the sirens to sound. Searchlights criss-crossed the night sky, lighting her way forward, and looking up, she saw tiny black dashes, stitching the beams together. Hundreds of bombs, falling like sleet. Suddenly she heard the unmistakable whistle of a bomb descending. Hurling herself on to the cobbled street, she covered her head. The explosion sent the stones rippling beneath her and windows from a nearby parade of shops shattered like a thousand chandeliers. Before the next bomb could fall, she leaped to her feet and ran, never stopping till she reached the railway arch. Not a moment too soon, she joined the crush of people inside, as the shock of another explosion ripped the night apart.

Families and couples were already settled into little encampments. Some had placed makeshift mattresses on to the rough wooden sleeping benches; others were bedded down on the floor. Children covered in blankets slumbered, in spite of the chatter and laughter that reverberated around the brick vault. But adults had less chance of sleep. Some were knitting, others reading by the light of paraffin lamps, and in one corner someone with a piano accordion had started up a sing-song. Peggy pushed her way through, looking for an empty corner.

'Come over 'ere, love.' A woman surrounded by six children, lying top-and-tailed on the floor beneath a striped blanket, shuffled over, patting a corner of the blanket. 'Plenty of room,' she said, grinning.

All night Peggy lay wakeful, curled on the edge

of the woman's blanket, listening to the alien snores and the fretful whimpering around her. It wasn't fear of the bombs falling that kept her awake, nor the thought of George, locked up only a few streets away in Tower Bridge nick, though she did wonder if they would have a shelter there. What had really shaken her was the exhilaration she'd felt as she ran through the raid, which had far outweighed the fear. She was no fonder of bombs than the next person, so the only other explanation for it was that she was facing it alone. She had felt free.

When daylight broke and the all-clear sounded, she stirred gratefully. Two smiling WVS canteen women entered the shelter with trays of buns and cups of tea.

'How about this for five-star service? Tea in bed!' one of them said, bending down to an elderly couple who were just sitting up and reaching for their dentures.

'Oh, look at this, love.' The husband shook his wife. 'Better'n the Savoy in here.'

Peggy thanked the woman whose blanket she'd shared and stepped round people packing up their bedding as she made her way outside, thick-headed, her mouth like sandpaper and her bones aching. A crowd of shelterers huddled round the WVS mobile canteen, while the woman serving struggled to keep up with the orders. After a night in the cold damp shelter, people's faces brightened as they sipped from the steaming cups, warmed equally by the tea and the smile of the woman serving. Peggy joined the queue and when the woman handed her the tea, she asked, 'Do you still need volunteers for these canteens?'

The girl in the green overall raised her eyes. 'Are you free to start now?' she asked, laughing.

After drinking down the hot tea, Peggy went straight to Southwark Park Road, without first going home. Her father received the news of George's arrest with an expression of determined calm.

'Well, he's been good to us and we'll stand by him,' he said.

But her mother was distraught. 'Of course we will, but what about our Peggy, what's she going to do without him?'

They were talking about her as though she wasn't there.

'There's cash in the house,' she interrupted. 'George's got a bit tucked away, and he's always told me to go to his mates if I ever get in trouble. You know George, everyone loves him.'

'Well, if you find you can't manage, you'll just have to come home, love,' her mother said.

But Peggy doubted she would ever go home again. Besides, her sister wouldn't thank her for crowding her out in the bedroom.

'He'll be out in no time,' her father said, patting her hand but avoiding her gaze. They both knew it would be much longer than that.

*   *   *

119

George was sentenced to two years. It might have been less if it had just been the clocks. The police had found jars of Hartley's jam and packets of tea and sugar in the lock-up, and they were clamping down on black marketeering of rationed goods. But worst of all they had found stolen ration books and identity cards. When she heard that part of the charge Peggy went cold. Her parents must never find out about it, for it was far too close to the crime that had robbed them of their last few days with Jack, and she doubted that their fondness for George would survive that knowledge.

Peggy was allowed to go to his holding cell, before he was sent down. She hadn't seen him since his arrest and she was shocked at the change in him. He sat, grey-faced and white-lipped, at a little table, a policeman standing behind him. When he saw her, he attempted the old cheery smile, but his eyes told her the truth. George was frightened.

'Princess, I'm sorry,' he said, reaching out for her hand. 'Suppose I should be grateful – it could have been longer. You'll be all right, though. Just go to Ronnie Riley if you're ever short. Ronnie'll look after you.'

'I'll be fine, George, don't worry about me. I can always go back to work.'

'No! There's no need for that,' George protested, but he knew as well as Peggy that the £500 fine which came with the sentence meant that her life as the queen of the Purbrook Estate was at an end. She wouldn't argue with him, not now.

'Well, look after yourself in there, and if your breathing gets bad make sure you see a prison doctor.'

She heard the constable give a small snort and looked up to see him smirking.

'You're entitled to see a doctor,' she said firmly.

George looked uncomfortable, but managed a smile. 'Yes, darl, I expect we get sent up Harley Street for our annual checkups an' all.'

When she left him, she felt an odd mixture of guilt and relief. Guilt for all the times she'd balked at his controlling ways, relief at the sudden expansion she felt as the cell door snapped shut behind her. It was as if a confining corset had been released and finally she could breathe. It struck her as odd that just as George was beginning his prison sentence, she was being freed from hers.

The next day she went to the labour exchange and signed up for war work. She filled in countless forms, name, age, marital status, husband's occupation. And Peggy felt herself blushing. Although it hadn't been her crime, she realized all at once that she would feel the stigma of George's.

'In prison,' she whispered, hoping that the people waiting to be seen couldn't hear. The woman filling in the form paused for an instant. 'Previous experience?' she asked, not looking up.

'Atkinson's.'

'Ah yes, they're looking for experienced women. They've started making cream for burn victims, very important work, or plane parts. Do you have any experience of soldering?'

'Well, yes, as a matter of fact I've done soldering on the talcum powder tins.'

The woman looked up, suddenly interested. 'That should come in handy. Women usually have to be sent on training courses. I'll recommend you for Atkinson's.'

Peggy's one fear had been that with her husband in prison she'd be considered a 'mobile woman' and shipped off to the other end of the country. At least now she could stay near her family.

After the labour exchange she went to the local WVS office. It was buzzing with activity. In one corner, overalled women were sorting piles of second-hand clothing. The unmistakable fusty smell of unwashed clothes hit her and she hurried past to the kitchen, where, through a serving hatch, she could see women bending over deep sinks, washing cups and saucers. An elderly woman, in WVS green, greeted her at a reception desk and asked what hours she could do.

'I'll be doing war work at Atkinson's, but I can volunteer around my shifts. I don't mind night work,' she said, thinking of the long nights ahead without George.

'Thank you, my dear.' The woman smiled and looked down at a rota. 'We're desperately in need of help on the mobile canteens' night shift. So many women have to get home for their children, you see.'

Again came the list of questions ending in 'husband's occupation?' And for some reason, this time her courage failed and she said, 'Forces.'

She was disappointed that she couldn't start right away, but in this, as in every other service, it seemed there was a uniform to be got. As she was being kitted out at the depot, with green frock and felt hat, along with a green woollen overcoat, she couldn't help feel that there was nothing here that George could object to. She looked the picture of respectability. The thing that gave her greatest pleasure, however, was the tin helmet. With that on her head, she began to believe that she really was part of the war effort.

She had to share her excitement with someone and decided that May would be the one to really appreciate why she needed to get involved. Her sister had changed since they'd lost Jack, surprising Peggy with her own campaign to be allowed to join up. May had always been the predictable homebody, and sometimes Peggy felt envious of her sister, for escaping all the expectations that their parents had piled upon her as the firstborn. Peggy, the pretty one, the one who had to marry and give them grandchildren and make them proud. She'd already failed. After four years, there were no grandchildren, and perhaps never would be. But her sister of late had begun to do the unexpected, and now it felt that she was beginning to surge ahead, leaving Peggy hurrying to keep up.

She waited in The Grange, opposite the factory

gates, and finally saw May walking towards her, chatting to a young man. Peggy didn't recognize him but this looked like another first for May, who'd been so boy-shy for all her teenage years and had never had a chap. He was dressed smartly in a jacket and tie and had one hand in his trouser pocket. Though his face was turned aside, she saw he had a strong profile, with a head of thick wavy hair, which he pushed back from his forehead every now and then. As he walked he didn't look straight ahead, but kept his gaze on May. They were so intent on their conversation that neither of them had noticed her waiting.

'Peggy, what are you doing here?' May gave her a look which forbade comment.

Peggy slipped her arm through May's and said to him, 'Excuse my sister, she'd never think to introduce us!'

She felt May's nails digging into her arm. He laughed, a pleasant, deep laugh, and put out his hand. 'Oh, she doesn't need to – you're Peggy, she's told me all about you! Bill Gilbie, pleased to meet you.'

He might know all about her, but she knew nothing of him. It was just like May to keep him hidden away. He fell into step with them and seemed as easy and relaxed as May was awkward. It was a mystery to the whole family why one of the local chaps hadn't snapped her up, but Peggy thought this one looked keen enough. She was intrigued.

When they reached Grange House, he stopped. 'This is where I live,' he said, waving towards the block of flats, and Peggy saw a look of disappointment cross May's face.

'Oh, see you tonight, Bill!' she said, stopping dead, as he paused at the block entrance.

'Yes, see you tonight, "Happy Days"!' He walked backwards, smiling at May, seeming to mime at playing an invisible piano. 'And lonely nights!' May pulled a sad face and laughed at what was obviously a private joke, so that Peggy felt like a spare part. As soon as he was out of earshot, May said, 'Trust you to embarrass me!'

'Oh, don't be daft. I had to say something to break the ice, you're so bloody tongue-tied. Anyway, you never told me you'd got a chap! Good-looking too!'

'He's not my chap.'

'Well, how come you're going on a date with him then?'

'It's not just me – all the Garner's girls go there. He's the piano player at the Red Cow.'

May blushed furiously and Peggy felt sorry for teasing her.

'Well, I didn't mean to break anything up. It's just I had to tell someone my news. I've got a job *and* I've joined the WVS!'

'Peggy! Blimey, you didn't lose any time, did you?' May said, and Peggy thought she saw a flash of admiration in her sister's eyes.

★　　★　　★

125

For the time being she was free to work both day and night shifts on the mobile canteen, at least until her job at Atkinson's was settled. She couldn't drive, so was paired with another woman who could. The next morning she reported for the early shift. After filling the urn with boiling water and stocking up the van with trays of cups, saucers, buns, cigarettes, matches and a hundred other things bombed-out families or volunteer workers might need, they set off. Her partner, whose name was Babs, was a middle-aged woman with a brisk, friendly manner. She was single, a bank clerk by day, and seemed a good driver, explaining to Peggy that she'd trained on ambulances in the last war. She'd moved here all the way from Devon, just so she could help in the worst of the Blitzed areas. She chatted non-stop, as they followed their set route around the bombed docks and streets of Bermondsey. They served tea, buns and sundries to whoever seemed most in need along the way. First stop was for some homeless families in a bombed street without a house left standing. Covered in a uniform white dust, whole families sat on the remains of their bedding, piled up on rubble mounds – all that was left of their homes. Most of them had escaped with nothing but the clothes on their backs.

At the sight of the tea van, the little groups stirred, children coming to life first, running over for pies and sandwiches. There was no time to worry about what she didn't know. She just followed Babs's lead and soon was hooking down cigarettes and ferreting out aspirin from all the clever cubby-holes built into the van.

'Orange juice and three teas, please.' A woman with a face full of small cuts, no doubt from flying glass, stood at the drop-down counter with a toddler beside her and a baby in her arms.

'Jenny Cole!' Peggy recognized the woman she'd once worked with at Atkinson's. They'd both married at the same time and been forced to leave their jobs.

'Peggy!' The woman smiled, her skin crinkling beneath a coating of brick dust. 'I thought I recognized you.'

'I'm so sorry, love. Is that your house?'

Jenny nodded. 'Was. That's me mum and dad – they lived on the top floor.' She pointed to an older couple sitting on a suitcase. 'Thank gawd we all come out alive. We was under the stairs.'

Peggy handed the woman the bottle of orange juice, looking down at the toddler who was hiding beneath the counter.

'These two your'n?' Peggy asked and the woman smiled, bouncing the baby in her arms. 'That's Archie and littl'un here is Alfie. You got any?'

Peggy shook her head. 'Not yet.'

'Lucky you!' the woman said.

But Peggy knew she meant the opposite.

Some Pioneer corps who were helping clear the rubble came up in a rowdy group and Jenny went back to her parents. Normally the sight of those two round-faced children would have stirred an unacknowledged longing, but she knew all the gradations of that particular desire and, today, it was not so fierce. Perhaps what she'd really wanted all along was simply to feel useful. And by evening, when they made their final stop for a group of exhausted firemen, fighting a warehouse blaze in Shad Thames, she had no doubt of her usefulness. But it hadn't been as easy as she'd imagined – even more tiring than a double shift at Atkinson's.

Before the end of that week, Peggy's nights no longer seemed so dark, lit as they were by the aerial play of searchlights, exploding bombs, blazing buildings, phosphorescence from incendiaries and also, by the faint glimmer of her own returning self.

CHAPTER 7

PLAY ON

February–March 1941

Life had gone on around them, and the leather works was almost back to full production. Persuading her parents to let her join the ATS was proving a more protracted battle than she'd expected, but meanwhile, determined to do something, May now took her turn with the other volunteer spotters on the factory roof. The weekly rota meant that she was often on Garner's rooftop at the same time as Bill Gilbie. They watched for enemy planes by day and fires by night, ready to give the warning for the factory to take cover or the fire service to spring into action. It was in those hours, patrolling the rooftop with Bill, that she began to lose her shyness around boys, or perhaps it was just this particular boy. Somehow it helped that most of her attention was focused on their common task – it was hard to be self-conscious when life and death hung in the balance.

It was a daylight raid. To save production hours these days the factory only evacuated once the bombers were almost overhead. She leaned her elbows on the roof parapet, binoculars scanning the sky.

Between shifts Bill had already taught her the difference between a German bomber and an English fighter, drawing little outlines of the planes and testing her afterwards.

Now he propped his elbows on the parapet too, raising his own binoculars. 'See the Alaska rooftop?'

'Yes, got it.'

She focused on the Alaska fur factory, not far off, in Grange Road.

'That's the highest around here, higher than Atkinson's or Young's. Alaska always spots 'em first. When you see their spotters running for it, sound our alarm sharpish!'

There was silence between them, and May heard Bill sigh. He seemed more subdued than normal.

'You're quiet today,' May said, for she'd discovered that she was never stuck for conversation with Bill.

He glanced at her, then put his binoculars back up to his eyes. 'I'm in a bit of a quandary, to be honest.' There was a pause and he seemed to make up his mind. 'Iris got in touch again.'

'Iris? Oh, *Iris*. Your old sweetheart?' She hadn't thought about the girl since he first mentioned her, but now she found she was intrigued by the woman who'd captured Bill's heart so young and then broken it.

'I can't make it out, May. She didn't take long

to get over me, you know . . . took up with someone straight away. That hurt at the time.'

'I'm sorry, Bill.'

He looked at her again, and the sadness in his eyes was evident. 'I'm long over it, May, but I just wish I knew why she's got in touch, now of all times, when I'm really . . .' he searched for the word, 'happy.'

'Do you think you'll pick up with her again?'

He didn't answer, but instead raised his binoculars and asked, 'Fancy coming for a walk dinner time?'

'OK,' she said, and saw Bill smile as he turned away to scan the eastern horizon.

She was surprised that a friendship could have blossomed in such unlikely, ruined soil, but since that fateful walk through the bombed streets of Bermondsey, she felt bound to Bill, by the tragedy they'd witnessed and by the tiny life that they'd saved. It seemed natural, after that day, that sometimes he would ask her to go for a lunchtime stroll. She didn't care if it drew knowing looks from Emmy or smirks from Dolly. She always had to put up with their cross-questioning later on, but, in truth, there was never much to report that would interest her curious friends.

Today, May and Bill set off down Fort Road, intending to stop for a drink at the Havelock Arms. She pointed out the ruins of the Labour Institute, which had suffered a direct hit.

'I used to belong to a club there, country dancing

of all things!' She grimaced, and catching Bill's look of astonishment, wished she'd kept quiet about it. It was the sort of thing her brother would have teased her about, and suddenly grief caught her. She bit her lip, distracting herself from the pain.

'You'll never believe it, but I used to go in for country dancing there too! Well, not for the dancing so much as the free jam sandwiches afterwards!'

May laughed, quickly brushing away a stray tear. 'Did you ever go to any of their concerts?'

'Oh yes, Dad took me once. He plays himself, not bad . . . he hits at least one in three notes right . . .'

Bill had a pleasant laugh, half throwing his head back, so that his dark blue eyes brightened in the noon sunshine. It was good to see he'd thrown off his earlier melancholy over Iris.

'It's nice to meet someone who appreciates a bit of classical. Mind you, I like the big bands too.' He smiled secretly to himself. 'Reminds me of my most embarrassing moment at school. Thing is I had a bit too much old bunny in class!' Bill said.

She laughed. 'That doesn't surprise me!'

'Me and my best mate, Stan, chatted all the way through one music lesson, so old Mr Credon gives us the choice, six of the best, "Or," he says, "you can sing for yer lives, you grubby little beggars!"

'Anyway he wanted a song from us, all the way

through, word perfect. "I'll String Along With You" was our favourite. We used to harmonize, pretend we had a big band behind us, you know.' Bill smiled and May could see the boy he'd been, with his full lips and fine eyebrows.

'It was a long one but we knew the chorus and all the verses too. Stood up in front of the class, did our turn, and I could see the old boy waving the bloody cane, getting ready to do a run up. We brought the house down!'

May laughed, asking for a demonstration and Bill sang, unembarrassed, while they picked their way through a stretch of glass-strewn pavement.

I'm looking for an angel, but angels are so few.
So until the day that one comes along,
I'll string along with you!

'Tell you what,' he said, breaking off, 'why don't you come to one of the lunchtime concerts at the National Gallery with me, on Saturday?' She hesitated a moment and he said gently, 'Go on, you need a break, May, with all you've been through . . . and it'll be my treat. They let you take in sandwiches – it'll be a sort of picnic.'

His lips were parted slightly, in an encouraging half smile. She knew he wanted to do something to ease her grief, and so she agreed. Because of the circumstances, she wasn't sure if this counted as being asked out – no doubt, Emmy and Dolly would enlighten her later.

And as she'd expected, the following afternoon she was plagued by questions from her friends.

'You just *talked*!' Emmy repeated, looking at her dubiously. 'Talking's all right for starters, and it's all right for afters, but it's no good for yer dinner, love!' And Emmy's husky laugh was full of innuendo, plain enough even for May to understand. Dolly too had plenty of her own advice to add and after a while May felt she'd had quite enough of it.

'Oh shut up, you two, he's just a really friendly chap. To be honest, I think he feels sorry for me, you know – he must do, to want to string along with me.'

'He's looking for an angel!' Emmy crooned, and May blushed scarlet. The words of the song must have lodged themselves in her mind and she cursed herself now for giving Emmy any inroad into that part of their conversation.

'What are you going beetroot for?' The two young women leaped upon her discomfort, like sharp-toothed little animals.

May knew that Bill's schoolboy story wasn't anything to get Emmy's romantic heart beating and besides, it was a confidence, an innocent tale you might tell your sister, or your best friend, and she didn't want to repeat it to these two, just so they could bandy it about the factory floor. So instead she told them about his invitation to the concert the next day and their faces lit up as they concluded that, indeed, she had definitely been asked out.

* * *

All the paintings had been sent away to the country – a bit like the children, May thought. But after standing for over an hour in the cheerful queue which had snaked round the corner into Charing Cross Road, May tried to keep her disappointment to herself. She hadn't realized the gallery would look so bare. It was stripped of all its grandeur, sandbagged, blacked out, pared back to its utilitarian shell, just like every other building in the capital. Of course, she knew that the raids didn't stop at Bermondsey or the docks, but she'd somehow hoped that some things had remained unchanged.

'I should have mentioned it,' Bill said, as they passed through the entrance and she'd commented on the absence of paintings.

'Oh, but it's the music we've come for!' she said, not wanting to seem ungrateful. But even Bill couldn't hide his disappointment when they were ushered into an airless basement. Unadorned, distempered walls, lagged with sandbags, were criss-crossed with water pipes and there was no natural light to relieve its gloom. Over three hundred eager concert-goers squeezed in and then somehow, more were stuffed around the edges, sitting and lounging on pipes and stone floors.

'Sorry, May, last time I came to one of these, it was held in a gallery with a beautiful great glass dome! Nothing like this.'

May shrugged. 'If there's an air raid we'll be glad of it. Besides, it's the—'

And Bill interrupted 'The music we've come for! Let's hope it's worth it.'

The basement room was warming up and Bill undid the top button of his collar. The more relaxed style suited him, but as he pulled at his tie, she wondered if he might be as nervous as she was. After all, the girls had assured her this *was* a date.

But then there was a pause in the shuffling and chatter. The dumpy figure of Dame Myra Hess crossed to the piano, and seated herself before it. May hadn't at first realized who she was, but now she found herself digging Bill in the ribs. She and her father had often sat spellbound, listening to Dame Myra on the wireless, much to her mother's disgust. She preferred her husband to play the old favourites on their upright piano, which had been bought, hire purchase, specifically for the purposes of impromptu parties after a night at the pub, or so her mother liked to think.

Bill pointed to the first piece on the programme and whispered, 'My favourite.'

Dame Myra launched into Mozart's Piano Concerto No 14, but it wasn't till she reached a slow movement of such sweet, almost unbearable yearning that May became entranced. Something about the purity and lightness contrasted so starkly with the forced ugliness of their surroundings, and the music seemed to push the basement walls away, so that May felt they were listening under a clear blue, spring sky. But when the howl of the air-raid siren penetrated the depths of the basement, breaking through the purity of the tripping melody, something seemed to break in May and for some reason she saw again the tiny baby they'd rescued from the wreckage of its mother's arms, all its years of innocence snatched away, and then she saw her brother's face, shining, just as it had on the day he'd got engaged to Joycie.

She felt Bill reach for her hand. He gave her his handkerchief and May bowed her head.

After the raid and the concert were over they walked out into Trafalgar Square. She was still clutching Bill's handkerchief.

'Thanks, Bill.' She smiled. 'I'll give it back . . . when it's clean!'

'Don't worry, May. Were you thinking of your Jack?'

She took in a long breath. 'Jack, yes, and our little baby's mother and Emmy's family and oh . . . there's too many people gone already, Bill, and that music was so sad, it just made me think of all the wasted lives . . .'

As they sat on the top deck of the bus crossing Waterloo Bridge they watched the tawny light of the setting sun turn the Thames liquid bronze and, without speaking, Bill put his arm round her shoulders.

The following week she made her decision. Emmy was surprised when May called at Dix's Place for her before work that day. It was something she never normally did – if she waited for Emmy to get ready every morning, she'd be docked half a week's wages.

'I've made up me mind, Em. Before Mum or Dad talks me out of it, are you coming to the labour exchange tonight or not?' she said, a note of challenge in her voice.

'What's it going to be, the ATS?' Emmy swallowed a last piece of toast, threw on her coat, then stopped to light up a cigarette in the courtyard. Blowing smoke into the billowing sail of someone's eiderdown, flapping on the line in the early morning breeze, she narrowed her eyes. 'If I go with you, you'd better not bottle out at the last minute!'

'I won't! But I think I can only go if you come too, Em.' She grabbed her friend's hand and squeezed it tightly.

Later, when she and Bill took their lunchtime walk, she told him her decision. His normal chattiness was silenced, and he walked for a few minutes beside her without comment, till she was forced to ask, 'Well, what do you think?'

She was horrified to see that he looked hurt. 'Why haven't you mentioned it to me?' he asked.

'Well, you knew I've been thinking about it for long enough.' she said, feeling that she was breaking some rule, knowing that whatever words came out of her mouth were not going to make this any less awkward. Not for the first time she found herself wishing she were more like Em and Dolly, who'd both already had a string of boyfriends.

138

The silence was horrible. She just wished that they could chat easily about this, as they'd grown used to doing about so many other things over the past months.

'It doesn't mean we can't carry on being friends, Bill,' she said, wanting only to see his face soften. 'We can see each other on leaves.'

But as she said the words the reality hit her. It was Bill she looked forward to seeing every day, it was Bill she hoped would be on her fire-watching rota, it was Bill she wanted to tell about her days or her family dramas and, in the moment she suggested that seeing him on her leaves would be enough, she knew it wouldn't be.

He seemed to pull himself together. 'Yeah, 'course we can, it's just that I've got fond of . . . us, you know, stringing along together.' Then came that wry smile of his, and she knew how truly disappointed he really was.

'I'll miss you too, Bill. It's hard to go, but—'

'I know,' Bill interrupted. 'You've got no choice.' He looked away. 'I'm sorry for making you feel bad about it.' He took a deep breath. 'It's not fair, seeing I'll be doing exactly the same.'

'What's that?' she said.

'I've got my call-up papers from the RAF,' he said.

'Oh, Bill, why didn't you tell me?' Now it was her turn to feel hurt.

'I kept thinking there'd be a better time . . .'

And she realized they had both, stupidly, being

trying to protect each other from the inevitable parting.

As the factory came into sight, Bill took her hand. 'May, let's promise to keep in touch. Let me know when your first leave is, won't you?' The muscles of his face were taut and his grip strong, and when she said, 'Yes,' it was a promise she fully intended to keep.

And it was a promise that echoed in her mind when that evening after work she, Emmy and Dolly took their places at booths in the white-tiled labour exchange. As she signed her name, May thought of Bill and tried to imagine what it would be like, seeing him only on leaves, or perhaps never again if the worst happened. But who could predict anything in this war? She banished the thought and took the oath.

CHAPTER 8

LEAVING

March 1941

It happened too quickly. Somehow she thought she'd have time to get used to the idea of leaving everything behind her. But only two weeks after signing up, her notice to join had arrived. Now she lay in her bed, eyes wide open, the pitch-black of the room weighing heavily upon her, like a palpable shroud. She knew that outside the moon was shining, for she had peeked through the heavy blackout curtains earlier, but now firmly fastened, they refused to let a sliver of its brilliance into the room. At least they would be free of a raid tonight. Whatever the rumoured inaccuracy of the ack-ack guns, the German planes would never risk the light of such a moon, as it washed the Thames with a light almost bright as day. Though the prospect of a night spent in her own bed instead of the damp bunk of the Anderson shelter would normally have filled her with relief, tonight there was none. Her heart matched the darkness of her room.

Why had she done it? She asked herself,

pretending not to know the answer. Neither Emmy pressurizing, nor the guilt-inducing government posters, could ever have persuaded her. It was for Jack; it was for her home. The constant bombardment of streets she'd grown up in, the school she'd attended, the factory she worked in, the church she'd been christened in – it was a destruction she couldn't leave unanswered. But it wasn't until tonight that she felt the reality of it.

She was leaving home for the first time. Going away from all she knew and she wished fervently that she was not. What made it even harder was that she was going alone. All the time she'd imagined it would be like Garner's but in a different place, because Em and Dolly were coming too. But when they got their notices to join, her friends had been ordered to report to a different station, on a different date, and in fact the two girls had left already. She felt her cheeks burn with the shame of her terror at leaving: in this world where the prospect of death on her own doorstep was so real, it seemed such a small thing to be frightened of, yet in the loneliness of the night it felt greater than the barrage of bombs she'd faced for the last six months. All that was familiar and certain would be left behind, and perhaps she would never find it again. She curled up with the wet handkerchief balled into her hand and tried to stifle her sobs.

'Are you crying, May?' Her mother's soft voice came from the open bedroom door.

'No, 'course not,' she choked.

'Oh, love, you don't have to pretend to be brave, not with me.' She sat on the bed and May sat up, and let her wet cheek rest on her mother's shoulder.

'It's only natural, you're sad to be going away.' Her mother gently stroked her hair.

'I wish I could change my mind and stay home.' May sniffed, grateful to be able to whisper her true feelings.

But her mother knew as well as she did that there was nothing to be done now. May had received her orders to report and all her mother could do was to soothe her fears, kissing the top of her head. 'You'll be all right, darlin', you'll find out you can cope with almost anything,' she whispered.

'That's what Granny Byron said.'

And May could only hope they were both right, for by this time tomorrow she would be in the ATS.

King's Cross Station was crammed with servicemen. May tripped over kitbags and sleeping soldiers, as she searched around for her contact. Her father had accompanied her this far, but at the station entrance she stopped him.

'No, Dad,' she said, taking the case from him. 'I'd better get used to doing things for myself.'

'But Mum give me orders, said I've got to see you on the train.'

They tussled with the case, but when she wouldn't release her grip, he let go.

'All right, you win. But don't tell your mother.' He kissed the top of her head. 'My little homing pigeon, never thought I'd see this day.' He held her tight enough for her to feel his beating heart and when eventually he let her go, she could see tears welling in his eyes.

'Bye, Dad, tell Mum I'll write, soon as I get a chance.'

She heard the tremble in her own voice and turned quickly, before her tears betrayed her. As she walked into the station alone, conscious of her father's eyes on her back, she knew it was for the best. Her goodbyes at home had been tearful enough, and her face was already puffy. She wanted to maintain at least some illusion of adulthood.

Where would she be travelling to? She had no idea. All she knew was that she was heading for 'Basic Training', but that seemed painfully vague. If only they'd given her a destination. She swallowed hard and forced herself to stand still. Then she spotted them, a huddle of girls looking anxiously about them, clutching cases and holding join-up cards, just like her own. May was relieved to see that they all looked as lost as she felt. She walked up to them.

'Oh, another one of the lost little lambs. Come here, sweetheart!' A young woman, with a strong Kent accent, a round face and brown curls, pulled her into their circle before she could say a word. She was older than May, perhaps twenty-five.

'I'm Ruby, from Ramsgate,' she said. 'We're waiting for the welfare officer.'

'Are we all going to the same place?' May asked, and another girl nearer May's age shrugged her shoulders.

'Gawd knows. I just hope they tell us soon. I've been awake half the night and I'm looking forward to a kip on the train!'

The girl introduced herself as Eileen, and by the sound of her accent May guessed she was from Bermondsey too. But the shrill whistle of a departing train drowned out the name of a third girl, who was tall and rather elegantly dressed. A troop of tin-hatted soldiers carrying full kit marched past, forcing the girls to flatten themselves against the platform gate.

'Do you think we're in the right place?' May asked Ruby, just as an ATS officer stepped up smartly, holding a clipboard.

'You're my lot, I think,' she said, calling out their names and ticking them off when they answered.

'All right, girls, fall in and follow me. You're off to Pontefract!' she said in a jolly voice, as though they were going on a works beano.

But May discovered soon enough this journey wouldn't be anything like a beano. For a start they had no silly hats to wear, and there was definitely no beer on board. After the officer had gathered together several more recruits, she took them to a mobile canteen that had been set up near the ticket office. They were each given a packet of sandwiches and told to make them last all day.

'All day!' Ruby hissed into May's ear. 'How far away is bloody Pontefract? These won't last me half an hour!'

Clutching their cases and sandwiches, they

followed the officer through milling crowds to the platform. With no train in evidence, the officer peered along the tracks, as if she could materialize one by the intensity of her glare.

'Damn! All right, girls, make yourselves comfortable while I go and see where our train's got to.'

May copied the others and sat on her case, watching the officer disappear along the platform. Steam billowed across from trains pulling in and out, and from high above the station roof came the faint drone of a plane. May hoped there wouldn't be a daylight raid. She clenched her hands, so that her nails dug into her palms. She desperately wanted to get the journey started. There was still a part of her that hadn't let go and, so long as she was still in London, she feared her homing instincts might ignite some irrational bolt back to Bermondsey.

May stood up and began to pace up and down in front of the other girls.

'Sit down for gawd's sake,' said Eileen. 'Your arse is making buttons!'

After half an hour the officer returned with the news that their train had been requisitioned for troop transport. There was nothing for it but to wait, so May sat, watching with envy whenever a train departed. As the morning wore on Eileen's eyes drooped and her head fell on to Ruby's shoulder; soon she was snoring softly.

'Lucky little bugger,' Ruby said. 'Wish I could drop off anywhere.' May too wondered at how the girl could sleep so peacefully. The station was a swirling maelstrom of bodies on the move. Soldiers with kitbags, clambering on to their trains, women with platform tickets, running along the carriages, hoping to wave off sweethearts. Groups of evacuee children, swamped by over-large boxes and cases, many clutching the hands of weeping mothers. May pressed her back against the tiled station wall, feeling dizzy and sick. Suddenly Ruby's elbow nudged her.

'Aye aye, Madam Butterfly's back again, looks like we're off.'

The officer scanned them, perhaps making sure none of her charges had thought better of it and wandered off back home. 'All present and correct?' she asked unnecessarily. 'We've got four minutes to get to platform six. Chop chop.' And she dashed away.

Ruby pushed Eileen awake. 'Whaa?' The girl stood up, zombie-like, grabbing blindly for her case.

'Train's leaving.' May set off at a half-sprint, following the officer, and before long they were all squashed into one carriage. The officer didn't get on the train with them, and May was disconcerted to realize that she was leaving them.

'Someone will be there to collect you from Pontefract Station and take you to the barracks. Good luck, girls, you're in the army now!'

With a grin and a jaunty salute, the woman strode away. The new recruits tried to make themselves comfortable, but with ten of them in the carriage, together with their bags, it wasn't easy. May had no idea where Pontefract was, just that one of the girls had said it was 'up north somewhere'. To May, it sounded like the ends of the earth.

They had wasted half the morning already and May felt herself relax as the train pulled out of the station with a scream from the whistle and a belch of steam. She leaned forward, eager to begin her journey and, with her head resting against the windowpane, she took in the last of London as a golden afternoon light bathed the war-scarred city.

The sandwiches ran out at Potters Bar. They'd all complained about them, but hunger had won out in the end. They were made of the vile grey national loaf and filled with what tasted like salmon paste, which Ruby said was actually mashed swede. 'That's all you get in the bloody army, you know, swedes and spuds and tea, that's what my sister told me.'

Eileen, who came from a family of ten in Dockhead, was disappointed, saying she'd only joined up for the three square meals a day. No one could tell them why, but they'd been shunted into a siding. As afternoon dwindled to dusk, they waited in the dimness of the unlit, crowded carriage with very little to do but eat and smoke. May felt like a smoked kipper, so when Ruby said she was getting up to stretch her legs, May followed her. They tumbled out of the carriage, on to the track, lighting up before the blackout came into force. Suddenly a little cheer went up, as a band of uniformed WVS ladies came into view, trundling tea urns on trolleys.

'My God, I do hope those char wallahs are destined for us!' The cut-glass accent caught May's attention and she turned to see the elegant young woman who had joined them at King's Cross. She'd seated herself by the corridor in their carriage and they hadn't yet spoken. Immaculately dressed in a trouser suit, with a gabardine coat draped over her shoulders, she stood as though on the deck of a moving ship, feet spread wide, with her hands shielding her eyes. Catching May's eye, she stuck out her hand. 'How do you do, Phoebe Fanshawe, call me Bee.'

They gathered round the tea urns, drinking mugs of steaming tea and eating rock cakes, until it was time to set off again. They had just settled back into their cramped carriage as the train chugged out of the siding, when out of nowhere a thunderclap burst above them – a thunderclap that shattered every window, showering them with slivers of stinging glass. May was heaved out of her seat, and tumbled, impossibly, into the luggage rack above her. She knew it couldn't be happening, yet she found her face pressed against the ceiling of the carriage. Shoving at it with all her strength, she pushed herself away, while what felt like a giant's foot crushed the carriage roof, buckling and creasing it, till she felt she herself was folded and squashed in its metallic embrace. The screech of crumpling metal deafened her. Suddenly screams pierced the darkness and May realized they were her own.

Then she felt herself falling, tumbling with the carriage as the giant kicked it away. Earth and black sky, earth and black sky, repeating as the carriage rolled down the embankment, till it came to rest with a groaning shudder. She blacked out, but only for a minute. The heat woke her, and acrid smoke pouring through the carriage, which was lit with the red glow she recognized too well. The train was ablaze.

She struggled, trussed still in the netting of the luggage rack. Kicking like a drowning woman, pushing against bags and bodies, she swam towards the smashed window. Grasping the jagged edges of broken glass, she pulled herself through, gasping for air, letting herself fall back on to wet grass. She felt an irresistible urge to sleep and closed her eyes. But something called her back, for she opened them to find herself staring into the blinding light of a spouting flame. Soil filled her mouth. She spat it out and registered sounds: someone moaning, another crying out for help, and from further down the train an incessant screaming. Pushing herself slowly to her knees, she crawled towards the whimpering huddled figure of a woman, face down on the embankment. Rolling her over gently, May saw it was Eileen, the girl from Dockhead. Blood was spouting from a gash in her forehead. She tried to listen for breathing, but if it was there, it was weak. May looked around desperately for help, calling to running figures, backlit by flames licking out of the carriage windows. With the train now a crazy jumble of carriages piled into the ditch, rescuers were pulling out bodies from wherever they could and dragging them away from the train. Clearly the fire was likely to take hold of it any minute.

'Help! Help, over here, someone's wounded!' she screamed, her voice scraping her throat hoarse. Unable to attract anyone's attention, May put her hands under Eileen's armpits and heaved. Halfway up the embankment she spotted another recruit from her party. It was Pat, a well-spoken but rather loud girl, who'd spent most of the journey standing outside in the corridor, being chatted up by a soldier with a seemingly endless supply of cigarettes.

'Pat, come and help!' May shouted hoarsely, still tugging at Eileen's shoulders, 'She's too heavy.' May shielded her face from the flames, which were getting hotter and hotter. 'We've got to move her away from the fire.'

But Pat's face was a blank, her eyes wide. She shook her head and took several steps back. She turned and ran.

'Pat!' May called after the girl, but she had seen such terror before. Sometimes it froze people to the spot; sometimes they ran. Pat was so petrified she probably hadn't even registered the wounded girl in May's arms. She turned back to Eileen. Finding strength, which later she wouldn't recognize as her own, she dug her feet into the soft earth and heaved. Straining every muscle, till the dead weight of the young woman yielded to her will, inch by inch, May dragged her up the rest of the bank. Nearing the top she felt her strength drain away, but with one last effort pushed Eileen out in front of her, up over the embankment. The last thing she heard was a boom, louder than all the ack-ack guns in Southwark Park combined. She rolled back down the embankment as a red flash seared her eyes and then there was blackness.

She came round, lying a few yards from the track.

'Eileen?' She looked frantically around.

The girl was nowhere to be seen. May pushed herself up and hot gimlets pierced her eyes. She shielded them from the light and the heat. The whole train was engulfed in flames, shooting out like tentacles of fire, ready to grab the nearest prey – which seemed to be May.

The embankment was clear of bodies and as she tried to push herself up, she realized her strength was spent. It served her right for leaving her home. She was about to give into the heat and the pain, lay her head on the soft yielding earth beneath her, when she heard a voice coming from the top of the embankment. Though her head felt too heavy to lift, she raised it, and outlined by fire she saw an ATS girl, pointing down the embankment to where she lay. It was Pat.

Feet in mud-caked boots surrounded her, then strong arms lifted her. Her cheek nestled against a rough khaki tunic. 'You're all right, love,' a gravelly voice reassured her, and she looked up into the soot-streaked face of a fire warden.

He carried her up the embankment, past ranks of wounded, and laid her on a stretcher. Job done, he turned to leave but not before May, with great effort, raised her hand to stop him. It shot fiery pain up her arm.

'Thank you!' she whispered, her voice hoarse from the fire.

'Thank *you*,' he said, crouching at her side. 'You're a brave young woman – you saved someone's life tonight.'

A Red Cross nurse wrapped her in an army-issue blanket and bandaged her hand. Then, as some Auxiliary Ambulance women carried past a body on a stretcher, May recognized Eileen's fair curls.

'Is she all right?' May called out. She tried to get up.

'Careful now! You're not going anywhere.'

May groaned and felt her head; it was sticky with blood.

'Can you tell me how my friend is?' she asked, before falling back into unconsciousness.

May awoke in the local cottage hospital. The night before had melted into a blur of flames and molten metal and pain. Was it a dream, or had giants really picked her up and hurled her out of London? After a confused hour, having her bandages checked over by auxiliary nurses, and lights shone into her eyes by a doctor, she was finally pronounced walking wounded and allowed to get up.

She found the rest of her ATS friends in the hospital canteen. They had largely escaped injury, and had decided to bed down in the hospital wherever they could find an unoccupied chair.

'Eileen?' May asked.

Ruby nodded. 'Doing all right, but she won't be travelling nowhere for a while.'

'Thank God,' May said and noticed that Pat, not so loud now, avoided looking her in the eye.

It took all May's courage to get back on a train going north. The girls were all far more subdued on this leg of the journey than they had been when they set out. She looked out of the carriage window at the ever-changing countryside and wondered how it was that she'd gone through months of the Blitz with hardly a scratch and yet the minute she left her home the heavens turned against her. She knew it was senseless, a combination of exhaustion and a crack on the head, but still, she felt it as a punishment for leaving. Yet there was a trickle of something else, running through all her murky misgivings, like a clear stream. She had been blown clear out of London and had survived. More than that, she had perhaps saved her new friend's life. She had stepped out of the bounds of all that was familiar, and nothing could ever be the same again.

CHAPTER 9

POPPIES AND PLANES

February–April 1941

It had been strange, going back to Atkinson's. When Peggy had left after getting married, she'd imagined such a different life ahead of her. She'd envisaged a couple of children by now; perhaps George giving up his dodgy dealings, going into some legitimate business; even a little house, out Bromley way. A car dealership, that was what he'd talked about, when he'd promised her things would be different once they were married. But now she wasn't sure if he ever intended to change his ways. Thieving, gambling, wheeling and dealing, it was all he'd ever known. There was a reason he'd grown up with the nickname Wide'oh.

The factory was situated at the end of a cobbled alley, just wide enough for a horse and cart. Too narrow for a lorry, the drivers cursed its awkwardness and had to leave their vehicles in Southwark Park Road when making deliveries. But Peggy had always loved the approach to the factory, for the smell was delicious. A heady mixture of wildflowers and roses, all the sweet essence of the countryside distilled, funnelled from the factory down this little alley. It was all the more surprising that Atkinson's should smell so sweet, since it was sited next to Young's gelatin works, with its knacker-yard aroma. Peggy, when she'd started work, had chosen Atkinson's primarily for its fragrance. She didn't know how May stuck it at Garner's, but by the time her sister had started work, there were far fewer jobs about and May couldn't afford to be fussy. Their parents had needed the money, with Dad in and out of work at the docks. But Peggy had always felt that it should have been poor May, the shrinking violet with her quiet, shy ways, working here and not herself. So she breathed deeply as she walked towards Atkinson's, for in a borough which had been the dumping ground for every foul-smelling industry, from tanning to vinegar brewing, working in this place was a luxury, and the alleyway was like the secret entrance to a sweeter world.

She'd assumed she'd be making plane parts, but after reporting in she found she'd be working on cosmetics. The factory was still producing face powder, cold creams, perfume and soap, though in smaller quantities than before the war and in the much plainer wartime packaging. Before the new intake of workers could start, they'd had to sit through a short rousing talk from the works manager. It was a well-rehearsed call to duty, about how they might not be in the forces, but they were doing valuable war work, not just those who would be making plane parts, but even those put on cosmetics.

'You'll be helping to keep up morale!' he said. 'What woman, even in the forces, doesn't feel better facing the day with a bit of war paint on! And what chap in the forces ain't cheered up by the sight of his sweetheart looking glamorous!'

Peggy heard a few groans coming from the other women starting with her that day. But she was just glad to be back at work, with the chance to earn her own money, make her own choices.

She and three other new women were sent to the powder room and as she pushed through the double swing-doors, she had to smile to herself, that a woman who'd been forbidden to wear make-up by her husband would now be making it for the war effort. She toyed with the idea of slapping some on and trying that line on George when she visited: 'Oh, I'm only wearing make-up, dear, because it's good for morale!' But she decided it wouldn't be fair to rub his nose in her newfound liberty. She was nervous enough as it was about his reaction to her return to work. She wouldn't be able to keep it from him for ever.

The forelady approached, leaving tracks like footprints in snow across the factory floor, which was coated in fine white powder. Peggy recognized her, Hattie Bustin. They used to work alongside each other, on the California Poppy packing line, though for some reason, the woman now pretended not to know her and made an unnecessary show of treating Peggy like any other new employee.

'This is where you load up your powder.' She led them along a row of high wooden hoppers, each with a ladder leaning against it. 'It goes down your chutes to the mixing and packing rooms, down there.' Hattie pointed a finger to the floor beneath them.

'Your powder gets mixed with the California Poppy, White Rose and Black Tulip, then the girls pack it. Now there's a war on, it goes in the brown cardboard boxes, saves tin.'

Peggy remembered the pretty talc and face-powder tins, printed with sophisticated women and bright flowers. It was a shame they had to go – it made the job drabber, without all those illusions of glamour in a tin.

'You work in twos. One of you gets yourself a bucket of powder, out the chests over there, you carries it up the ladder and tips it in the hopper. The other one holds the ladder steady. Got it?'

They all nodded. Hattie's nickname was Hatchet-face. Unsmiling, square-jawed, straight-lipped, she didn't have the sort of demeanour that invited questions. But Peggy knew all there was to know about the simple task required of them. She also had a vivid memory of aching calves and shoulder muscles, after a day spent filling the hoppers. The best thing about working on this floor was the freedom. Once she'd set you up, the forelady didn't hang around. There was nothing for her to supervise, and she would leave them alone for the rest of the day. The three other women had never worked at Atkinson's before, so once Hattie had disappeared and they'd paired up, Peggy explained.

'So long as we keep the powder coming for them downstairs, nobody'll bother us. When the hoppers are nearly full, we can take a crafty break. Once they're half empty, we'll start again.'

The young girl she'd paired up with looked a bit worried.

'Trust me, love, you've got to pace yourself, otherwise your legs'll be falling off you by the end of the morning.'

Peggy volunteered to be the one going up and down the ladder; in the afternoon they would swap. She scooped up a bucket of powder, and started up the ladder, the first of many trips which, by clocking-off time, had her ruing the day she ever thought she should go back to work. But that night, when she stretched herself out across the empty bed, Peggy found that she didn't mind her aching legs at all.

After a week on days, hatchet-face Hattie came to her with a request. 'We need you on nights for a week,' she said unceremoniously.

'But I said I only want days. I'm doing voluntary work on the canteens at night!'

Hattie jerked her head in the general direction of the offices. 'They say it's urgent. Everyone's got to do Saturdays and nights till the order's got out.'

'How can a tin of talc be more urgent than looking after the poor sods who've been bombed out?'

Peggy wasn't at all sure the order had come from the office.

'With your old man in the nick I'd have thought you'd do anything to keep this job. Ne' mind about voluntary work! Anyhow, the talc's for soldiers' packs, going out to the Far East. That useful enough for you?'

Peggy wasn't sure what she'd done to upset Hattie, but she'd obviously made up her mind about a woman whose husband was spending the war in prison. The forelady was right about her needing the job, but for Peggy being back at Atkinson's still felt less like work than a sort of holiday – from her old life and that perfect little flat.

She could have wished for a more efficient partner, but she was stuck with Ada for a week of nights. A sweet young girl, who turned out to be a niece of her parent's neighbor Flo, she was so nervous of heights that Peggy was the one spending most of her time atop the ladder.

On their last night shift, as she was standing on the top rung, leaning forward to tip a bucket of white powder into the hopper, the room suddenly exploded. The wooden boards of the hopper blew outwards, the ladder toppled backwards and Peggy found she was swaying on top

160

of it. Any minute she would crash to the floor below; instinctively she threw all her weight in the opposite direction. The ladder sprang back towards the hopper, but instead of the comforting thud of solid wood against the ladder, there was only air. She could see nothing. The room was filled with clouds of choking white powder, and from her unsupported perch, she glimpsed through the high windows what looked like swirls of snow. Time seemed to freeze, the blast turning the room into a snow globe, and she was trapped inside. Peggy screamed for help, but her mouth filled with talcum powder as she fell forward. Bracing herself for the bone-crunching landing on the hard factory floor, she felt instead a soft thud, as if she had fallen on to Granny Byron's feather mattress. She had landed on top of a yielding mound of talcum powder, spilled from the hopper. She lay spread-eagled, mouth, eyes and ears full of the cloying snow. Her hands curled into it. She didn't know if she were facing up or down, or if anyone else had survived the bomb blast. For now her senses were returning, she knew a bomb was the only explanation.

She spat clay from her mouth and shouted. 'Help! Anyone there?'

Immediately she felt a hand grip her ankle. 'You're all right, Peg, just let yourself fall.' The small hand pulled her firmly down the side of the snowy mountain of powder, till her feet touched the floor and she was helped to unsteady feet. As she rubbed her eyes, she could see it was her young helper, Ada.

'Christ, you look like a snowman, Peg!' she said.

Wiping powder from her lashes, Peggy looked at her rescuer. 'And you look like a bloody ghost!' Putting her arm round Ada's shoulders, she hobbled across the powder-strewn floor to where the door should have been. It had been blown clean off and now she could feel a draught. The back wall of the factory was breached and she saw it was raining outside. As sheets of rain blew in through the powder room, the mountain of talc began to turn into a slushy china clay.

'Come on, Ada, let's get out of here.'

Outside they were greeted by a scene of panic. They had been hit with a lightning raid. It seemed there had been no warning, perhaps because of the moonless night and the driving rain, the spotters hadn't seen the plane coming. But the ARP wardens were now in action, stretchering the injured and leading the walking wounded slowly out of the building. Out in the street, shivering with shock and cold, she found herself being draped in a blanket and guided towards a Red Cross van. But before she reached it, she noticed that Babs had already turned up in the mobile canteen and was doling out mugs of tea to walking wounded and rescue workers.

'You go on, Ada,' she said, straightening up. 'Looks like I'll be on the canteen tonight after all!'

She rolled up her sleeves and, still covered from

head to foot in white powder, got into the back of the van – much to the amusement of Babs.

She should have been exhausted. For weeks she kept up a relentless routine of working all day at the factory, dashing home for her tea, then spending most evenings out in the mobile canteen. If she was lucky, she'd get a nap before setting off for the WVS station and then try to catch a few hours when her stint had ended. But she was exhilarated more than exhausted. Since returning to Atkinson's she'd been moved all over the factory. Working in the powder room was the most tiring, and she found herself praying to be sent to the perfumes section, where the only part of her that was exercised was her index finger. As rows of filled bottles of California Poppy passed before her on a conveyer belt, Peggy had to dip her finger into a pile of black bottle-caps and dot a cap on to the open bottle-top, ready for a woman further down the line who screwed on the top. It was so monotonous that sometimes Peggy's eyes closed and she did the work almost in her sleep. But the foreladies were like ferocious guard dogs prowling the lines and wouldn't hesitate to dock her pay if she was found to be slacking.

Yet nothing about her new life could dampen her spirits. Whatever boredom she experienced during the daytime was more than made up for in the drama-filled nights, as she went about from bomb site to shelter, dodging incendiaries and skirting blazes. Between the factory in the day and the canteen van at night, she felt that her life was fuller than it had ever been. She loved the camaraderie of the girls she worked with during the day. They would bring in their stories on Monday morning about dances and the chaps they'd met. Even the married women, with their men away in the forces, seemed to be joining in the free-for-all. It felt as if the restraints of pre-war days had been loosened, that with death always at their shoulder the priority had become living life to the full. But she had no time or interest in straying. In her secret heart of hearts, she was glad to be solitary.

It was Saturday afternoon in late spring, a half-day at the factory, and she was making the weekly journey to Brixton to visit George. With buses frequently cancelled and roads often blocked by debris or closed because of unexploded bombs, it was a laborious trek, sometimes lasting two hours, all for an hour's visit. It was a duty she was determined to keep up: whatever she was learning about herself in his absence, George was still her husband and she had promised to stick by him.

She hated the sight of the ugly brick slab of a building, with its rows of identical barred windows. The worst part for her was the feeling of claustrophobia as she walked under the arched entrance, though whether this came from entering a prison, or from the prospect of seeing George, she couldn't tell.

As usual, he was sitting behind the table in the visiting room. He was thinner, his pale face touched with high colour on his cheeks, his eyes bright, eager as always to see her.

'Hello, princess! Have you missed me?'

'Of course I've missed you! How've you been, love?'

'Oh, you know, can't grumble. Grub's not getting any better, but the blokes in me cell are decent enough.' He leaned forward, lowering his voice. 'Matter of fact we're pulling a fast one, and you can help me with it. Got a screw in me pocket, gets me in whatever I like. But it's fags we need.' He was growing breathless.

'Well, I hope you're not smoking them yourself – your breathing don't seem any better!'

'What yer talking about, fags do me good, clears me chest. Anyway, that's not the point. Can you get your hands on any, from that WVS van of yours?'

She looked at him askance. 'What do you mean? You want me to nick some for you?'

'They get boxes and boxes delivered to their depots. They're not gonna notice the odd one here and there.'

Peggy was silent, genuinely shocked. She knew that George had purposefully avoided involving her directly in his thieving. She wasn't an innocent; after all she'd lived on the proceeds. But he'd always seemed to want to keep her 'clean', maintaining the illusion that she was a cut above all his dodgy dealings.

She shook her head. 'No, George, I'm sorry but

I'm *not* doing that! Half our stuff's donated, by people worse off than us sometimes, and I'm not nicking nothing from the WVS.'

It was only when she registered George's look of surprise that she realized she'd just said 'no' to him.

'Well, I never wanted you volunteering for them anyway!' He took in a wheezing breath. 'Least you could do is make it a bit easier for me in here.'

His high colour intensified as he took a few short, angry gulps of air. 'You was glad enough of all the bent money I made, though, wasn't you?'

Peggy scraped her chair back and a look of alarm crossed George's face.

'You're not going yet, are you?'

'No, but I will if you keep on about it, George.'

'Sorry, princess, but it's not easy in here. You don't know what it's like,' he said morosely, 'when you've been used to coming and going as you please, and then someone's on your back day and night, telling you what you can and can't do.'

Peggy wanted to tell him that she understood perfectly. But instead, she sat down again and asked him about his visit to the infirmary, where they'd told him there was little they could do to help his breathing. Conversation was always hard work on these visits, and like a dog with a bone, he returned to his usual complaint.

'I'm not keen on you joining the WVS, but it sticks right in my throat, you back at that factory.

I never wanted a wife of mine working in a shithole like that.'

'Oh, for Christ's sake, George, give it a rest,' she said, her face flushed with uncharacteristic anger. The warden looked their way and she lowered her voice. 'It's not so bad as some places, and you need to get your head out of your arse! There's no money in the house and I haven't seen hide nor hair of Ronnie Riley, nor any of your other so-called friends. It's only my wages paying the rent, so if you want a home to come back to, then you'll just have to get used to it!'

George banged his fist on the table and she flinched away in fear.

Peggy had always been grateful he'd never been physically violent towards her, but his outburst made her realize there were other ways to be a bully, and she remembered all those times he'd sapped her confidence, controlling every choice, from her clothes to the food she ordered in a café, so that now she hardly knew what sort of person she could have been if she'd never married him.

She stood up, hoping that her trembling legs wouldn't betray her.

George ducked his head. 'Sorry, Peg. Don't go yet.'

'I've got to, I'm on the van tonight,' she said, turning to leave without her customary kiss on the cheek.

'Don't go like that, Peg!'

But she didn't look back. Was it that she had changed, or did her bravado spring only from knowing that he was locked up? She didn't care. All she knew was that she had defied George in a way that would once have seemed unthinkable.

In fact, she'd been thinking of asking for an evening off from the canteen round, but the van was beginning to feel more like home than the flat and so, as soon as she got home that evening, she changed into her uniform and reported in.

But it was a tough night. The German air force seemed to be throwing every last bomb and incendiary at them. The papers had been full of the unbreakable spirit of Londoners, and how after nearly eight months of bombardment Hitler was getting desperate to break their morale. On this particular night it seemed to be raining fire, as they drove to Butler's Wharf. Babs put her foot down, speeding through a gauntlet of flame which leaped from warehouses, the contents of which were spreading into a molten river across the road. It was probably from the sugar store, as the smell wafting up from the amber lava flow was just like toffee apples.

'Don't want that stuff sticking to our tyres!' Babs said, as she swerved suddenly to avoid a lake of toffee.

Peggy hung on tight, glancing back into the van's interior, where a couple of bun trays had toppled over. 'Steady on, Babs, or we'll have nothing left to give 'em by the time we get there!'

'Oh, those boys'll be filthy by now, they're not going to worry about a bit of dust on their buns!'

They'd been told about a crew of Tommies, seconded to rescue work down by the river, who'd been clearing debris without a break for almost twenty-four hours. Without street lamps and only the merest slits for headlights, they relied upon the incendiary fires to light their way.

'There they are!' Peggy had spotted them, at the remains of a warehouse, a chain of tired-looking men, passing bricks and lumps of rubble from hand to hand across the ruin.

They pulled up and Peggy ran out to lower the counter. Within minutes they were surrounded by dusty, parched soldiers and the work of supplying endless cups of tea began. She and Babs had a well-oiled routine going. The cups and saucers, all pre-washed at the previous stop, were laid out by Babs, while Peggy filled the cups from the urn, then she served the men tea and buns, while Babs took orders for cigarettes, razor blades and even stamps. The men were haggard but cheerful, every crease in their faces accentuated by a thick coating of mortar dust.

In one face, a pair of blue eyes of startling brightness caught her attention. He was at the end of the queue, and she took his order, noticing the dented helmet he wore at a jaunty angle.

He must have followed the direction of her gaze, for after taking a long gulp of tea, he rapped the helmet and said, 'Took a direct hit!' With the cup

169

still in one hand, he spread his arms wide. 'Rock as big as this. Good job I had the tin hat on, or that would've been the end of my war!' He looked at her, with a bold amused look as he sipped at the tea, and for some reason, perhaps because the night was so dark, or his face so white with dust, his eyes seemed lit from within, like clear blue skies on a summer day.

She realized that she hadn't said a word and now she smiled foolishly. 'You were lucky.'

'Well, I'm alive.' He gave a rather sad, slow smile. 'And the things I've seen . . . well, that counts as lucky these days.'

She would have liked to delay him, to carry on talking to him, for the bold look and the sad smile had acted like two tiny hooks and as she leaned forward to take the cup from him, his fingers brushed hers. Some impulse made her want to take his hand. But before she could, Babs called back from the driver's seat.

'Time to shut up shop, Peggy.'

'Goo'night, Peggy.' The soldier smiled again and she noticed perfectly arched eyebrows framing those bright eyes, the corners of which crinkled beneath the dust coating his face. The long smooth jaw, was shadowed by stubble and weariness. 'My name's Harry. Will you be coming this way tomorrow?'

Peggy nodded.

'I'll be here too, clearing the site.'

'Peggy! Get that counter up. I want to get home to my bed!' Bab's roared from the front.

Harry pulled a face. 'Sergeant Major's calling. Here, let me help.'

He lifted the counter for Peggy, who, before she locked it into position, put her hand through the gap and waved.

'See you tomorrow, Harry!'

She felt her hand being taken, and the fingertips kissed by an invisible Harry. Without warning, Peggy felt a dangerous sweetness flood her and she was glad of the van's dark interior to hide the flush she knew was rising to her face. Within a heartbeat she had given a name to her feeling and realized that it was neither safe nor comfortable, let alone resistible. She pulled in her hand, locked up the counter and slipped into the cab.

'Drive, Babs,' she said. 'Drive.'

Peggy saw Harry every night for a week, but she learned only the briefest details of his life. Originally from Camberwell, he'd moved to Bermondsey before the war and been called up in 1939. All the way through the canteen round she found herself thinking of nothing else but the stop down by Butler's Wharf. She anticipated, almost painfully, the brief sensation of his fingers brushing hers as she handed him the cup of tea. She knew it was deliberate, and for the few moments that their hands touched, Harry held her gaze with those bright eyes. The effect of these small encounters was so powerful she was ashamed of herself. She'd walked out with a few boys before marrying

George, but had never felt this demanding draw to a man. She felt almost as virginal as her poor sister May, whom she'd teased for her inexperience. If first love was foreign territory to May, then this passion Peggy felt was like an undiscovered continent. And she had no one to help her navigate this foreign, forbidden land.

On the fifth night Harry told her his squad would be moving on to another bombed area the next night. They were being placed wherever they were needed, while waiting for a regular posting, which could be anywhere, he said, even overseas. He wondered if she would meet him for a drink somewhere, before they left. And if it hadn't been for an encounter with Ronnie Riley earlier that day, she was pretty sure, in spite of her attraction to Harry, she would have said 'no'.

But that afternoon Ronnie had been waiting for her when she'd arrived home from work. As she was walking towards the block entrance, she heard a loud whistle and then a gravelly voice called down to her from the landing. 'Oi, does your old man know you're out?'

She looked up sharply to her flat on the first floor, annoyed to see Ronnie looking down at her, leaning his beefy arms on the landing railing. She dashed up the stairs, planning to get rid of him. She wasn't going to waste her precious hour before going out on the canteen making small talk with one of George's cronies.

'Hello, love, sorry I ain't been before,' he said,

as she put the key in the door and walked into the passage. She turned towards him, holding the door open, but not asking him in.

'That's all right, Ronnie, but I'm in a bit of a rush. Got to have my tea and get ready for WVS duty.'

'George said you was keeping yourself busy. Lonely, he reckons you are.' He grinned, squeezing his camel-coated bulk past her into the passage.

'Anyway, he asked me to make sure you was all right. I'll just stop for a quick cuppa.'

She sighed. It was no good being nasty to Ronnie. He was only the messenger.

She offered him some of the cold meat and pickle which was all she had time for and he tucked in, finishing the last of her bread as well.

'Anyway, love, he don't want you going short. Asked me to give you this.' Ronnie took a large bite out of the bread and pushed a roll of notes across the kitchen table.

'No! I can't take that, Ronnie.'

'Go on! Take it.' His mouth was full of bread. 'Now don't offend me.'

She felt cornered and as she'd often done since marrying George, she took the money, and tried not to imagine how it had been come by.

'George'll make sure you get it back . . .' she said weakly.

Ronnie waved his hand. 'Don't worry about it. He's me mate. I promised I'd keep an eye on you, and I will.'

He sat back, giving her an appraising look. 'You're a good-looking woman, even in that clobber.'

She hadn't yet changed out of the red siren suit which she found more practical when climbing ladders in the powder room, and she was still wearing the dark blue polka-dot scarf, which she tied turban-style to protect her hair from the powder.

'I expect you've got a few fellers sniffing around?'

Peggy bristled, realizing that her material needs were not all that he was checking up on. George had sent him to be her jailer. She got up abruptly.

'I'm doing ten-hour days at Atkinson's and out most nights on the van. Do you think I've got time to look at fellers?' she said frostily and Ronnie put up his hand, aware that he'd gone too far.

'Sorry, Peg, didn't mean nothing by it. It's just George. He's a bit windy stuck in there with you out here on yer own. But I told him not to worry. You're a different class, Peg. Not like these old brasses drop their knickers for anyone in uniform. Enough said.'

He shrugged on the camel overcoat that he'd draped over the kitchen chair. She waited till he'd gone before she stuffed the roll of money into a drawer, wishing it was as easy to wipe away the notion that, even from prison, George had her tethered. She changed quickly into her WVS uniform and didn't feel she could breathe properly until she and Babs had loaded up the van and were on their way.

So, fuelled by anger at George's mistrust and defiance at Ronnie Riley's surveillance, she agreed to meet Harry for a drink the next evening after work. But she was determined not to let her anger and rebelliousness take her anywhere she would regret going. It would just be a drink, a goodbye drink – passion would be a fire she viewed from a distance. She had no intention of getting burned.

CHAPTER 10

THE BROKEN BRIDGE

Spring 1941

It had taken them two and a half days to get to Pontefract and the town did not greet them with a smiling face. During all the long delays at stations and interminable stops at halts, they'd gleaned what information they could about the town they were heading for. May had heard of Pontefract cakes, the liquorice lozenges the town was famous for, and Pat, who seemed familiar with the place, declared that Pontefract meant 'broken bridge', which May thought was ominous. It certainly felt as if every bridge between here and her old life was tumbling down. The further north she went, the more she realized how little she knew of her own country, the one they were all meant to be fighting for. It was an alien landscape. The too wide, unbroken skies made May feel dizzy, used as she was to Bermondsey's crowded skyline. When the train, with an almost disapproving snort of steam, finally chugged into Pontefract, May was astonished at how different the place looked from any other she'd ever been.

It sat bleakly in the folded brown and grey countryside. Built of unfamiliar, soot-blackened stone, the place felt hard and cold compared to the warmth of London's brick.

'Thank God we're not stopping long,' she remarked to Ruby as they stepped off the train into a mizzling rain, which immediately soaked into her woollen coat. She saw a sergeant approaching them. Bee had had the presence of mind to telephone the barracks from the hospital, so at least they were expected. The sergeant's face was fixed, but May could see from his eyes that he wanted to laugh. They must look an absolute state.

'Ah, the reinforcements have arrived! Come on, *ladies*,' he said with exaggerated politeness, 'your chariot awaits!' And he beckoned them onward.

They were a raggle-taggle band of already wounded soldiers that clambered up on to the back of the covered army lorry. May with her bandaged hand, Ruby with an impressive head bandage and Bee with her immaculate gabardine ripped all the way up the back. The only apparently unscathed one of May's travelling companions was loud Pat. As they were jolted along slick, grey streets to the barracks, May held on tight, trying to keep her bruised ribs away from the side board. She hadn't known what to expect, but the fort-like barracks, when it came into view, reminded her of something Jack had played with as a boy, with its square turrets and window slits. She peered through the open end of the lorry at a parade ground which seemed to go on forever. The hoarse commands of a drill sergeant were confusing a group of uniformed women, as they attempted a quick march across the square.

'They don't look in step, do they?' Ruby whispered.

'Ee-eyes right!' came the barked command, and the girls generally turned their heads in the correct direction.

'It's probably harder than it looks,' May said, thinking of her own attempts to learn country dancing at the Labour Institute.

'They're useless,' came a grating voice. 'My father's in the army and he'd have them out here all day till they got it right.' May ignored Pat's damning comment, but a few others in the lorry sniggered.

Half a dozen other lorry loads of freshly arrived recruits were congregating outside the main building. They were told to form a line and were quick-marched to a long, low canteen hut, where after a ten minute stop for sandwiches and tea, served from a huge urn, they were ordered to follow the sergeant to the stores. The smell struck May as soon as she entered: wool and leather and polish. In another life she might have protested at having to parade past a male corporal, who eyed them up and without even asking their sizes, pushed skirts, tunics and shirts across the counter. May felt sure the skirts she'd been given must be two sizes too big; she was damn sure her hips weren't that wide. But she sensed it would be pointless to argue: it might be the ATS, but it was still a man's army. She noticed that even the shirts and tunics fastened left over right. Shoes were the only thing they were allowed to try on and thankfully her brown tie-ups, though unflattering, did seem to fit. Poor Ruby was having no luck, as her stocky frame extended to unusually wide feet.

'Take these for now.' The corporal slid a pair across the stores bench. 'We'll put in for an extra wide later on! VIP treatment for Private Cobb!' he said, licking a pencil and making a note on his order pad.

They passed on to the next storesman who, to May's deep embarrassment, handed her two pairs of salmon-pink brassieres and the largest pair of knickers she'd ever seen. These must be the famous khaki passion killers, but nothing could have prepared her for the sheer hideousness of the garments, which would certainly reach to her knees. They came with another pair of white woollen under-bloomers. May thought it was just as well she'd have all that room in the skirt after all, what with the double knickers they seemed expected to wear.

The kit for keeping themselves smart was impressive and obviously an army priority, for there was not only a brush for their hair, but one for their teeth, another for shoes, and another one for buttons. With uniform and kit balanced on their arms, they were marched at the double to rows of Nissen huts by the parade ground and then peeled off in eights to each hut.

She was glad to be allocated the same hut as Ruby and Bee, but not so keen on Pat's joining them. Still, any familiar face was better than a camp full of strangers. The others in their hut included a large, freckle-faced woman called Jean who spoke with a strong Scottish accent. When the door closed behind them, the curving interior of the hut felt a welcome refuge from the shouting of the drill sergeant, the tramp of boots on tarmac, the high-pitched chatter of a thousand women and the continual roar of army lorries coming and going. At least, May thought, there would be peace for tonight. She pushed a flat hand on the mattress. It was hard as a plank of wood and ludicrously designed in three separate sections.

'How are you meant to get a night's sleep on this?' She held up the three pieces for Ruby's inspection.

'They're called biscuits!' Pat said knowledgeably. 'The trick is to wrap them up tight in the sheet like this, so they don't move.'

Pat's voice reminded May of one of her old schoolteachers, and it would certainly have carried to the back of any classroom.

'Thanks,' May said: the girl might be a busybody, but it did seem like the only way to keep the bed together.

'Army brat,' Pat explained, and May wondered how proud her army dad would have been of her behavior at the train crash. They'd talked little about Eileen on the rest of their journey, but it seemed doubtful she'd be joining them now. Her leg had been shattered and she'd lost so much blood, the nurse had said it was touch and go during the night.

'Rube, look at the size of this skirt, will you?' she said, turning to the girl, who was already trying on her new uniform.

'It's too big, sweetheart. Your'n would fit me better than the one they give me. Look.'

They decided to swap skirts and then spent the rest of the evening making alterations to the rest of their uniforms, putting tucks into baggy shirts, and moving tunic buttons. The one thing May really couldn't bear was the soft peaked cap.

'This looks like one of me mum's meat puddings!' she said, perching it on her head and making Ruby laugh with the accuracy of her description. It took May half an hour of pulling, pushing and folding till the cap sat at a jaunty angle and she was pleased with it. The cap badge had to be polished till it gleamed and then all the buttons buffed with polish and a small stick till they shone. May stayed up till the last minute before lights out, making sure every smear was eradicated and every crease ironed to a knife-like edge. She was a naturally smart and tidy person – the girls at Garner's had teased her for coming into the leather factory every day looking like Ginger Rogers, with her golden hair carefully rolled under at the back. But there was something other than pride in her appearance behind her efforts. She dreaded the coming of lights-out and the long night ahead.

When the bugle sounded and the lights went off, she finally lay down on the hard 'biscuits' with a scratchy blanket up around her ears. For the first time in three days she allowed herself to think of home. It was a mistake. She'd heard of this sickness, of course she had, but never had cause to feel it. Why had no one ever told her that it was a pain, not a sickness. The pain was centred around her heart. An iron fist seized it and squeezed, till she choked, and the more she told herself not to be a baby, the tighter it gripped and twisted, forcing silent shudders up through her shoulders, till there was no help for it, and she began to sob, as silently as she could. Soon her cheeks were wet with tears and the pillow that she clutched was soaked. She wanted to go home.

But hers were not the only tears being shed that night. Other stifled sobs joined her own and before long there was an unashamed chorus of sorrow filling the hut. The only privacy was the darkness, yet at least in the morning they could each pretend it had been someone else crying themselves to sleep.

At kit inspection the next day the captain made a special visit to their hut. After checking the beds had been 'barracked' to her satisfaction and that all their buttons were gleaming, she asked for their attention.

'Now, girls, you'll be pleased to hear that I've had a report from the hospital and Private Eileen Turner is making a splendid recovery. And I understand it is all due to your prompt action, teamwork and steadiness under fire that she was removed from the wreck in good time. You're to be congratulated!'

The captain beamed, and Bee said, 'It wasn't us, it was—' but she was cut off mid-sentence and all eyes turned on Pat as she replied, 'Thank you, ma'am.'

The next few days passed in a blur of square-bashing, spud-bashing and ear-bashing. But apart from the blisters caused by the too-hard leather of her army shoes, May found she didn't mind the drill too much. It wasn't long before she could mark time and change step on the march, she certainly never ended up, like poor Ruby, the lone soldier in one corner of the parade ground, having turned right when she should have turned left. When it came time, at the end of the day, to soak their feet in bowls of warm salt water, May's services were sought out. Her job in the tannery had taught her how to work at unforgiving leather and now, with nothing but the back of a spoon or a knife handle, she patiently worked the rigid heel backs of her hut-mates' shoes, easing them out till they were soft and malleable.

Jean, the copper-haired Scottish girl who now went by the name of Mac, even though her surname was in fact Brown, held up her size tens admiringly. 'Soft as the finest kid! Thanks, hen, you're a loss to the leather trade!'

May laughed and raised her eyes. 'Tell that to my foreman – I never got much praise off him!'

And May realized with a shock that she hadn't once thought of Garner's since arriving at Pontefract. Of course she'd been busy physically – there was never a day without some pay parade, church parade or route march. But she knew that what had banished the factory entirely was the experience of having her mind fully occupied for the first time since school. She found that she loved the lectures, even those the other girls labelled dull. But still, every night brought a return to misery. It was then, as she tossed and turned on the hard 'biscuits', that the faces of her family came to her, and then another face, that of Bill Gilbie.

They'd both promised to keep in touch and meet for a drink when they had leave, but the only letter she'd managed to send was one of the pre-printed cards they'd been issued with, to notify their families of their safe arrival. Paper shortages were so bad she'd had to wait almost until the end of their basic training before the NAAFI received a stock of writing paper. Their third week had largely been taken up with aptitude tests designed to determine which trade they'd all end up in, so it wasn't until the end of those that she had a spare hour to write her letter to Bill. But what could she say? They had left so much unsaid and she wasn't even sure he would want to carry on their friendship. Bill had certainly seemed disappointed she was going away, but there had been no promises made and he'd had to leave for basic training in the RAF before she did. She had no idea where he'd ended up. She could write care of his mother's, but she'd rather have heard from Bill first. She sat with her pen hovering over the paper, a glob of ink collecting in the nib. She put it down, unwilling to spoil her precious paper, yet why else had she bought it? There was no telling if they'd even see each other again – perhaps she should just leave it. He might be posted abroad and never come home. He might have forgotten her in the six weeks he'd been away. Yet the brief friendship they'd shared had been such a sweet connection, that however tenuous the tie, she knew she did not want to sever it, and when it came to bridges, she found it was the one between her and Bill Gilbie that she least wanted to break.

It was the country dancing which helped her out. She simply thought it was something he'd like to hear about, remembering how he'd been roped into country-dancing lessons at the Labour Institute when he was a boy. She decided to tell him all about the Princess Royal coming and how she'd been expected to show off the ATS girls' more gentle side in the presence of royalty.

She'd found out about it from the drill sergeant, who, that day, seemed a little disappointed that they'd finally got to the stage when they could all end up at the right end of the square roughly in step. He had them marking time on the spot, then quick-marched them from one end of the square to the other and back. May wished he'd just let them go, the soles of her feet were burning, sweat soaked the back of her tunic and the hatband seemed like an iron vice round her forehead.

'Quiet, you lot!' he screamed, though none of them had squeaked.

'Anyone done country dancing? Take one step forward.'

May stepped forward and heard a warning hiss, too late, from Bee at her side. She looked nervously along the line. It seemed she was the only one who'd confessed to being a country dancer.

'Important announcement! Lloyd here is going to instruct you 'orrible, uncoordinated clodhoppers in country dancing. You will put on a display for the Princess Royal, who is paying us a visit. One week to prepare. Carry on, Lloyd! Dismissed!'

May wasn't quite sure what had happened, but she knew it was bad when she saw a smirking Pat strolling towards her. 'You clot, May. Don't you know the first rule of the army? Never volunteer for anything!' she said, grinning. 'Well, you can count me out. I'll sit in the audience!'

Bee and Ruby were at her side in an instant.

'Surely he didn't mean I've got to organize it?'

'I think he did, darling,' said Bee, putting her

arm round May's shoulders. 'But we'll lend a hand, won't we, Ruby?'

Looking at Ruby's unathletic figure, May doubted she'd be an asset.

'I'll have to talk to the captain. I'm not up to it. I've got to get out of it!' May felt true panic grip her and she thought she was going to be sick.

At dinner May picked at her food and gave her bread-and-butter pudding to Ruby. The other girls from her hut were keen to offer suggestions.

'I can do the Gay Gordons,' Mac offered, raising her arms above her head in demonstration.

'That should look good – with your size tens, you'll be tripping everyone up!' Pat said and Mac's freckled face turned red. May knew she was conscious of her large frame.

'Thanks, Mac, that's really nice of you,' May said, turning away from Pat. The girl was beginning to get under her skin, but May hated conflict and besides, she was determined to get through basic training without trouble.

'I only know a few, Knole Park and Strip the Willow. How many country dances does a princess want to see?' May put her head in her hands and groaned.

What on earth had possessed her to step forward? She knew the answer to that. It was a memory. A sweet memory of a sunny day in the school holidays, when she was about thirteen. It had been such a hot summer and the little playground at the side of the Labour Institute was a rare and inviting open space. All summer long they had been learning country dances there, the boys leaping over wooden staves, then interlacing them to make a great star, held aloft with a triumphant shout at the end of the dance; the girls weaving and dipping beneath arms, linked to form a low tunnel. The golden light playing on her friends' faces, their laughter and energy, the teacher's shouts and the music from the gramophone bouncing around the little yard. It captured a moment in time; the end of her childhood. For after the class she'd gone home to find her mother holding a letter in her hand.

'You've passed the scholarship exam,' she'd said and May's heart had lurched. College! Her future flashed before her. Something other than a factory girl – she could work in an office, perhaps even be a teacher.

'Oh, Mum.' May had rarely felt such excitement; she could barely breathe. 'Can I go? Will Dad let me go?'

Her mother had paused and looked down at the letter. 'I'm sorry, May, we just can't afford it. Even with the scholarship, there's your tram fare and books – the fact is, love, you can get seven and six a week at Garner's.' She put the letter back in its envelope. 'It's been such a struggle, you know, with your dad in and out of work.'

Then May realized she wouldn't be going back to school at all, and it was a moment she preferred to forget. Instead, she remembered the country dancing, the carefree day, when she was still a child and the future lay bright and untrammelled before her.

And that was why, when she should have stayed firmly put, she took one step forward and landed herself in this pickle. She didn't know why she'd lied to Bill about taking the exam, why she'd downplayed her own dreams. But now, as she picked up her pen, she decided to tell him about the country-dancing debacle and the truth about her dreams.

Dear Bill, she began, *I have a confession to make . . .*

CHAPTER 11

GUNNER GIRLS

Spring 1941

After a miserable, sleepless night, spent wracking her brain trying to remember the convoluted dance moves learned so long ago, the last thing May was ready for was PT parade. Out into the chilly grey morning, they tumbled, breath pluming, shivering in gymslips. They spent half an hour jumping up and down, swinging their arms and touching their toes till May felt sick. But it was only after they were dismissed that she had cause to bless the PT instructor, who had up till now not been May's favourite person. She was eagerly hurrying towards the cookhouse and a hot breakfast when she heard her name being called.

'Private Lloyd? A word?'

She did an about face, worried that she'd committed some PT misdemeanour. The army was so crammed full of rules that even May's retentive memory struggled to remember them all.

'At ease, Lloyd. It's about the country dancing. I've been put in charge.'

'Oh, thank you, thank you!' May could have kissed the woman's feet.

'Don't be too quick to thank me, Lloyd. I haven't done anything yet.'

'Sorry, ma'am. It's just that the sergeant told me I was in charge.'

The woman let out a sharp laugh. 'No wonder you were looking green all through exercises. I think Sarge was having a bit of fun with you, Lloyd. No, you and a couple of other privates are detailed to work with me. Here's a list of dances we'll be performing. It's your job to get huts one to six in shape and then we'll have a rehearsal all together. Can you manage that?'

'Yes, ma'am, of course.' She smiled with relief and the PT instructor gave her a puzzled look. 'You really like country dancing then? Can't stand it myself.'

And the woman strode off across the parade ground, leaving May to make her way to the cookhouse with a skip and a flick of her toe, taking a turn with an imaginary partner. Perhaps it wouldn't be such a disaster after all.

The practices took place between lectures and route marches, but the girls were so keen to impress their royal visitor that they even agreed to use off-duty time to learn the dances. They met in the recreation hut. First May organized her girls into pairs, letting them sort out who would be the man. She'd found a violinist and pianist amongst them and handed the sheet music out. They

191

started with 'My Lord Byron's Maggot', a dance that May didn't know but couldn't help being pleased about, as it seemed to be named after her wayward grandfather. The 'men' and 'women' spent most of the time clapping hands with the wrong partner and casting off at the wrong end, which May feared was due to her inexpert calling. At the end of the evening she doubted they'd ever be able to distinguish between a cast-off and a cast-down, but still, their laughter at their own incompetence was infectious. May suddenly realized she had begun to enjoy leading the little troupe, her usual shyness banished by the challenge of getting six huts of girls in step and synchronized in only seven days.

As she called the final beat, and the dancers began to leave the floor, the pianist, a girl more used to pub playing than the military strains of 'Lillibullero', broke into the 'Boogie Woogie Bugle Boy', the violinist joined in and May felt herself grabbed from behind. It was Ruby.

'Come on, May, let's show 'em how it's done. Better'n that Maggot!'

She whirled May off into a jitterbug. Ruby was light on her feet and seemed to know all the steps. She spun May like a yoyo and soon other couples joined in. Before long the floorboards of the old wooden hut were bouncing and the loose windows rattling in their frames.

They twirled and hopped wildly to the music, the more athletic of them even swinging their partners over their shoulders. May was swept away too, by the sudden sense of freedom. After weeks of having every footstep controlled, every arm movement criticized on the parade ground, their limbs had mutinied, demanding to be set free. She never heard the drill sergeant come in, not until his parade-ground roar succeeded in silencing the piano and violin. At that very instant, May was being swung through Ruby's outstretched legs but at the sergeant's bark, Ruby let go. May slewed across the floor, coming to an ungainly halt at his feet.

'What a shower! On your feet, Ginger. If this is country dancing, then my name's fuckin' Fred Astaire!'

May leaped up, pulling down the khaki skirt, which had ridden up to reveal rather too much of the unattractive lisle stockings.

'Sorry, sir,' May said, to stifled giggles from the other girls. He stared at her, eyes almost invisible beneath the cap, ram rod straight and unsmiling.

'You lot, get back to your huts. You,' he inclined his head, 'stay put.'

He watched the last of the girls as they left and when the door clicked closed turned back to May.

'You're an utter disgrace, Lloyd. If you're put in charge, you're meant to set an example, not act like an old scrubber from Bermondsey!'

May flinched.

'Oh,' he said, curling his lip. 'But that's just what you are, eh, Lloyd?'

She could only guess that he'd had some bad experiences with some of her fellow Bermondsey girls, but it didn't seem fair she was being made to pay.

'Sorry, sir, I thought it would be good for morale!'

'Don't be fuckin' clever with me, Lloyd. And while we're on the subject, I hear you've been excluding soldiers from your little display, so how good is that for morale?'

'No, sir, no one's been excluded.'

'Don't argue with me, Lloyd. Private Sands has told me she's been left out and if you're calling her a liar, then don't. I know her father, good pal of mine. You *will* include her, understand?' He prodded May in the chest.

'Yes, sir,' she said, sticking her chin out. Perhaps her five weeks in this place really had toughened her up after all, for she felt only defiance.

So Pat had put the boot in. But it was a mystery to May. What had she done to the girl, except witness her fear?

May had spent her life as the peacemaker in her family. If Peggy and Jack were arguing over who sat nearest the fire on cold winter mornings, it would be May who gave up her own place to avoid an argument. Now, faced with such obvious animosity from Pat, it was hard for her not to hold out the olive branch. Before lights out, when the girls in her hut gathered round the stove, enjoying the dying embers of their meagre coal supply and drinking mugs of cocoa, May went over to Pat's bunk.

'The sergeant just told me you felt left out of the country dancing. I thought you didn't want to join in.' Pat said nothing, but May persisted. 'Sorry if I got the wrong end of the stick. I can do with all the volunteers I can get.'

Pat lay back on the bunk with her arms behind her head. 'Too late. I've missed the practices.'

'Well, the sergeant's ordered me to get you involved. I'll go through the dances, but we've got odd numbers now, so . . . I'll have to be your partner.'

Pat gave an exaggerated groan. 'Perfect,' she said and rolled over.

May felt dismissed and went back to join the cocoa drinkers.

'Very diplomatic,' whispered Bee, and Mac said, 'I'd have told her to take a long skip and hop off a short plank!'

Ruby handed her a cocoa, and May found herself feeling perversely sorry for Pat; with her prickly back turned to the group, obviously not asleep, she must be hearing the whispers. May decided to change the subject.

'Did I tell you that my old grandad has got a country dance named after him?' And then she recounted the story of how Lord Byron had earned himself an extra six months in jail.

'That's priceless!' Bee said, blowing on her cocoa. 'Fancy risking an extra six months! Spirited old chap.'

'Tell that to my nan! She says being married to aristocracy's not all it's cracked up to be!'

Ruby took the tin mugs out to wash them in the ablutions block, and before lights-out sounded, May got out her precious store of writing paper.

Well, Bill, who'd have thought I'd join the army only to end up organizing a country-dance display for a princess! I wonder if the RAF recruits have to do anything as soppy? I doubt it! Wherever you are, Bill, I hope you've settled in to forces life and have made some friends. Tomorrow we get assessed for our trades and I can hardly believe myself, because after all the training and lectures, do you know what I'd really like to be? A gunner girl!

She didn't know when she'd decided that ack-ack guns were where she'd feel most useful. She suspected the notion had been born during that chance encounter with the ATS girl in Southwark Park who'd mentioned the rumours of mixed batteries. The girl had been right: they'd been told that some of them might be joining the artillery brigades, training to use the tracking instruments. She was sure her family hoped she'd end up cooking dinners for officers or organizing stores. The idea of homebody May anywhere near a big gun, even if she'd never technically be firing one, would horrify them. But if she could stop a few bombs from reaching Bermondsey, then to her mind, she really would be fulfilling the vow she'd made to do her bit.

And so, next day when the lectures were all done and her final assessment had arrived, May sat outside the captain's office, waiting to go before the panel. She'd been told by more experienced girls to express no preference – if you indicated that you'd like to be a clerk, they'd make you a cook. But May knew she'd done well on the instruments used on ack-ack gun batteries; surely they wouldn't ignore that. With night vision sharper than a cat's she had an advantage in using the spotter and the height finder, but she was best at operating the predictor, the machine which calculated just when the guns should fire so as to hit their target. She'd surprised herself with a talent for maths too. Although she'd done well enough at arithmetic to pass the scholarship exam, it had never been her favourite subject at school. All she knew was that no shopkeeper ever shortchanged her. As a child, when her mother would send her to Joe Capp's for groceries, she'd know as soon as the coppers touched her palm whether the change he'd given was correct. Joe had told her mother once, 'You couldn't get away with being short a brass farden, not with that gel of yours. She's cute she is, very cute.' And now the years of mental arithmetic seemed to be paying off.

The only thing she had failed at in practice was projecting her voice, so that the men firing the guns could hear her commands. Time and time again the training sergeant had hollered at her, 'Speak up, Lloyd, you're not in fuckin' church now, you're on a gun battery! When you shout out the fuse, he'd better bloody hear you or Gerry's already up the Thames and bombed the effin' 'Ouses of Parliament before you can say Hail Mary full o' grace!'

'So, Private Lloyd, what trade would you like to follow?'

May took a deep breath and replied as convincingly as she could. 'PT instructor, ma'am.'

The captain flicked through her assessment results.

'Hmm, I see you're helping PTI Thomas with the country-dancing display, a good report from her – but hang on, there's a note from your drill sergeant, seems there's a question mark over your ability to impose discipline on a large squad.

'No.' The captain shut the file. 'Request denied. Looking at your test results, Lloyd, I think you'd be better off in a heavy artillery mixed battery.'

May suppressed a smile. Pat had done her a favour in complaining to the drill sergeant. She was going to be a gunner girl!

It was like swinging a sack of flour around. Pat really was a lumpen dancer and what's more, May was convinced she was taking every opportunity to tread on her toes. She'd picked up the dance steps well enough, but there was no life or exuberance in her movements. At least May, being the man, had some control over her, and chivvied her along, kept her moving at a reasonable tempo, but it was exhausting, like stripping the willow with the brakes on.

Two hundred of them, in thin gymslips, were making a slow circuit of the vast parade ground. After each dance the groups moved counterclockwise, so that eventually all of them had an opportunity to perform directly in front of the princess. May was doing double duty as dancer and caller, and when their group came to face the podium she glanced up. All the brass had arrayed round the small, uniformed figure of the princess. May began calling 'My Lord Byron's Maggot', but after the first beat Pat decided to trip. Unfortunately, it was at a point in the dance when May wasn't holding on to her hand, and May watched in horror as the trip turned into a stumble, which turned into a careen in the direction of the podium. May kept on dancing as Pat landed head first beneath the Union Jack skirting the dais. May waited for the girl to emerge again, but whether from injury or embarrassment it seemed she'd decided it was best to stay hidden under the dais and May finished the dance solo.

The princess in true royal style kept a straight face throughout, and applauded duly at the end of the display. The top brass disappeared, the girls trooped off the parade ground and only then did

May allow herself a quick look back. Pat's head was poking out from under the red, white and blue drapes. The girl's cheeks were burning and there was murder in her eyes.

The minute they were back in their hut their laughter exploded.

'That's the fastest I've seen her move all BT! I thought she was gonna take off!' Ruby said. Bee doubled over and there were tears streaming from Mac's eyes.

'I bet you a pound to a penny she makes it my fault, though,' said May.

'Oh, don't be daft, Ginger, if it hadn't been for you she'd never have made it through the first dance!' said Bee.

'Well, you didn't see her face. Thank God after today I'll never have to see her again.'

'I wouldn't be too sure of that, darlin'.' Ruby looked like a plump caterpillar as she sloughed off the tight green gymslip. 'I heard she's coming to Oswestry with us. She's going on the ack-acks too.'

'Oh, no! I thought she wanted clerical?'

'Well, she might have been stupid enough to ask for it,' Bee said, 'but you know what the ATS motto is?'

'Ask and you shall not receive!' came the answering chorus.

May had been overjoyed when Bee, Ruby and Mac had all been given the same posting to the heavy artillery training camp. It hadn't occurred to her that Pat would be coming too. But once again she felt an unwarranted sympathy for the girl.

'She's not suited, though,' was all she said, remembering Pat's white-faced fear at the train crash. May didn't doubt that Pat would be dreading standing only yards from exploding guns, with Heinkels dropping bombs over her head.

Still, she wasn't going to let the news spoil her mood. She'd finished her basic training and tomorrow they'd be travelling westward into the Welsh border country. Wales sounded even more like a foreign country than Yorkshire, but the sooner they got to Oswestry, the sooner she'd be on the guns, and now that she knew what her future held, she was eager to meet it.

That night May and her friends got a lift into Pontefract and swapped country dancing for the foxtrot at the Assembly Rooms. Some of the Yorks and Lancs had formed a dance band and were playing 'What Will I Tell My Heart?' as the girls entered the brightly lit, barrel-vaulted space. May was surprised by the impressive ballroom, with its wide stage and galleries. Couples were already circling the floor, and though she was quite happy to partner up with Ruby, May soon found herself whisked away by a corporal from the barracks. He was a friendly chap, and a good dancer, but she felt her old shyness returning and spent the dance looking over his shoulder, desperately trying to think of something to say and all the while wondering what it would be like to be guided round the dance floor in the arms of Bill Gilbie. When the music changed to a slow foxtrot to the tune of 'I'll String Along With You', the memory of Bill's childhood story came flooding back and a sense of loneliness washed over her so strongly that she excused herself from the next dance and sought out Bee and Mac, who were standing unpartnered on the sidelines.

'Why did you leave your corporal stranded?' asked Mac. 'He's a good dancer, and a bonny-looking chap, and you have to take your chances these days, hen.'

May smiled weakly. She had no answer for Mac. She couldn't tell her she already had a chap, because she didn't. She'd had such a short friendship with Bill that at any other time the slender connection might have just melted away, but magnified by the glare of searchlights and the thunder of guns, it had begun to feel as if Bill had carved out a place in her heart which fitted no one else.

The train journey to Oswestry wasn't as slow as the one to Pontefract, but it was much duller. They seemed to change at every station, zigzagging their way westward, spending hours staring out of the window at unknown landscapes, being served tea and sandwiches at strange-sounding halts, by women speaking in incomprehensible Liverpool accents.

When they arrived it was raining. At least Granny Byron had read one thing right in her tea leaves

– wherever she went it rained. The camp was spread out over a huge area, covered by double rows of long, low wooden barrack huts that faced each other in 'streets', with separate ablution blocks. May was relieved to be billeted with her friends, and the fact that Pat was amongst them was almost a comfort. Somehow it felt as though she had formed a new family in Pontefract, including the difficult, annoying sister, and now, thrown into another completely alien world, anything that was familiar was welcome.

Before they could sleep, they unpacked kitbags, tidied lockers and 'barracked' their beds ready for inspection. The huts were much bigger than at Pontefract. May counted at least sixteen bunks, but the friends made sure their bunks were all next to each other. She spent her first half an hour teasing her pudding-shaped cap back into the jaunty style she preferred, ignoring all the jokes at her expense.

'Well, just because it's the army, don't mean we have to look like frumps! Come here, Bee, and I'll do your back curlers.'

May had been dubbed 'Ginger' ever since the drill sergeant's dressing down at country-dance practice, and it had stuck, even though she'd been forced to get her shoulder-length, Ginger Rogers victory roll cut to regulation length. She still made sure she put in her dinkie curlers every night. Ruby couldn't be bothered, and kept her hair straight, but Bee always joined May in the nightly rolling routine, each doing the other's back curlers before lights out.

'Do you think we'll get any leave while we're here?' May asked, as she curled a lock of hair round the flat metal prong and clipped it tight.

'Ouch!' Bee jumped. 'That's my head not a pincushion!'

'Sorry, Bee!' May loosened off the curler.

'I heard we won't get any till we've finished here, might even have to wait till the end of firing camp.'

'Oh no, that's another month away!'

'Why? It's not as if you've got a sweetheart to go back to, unless there's something you're not telling us!'

'No, no . . . suppose I'm just still a bit homesick.'

May knew she'd never really lost that pain. It had only been masked by activity and novelty, and that was why she liked to keep busy. She was the one who invariably stayed up the latest, ironing shirts and polishing buttons, and when she was finished with her own kit, she started on the barrack room, which meant that their hut had always been praised for its neatness. Bee called her 'the maid'.

'Well, darling, if you think this is bad, try being sent away to boarding school at seven, then you could talk about home sickness.'

'I don't know how your mum could've done that, Bee,' May said, giving Bee's shoulder a sympathetic squeeze. 'But at least it means you're used to it now. I'd never even slept in a bed on my own before!'

'Oh, stop moaning, will ya!' someone shouted from the other end of the hut. 'At least you ain't got that Garner's stink up your nose all day!'

May whirled round, pulling on the curler caught in Bee's hair and eliciting another yelp from her. She knew that voice.

'Em!'

Emmy Harris charged up the middle of the barrack room and in an instant she had swept May up in a bear hug, bouncing her up and down, so that May's tin hat fell off the top of her locker and the curlers and pins scattered across the floorboards. Emmy let out her familiar throaty laugh.

'Trust me to come and mess up your tidy corner!'

But it was a mess that May welcomed with open arms. For the sight of Emmy had been like coming home.

'Oh, Em, I'm so pleased to see you! But how did you get here?'

Her friend was grinning from ear to ear. 'I was sent here, same as you!'

May looked at her friend, conscious that she must have the same silly grin on her own face, but didn't care.

'Em, you look so good in uniform!' And May realized that Em also seemed much healthier – she'd filled out and her normal pallor had been replaced by a sun-browned glow. She was wearing battledress and even the slacks suited her.

'Army life's not so bad, love. It's better than

hanging up stinking hides all day, I'll tell you that for nothing. And you've grown up all of a sudden, look at you!'

Emmy took May's hand and spun her round. 'But all your lovely barnet's gone – you look so different!'

All the while May's friends were looking on, smiling at their joyful reunion – until Bee, pointing to her own hair, said to Emmy, 'Excuse me but could you spare my hairdresser for half a mo'? I'm only semi-curled!'

'Sorry, love, she's such a skiver!' Emmy laughed and May made the introductions. As she finished rolling Bee's hair, and then got hers done, Emmy recounted tales of her own basic training, which sounded much like May's. When it was time to go to the ablution block, May took Emmy with her. They walked to the end of the row of barrack huts, wrapped in their overcoats, and May put her arm through Emmy's. She pulled the girl in close. 'Em, it's almost as good as getting leave, having you here.'

'Poor May, Granny Byron told my mum she thought you'd take it hard, being away. But, tell the truth, I'm loving it. Look at that!'

Emmy pointed to the wide blackness of sky and the thousands of stars dusting it. 'You don't get stars like that in Bermondsey, do you, love?'

Just then, a streak of light shot low over the far barrack huts.

'Shooting star?' Emmy asked.

'Duck!' May pulled her friend to the ground as the incendiary bomb exploded yards from the huts.

It seemed the Luftwaffe wanted to get the gunner girls before they'd even seen a gun. They sheltered low in the lea of the ablution block, scanning the sky.

'Looks like a lone one, dropping its load,' May shouted as the camp erupted around them. But May and Emmy were so familiar with the drone of German planes that they knew it was receding. 'On its way back home, I reckon. Come on, Em, let's get in the ablution block while everyone's in the shelters.'

The ablution block was spotless and spartan. Standing in front of the small mirror, Emmy put her hair into a net.

'This reminds me of all those false raids in Garner's. We used to run Bill Gilbie ragged, didn't we? Him trying to get us in the shelter, us dawdling along rabbiting. Did you keep in touch?'

May knew it wasn't as casual a question as Emmy made it sound.

'I wrote to him, sent the letter to his mum's, but I haven't heard back. He went in the RAF, you know, probably finished his BT. He could be anywhere by now.'

'Well, you soppy mare, you should've made sure you got his forwarding address, shouldn't you?' Emmy said unsympathetically. 'Should have grabbed him while you could.'

They finished brushing their teeth and walked back through the silent camp to an empty barrack room. All the girls were still in the shelter. The blackout boards were over the windows, so it was pitch-black, but from somewhere in the darkness came a soft choking sound.

'Who's there?' May asked, using her night vision, which was much better than Emmy's, to make her way along the bunks. 'Everything all right?'

She came to a halt in front of a seemingly empty bunk, but the sound was definitely coming from there. She hunkered down. Feeling around under the bed her hand found a foot, then a leg. She tugged it, only to receive a sharp kick in the face.

'Sod you!' She rubbed her cheek. 'Come out of there.'

Emmy came to kneel beside her, and between the two of them they pulled the resisting figure out from under the bed.

'It's the bombs – I get so that I can't move. I'm so ashamed of myself.' The voice trembled.

May edged forward. 'You shouldn't be. It's natural to be scared. It's only that me and Em's got used to it, where we come from.'

The girl reached out, gripping her overcoat. 'Don't tell anyone, please!' she begged, and in the darkness May reached out, to find a face wet with tears. 'It's all right, Pat,' she said. 'We won't tell.'

CHAPTER 12

DEFENCES

Late Spring 1941

'No woman shall ever fire a gun,' the instructor said, looking at them with a bullish, defensive look. 'The rule is clear.' May felt a moment's defiance as he glared at them, daring one of them to contradict him. But May was learning the ways of the army, and often things were not called by their true names. They were destined to serve not in anti-aircraft companies, but in ack-ack; the guns were archies, their mattresses were biscuits and church parade was knee drill. When they paraded in full kit, they were on Christmas Tree order. And so when the instructor told her she wouldn't be firing a gun, she immediately translated that into what would actually happen. In training sessions she'd learned that controlling the predictor was firing a gun in all but name. The machine, a square black box, with eyepieces and dials on each side, was used to calculate the exact time when the gun should fire in order to hit the moving aircraft. A team of girls manned the predictor, following a small moving image of the plane through the eyepieces. At the optimum moment the Number One on the team would call out 'the fuse' to the gunner sergeant, effectively ordering him when to fire at the target.

Over the past four weeks, May had learned to distinguish enemy planes from their own, she'd learned how to use the telescopic identification instrument for spotting enemy planes and she'd learned to plot their position on the height-and-range finders, which were like huge double telescopes. But manning the predictor gave her the greatest satisfaction. It was the closest she would ever come to actively engaging the enemy who was destroying her world.

When she looked through the eyepiece at the tiny image of the plane, when she shouted 'the fuse' at the top of her lungs, she did not – could not – allow herself to see a man in the cockpit of the plane above. She hadn't travelled that far from herself. She knew that most of this new self would hardly be recognizable to the old May – that peace-loving, home-maker would be horrified. And yet, for her, there had been no other possible response to her brother's death but to dismantle the broken parts of herself and rebuild them into this woman with a steel core that she barely recognized. Jack's death had propelled her forward with the force of a shell bursting from one of the big guns she was now directing.

She suspected that such a change in a person

would normally take a lifetime, but hers was no ordinary lifetime, that much she knew. Born into a time of bitter conflict, all ideas of what was normal had vanished that first day of the war, when she refused to go to the shelter because she had to put the Sunday dinner in the oven.

Her instructor was a broad-shouldered man with no neck and a broken, concave nose. However much he might balk at the idea, ATS women were now considered essential to the war effort and had been, if not exactly welcomed, then grudgingly accepted into the Royal Artillery. From now on batteries were going to be mixed, with men loading shells and manning guns and women taking over the tracking instruments. And if the RA wanted to cling to the notion that women never fired the guns, then let them. May didn't care.

Soon she would be leaving Oswestry and crossing the border into Wales proper for the last phase of her training at Ty-Croes, the firing camp on Anglesey. They would practise as teams on actual guns. From the minute they arrived in Oswestry, they had been drilled in the teams which they would stay with for their final Company postings. It was essential, the instructor said, for them to work like a 'well-oiled' machine – the spotters to identify, the height-and-range finders to feed the position to the predictor girls, who calculated the right time to fire, shouting the order to the gunners. They had to be able to rely on the split-second reactions of each other. There were no

211

second chances – once the German bomber had passed beyond the searchlight's glare, it had escaped to destroy another house, orphan another baby, kill another Jack. May felt her focus sharpen to a pinpoint of light as she honed her skill on the predictor. There was a freedom in it. Everything else fell away – her grief for her brother, her thoughts of Bill, her fears for her family at home. She was free, and it seemed her freedom gave her an accuracy that had drawn the attention of her instructor.

After the lecture was over he called them up one by one to be placed in their final teams and given numbers within their group. May waited anxiously, both fingers crossed behind her back, hardly daring to admit what she wanted, out of some superstitious remnant from her father's teaching. 'Never,' he had taught her as a child, 'never look forward to anything. That way you'll never be disappointed.' So now she concentrated on not looking forward to being made a predictor operator. When her turn came she stepped smartly forward to the instructor's desk. Glancing down at the sheet in front of him, she looked for her name but couldn't see it. She hoped she hadn't failed out.

'Lloyd? We're recommending you for Number One.' He paused.

Yes, but Number One on what? She clenched her fists, squashing down hope.

'Once you get to Anglesey, you'll be in charge of A-team on the predictor. Are you up to it?'

'Yes, sir! Thank you, sir.'

She felt her stomach contract, recognizing not apprehension, but eagerness, and she almost ran from the room.

Outside the lecture hut, she waited for her friends. Girls who'd already learned their fate were waiting in little groups, congratulating each other or commiserating. One after the other her friends came out. Bee, Mac, Emmy and Ruby were all on her predictor team.

'For once the army's showing some sense!' Bee said, clearly relieved. 'You couldn't get a more well-oiled team than us!'

'Well-oiled on gin and its – that's us!' Mac retorted.

Pat came out of the hut and wandered over to them. 'I'm on TI. Sarge said I was a natural for it,' she said, smiling nervously at May.

'Good for you,' May replied, happy to let her have her moment, and only too relieved that Pat was going to be a spotter and not on her predictor. She and Emmy had tacitly agreed never to mention Pat's terror on their first night in Oswestry. But May feared that Pat was like a cracked china cup, just waiting for the day when full of hot tea, it would break, scalding whoever was holding it. May was relieved that her predictor team would not have to be holding Pat when she broke. Still, the girl had definitely changed since that night and it had made for a pleasanter atmosphere in the hut.

On the way back to the cookhouse for their dinner, May stopped off in the camp post office. There were times when she almost forgot about Bill, but now, in the glow of her success, she found herself longing to be able to tell him about it. She had received no reply to her letter sent from Pontefract. But other girls in her hut had similar long delays: with people being moved at a moment's notice all over the country, it wasn't unusual for letters to take weeks in arriving. She found a letter there for her, but it wasn't the reply she was hoping for. The handwriting on the envelope was her own, and marked in thick blue crayon on the front was: *Return to sender. Not known at this address.*

Her stomach lurched. Emmy had been right – what a fool she had been not to get his forwarding address. His family had obviously moved from Grange House, perhaps bombed out, perhaps evacuated, who knew these days? Although she'd told Bill that she lived in Southwark Park Road, she couldn't remember ever giving him the house number. And it was a long, long road, looping like a necklace across the heart of Bermondsey. At least four hundred buildings: there were shops, pubs, schools, factories as well as houses, and hers was up at the far end, in the three hundreds. Would Bill care enough to knock at each one? It would be quite a search. And if she tried to find him, would the neighbours in Grange House know where his family had gone? She felt bombarded by all these questions as she emerged from the camp post office. She crumpled her letter, feeling sick with misery. Too miserable for company, she certainly didn't feel like facing any more of Emmy's 'told you so's'. She needed to be on her own, but where?

The post office was near the bike store, and on impulse she borrowed a bike, setting off on the road out of town, heading for the old hill fort, a huge circular earthworks they'd passed on their last route march. It had loomed above them, vast concentric rings of dykes and ditches, impressing her with its ancient, immovable strength. She'd looked up at the high green ramparts of the ancient defensive fort, built to keep long-dead raiders at bay, and she'd felt a connection. She knew what it was like to be part of that endeavour. The gun batteries she was becoming familiar with were no different. Whatever gun site she ended up at would only be a modern-day version of these ancient defences. Artillery, gunpowder and shells replaced stones and spears, but at heart it would be a hill fort, high and forbidding, declaring: *Thus far and no further.*

She didn't know what had drawn her there now. But as she approached its lower slopes, she leaped off the bike, letting it fall to the ground. She began climbing, trudging up the steep slopes, one after another, up and up again, ever higher, till at the top, it seemed that all of Shropshire and half of Wales was spread out before her. Spinning, with one foot on the ground, the other propelling her round, a step she'd learned in an old English dance, she surveyed all the hills and valleys, calling silently on the spirit of the place to give her strength; imagining all the ancient defenders, rank upon rank of them on the old earthwork, each one ultimately alone, in the face of their enemy.

She stayed up on the green banks till the distant hills turned purple in the dusk, and the chill of evening got into her bones. She knew that for now, she had to concentrate on becoming the best defender she could be. Romance and love, surely that was for a time of peace? On her ride back to camp, she realized that she would not look for Bill. She had already lost one dearly loved boy to the war, and she feared that if she found Bill only to lose him too, she'd never be able to bear it. Better to leave what they had as a sweet memory of her earlier, softer self. For now, she felt one with the warrior bones buried beneath that hill fort and it would be her entire focus till the war was, one day, over.

'Em! Can you believe it? We're going home!'

Before their final training at the Anglesey firing camp began they'd been granted a few precious days' leave. Excitement bubbled up so that May had to grab Emmy's arm as they were jolted by the rocking of the lorry on its way to Oswestry train station.

The only contact she'd had with home since leaving had been the regular letters from her father and the parcels from her mother. Each of the parcels had made her cry – carefully saved rations of chocolate and clothes' coupons, a crocheted cream shawl that her mother had made in the long hours spent sheltering at London Bridge Underground Station. Since losing Jack, Mrs Lloyd's nerves had shredded, and she no longer slept in Southwark Park Road, preferring to line up half the day for a sleeping place in the deep tunnels beneath the station. Her father slept at home, but most of his nights were spent on ARP duties anyway. If May had been there, perhaps her mother might have been stronger, but May had to believe she was where she was meant to be.

'Do you think it will look different?' Emmy asked.

'Well, the bombing hasn't stopped while we've been away, love, so yes, I think it will.'

'Are you going to look up Bill Gilbie?'

May hadn't told her friend about the returned letter, out of embarrassment more than anything else. But now she did.

'Oh, May, you never know, you might bump into him on leave.' Either Emmy had become much more tactful or her own face had betrayed enough disappointment to deter her usual teasing. The lorry stopped outside Oswestry Station and Emmy picked up her kitbag.

'I might,' May said, reaching for her own, 'but perhaps it's just as well. We've got work to do, haven't we, and anything else, well, it might just get in the way.'

'But we've got to live. I think we should have a bloody good time on leave.' Jumping down from the back of the lorry, Emmy grinned and held out a hand to May. 'And if we meet any fellers, well, we should enjoy life while we can!'

May couldn't argue with that. She followed Emmy and they leaped on the train with seconds to spare.

They spent half the journey planning outings for their leave, which Emmy was determined to make the most of. But long delays and an unscheduled overnight stop had taken the edge off their excitement and left them both bone-tired. When their train eventually passed along the viaduct through Bermondsey, May was able to judge just how much her home had changed. The viaduct itself had been shored up where bombs had found their targets. Battered streets, bombed into a different geography, were unrecognizable. Sometimes all that remained were small mountains of rubble or canyons of bomb craters, with a few truncated houses, shored up by timber frames. It was a sight that tightened her throat with dammed-up tears. It had never been beautiful, not unless you counted the river, but it had been home, and she had loved every sooty brick and stone of it. She had been proud of every attempt to make it look better: women like her mother whitened their steps and cleaned their windows with vinegar and newspaper, or men like her father repaired rotten window frames and dug over dusty backyards to grow a few flowers. And the council, too, had played its pioneering part, planting trees and flowers, replacing slums with new flats, public baths and health centres. All that effort and civic pride – torn down, undone, blasted by the twisted will of a raging madman across the Channel.

The destruction appeared demonic and yet upon its surface she saw ordinary life persisting. There were already long queues of women gathered in the early morning light, waiting patiently to buy oranges or fish, whatever foodstuffs or material had suddenly made a reappearance in the shops. Then, as they neared the station, from the high viaduct she could see clear to the docks where a large vessel was being unloaded by cranes, and she glimpsed the river, visible through gaps made by destroyed warehouses. As the train shunted to a halt and they were held on the viaduct, waiting for a troop train to pull out of the station, she looked down from their position high above the street at crowds of suited office workers, picking their way over ruins, following the well-worn route across London Bridge to the City. She realized that beneath the fallen stones was an invisible magnetic pathway, drawing them into their daily routine, in spite of the surrounding devastation, and May had learned in her army training how strong a force that could be. Routine kept her steady at the predictor, as gunfire erupted around her, routine kept her mind from her mother's distress, routine kept her marching when she'd rather be weeping, and routine got her up in the morning with reveille when she'd rather stay with her head under the covers because she'd cried half the night mourning her brother.

Finally the signal changed and they were allowed to pull into the station. The machine-gun rat-a-tat of countless carriage doors being flung open, banging back against the carriages, announced their arrival like a hundred-gun salute. Tommies shouldering kitbags, RAF boys and sailors leaped down first, eager to get into London and start their leave in earnest. May and Emmy stepped down into the mêlée and were swept along the platform. After they'd passed through the gate, Emmy offered her a cigarette and lit a match, cupping it with her hand. May dipped her head, and as she did so her eye was caught by the figure of a woman at the next platform. She was wrapped in the arms of a soldier who had dropped his kitbag to the floor. It was a normal sight, these days: couples, oblivious to their surroundings, not caring who witnessed what might be their last goodbye. The couple's kiss seemed endless to May, as if they were gathering all that they were and passing it to each other for safe keeping. She had time to straighten up, inhaling and exhaling a long thread of smoke, before Emmy noticed her stare. Her eyes followed May's.

'Jesus,' she whispered, 'is that your sister?'

CHAPTER 13

LEAVE IT TO LOVE

Late Spring 1941

'Come on, Em,' May said. 'Let's get out of here.'

Picking up her kitbag, she hurried for the stairs leading down into Tooley Street. Neither of them spoke until they reached the bus stop opposite.

'Blimey, May, are you going to say anything?'

'To Peggy?'

'No, to George!'

'I don't know. I can't believe she's done this to George. He idolizes her.'

'Might be best to leave it. What he don't know can't hurt him, can it?'

'He'd do anything for her, though. It *was* Peggy, wasn't it? I didn't just imagine it?'

'Gawd, you're like a tit in a trance! Come on!'

Emmy pulled her on to the back board of the bus, which had arrived without May even noticing. She followed her friend blindly along the crowded lower deck till they found two seats at the front. Slumping down, kitbag perched on her lap, she replayed the scene on the station – Peggy's head tilting as the young soldier kissed her, his hand pressing into the small of her back. She had seen her sister's closed eyes, her rapt expression. It didn't look like the Peggy she knew. She'd always seemed so unsentimental, sometimes almost cold. For May it had been like witnessing some passionate stranger; perhaps the best course of action would be to pretend Peggy was just that, a stranger, and to say nothing at all.

Finally, she said to Emmy, 'It'd finish Mum off if she found out. She'd never forgive Peggy for this. You know how Mum loves George.'

'Well, she might love him, but it don't look like Peggy does.'

Emmy's blunt statement was too much for her. 'She does, though!' May protested. And then she remembered scenes, conversations with Peggy, that told a different tale. Perhaps her sister had been less happy to play the role of cosseted princess than everyone had assumed. May remembered her sister's joy when she'd came to tell her she was going back to work, and how proud she'd been of her WVS uniform.

'I wish I'd never seen them.'

'Well, act as if you didn't then,' Emmy said, with her usual practical refusal to be brought low by anything. 'Anyway,' she went on, 'it's none of your business, is it? Best keep your nose out, love, even if it is your sister.'

'Perhaps.' May rubbed knuckles into her tired

eyes. Their train should have arrived late the previous evening, but instead they'd had to spend the night in a siding near Reading and May hadn't slept.

'My stop next. Listen, don't let it spoil your leave,' Emmy said. 'We're still going dancing next week, ain't we?'

'Of course!' May said, more brightly than she felt. But what would be the point in moping at home? Emmy got off at Grange Road, waving to May as the bus moved off. She leaned her head against the window, giving into the swaying motion, her eyelids drooping as they passed the familiar shops in the Blue. Grants the toyshop, with its front boarded up, no kids peering in through the windows today. She smiled to herself. Then the Home and Colonial, where she'd sheltered on her first time caught out in an air raid. It seemed so long ago. Then the Blue Anchor pub and finally, where the railway viaduct crossed the road, the patched-up John Bull Arch, the very name on her lips, as she whispered it, bringing back all the heaviness of loss. She closed her eyes tight against the memory. Tiredness and the rocking of the bus must have caused her to doze off, for she narrowly avoided missing her stop.

When the clippie called out, 'Southwark Park!' she stumbled off the bus, banging her kitbag against standing passengers, her legs weak, her strength all but drained. She hadn't felt so tired in all those solid nights and days of training.

Trudging towards her house, she tried to push Peggy to the back of her mind, hoping to regain the sense of excitement she'd felt when she'd started her journey. She was nearly home, she told herself, nearly home!

Her father opened the door.

'What sort of bird am I?' she asked, falling into his outstretched arms, letting him pull her into a tight embrace.

'It's my little homing pigeon!' he said, with a catch in his voice, squeezing her till she laughed. 'You'd better let me go, Dad, I can't breathe!'

May peered down the passage. 'Where's Mum?' She looked searchingly at her father.

'She'll be down later, love. She don't get much kip of a night. Here, let me carry that.'

He took the kitbag from her and she didn't bother protesting, even though last week she'd had a try at lifting some shells, for emergency drill, and she was sure they must have weighed five times her kitbag.

'Look at you!' her father said, once she was seated in the kitchen with a cup of tea in front of her. 'You look . . .' he searched for the word, 'older.'

'Oh thanks, Dad!' Tact had never been his strong point.

'No, I don't mean older, I mean, well . . . grown up.' But although he was smiling, his eyes looked sad.

May bent down to retrieve a tin from her kitbag. 'Here. Cakes to go with the tea,' she said, smiling.

'Cakes?' Her father examined the tin.

'Pontefract cakes, but they're really liquorice.'

'For me?'

'Yes, for you – but you can share them with Mum if you're feeling generous!'

They were both chewing on the liquorice when her mother came in.

'You're home! Why didn't no one get me up?'

May spun round and a small cry of alarm burst from her at the sight of her much-changed mother. She jumped up, hoping that Mrs Lloyd had taken her cry for one of surprise. As she enfolded the woman in her arms, she tried to hide her shock at her mother's appearance. She had faded, wasting away in just a couple of months, so that she seemed half the size May remembered. As May hugged her, she felt her shoulder blades, bony wings protruding through her mother's wrap-around pinny. The pinafore, a tight corset-like covering, normally announced that Carrie Lloyd was ready for all manner of work: cooking; cleaning; washing or ironing; caring for whoever needed it. It was just as much a uniform as May's own khaki, and proclaimed, like Joe Capp's sign, that she was carrying on business as usual. But today the floral-print pinny hung upon her bones like a sail in a windless ocean; her mother, it was clear, was still becalmed on a sea of grief.

'I've only just got here. And anyway, we didn't want to wake you up! Dad says you've not been sleeping.'

Her mother slumped in the chair opposite May, still holding on to one of her hands.

'Oh, take no notice of him . . . I can sleep when I'm dead!' she said, a small smile on her lips as she stroked the back of May's hand. 'I'm so glad you're back, darlin'.'

May looked into her red-rimmed eyes, seeing more than tiredness. There was a blankness there, which belied her assurances.

'But let's have a look at you. Your lovely hair! You've cut it all off.'

May put her palm to the bottom of the new waved style, rolled just above her collar. 'Regulations. I like it, though.'

'I think it suits her,' Mr Lloyd said, and May flashed him a wide black-toothed grin so that even her mother had to smile.

'Well, I've got to love you and leave you or I'll be late for me shift,' her father said, kissing the top of her new hairstyle.

When he'd gone her mother insisted on making May a cooked breakfast, which she thought must have contained the whole family's monthly bacon ration. Afterwards, she and her mother washed up plates in the scullery.

'Peggy said she'll try to get round and see you tomorrow, after work.'

'Oh, that's good,' May said, trying to sound

unconcerned. 'I bet she's been finding it hard without George.'

'Oh yes, she's lost without him,' her mother said wistfully. 'Well, he was everything to her, wasn't he?'

But May suspected her mother was thinking more about her own loss than Peggy's.

'Still, she's enjoying being back at Atkinson's, and her WVS work?'

Her mother polished the plate again, which she had already dried once. 'She's wearing herself out with it and it's not necessary. Atkinson's counts as war work. It worries me sick, her out all night in that canteen, down by the docks, bombs falling and gawd knows what.'

'Perhaps she's lonely at night, without George I mean. She might want the distraction,' May said, secretly feeling Peggy might be getting distraction enough at the moment. 'Does she get up to see George much?'

'Oh, regular as clockwork. Never misses a visit. No, she's a good wife . . . well, as good as she can be with him in nick.'

May was getting uncomfortable with the direction of the conversation. 'What about you, Mum? Are you going up London Bridge every night now?'

'I have to! It's the only way I get any sleep. It's been terrible here since you left – well, you've only got to look at the streets. Not that you get much sleep up there, what with the kids larking about and the chatting. But at least I feel safe enough to close me eyes, which I never do at home, not no more.'

She was silent for a moment, her eyes fixed, as if searching out a time when sleep came easily. She shook her head.

'No, I'd rather line up and get me spot on the platform. There's a few of us got our regular places. Mrs Collins is always there, and sometimes Flo comes with me. We takes our eiderdowns and a primus so we can make a cuppa. The only thing you can't do nothing about is the filth. Everything comes home grubby. I'm forever washing. You coming with me tonight?'

'Mum! I'm not wasting half my leave queuing up for a shelter. Anyway, I've got to get used to being out in a raid, now I'm going on the ack-acks.'

'Don't talk to me about it. I don't want to know.' Her mother turned away abruptly and May followed her back into the kitchen. She was glad to have her mother to herself. It was obvious that her letters to May had masked her real state. They sat drinking more tea at the kitchen table.

'Mum, you've got to stop worrying about me. That's what all the training's been for, and don't forget, I'll be the one behind a bloody great big gun! Now that should make you feel better, eh?'

May was trying to be light-hearted, but the furrows in her mother's forehead only deepened.

'I've already lost one child. I don't want to lose another.'

May grabbed her mother's hand, squeezing it tight. 'And you won't. I promise.'

'You can't promise me that,' her mother said flatly and for the moment, May gave up trying to ease her worries.

'How's Nan? Does she go up London Bridge with you of a night?'

'No fear! Not her – she shakes her bleedin' fist at them when they fly over, won't even go near a shelter.'

May laughed. 'We can't all be brave like her.'

'Brave? No such thing – she's seen it in the leaves! Says it's not her time to go . . .'

May was silent, remembering her grandmother's reading of the leaves before she'd joined up. Granny Byron had not, she was sure, revealed everything, and May wondered if her own 'time to go' had been written in the leaves on that day. But only Troubles, the dog, would hear of it, for her grandmother was adamant that there were things in the future it was really better not to know. Perhaps May had been right not to try to wheedle any more out of her. For May had been feeling her own youth far more acutely since joining up, and when she reported to her battery after firing-camp training, she wanted nothing to hold her back from living her own present. In spite of the war, there was never going to be another time when she would be this young again, and Jack's death had convinced her that life was too precious to waste. Come bombs and destruction, come gunfire and danger, she knew that youth was on her side and, if that hadn't made her exactly reckless, like her poor brother Jack, it had made her heedless of whatever perils lay ahead.

May went upstairs, and after unpacking, she spent the rest of the day with her mother, exploring the old house as if it were some new country, wondering at how small her bedroom was and how tiny the backyard and how close the next-door house was to theirs. Wherever she went she saw the familiar in a new light. At one point there was a loud bang and May noticed her mother flinch at the sudden noise. But it was only Flo knocking on the front door. She walked straight in through the unlocked door, calling from the passage, 'It's only me. There's fish down the Blue!'

When her mother didn't answer, May called back unnecessarily, 'Come in, Flo!'

'Oh hello, love! Stand up, let's see your uniform then.'

May happily walked round the small kitchen, modelling her khaki shirt and skirt, and even put on the cap.

'You look so smart!' Flo exclaimed, glancing at Mrs Lloyd. 'Don't she, Carrie? Anyway, you coming down the Blue?'

'I don't think I can be bothered, Flo, not today.' She sat at the kitchen table, fingering the cloth absent-mindedly.

'Not bothered! Your old man won't thank you

when every one else's got fish for their teas and he's got potato pie!'

May was shocked. Her mother had always been a woman who showed her affection for her family in the size of the portions she dished up at dinner time. Before rationing, if a recipe had called for an ounce of butter, she would contrive to put in two, on the principle that more was always better. And in the early days of the war she'd cheerfully stand in line all day for fish.

'Come on, Mum, it'll do you good to get out. I'll come with you.'

Mrs Lloyd let out a small sigh and shook her head. 'No, you don't want to waste your time.'

But May saw her glance at Flo; she was wavering.

'It's not a waste – it'll give us a chance to chat. Besides we'll need more tea, the amount I've drunk this morning!' She plucked the coupon book down from the kitchen mantlepiece and handed it to her mother.

'All right, love,' Mrs Lloyd said, her face brightening.

'Thanks, Flo,' May said, as her mother went to fetch her coat.

'No trouble.' Then, dropping her voice, Flo said, 'She's not been very good, May. But she's been talking about your leave all week. You're a good girl – try and jolly her along a bit while you're home, won't you?'

May assured Flo that she would and as they walked towards the fish shop in the Blue, she linked arms with her mother. Though this wasn't the way she'd imagined her first day's leave, she found herself actually enjoying queuing with the gossiping, bantering women. When the woman in front of them asked Ray, the fishmonger, if he had any skate's eyeballs, Flo said in a loud voice, 'No, love, he keeps his balls under the counter, for the *special* customers, don't you, Ray?' The queue erupted into laughter, and May was grateful to the woman for drawing out her mother's once ready laugh.

The next day May woke up with a sense of unease: she really was dreading her meeting with Peggy. Always good at hiding her feelings, May now worried that her discovery of Peggy's infidelity might somehow betray itself in her manner. As it was, she needn't have worried – in fact it would have been more suspicious if May hadn't acted shocked. Her sister was so changed that May couldn't take her eyes off her. Straight from her Saturday morning shift at Atkinson's, she walked into the kitchen, where they'd just finished dinner, and threw off her coat to reveal a red siren suit, which looked almost elegant on her long-legged, slim frame. May only wished she looked half as good in those baggy, battledress trousers that she kept ironed to a knife-edged crease in an attempt to make them look stylish. Peggy's fair hair was fashionably waved, and there was no sign of the net that used to confine it.

'You're wearing make-up!' May said, astonished.

'You're wearing uniform!' Peggy laughed and it felt to May like the sun coming out on a cloudy day. Her sister was happy, and it wasn't just because she'd been able to go back to work. How could her mum believe that Peggy was 'lost' without George? Her mother's own retreat from life must have clouded her judgement; she simply couldn't see beyond the closed room of her own grief. But May saw it. Peggy had crept out of a dull chrysalis and spread her wings.

The sisters hugged and May stepped back, looking for any sign of guilt or shame, but Peggy wasn't hiding anything. Her face was an open book to May, and on each of the leaves was written the same story, Peggy loved everyone. She had patience with her father, who pestered her for news of George; she was unusually gentle with her mother and she seemed more involved in the family than she'd ever been when George was around. It seemed that Peggy had been hiding in the wings all this time, curtained off by her husband's popularity and notoriety, but now she had stepped on to the stage – though May knew there was more to it than that.

'I've been hearing all about you and your big guns!' Peggy squeezed her again. 'My little sister, a gunner girl. I'm so proud of you, May.'

May was pleased by the praise, for her elder sister had never been lavish with it. May had sometimes suspected Peggy might envy her, though the reason was a mystery.

'I reckon you've got it harder, Peg. Working all day in the factory, *and* all night on the canteen, you must be exhausted . . .' But even as she made the comment, May could see it wasn't true.

'No, you don't need as much sleep as you think you do. You must be up half the night yourself.'

May shook her head. 'Not yet, but I will be once I get on active duty. It'll be a case of sleep when you can, and be ready to jump up when the alarm goes.'

May's mother was looking, in a bemused way, from one daughter to the other, as if she no longer knew either of them.

'Well, I've got this afternoon off and I wondered if you wanted to go out, over the other side, make the most of your leave? My treat,' Peggy asked.

May hesitated, conscious of her mother's eyes on her. She remembered Flo's plea and said, 'I haven't seen much of Mum.'

But Mrs Lloyd urged, 'Go on! You two get out and enjoy yourselves while you can. You're a long time dead.'

So that afternoon, May found herself sitting in Lyon's Corner House opposite her sister and, after answering a hundred and one questions about army life, she finally broached the subject that had been on her mind ever since she'd seen Peggy's passionate farewell scene with the young soldier. The previous night, lying awake in her old bed, May had gone over the scene again and again, wondering if there was anything to be gained by

234

confronting Peggy. And she'd decided to stay silent. But now, faced with a sister so changed as to be almost unrecognizable, she found herself intrigued. What was so special about this man that now Peggy seemed so full of life? May needed to know, for selfish reasons. With Bill, she knew she herself had begun to skirt, cautiously, the unknown world of love, but she needed to know why, for the right person, it was worth risking everything.

'Peggy, you're so different . . . happier,' she said, in a rush, before she lost her courage. 'What's changed?'

'Different? Am I?' A blush was creeping up Peggy's neck. 'The only thing that's changed is George's in prison, I suppose. Terrible really, if that's the reason I look happier.'

'Is that it then? You prefer life without your husband?'

Peggy was fiddling with her coffee glass. It was a tall tumbler, with a stainless-steel cradle and handle. She twisted the glass round and round in the cradle before answering.

'It's freedom. That's what it is. You wouldn't understand, May. You're single and you've got all your life in front of you. But I've already made my choices . . .'

'What, and they were the wrong ones?' May said in a hushed voice. Suddenly the chatter of the crowded corner house seemed to recede and a confessional quiet fell over their little table.

'Don't get me wrong, May, I've wanted for

nothing since I married George. It's just that I kept feeling something was missing, and that seemed bloody ungrateful . . . you know, look around at the poor cows on the Purbrook with a dozen kids and an old man living up the pub . . . I thought, perhaps if we had a baby. But it's only since I've been coping on my own that I realized. I didn't have nothing to get up for, and now I do. Mum's worried I'm worn out, but I'm loving it! You know how we always used to moan about work, but even Atkinson's . . . I look forward to going in! But the WVS is the best thing I've ever done.'

She finally sat back and took a sip of the coffee. 'I feel useful, I suppose, that's what it is.'

May could understand that; it was why she'd joined up herself. But there was no avoiding the fact that it wasn't the only thing contributing to Peggy's newfound happiness.

'Peg,' May took a deep breath, 'I think you should know . . . I saw you at London Bridge.'

'When?' Her sister blanched, the newfound bloom fading, quickly replaced by fear.

'Yesterday morning, when we got off the train. You were on the next platform – with a soldier.'

Peggy looked away, still fiddling with the glass coffee mug. 'Don't look at me like that, May,' she said finally.

'Like what?'

'Like I'm a slut.'

May had been careful with her expression, but

perhaps a part of her had already condemned her sister.

'I don't think that, Peg. I just want to know why.'

'Have you ever been in love, May?'

Now it was her turn to feel uncomfortable.

'No, I thought not. Well, if you had, you wouldn't even have to ask why, love. I wasn't looking for it, I'll tell you that. I know it sounds selfish, but I was just enjoying being on me own. No one looking over my shoulder, telling me what I could and couldn't wear, watching my every move.' Peggy sighed.

'I met him one night, on the canteen round. His platoon was helping clear up a bombed street. They'd stopped work . . . unexploded bomb. He came up, face covered in dust from the rubble.' Peggy smiled. 'He looked like someone had dropped him in a hopper full of face powder! But when he held out his hand for the tea, his poor fingertips were ripped to shreds. Bleeding, broken nails, where he'd been digging out some poor soul with his bare hands. And he was shaking. So I got hold of his hands and put the cup in them and when he looked at me, that was it.'

'That was it? What d'you mean, you fell in love there and then? But you hadn't even spoken to him.'

'I didn't need to.'

This was nothing like her experience with Bill. They'd done nothing *but* talk. So perhaps what she'd felt wasn't love, or being 'in love'.

'But then he was there the next night, and the next, and one night he asked me out for a drink . . . It just went on from there.'

'But didn't you think about George?'

'Of course I did! But me and George – Oh, May. I made a mistake, all right.'

'What, with your soldier?'

Peggy gave a bitter laugh. 'No, love, by marrying George in the first place.'

It was as if another of the foundations of her life had collapsed. Images of Peggy's wedding, with herself as bridesmaid, of George moving heaven and earth to find Jack; Wide'oh filling their kitchen with his wheezy presence and his dodgy goods. She felt a surge of anger towards her sister. As if the war wasn't enough to tear their world apart, she had to turn everything upside down.

'Poor George,' May said.

But her sister's stricken face stopped May from saying anything harsher. Peggy might be happy but a part of her was also suffering. May stretched a hand out to Peggy. 'Poor you.'

'Don't feel sorry for me, love, I don't deserve it.'

'So you and him, on the station. Was that the end of it?'

Peggy's soldier had been carrying full kitbag and webbing. It didn't look like he'd be coming back soon. She was surprised at the defiant look Peggy flashed her.

'You really haven't got a clue, have you? Some

people wait a lifetime for what I've got with Harry. No, it's not the end.'

'But don't you care what this'll do to the family?' It was incomprehensible to May that anything should come before that.

Peggy's face grew redder, but not with shame. 'See, that's your problem, May. The war's not taught you nothing, has it? We've only got one life, and that's short enough. Look at our poor Jack. You need to start living your own life. I thought you might have changed – the fight you put up to join the ATS – but if you want to live your life around other people, that's up to you. One day, if you're lucky, someone'll come along that'll mean more to you than anything, or anyone.'

She hadn't expected to be the one under fire, but now her thoughts returned to Bill. Would she give everything up for him? Peggy's look sharpened.

'What about that feller you was seeing, at Garner's?' May felt suddenly like a German plane caught in a searchlight beam.

'We lost touch.' And to hide her confusion, she took a sip of the cooling, bitter chicory that pretended to be coffee.

'Well, the way he was looking at you that day I met him, I'd say you've already let your someone special slip right through your fingers.'

'I've got no way of finding him.'

'Too scared to, more like.'

'We're not talking about me, we're talking about

239

you and the mess you're in,' May said, feeling too exposed for comfort now.

'Listen, May, I've made some bloody bad choices in my life, and I daresay I'll make a lot more, but at least now I know that if you find someone who makes you happy, you bloody well hold on to them. For me it's Harry, and if you think it's Bill for you – then get out there and find him!'

CHAPTER 14

NO TASTE IN NOTHING

Summer 1941

She really should say goodbye to Granny Byron before she left. She had spent most of her leave with her mother, trying to lure her back into some life which didn't centre around sleeping at London Bridge Station. She'd been unable to persuade her to sleep at home, but it did seem that her mother was making more effort to get out of bed in the morning now that May was home. Her father had told her that Mrs Lloyd sometimes stayed in bed all day, until it was time to queue at London Bridge.

But one morning, after the bombs of the previous night had been particularly vicious, she emerged from the shelter to the sight of smoke spewing in heavy plumes from the direction of the river, and the occasional spout of flame stoking the sky with lurid light. May's first thought was for her mother – she hadn't come home.

Her father was still out on ARP duties and she could only imagine what devastation lay between here and London Bridge. She couldn't bear the thought of her mother battling home on her own, so she dressed hurriedly and set off to find her. She shuddered as she walked under John Bull Arch. She could never now pass beneath any of the railway arches bisecting Bermondsey without a shiver of fear. All the bombed arches – John Bull, Joiner Street, Stainer Street, Druid Street – were like a litany of destruction. She broke into a trot. No thunder of trains echoed overhead, only a sepulchral silence filled the vault. Perhaps the railway viaduct had been hit, further up or down the line; please God, she prayed, not another arch.

As she emerged from the tunnel into the light, she heard the toot of a car horn, then someone calling her name. It was her father, leaning out of the window of an ARP van, which came to a halt beside her.

'Where've you been?' he asked, worry lines creasing his forehead. 'When you wasn't at home, I thought something had happened to you!'

'You shouldn't have worried . . . you know what sort of bird I am!' She smiled crookedly.

He raised his eyes. 'I know, I know. I was worried about Mum. But I'm needed over at the docks – there's a big one gone off down there last night. She's probably all right, but can you go up London Bridge, and turf her out of there?'

'That's where I was going!'

Her father's grey face revealed more worry than his words did.

'Don't worry, Dad, I'll find her.'

'Get in then, we'll give you a lift as far as Dockhead.'

She got into the back of the van, making a space amongst the spades, buckets of sand and stirrup pumps. It was a short, uncomfortable ride to Dockhead, where the air was thick with acrid smoke, and she choked as it caught in her throat. 'Bye, Dad!' she croaked, jumping out of the van and putting a scarf to her face before waving him off.

From Dockhead she walked to London Bridge, skirting a little lake that had formed above a burst water main. Just a few streets away was where she and Bill had found little Jack, and she wanted to turn aside, to see what was left of the place, but instead she hurried on and was soon making her way against the tide of commuters coming out of the station.

She went down to the Tube, passing a few shelterers still wrapped in their blankets on the stairs. Those too late to find a place on a platform would use escalators and staircases for their beds instead. She picked her way down through the central space they'd left, checking each face. But her mother was not among them. Down and down, she went, to the Northern Line platform.

The trains had begun to run, and a blast of warm air blew up from the tunnel entrance as one pulled in. Commuters stepped off and over the sleeping bodies, without a second look. May was amazed at the number of people still asleep on the platform. She wrinkled her nose as the smell hit her, an unsavoury mix of unwashed bodies, damp blankets, urine and fear. Compared to this, their Anderson shelter was luxury, and she wondered how her mother stood it. But May could only think that this, the deepest of all the Tube lines, with the weight of all that London clay above them, was the only thing that could appease her mother's terror.

As she walked the length of the platform, more and more people began gathering up their cases and blankets, and retrieving their coats and hats, which were hanging from any available hook. She walked against the tide of shelterers trudging back up to the surface. It wasn't until she neared the tunnel mouth that she found her mother, sitting on her blanket, knitting.

'Mum? Ain't you coming home?'

At first Mrs Lloyd didn't look up, but kept on knitting till she reached the end of the row. She turned her knitting round and only then looked up, with watery, dark-ringed eyes.

'Oh hello, love!' Her voice was a whisper, and she bent her head almost immediately, carrying on with the knitting as though May wasn't there. Her case was close by and May sat on it, noticing the carefully spread newspaper beneath her mother's blanket. But still, dirt and oily fluff balls had blown in from the tunnel mouth, a fact that her houseproud mother seemed oblivious of.

'It's time to come home, Mum, Dad's been worried.'

Mrs Lloyd shook her head and May noticed that her hair was now almost entirely grey. She'd had such beautiful, glossy dark hair; the shine, she swore, was down to Sarson's vinegar, the secret ingredient in the rinsing water.

'I think I'll stay here, love.'

'Mum! What are you talking about? You can't stay here all day!'

Mrs Lloyd turned her knitting again and looked into her daughter's eyes. 'No, May. I don't want to go out there.'

And May realized that grief and naked fear of the relentless, pounding bombs had finally transformed her sturdy, rock-like mother, pulverizing the strength at her core, till all that remained was a fine and insubstantial sand.

She began to panic. What if she couldn't persuade her to go to the surface; what if her mother really did intend to live down here. She glanced down the platform and spotted a little tea stall, with the familiar green-uniformed WVS ladies serving drinks to shelterers and commuters alike.

'Do you fancy a cup of tea, Mum?'

'Oh yes, love, if you're making one.'

'Yes, I'm making one,' May said gently.

She got up and as she was walking to the stall a woman stopped her. Rolling up her bedding, she said, 'You her daughter? She shouldn't be down here on her own.'

'I know. She says it's the only place she can sleep,' May explained.

'Well, she's had no sleep last night. Every time I wakes up there she is, clacking away with her knitting, wants to tell me all about her son, coming home from the army.'

'Sorry she kept you awake,' May said, grieving for her poor, broken mother.

'Oh don't worry, love, none of us sleeps much these days, do we?' The woman smiled cheerfully.

At the tea stall, May bought two teas and a bun, and explained to the green-uniformed volunteer the problem with her mother.

'She just won't leave, but if you could come up in about five minutes and say you've got to clear the station, I think she'll listen to you.'

Mrs Lloyd had always been in awe of anyone in authority, eager to do as she was told, apart, of course, from the odd misdemeanour involving George Flint's knocked-off stuff. May knew that anyone in uniform would impress her.

They sipped the hot tea and her mother seemed to rally. 'Oh, did you get that rabbit?'

May's hand flew to her face. She'd been charged with getting rabbit from the butcher's in the Blue.

'The rabbit! It's been out on the side all night. I had to run to the shelter and leave it. Do you think it'll still be all right?'

Her mother seemed to perk up, now there was something practical to consider. 'Oh yes, love, right as rain. We'll have that for our tea tonight, love. Jack always likes a bit of rabbit stew. Just give me a minute to finish me tea and I'll go and peel the potatoes.'

May heard the WVS lady approaching and looked round.

'I'm afraid we've got to clear the platform, orders from the high-ups!' the woman said in a bright, loud voice.

Her mother, meek as a lamb, put away her knitting and stood up. 'Come on, love,' she said to May, 'that rabbit's not gonna get cooked with me sitting here all day.'

She was thinking of her mother's vague pale face, just as Granny Byron answered the door, Troubles scampering excitedly around her ankles. The contrast was stark. A smile creased her grandmother's walnut-brown face and the golden hoops flashed as she beckoned May in.

'I was just this minute thinking of you!' She laughed. 'And you say my gift's a load of old cods – well, explain that!'

May was always amazed at how Granny Byron could find significance in the smallest coincidence.

'What were you thinking?' she asked, taking off her cap and dipping to check her hair in the low mirror, which was adjusted to her grandmother's height.

'I was remembering when you was a kid and you went blind, and I was thinking to meself, maybe that's why you don't see too clever now.'

Her grandmother dumped the kettle on to the range and May laughed.

'Well, you got that one wrong, Nan. I had my vision tested by the army doctor – A1! That's why they put me on the predictor. And when it comes to night vision, I can see better than any of the girls.'

'I'm not talking about these!' Granny Byron pointed two fingers at her eyes. 'I'm talking about this.' She patted her heart. 'There's none so blind as cannot see! Peggy tells me you're in love and you don't even know it.'

May flushed. It didn't seem right for a woman as old as her grandmother to be seeing into her heart.

'Peggy should think more about her own bloody eyesight,' May said, immediately regretting it as Granny Byron cocked her head to one side.

'Don't look so guilty. You've not let the cat out of the bag. I know what's been going on with her.'

'Promise not to say anything!' May added hastily, but her grandmother waved at her like an annoying fly.

'I'm not stupid. I haven't even let on to Peggy I know, and would I say anything to your mother with her nerves the way they are?'

May was frightened to ask how she knew. She certainly didn't want to hear that Granny Byron had seen it in the leaves.

'It's what happens in a war. I've seen it all before. People start to wonder what they've been doing with their lives, start swapping around, this one and that one. In the last war there was babies being born at all the wrong times. The men used to come home and they wouldn't say nothing about it. Just bleedin' glad to get out of it alive most of the time. No, I don't worry about Peggy, but I do worry about you, love. You was always a bit slow in coming forward. If there's something you want, you've got to take it, o'ss you'll end up with *nothing*, and you know what they say?'

There were a thousand things that 'they' said and May was sure Granny Byron would enlighten her. She shook her head. 'What?'

'There's no taste in nothing!'

She left her grandmother's, wondering why the old woman wasn't worried about Peggy, whose life seemed to be in far more turmoil than her own. Peggy hadn't even asked May if she planned to tell her secret to George or their parents, but perhaps her sister knew that May would do anything to keep the peace at home. She wondered why she couldn't feel more outraged at her sister's behaviour. But although Peggy had accused May of learning nothing from the war, that wasn't true. May *had* started putting herself before her family. Wasn't that what she'd done by joining the ATS? She should have stayed home and looked after her grieving mother, but she had wanted her own response to Jack's death and now, on this final day's leave, she found herself standing outside

Bill's old home, contemplating another step towards her own destiny.

Grange House was only a short walk from Granny Byron's in Dix's Place, and one of the first of the new blocks of flats built during the previous decade. May remembered the time when many of the old slum streets, where three or four families would share one house, had been demolished, and Bermondsey had become one big building site as new blocks of flats sprang up all over the borough. Most people kept their flats like pristine palaces, such was the novelty of having a kitchen and a bathroom and more than one bedroom. Even now there was a tenant outside Grange House, on her hands and knees, scrubbing the entrance to the stairwell. Every block had a rota, and it was the greatest of social sins to miss your turn at cleaning the stairs and landings. May was pretty sure Bill hadn't lived on the ground floor, for she'd heard him talking about watching out for planes from his landing.

'Hello, love, wanna get up the stairs?' Sitting back on her haunches, the woman wiped her forehead with the back of her hand and pulled the zinc bucketful of disinfectant water out of the way. May skirted round it.

'I'm looking for the Gilbies. I think they moved away. I don't suppose you know where they went?'

'Hmm, Gilbie . . . Gilbie. Lovely family, three boys?'

'Yes, that's them.' Perhaps this was going to be easier than she'd expected.

'No, I haven't seen them, not for months, but I couldn't tell you where they've gone, love. Could 'ave moved out to relatives. There's lots in these flats went out of London, and 'course we've got all new bombed-out families coming in here now and some of 'em don't know what a bucket and mop's for,' the woman said, pointing to the stairwell. 'I despair of keeping it clean, what with all the dust and soot and gawd knows what from the bombs. Still . . .' she heaved herself up, 'you've got to keep up yer standards. Try on the first floor. The Gilbies had the end flat if I recollect rightly.'

May thanked her and made her way up to the first floor. As she walked along the landing to the end flat, she ran her hand over the railing. It had a thick coating of sooty ash carried on the wind from the latest conflagration. The poor woman was fighting a losing battle. Crouching in her path was a small child banging a battered tin box with a stick. She kneeled down. 'Is your mummy in?' she asked.

The little boy nodded. 'Mum!' he yelled and his mother darted to the front door.

May explained why she was there, but the woman was one of the newer residents, bombed out of her house in Rotherhithe. She'd found temporary sanctuary in The Grange, though she told May they'd be moving out to live with a cousin in Surrey soon.

'There's nowhere safe, I know, but you don't

251

have to put yourself in the firing line unless you can help it. You look as if *you* have, though.'

The woman was eyeing her uniform. 'You could ask old Mrs Martin, at the other end of the landing, about your friends. She's been here since the flats was built.'

May tried the flat, but the old lady was deaf and thought she was her own granddaughter. May could get no sense from her.

As she left the flats she passed the Red Cow on the corner. On a whim, she pushed through the side door and, before she could change her mind, slipped through the crowd of off-duty soldiers to the bar. Keeping her eyes firmly fixed on the publican, she pretended not to see the stares she'd drawn. But she couldn't help hearing their remarks.

'There's one for you, Sid. Drop their passion killers for nothing, they will.'

'Oi, oi, have a few manners, she's in uniform!' the landlord shouted across to the soldiers. ''Scuse 'em, love, they don't come from round here.'

May began to inwardly curse Peggy. This had been a stupid quest.

'What can I get yer, love?' he said, leaning on the bar.

She ordered a gin and bitter lemon, feeling she couldn't walk into a pub without drinking something.

'You're lucky. Just got some in!' He pointed towards the optics behind the bar, half of which were empty, but the green gin bottle was reassuringly full.

When the publican placed her drink on the bar she asked her question.

'Gilbie? Yes, I know young Bill, used to be our piano player before he got called up. I believe his family moved over St James's Road way, but I couldn't tell you the address. Sorry, darlin', it's like the whole bleedin' world's on the move. Like them fellers over there.' He nodded towards the soldiers. 'Wouldn't know 'em from Adam.'

May finished her drink and went out into the early evening. Just as her father had taught her, she hadn't got her hopes up, so why was it that she felt so disappointed not to have tracked down Bill's family? For others, bolder than herself, the little tour she'd just made might be a small thing, but a few months ago she couldn't have done it. Perhaps it had something to do with the army's toughening her up, but her fruitless search had convinced her that she valued Bill enough to overcome her shyness, certainly too much to let him vanish out of her life altogether. And by Peggy's definition that meant only one thing.

They travelled from Oswestry to Anglesey firing camp by train, first travelling north towards Chester, then changing trains to hug the north coast of Wales, till the line reached the island in the west. Army lorries were waiting to take them to the far west coast where the firing camp lay, a

253

sprawl of brick huts and gun encampments. When they arrived, it was raining.

'Bloody hell, my nan said everywhere I went it would be raining, and look at that, it's peeing down!'

May wiped condensation from their barrack-room window and Bee came up beside her.

'Not very promising. We'll be out on parade first thing. Christmas Tree parade it says on the board. Be lovely if it's like this!' Bee said, peering over her shoulder at the banks of grey cloud rolling in from the seaward side.

'And we'll spend all week getting our kit dry with that useless lump of tin they call a stove.'

They turned away and went back to the central stove, where the full bucket of coal waited, unused.

'Stupid bloody army rules. Why do we have to wait till six o'clock before we can put a bit of coal in it – be more sensible to put it on when it's cold!'

Summer had barely arrived, and yet this country was cold as well as damp. May looked at the clock: still half an hour to go before they could get any heat.

'Well, you know what they say about this place,' Bee told her. 'If you're looking across the Menai Strait and you can see the other shore, then it's going to rain. And if you can't see it, then it's already raining!'

May smiled weakly and was about to suggest breaking the rules and shoving on a surreptitious shovel of coal when the hut door opened and the sergeant entered. They all hopped back, standing at the ends of their beds as she walked the length of the hut.

'Very good. Glad to see you've got yourselves settled in. Parade and duty rostas posted here.' She indicated a board at the end of the hut. 'And in case you thought you'd be getting away with it on your first night, you're mistaken. You're on guard duty tonight, and it's A-team first.'

May shot a look at Emmy in the opposite bunk and mouthed 'just our luck!'

'What's that, Private, got any thoughts you'd like to share with us?'

'No, Sergeant.'

'Good, and make sure you keep them to yourself or you'll find yourself on guard duty every night! I know you're all anxious to get on the big guns, but don't forget that a camp can only run when we all pull together. You'll still be expected to do guard duty, kitchen duties and drill. But you *will* be excused PT in the mornings after a night on the guns.'

That's big of *them*, May thought, but kept her lips firmly pressed together.

But the Welsh rain was still falling that night, soaking through them as she and Emmy stood on guard duty at the camp entrance. It was a penetrating fine drizzle that seeped through their overcoats. After a day's travelling and an evening of kit cleaning, she would have welcomed just collapsing on the hard biscuits tonight. Not that she'd expected to get much sleep. She was too excited about the coming day.

Next morning May got her first taste of the guns. They had been ordered to assemble around the gun emplacements and here they first met the men who would form the other halves of their gun teams. They were shown every shell and firing pin, even though their positions with the predictors and height finders would be twenty yards away from the guns themselves. When they finally got to practise firing it was a shock. Nothing in training had prepared May for the noise – worse than the bombs that rained on Bermondsey, worse than the guns in Southwark Park. First came the blinding flashes, lighting the sky, followed by the noise of a hundred thunderstorms rolled into one. Without any ear muffs, the clamour set her ears ringing, so that she could barely hear herself as she shouted out 'Target!' at the top of her lungs.

They stood for hours on the cliff tops, buffeted by wind and rain, waiting for the moment when a small plane was sent over the site. Towing a sock, which billowed out behind it, this was a clearly visible target, nothing so difficult as the small black dashes caught in searchlight beams that would be their real targets. But as May pinned her eye to the predictor and turned dials with trembling fingers, she felt as if she were trying to catch a whale with a fish hook in the middle of a hurricane.

They fired round after round, till May felt as though every cell in her body was vibrating to the quaking of an earth and sky set in motion by the shells. In the afternoon, they sat in a classroom, with ringing ears and tired eyes, to have their results assessed by the instructor. Mostly they'd missed the target drogue, but it turned out that was preferable to them getting so close they actually hit the tow plane and put it out of action.

'A-team predictor operators, well done, you were the ones with the closest hit. If it had been a Heinkel, it wouldn't have got back to Berlin to tell the tale! Commendation for you at parade tomorrow. Keep up the good work.'

May blushed with pride. An 'almost' direct hit! And then a vision struck her: falling from the sky, whirling down to earth with his plane, a boy, a flyer, perhaps no older than Jack or Bill, falling in flames over the sea. She shook her head to rid herself of the vision. It couldn't be helped, and the Germans had started the blasted war, hadn't they? She would have to deal with it, the part of her that wanted to see everyone else's side. She had always been that sort of person. No one was right, no one was wrong, people were just different, or so she'd told herself. But now she had been forced to take a side. She would just have to imagine that every plane was heading for Bermondsey, every bomb destined to drop on her house in Southwark Park Road, and it was up to her to stop it. It was the only way she would get through this.

CHAPTER 15

ENGAGING THE ENEMY

Summer 1941

Essex was a convenient posting, certainly easier to get home from on leave than if she'd been sent to Scotland or Hull. But thick fog and troop movements, coupled with a forced stop during an air raid, delayed them and it took all night to reach Barkingside. They had been given three days' leave before reporting to the base, which May largely spent keeping an eye on her mother and sleeping. Their orders were to assemble at Liverpool Street Station and she'd arranged to travel there with Emmy. The meeting with their battery at Liverpool Street was like a sort of homecoming. It was comforting to know they'd all be going into the unknown together. Bee was there and Ruby, but Mac would be coming down from Scotland, so it wasn't until they arrived at the gun site in Barkingside that they were all reunited and had the chance to properly swap leave stories.

As they drove into the camp in the back of a lorry, May pulled aside the canvas and peered across a field to the command centre, where the massive bulks and long snouts of the ack-ack guns circled like long-trunked elephants. But May knew, once those snouts were lifted skyward, they'd become more like fire-breathing dragons. She was relieved to see that the gun emplacements were situated a fair distance from the 'spider', which was army slang for the web of huts connected by duckboards to a central ablutions block, which would be their home. If there should be a direct hit on the guns one night, at least those asleep in the 'spider' would be spared. She tried not to think about what would happen to those manning the guns at the time.

May was the first one to jump off the lorry and pushed open the door into their hut, which could house fourteen girls. She was greeted by the familiar soft Scottish burr.

'Come in, hens, I've got your cocoa sitting on the stove!'

'Mac!' May rushed to embrace the girl. Although she'd known her only a few months she felt the same delight as if she'd come across her own sister. Soon they were all sitting round the stove, sipping the still warm cocoa. Mac had spent her leave on her parents' small farm up in the west of Scotland. Of all the girls, May felt, she must find this new life the most difficult. Mac said there was nothing but sky and sea surrounding their farm.

'Ohh, and the *quiet*, I was drinking it in, trying

to get ma fill, before comin' here to be deafened!' she said.

But the best leave story was from Ruby, who informed them that she'd met a feller and was determined to get him to pop the question before he went overseas the following month.

'That's if I can get "passionate leave", of course!' she said, to a chorus of laughter.

There were new girls to get to know and May was conscious too of Pat, hovering awkwardly on the edges of the conversation. She turned to her and asked, 'What about you, Pat, where did you spend your leave, at home?'

The girl seemed surprised to be addressed, but moved closer to the group. She had changed, May thought. She'd offered no loud opinions and hadn't tried to dominate the conversation as she once would have.

'No, I didn't go home. Well . . . haven't really got one. Dad's overseas and Mum's dead.'

May immediately felt guilty for every unkind thought she'd had towards the girl and, nudging Emmy to move over, she picked up a nearly cool cup of cocoa and offered it to Pat.

'So where did you go?'

'Stayed with my uncle, out in the sticks. Leave was all right. Not so much fun as Ruby's, though!'

May was relieved to see some of the others softening, if for no other reason than, as part of their gun team, it would help to have Pat on their side.

The hard biscuits on the iron bed kept her awake for what was left of the night. It was surprising how quickly she'd got used to the normal comforts of home, but it was just as well she'd spent so much of her leave catching up on sleep. When the bugle sounded reveille at six-thirty she'd forgotten where she was, and it was only when she heard the clatter of feet along the duckboards as people rushed to the ablution block that she remembered she was back in her other life. She groaned when Emmy came to roll her over and out of the bed.

'Come on, love, can't let the hut down on the first day. Don't want 'em saying the Bermondsey girls are sweatin' in the bed half the bleedin' morning!'

May grabbed her toilet bag and toothbrush and moved, heavy-lidded, towards the ablutions. Outside the wind whipped across the field, stinging her eyes. She squinted at the guns, silhouetted now in the grey morning light. The truth was, she was sick with apprehension. She still didn't know how she'd stand up to real action. How would she cope when the fire-breathing dragons finally opened their great jaws?

But however convenient, Essex wasn't an easy posting, positioned as they were in the direct flight line of Heinkels searching out the Thames Estuary, following the guiding light of the river straight into London's heart and beyond. They were supposed to have a week or so familiarizing themselves with their positions on the gun encampments, but that night, after only a day at their new posts, the alarm sounded.

A raid so soon? She didn't feel ready, and found her breath coming in shallow gasps as she jammed on the tin hat and then fumbled with her leather jerkin. With gas mask slung round her neck, she joined her steps to the thundering feet on the duckboards. There were a few cries as some girls slipped off the edges, turning ankles, but there was no time to stop. May sped across the field, blessing her keen sight, as she avoided uneven ground, to arrive safely at the predictor machine, before standing to attention. There were eight big guns spread out in two semicircles in the centre of the field, with the instruments for each gun set up twenty odd yards away within concrete bunkers. At the bunkers her team stood ready, two spotters with binoculars and another two girls manning the huge double-ended telescopic identification instrument. Four were on the height-and-range finder and before she knew it her predictor team was flanking each side of the large, dial-covered, metal box. She had no time to be nervous, for almost immediately a searchlight operator shouted 'Expose!' There was a loud hum and searchlights pierced the blackness above with their silver arrows. The sky soon thrummed with the noise of a hundred enemy engines, and when one was caught in the net of beams cast across the sky, the spotter yelled, 'Plane sighted!' May's focus then became as bright and sharp as the beams etching the sky. She bent to the eyepiece and saw the tiny image of a plane. Keeping her eye fixed on the image and alert for the shouts from the height-and-range finder, she waited, aware of a fine trembling throughout her body. Suddenly there was a high-pitched whizz and rumbling explosion, as the whole gun emplacement shook.

May flinched, along with the other girls, as earth and shrapnel shot their way. But they held their positions and May called out to her team, 'Steady! Steady!'

What was going on? They hadn't even had time to fire. One plane amongst the swarm above them must have decided to start dropping its bombs early, and it seemed they were the target.

She heard numbers, shouted in the rather shaky voice of Number One on the range finder. A few short months ago, they would have been incomprehensible to May, but now she had a clear image in her mind of the plane and where in the sky it would be.

'On target!' came the call as May's team sprang into action, spinning dials, swiftly pinpointing the plane, and calculating how long to set the fuse. The calculation was done in seconds, then May roared at the top of her lungs. 'Fuse! One point eight!'

From over at the gun came the answering call from the men, 'Fuse! Fire!'

A ball of flame exploded from the barrel, sending up clouds of eye-stinging acrid smoke. As more planes were spotted, all the guns joined in an unending chorus: booming, bellowing, belching flames in a hellish glare that, instead of confusing May, seemed only to sharpen her concentration to a diamond-hard point.

All night the planes came. They stayed at their posts until dawn, when the all-clear sounded, and May finally stood up from the predictor, arching her back in a long stretch. She looked up at the wide Essex sky, streaked with smoke, pewter and rose, above a low horizon broken only by the black rim of the forest. May and her friends linked their arms round each other's waists, walking in companionable, drunken tiredness towards the hut to catch up on some sleep. Something had changed between them, and suddenly, she knew she could trust these girls with her life. Even Pat. Although May had spotted her almost cuddling a sandbag at one point, the girl had controlled her terror just long enough to identify the planes. May didn't have time to realize, until later when she was lying in bed, ears still ringing, that though she might not have shot down an enemy plane that night, she had finally engaged the enemy.

As the raids on London gradually decreased, those on the rest of the country increased and the Thames Estuary was the bomber's favourite highway from the Channel. They saw action almost every night for months. As May shouted herself hoarse each night, she sometimes forgot who she was. She became the thunder in her ears, her only concerns angle, bearing, height, range. The target was all and yet that almost ceased to be a physical thing, flying through the sky above her, and became merely an image on a screen, which at all costs had to be eradicated. Not even the hot shrapnel raining down, pinging on to her tin hat, had the power to deflect her. And she knew her teammates felt the same. Becoming an amalgam of each of their skills, the parade-ground drill which had been dinned into them, making them one marching unit, now made them one fighting unit. May became the eyes and ears of the fire-breathing dragon and sometimes, in the early hours, when there was a brief lull in the shelling and they were allowed to sit below in a bunker, it took her what seemed like forever to come back to herself.

She was in the bunker, in that semi-state between fighting and resting, wondering if she had either the energy or the courage to read a letter from Peggy that she'd tucked inside her tunic before coming on duty, when she heard the bomb fall. The roar ripped through the sandbags and the concrete, making the earth beneath the bunker shudder. She leaped up and scrambled to the surface, followed by Mac and the others. Their own guns were silent, but the sky was lit by a lurid, orange glow coming from across the field, where a 'spider' was ablaze. It looked to May as if the huts had taken a direct hit, one of the men's spiders further up the field. For a moment she was paralysed, fearing that her trembling legs wouldn't carry her, knowing she had to move and yet unsure which way to run. She looked about her, then heard shouts coming from the other side of the guns. Should they man their positions or run towards the huts? There was chaos, with shouted commands ringing through the darkness. The German bomber had taken them all by surprise, no doubt a stray, left behind, getting rid of its load on the way home. By now it would be long gone.

'Get over there and help them!' It was their gunner sergeant.

As she began to run, there was another explosion as one of the girl's ablution blocks went up in flames. Crackling fire expanded, snapping at them, and necessity chased away the remnants of fear as she heard screams coming from one of the huts. Her teammates were running with her and other frantic figures, black against the bright conflagration ahead, were converging from different directions. But when they neared the huts she heard an anguished cry as one of them tumbled headlong on to the grass. May tripped over her. It was a corporal she recognized from another team. She was on her back, her face livid in the glare from the blaze, eyes wide with shock. She shook her head. 'Leave me. I'm all right. Go and help the others!'

But May could see enough to know she wasn't

all right and looked around desperately for help. Just then Pat ran past, charging in the opposite direction from the huts. May grabbed her hand but as she tried to pull away, May held her tight.

'What you running that way for? Pat, for God's sake, you're not doing this again – you've got to help me, look at her!' The corporal's tunic was soaked with blood, a jagged piece of wood protruding just above her elbow, from where blood was pumping in a steady stream.

'If we don't get her help, she'll bleed to death! Now you bloody well hold her legs, while I take her arms.'

Pat hesitated, then seemed to make a decision. She picked up the corporal's feet. May took her under the armpits, and ignoring her cries of pain they carried her towards the medics.

'You'll be all right. Just hold on, we're nearly there!' May spoke to the corporal, more as an encouragement to herself, for the woman wasn't responding.

A small triage station had been set up on the edge of the gun site and they carefully laid the corporal down, while a young medic checked the projectile still poking from her arm.

'We'll need this out pronto. Stretcher here! Out of the way, you two, go and make yourselves useful.'

Dismissed, May paused, scanning the chaos. Fire crews were aiming jets of water into the blazing huts, and the stench of charred wet timber came to her on the wind. It felt like being back in a night raid in Bermondsey – the smells were the same, and the sounds, the shouts, the thuds, the screams. They were nothing she hadn't seen before and the memory of why she'd joined the ATS came to her with a vivid burst of flame, the thought seeming to renew her courage There were still bodies, unattended. She ran towards an unmoving figure closer to the guns. To her horror, she realized it was Emmy. She must have been running behind May and taken a hit.

'Oh, Em, hang on, love. It's May. I'm here!'

Looking round for Pat, she realized the girl hadn't followed her. She would just have to move Emmy herself. Just then, she heard an approaching 'rat-a-tat-tat'. Glancing back, she was horrified to see just behind them clods of earth exploding in a double row, like so many small underground explosions, accompanied by bursts of fire. They were being strafed! A German plane must have circled back and, seeing them vulnerable, was hunting down easy pickings by the light of the fires. May gathered up Emmy into her arms. Making her own body into something resembling a magic carpet, she rocked herself into motion, and with one massive effort rolled them out of the path of the bullets. Time stood still, as she waited to be hit. Holding her friend in a grip tight as death, not daring to move until the machine-gun fire had receded, it suddenly occurred to her the plane might come round again. She certainly wasn't going to be waiting for it, and with strength that seemed to come from outside of herself, she dragged Emmy back into the shelter of a bunker. Hunkering as close to the sandbagged wall as she could, she knew she was spent. Her chest heaving, her muscles screaming, she held the still unconscious Emmy in her arms until the night fires died down to be replaced by a bleak dawn.

For their part in the night's drama, May's team was mentioned on parade and May earned herself a commendation and a promotion to Lance Corporal. Pat came up to her as they left the parade ground.

'May, wait!' The foghorn quality of Pat's voice could still make her wince, but May was more forgiving these days. After all, the girl had battled her demons and helped save someone's life last night. Pat, surprisingly, flung her arm round May's shoulders as they walked.

'Listen, May, I just wanted to say thanks . . . for last night. I never thought I'd be able to do something like that. I'm glad you made me stop and help.'

'I know it's harder for you, Pat, harder than for any of us, I reckon, but you deserved the commendation just as much as me.'

But Pat shook her head. 'You know as well as I do, I was running the other way. I've tried, but I'm not cut out for this, May. I've asked for a transfer to stores.'

May was inexplicably disappointed. Pat, for all her faults, was one of the team now.

'What about all your training?'

The girl shrugged. 'I'll be more use in the stores, and if you ever need anything, you just let me know!' She winked and walked off in the direction of the stores.

'I will!' May called after her.

In stark contrast to the high drama of the previous night, May spent the morning on kitchen fatigues, scouring pots, her arms elbow-deep in greasy soda water. It seemed that even a heroine's place was still in the kitchen.

After fatigues, she made her way to the infirmary. She'd heard that Emmy had been lucky, concussion and a broken collarbone. But the sight of her battered friend made her realize how close she'd come to losing her, and she gave her a relieved hug.

'Blimey, May, you're doing more damage than Gerry,' Emmy said, wincing. Then she grinned. 'Always a silver lining, though.' She turned in the bed to get herself comfortable. 'Guess where I'm going?'

'Not home?'

Emmy stifled a painful laugh and nodded. 'They said this'll take weeks to heal. I've got early Christmas leave!'

'You lucky so-and-so!'

But Emmy's expression was serious and her usual flippant reply didn't come. She took hold of May's hand. 'Wouldn't have been lucky if it weren't for you, May. Thanks, love.'

May spent half an hour with her friend, so it wasn't until her off-duty hours that afternoon, when she was sewing her first stripe on to her uniform, that May remembered the letter from Peggy. After making sure the stripe wasn't crooked, she fished the letter from her tunic pocket. It smelled of fire smoke and something indefinable. She put it to her nose. California Poppy! The sweetest smell in Bermondsey. It transported her back to Southwark Park Road and her sister's tangled life.

The first paragraph was all about her mother. Mrs Lloyd was getting worse and one morning last week their father had been forced to go to London Bridge and bring her home. She'd decided she might as well stay there all day. But it was the second paragraph that caused May to let out a long groan.

CHAPTER 16

PASSIONATE LEAVE

Autumn 1941

The red siren suit was too revealing. Peggy stood in front of the mirror, looking at herself from the side, and tried tightening the belt, which only made her swelling stomach more obvious, at least to her. She would have to go back to wearing frocks at work, but the new utility styles were so ungenerous, with all excess folds and pleats forbidden, that soon she'd be showing even in dresses.

She had only told one person – her sister May – writing to her in the first sickening realization that she was pregnant. Perhaps she shouldn't have, but she'd felt so alone, with Harry already posted to Southampton.

But although May was the only person Peggy had told, she wasn't the only person who knew. Somehow Granny Byron had found out, using her own intuition and God only knew what other methods, a crystal ball for all Peggy could tell. Her grandmother had been waiting for her one evening, outside Atkinson's, and Peggy had been so shocked to see her there, she'd assumed there'd been some sort of accident.

'What's happened?' She'd rushed up to the incongruously colourful figure, with her hoop earrings and wide-brimmed feathered hat.

'Nothing!' Granny Byron had her arms folded, a large black handbag over one arm. 'I've just been to see Mrs Tucker, up Alma Grove, bedridden now, poor old cow, so I do her a home reading now 'an again. I had a feeling I'd bump into you.'

Peggy was mystified. Her grandmother never came to see her at work.

'Come for a drink with your old nan,' she said and it was more a command than a request, as she led the way towards the Turk's Head. The narrow old pub, with its Ottoman-looking cupola stuck incongruously atop one corner, stood on the corner of the alley leading to the factory and was a favourite drinking place for the Atkinson's workers. She felt slightly embarrassed to be dragged in there by her grandmother. But Granny Byron liked a drink and insisted that she had been weaned on Guinness. Peggy knew that May sometimes asked their nan for a reading, but she never had. Perhaps she was less captivated than May by the Romany family heritage, failing to see how being born in a caravan had any merit at all.

But that evening Granny Byron bore out her claims to 'the sight'. Taking a sip of the creamy-topped Guinness, wiping the foam from her top lip, putting the glass down deliberately and leaning forward over the large bag that sat in her lap, she asked, 'How far gone are you then? Three months?'

'Nan!'

Peggy looked swiftly round. She'd already spotted a few women from Atkinson's, meeting their chaps here after work.

'Keep your voice down. How do you know that? Did May tell you? Have you told anyone else?' Peggy was panicking. She knew it had to come out, but not yet. She wasn't ready.

'May's not said a word. I knew you was carrying on, ages ago. That didn't take no crystal ball, what with your new clothes and your make-up, and gawd knows what. I've seen that look in a woman's eyes before, when they come to me and want to know "Does he love me?" Weeks and weeks you've been miles away. Anyway, don't matter how I found out you're expecting. I've told no one. But before the balloon goes up, what I wanted to say to you is this . . .' She tapped a tobacco-stained finger on the edge of the beer-shiny table. 'You can always come to me. Don't matter what your mother says, nor your father, nor George. If you need anything – you come to me.'

Peggy covered her face with her hand as she felt tears threaten. After a minute she drew her hand down, as if wiping away all trace of weakness.

'That's it, gel, you're like me, tough as old boots. You'll manage. Have you told the feller?'

Peggy shook her head.

'Well, I don't know as you'll get any satisfaction

there, love, but if you want to keep him as well as the baby, you'll have a tussle on your hands with Wide'oh.'

Granny Byron always referred to George by the name he'd earned growing up.

'He was never no good for you, love, you always give in to him too easily. But you might think twice about going it on your own. Look at me. I might as well not ever been married, for all the help I've had from my old man over the years. Still, at least I've lived me own life, he don't get it all his own way.' She paused, letting the comparison with Peggy's marriage sink in. 'I'm not saying it'll be easy. It's bloody hard work on your own, but something tells me you'd be better off.'

She got up, adjusting her wide-brimmed hat. 'Don't leave it too long before you tell 'em. It's only worry making you feel sick.'

She bent down to kiss her granddaughter, the green plume of her hat falling forward, brushing against Peggy's cheek.

'Thanks, Nan,' Peggy said, looking up into her creased old face. 'I'm glad I've got you.'

Now, as she gazed at herself in the mirror, Peggy realized it was time to heed her grandmother's advice and tell her parents. She suddenly felt a wave of nausea and dashed for the bathroom. Leaning her arms on the basin, she waited for the sickness to pass. It may have been morning sickness, but she suspected it was more the thought of telling her parents, and afterwards George, that was the cause this time. And yet she couldn't regret what had happened. She'd lived an entire lifetime in these past months with Harry. She'd felt every emotion from ecstasy to despair, and she knew that her life up until this point had been only half lived. She had not thought of getting rid of the baby; the only question was whether she'd have to bring it up alone. For Harry didn't know she was expecting his child and there was no guarantee he would want to take them both on when he came home – *if* he came home. He'd had a couple of brief leaves since going to Southampton and she didn't know if he'd get another before he sailed for North Africa. For now, all she had left of him were the memory of his bright eyes and the child growing inside her. Fruit of her war, waiting, like an unexploded bomb, to blow her family apart.

She sighed and pulled on the new frock, which had taken almost all her coupons. A green print, with a blouse collar and a too-tight belt at the waist that would soon have to be let out. She'd made her decision. Today would be the day she told her parents and she would do it before her visit to George this afternoon. She spent the morning at work with a stomach screwed into knots. She'd finally been transferred to real war work, only to find that it consisted of stamping serial numbers on to metal plane parts. What the numbers meant she had no idea, but the works' manager assured them that those numbers were vital to the war effort. The task was repetitive and far duller than working on cosmetics, and she could have wished for a ladder or two to climb, just to keep her mind off the interview ahead. She knew that if only she had her parents' support, if only they would stick by her, then she could face George. But without them, she doubted her courage could carry her through. As she stamped another number and then another on to the metal plates, she realized she didn't fear that George would disown her; what she feared was that he wouldn't.

'You look pretty, love!' her mother greeted her at the door. Peggy noticed the little suitcase standing in the passage, packed and ready for her night in the Underground.

They hadn't seen a real raid in months, for London's respite had been other cities' misfortune as the German bombers turned their attention elsewhere in the country. But that hadn't made much difference to Mrs Lloyd. Bermondsey still had plenty of false alarms and lightning tip-and-run raids, which gave her mother's frayed nerves no real chance to heal, and she still insisted on sheltering in the Underground at night.

'I get fed up of seeing you in those trousers all the time!'

'I fancied a change.' Peggy forced a smile.

'We've just finished our dinner. Do you want

something?' Her mother seemed in a brighter mood, and Peggy wished she didn't have to spoil it.

'Just a cup of tea'll do me.'

Her father was sitting in his usual after-dinner chair by the fire. Sleeves rolled up, contentedly puffing away on his pipe, matches to the ready on the arm of his chair, his bright smile when he greeted her was like a knife to the heart. This was the worst part of 'living your own life', as Granny Byron had called it, the hurting of those you loved in the process.

'You all right, love? You're doing too much if you ask me,' he said, as she kissed him and sat down in the chair opposite. When Mrs Lloyd brought in the tea, Peggy hesitated. It was now or never.

'I've got some news to tell you.'

They lifted eager faces.

'I'm expecting.'

She saw a flash of joy on her mother's face, such as she hadn't seen since before Jack died. And then almost immediately, it faded, replaced by horror. Peggy looked at her father. He'd understood straight away and his expression, robbed of its earlier warmth, hardened. He stood up, without a word, and took down his coat from the hook at the back of the door. He went to walk past her mother, but stopped.

'You've broke her heart, what she had left of it,' he said, placing his hand on his wife's shoulder, before walking out.

The two of them sat, in silence. Peggy wished that her father had shouted at her, shown any other emotion but the contempt written on his face. She, who had lived her life to fulfil their expectations, had succeeded only in destroying them in the worst possible way.

Her mother's face was blank with shock. 'Oh, Peg, how could you do this to poor George? He's been so good to you.'

'I met someone, Mum. It's not just a fling – he means a lot to me.'

Her mother let out a small cry of impatience. 'What's that got to do with anything? George is your husband!'

She made it sound so simple, as if Peggy had no choice in the matter. As if there was a ration book for love, and she had exceeded her points in marrying George. To want anything else was not just greedy; it was illegal. Ironic really, as George was the one who'd grown up breaking every rule in the book, especially the one that governed rationing. She smiled grimly. George might have given her the best of furniture, all the latest appliances, but where her own heart was concerned it had been a utility marriage, stamped all the way through with the C41 mark, and now she would pay for wanting more – extra pleats, superfluous material, unnecessary frills. She found herself growing angry. Why shouldn't she have the choice when it came to love?

'Well, he might be my husband, but he's not

here, is he? And he was the one made the choice to nick the stuff. He never asked me, did he?'

It wasn't what she'd meant to say.

'It's nothing hundreds of others ain't doing. And look how good he was to us, helping us find our Jack.'

Peggy couldn't bear it, that she used this against her. 'I don't love him, Mum.'

'He's not a well man, Peg. This'll finish him off – have you thought of that?'

How could she say that she hadn't thought of anything at all, that it hadn't been a matter of thought, none of it.

'But what about me?' Peggy's voice rose, trying to penetrate the fortress of respectable objections.

'Don't you raise your voice to me. You're the one in the wrong here. You better go and see if your husband will forgive you because I don't think me or your dad ever will.'

Letting the door click shut behind her, Peggy stood on the front step of her one-time home, panic tightening her chest. Yet she feared that this was only the smallest of tremors, nothing compared to the direct blast that was to come. There was no turning back; she might as well wish all the bomb damage around her undone. Her life was about to become one of the ruins and she only hoped that, somehow, there would be a way to salvage whatever was precious in it.

★   ★   ★

The journey to Brixton this week was straight-forward – no unexploded bombs, no delays – which was ironic, as today she wished the journey might go on forever, so that she never had to get off the bus or face George. But all too soon the tall chimneys of the prison rose up, black against a leaden sky, and she filed through the entrance with all the other visitors. She'd witnessed emotional scenes in the visitor room before now and had always looked away, pretended not to see and hear when domestic dramas had played out in full painful view. Today it would be her turn. She had rehearsed a thousand times what she would say, yet sitting opposite him now there seemed only one way, and without preamble she spoke.

'George, I'm sorry, but there's something I've got to tell you – I'm pregnant.'

'You're *what*?'

There it was, the instinctive moment of joy she'd seen on her mother's face, followed by shock and a look of disgust, as if he'd swallowed bitter aloes and would like to spit her out.

He lunged at her across the table, only to be hauled back by a quick guard, who perhaps, seeing the signs – she pale and shame-faced, he shocked rigid – was already on the alert.

'Steady on, Flint. No need for that, or your wife will have to leave.'

'Fuckin' suits me, the slut,' George said, shrugging off the hand of the guard. 'She's no wife to me.'

George walked out of the visiting room without looking back. He left her there, face burning, hands trembling, as she held her handbag. He had managed to catch her cheek with the back of his hand. She felt its smart and, ducking her head, avoiding the eyes of the other visitors, she ran out of the prison. Outside, she leaned against the smoke-blackened, brick wall, sharp, shallow breaths raking her chest. It was done. She pushed herself off from the wall and walked shakily to the bus stop. Fearing that her legs would give way, she held tight to the stop sign until the bus came into view.

Once on the bus, she slumped into the nearest seat, closing her eyes and trying to breathe deeply. She'd imagined that she'd have to be brave to face him with the truth, but perhaps she was a coward still, for George's imprisonment had spared her the full force of his anger, hurt and disappointment. He didn't deserve such treatment from her, it was true, but didn't she deserve love?

She opened her eyes as the bus passed through devastated streets. Gazing at ruined buildings, mere gaunt, blackened skeletons, their eyeless windows staring blindly back at her, she shuddered, wondering what sort of a life she had chosen for herself and her unborn child.

The following day, she guessed she wouldn't be welcome at her parents' for the traditional Sunday family dinner. Instead she went to Granny Byron's, who was out, having her Sunday lunchtime drink at the Red Cow. Peggy waited in the yard in Dix's Place, watching as some young girls sang '*The big ship sailed on the alley, alley-oh*', linking arms in a writhing tangled mass. A ten-year-old, wearing pigtails and a too-small dress, was attempting to attach an unwieldy gas hood over her baby brother in a pram. Peggy went to help. Not many people bothered with gas masks these days. Peggy looked under the hood. The baby was wide awake, chewing on a teething ring.

'Me mum says we've got to practise, just in case. But by the time we get it on we'd all be dead anyway.'

The little girl smiled brightly, as if this were just another street game, like alley-oh.

'Where's your mum?'

'Up the pub. I was trying to get him off to sleep, but he won't go.'

And Peggy wondered who would look after her child while she was at work. There were a million things she hadn't thought through, but at least the war had meant an increase in nurseries. She knew that the WVS ran kindergartens for women in war work; in fact she'd thought of volunteering for one herself if the mobile canteens hadn't wanted her. Money would be tight, but there were cheap 'British Restaurants' being set up for war workers and there were second-hand clothes coming into the country by the baleful. If anything, the war would be her lifeline, but the only thing the WVS couldn't supply was a degree of tolerance among her neighbours. She'd be branded a whore, for certain, but even that wasn't so uncommon an insult as before the war. Even her poor sister May, pure as driven snow compared to Peggy, had been labelled a scrubber by some for the offence of joining the ATS. It didn't seem fair.

Peggy was about to give up and leave, when Granny Byron came rolling along with her drinking pals, Troubles trotting along beside her. The women were laughing loudly, Peggy knew, at some rude remark, probably made by her grandmother, and they all seemed a little unsteady.

'Hello, me darlin'!' Granny Byron opened her arms wide as she walked towards Peggy. 'It's me granddaughter!' she explained to her friends, who all knew her anyway. 'Beautiful, ain't she?'

Peggy smiled. Thank God for Granny Byron.

She had no contact with her parents for over two weeks. Granny Byron had advised waiting for them to come to her, but Peggy had begun to despair of that ever happening. These days she was even more grateful for her night-time work on the canteen van, which kept her so busy that she had little time to think or regret, and she was so exhausted when she finally got to bed that she never lay awake worrying. One night, towards the end of November, she went home in the early hours, feeling her way along the railings with only the stars and a sickle moon to light the pitch-black street. She was so tired that as she put the key in the lock, her eyes were already closing. The blackout curtains were drawn, and even with eyes open, she had to feel her way. But something made her stop dead. She felt a presence, a stillness in the corner, an area less than black, in the shape of a man sitting in the armchair by the unlit fire. She stood on the threshold of the room, gripping the door jamb, unsure whether to scream or run. Then the ghostly shape stirred, its head rising, so that a thin seam of moonlight penetrating the edge of the curtains caught it, the sliver of light glancing off bright eyes that regarded her intently.

She threw herself across the room and into his arms. 'Harry!'

His name on her lips was smothered by his kisses. 'Oh, Harry.'

When she finally pulled away she searched his face, wanting to reacquaint herself with all its planes and lines, the curve of his mouth and the long line of his jaw. But most of all, his eyes told her that nothing had changed, that his heart was still hers. She hadn't seen him since his last leave in August and the letters, no matter how fond, had never been able to say all that his eyes had conveyed in just these brief minutes together. She led him into the bedroom and to the bed, which no longer smelled of George, and as she melted at the merest brush of his fingertips on her skin, Peggy remembered why she was risking everything for the man in her arms.

It wasn't until the following morning that she found out how he came to be there, just at the moment she'd needed him. He had received his overseas posting and had been granted what he laughingly called 'passionate leave', though Peggy didn't laugh – it was too near the truth for her. She made him breakfast and, while he ate, feasted on the sight of him sitting opposite her.

'How long have you got?' she asked.

'Only a forty-eight, darling, and it took me practically all day to get here. I'll have to leave tonight.'

'Oh no!' She wanted to cry. 'I've been without you for so long.' She put out her hand and they linked fingers across the table.

He stroked his thumb across her hand. 'It's better than not seeing you at all.' And he pulled her round the table, to sit on his lap.

'I'm taking the day off.' She smoothed strands of his dark blond hair, kissing the top of his head, stroking the back of his neck.

'You'll get the sack.'

But he didn't wait to hear her say that she didn't care. He lifted her into his arms and took her back to bed. They stayed there as the morning wore on, and once, when she had to get up, he reached his arm towards her, holding on to her hand, till her fingertips slid from his own, and she wondered at how being tethered to him could seem like such a joyous freedom.

It was only when the afternoon light began to fade and she knew that he must leave, that Peggy told him about the child, and for the first time, she didn't see that initial light of joy fade to disgust or anger or bitterness. Instead she saw it change to something far more complex. His expression was both tender and sad. 'Oh, darling, I'm sorry I wasn't here. Why didn't you write and tell me?'

'I couldn't, Harry, not in a letter. I needed to see your face . . . when you heard the news. I needed to know it would all be all right.'

He gathered her in his arms. 'It will be all right. I promise, but it's not going to be easy for you, sweetheart. It'll be easier for me off in Africa than it will be for you, my love. I'm so sorry.'

She told him about George and how she wasn't sorry that he'd washed his hands of her, and she tried to make light of the painful sense of separation she had from her family, all except her one ally, Granny Byron.

'We'll get married as soon as we can, Peggy, if you'll have me? We'll be together, I promise, love, but I don't know when I'll get leave again.'

He was up now, packing kit absent-mindedly, the demands of duty already claiming a part of him. 'I'll send you money, whatever I can. But there's something else you should know.' He sat down next to her, after strapping up his kitbag.

'Come here, my love. There's something I haven't told you.'

CHAPTER 17

FOUNDLINGS

Christmas 1941

May couldn't wait to get out of her uniform and into civvies. Two whole weeks of wearing whatever she liked, and she was going to make the most of it. She still took pride in the uniform, drawing jokes from her pals and praise from her officers for the knife-edge creases and spotless buttons on her uniform, but she had come to the conclusion that khaki had to be the most boring colour in the world. Not that she had many civvies to choose from. She'd saved up enough coupons to buy a new dress for this Christmas leave, a rich royal blue with boxy shoulders, and an A-line skirt. The trimmings were minimal, but army life had certainly improved her figure and when she looked at herself in the wardrobe mirror, wearing make-up courtesy of Atkinson's seconds from Peggy, she was pleased with what she saw. She looked like a woman now, no longer the shy girl who had left home for the first time last year.

But it would not be an easy Christmas for any

of them. The anniversary of Jack's death had just passed, and then there was Peggy. The family had fallen into two camps: those who would speak to Peggy, and those who would not. May and Granny Byron were the only two in the former camp. When she'd seen Peggy and Harry kissing that day at London Bridge, she'd initially condemned her sister as selfish, unkind and spoiled, her sympathies firmly with George. But Peggy's letter, confessing her pregnancy, had been heartbreaking in its appeal to May. *I know I'm burning my bridges*, she'd written. *I'll be on my own and I don't even know if Harry will still want me. But it's a child, May. You might not know how much I've wanted one. How can I give up a child?*

And May had immediately decided that, whatever her parents thought, morality could have no argument against a mother and her child. She would stick by her sister. She'd arrived home from Essex on Friday and had made the mistake of asking, on Sunday morning, where Peggy was, assuming she would be coming for Sunday dinner as usual. It was frightening to May how cold her father became at the mention of her sister's name, as if the winter chill outside had invaded his heart. May decided it was better not to speak of her sister again to her parents. But that didn't mean she wasn't going to see her.

So that Sunday evening, May let her mother believe she was paying a visit to Emmy. Her friend was still on sick leave, but the broken collarbone had almost healed. May did plan to visit Emmy, but not until she'd made sure her sister was all right.

'May!' Peggy pulled her into the passage of her little flat and squeezed her tightly. 'I didn't know you were home!'

'Just got back on Friday. I've got two weeks' leave! Can you believe it?'

'It seems strange to see you in civvies. You look lovely! Lipstick as well, wonder where you got that from!'

'You've got your uses.'

They laughed and May thought how good it was to see her sister smiling. She'd imagined her sunk in solitary gloom. But she still had the brightness about her that May had noticed last leave.

'What have you done to the flat?' she asked, looking round. It looked so different, less sombre somehow.

Peggy looked puzzled. 'Nothing,' she said. 'Oh yes, I did get rid of some of that heavy old furniture George's pals nicked from Heal's. Gave it to a young couple down the landing. They hadn't got a stick, and there was nothing in the shops for them to buy. I didn't need all that stuff cluttering up the place.'

'But what about George, won't he be angry with you?'

Peggy gave a rueful little laugh. 'What, you

mean, even more angry with me than he already is for getting pregnant by another man?'

May blushed with embarrassment at her own stupidity, but also at Peggy's frankness. But what was the point of pussyfooting around the subject?

'Have you seen George?' May asked, taking off her coat.

'Just the once, to tell him . . . you know.' Peggy turned away from her. 'Sit down, love, I'll make us some tea. You're frozen.'

May waited, leaving Peggy to make tea in the kitchen, while she sat in the much-changed living room. It was sparer, certainly, but the cushion covers were brighter and an embroidered table-cloth now softened the heavy oak table. One of the sideboards and an overstuffed chair was gone, and most of George's knocked-off items had disappeared.

The grey afternoon light was already fading to twilight and when Peggy came back with the tea, May could see she had been crying. She turned away, pulling the blackout curtains and turning on a standard lamp, which glowed warmly in the corner.

'Oh, Peg, love, come here.' May got up and held her sister, who tried to wipe her tears away.

'I'm getting so emotional. They say it happens, when you're expecting.'

'Peggy, you don't have to pretend with me. If Mum and Dad was treating me like they are you, I'd be crying too, pregnant or not!'

'Thank God I've got you and Nan,' Peggy said, blowing her nose.

'Have you told Harry?'

'Harry?' A smile broke through Peggy's tears. 'He was the only one that was happy about it. Everyone else got so upset and angry, but I just wanted someone to be pleased.' She held May's gaze, as if gauging her reaction. 'I must seem so selfish.'

'I was upset with you at first. But . . . well, life's short, you learn that in the army. A few weeks ago I nearly got blown up, and I had your letter in my pocket. Peg, I might never have read it, could have been like the other poor buggers that didn't make it that night. So when I read it next day, there was blood on your letter . . .'

Peggy gasped and May hurried to reassure her. 'Not mine! Some poor corporal. It made me see things differently.' She shook her head sadly, and repeated, 'Life's short. It's too precious to waste living a lie.'

Her sister was looking at her with admiration. 'You've grown up, May.'

May shrugged. 'I suppose I have.'

'Well, there's something else I've been waiting to tell you.'

'What now!' May almost didn't want to hear. She wasn't sure if she could cope with any more surprises from her sister.

'It's nothing bad, not really. It's just that Harry hadn't told me everything about himself. There

I was, feeling like I'd known him all my life, but I didn't know the most important thing about him.'

'Don't tell me – he's married!'

May couldn't believe her sister had been so naïve. Peggy was meant to be the experienced one.

'No, that's not it. He was married, but she died. The thing he didn't tell me was that he's already got a child!'

'He's got a kid, and he never told you! But why keep it to himself?' May felt immediately suspicious.

'I'm not sure, love. He said he never found the right opportunity, and then he just left it too long. I think he was frightened I'd pack him in if there was a kid involved.'

'It's sad, about losing his wife. But where's the child?'

'Well, this is the strange thing, May.' Her sister leaned forward eagerly. 'His wife died in the bombing, early in the war while poor Harry was posted away. So he was going to put the baby in an orphanage. But then he met this lovely Bermondsey couple, who offered to take the little boy on, look after him for the duration.'

May felt a moment of relief, for her sister's sake. 'Good, that's good. I don't think you'd be able to manage two kids on your own!'

'No, he doesn't expect that of me. Well, not right now . . . But, May, this is what I've been waiting to tell you . . .' Peggy's face lit with excitement.

'The name of the couple, it's Gilbie . . . it's only Bill Gilbie's mum and dad!'

'Bill's? How can you be sure? There could be other Gilbies in Bermondsey.'

'I can be sure because Harry knows Bill.'

'Really! How?'

'May, can't you guess?' Peggy was beaming.

Now that Peggy had mentioned Bill, May's interest was even more piqued. 'No, I can't guess. Will you just spit it out.'

'Harry's wife died when their house was bombed. The police told him the only reason his child had survived was because a young man and a girl had rescued him from the ruins. They gave Harry the man's address . . .'

May shivered, as a tingling snaked up her spine. 'It was Harry's baby we saved? And the mother . . . Harry's wife? Oh, Peg, that poor man, if you'd seen her . . . cradling her baby. I always wondered about the baby's dad . . .' her voice was hushed, as though in a church, 'and how he would feel, that only one of them had been saved . . .'

May was aware of the clock ticking and of her own beating heart, noises that only emphasized the palpable stillness surrounding them.

'And what did he say, when you told him it was me found the baby?'

'Do you know, love, he didn't seem as surprised as you'd think. He just said, "It's the war, it brings people together."'

May shook her head in wonderment. 'Strange,

but I think he's right, Peg. On that day, I just felt something was leading me to that very spot, and when Bill said it was a cat, I said no, and made him go in. I just knew . . .'

Her voice was trembling, as was Peggy's hand when she took it. They held on tight to each other, as though they were making a pact.

'Maybe you've got more of Nan's gypsy blood in you than you thought. She'd say it was the sight. But listen, May, Harry gave me this.' And Peggy went to the mantlepiece, where from behind the old clock she pulled out a piece of paper.

'Here. It's the Gilbies' new address.'

May knew that this would be the measure of how grown-up she'd become. Once before she'd gone looking for Bill, and she had given up. Now the lines of their lives had intersected once again, caught like two planes in searchlight beams, criss-crossing the night sky. She knew there would only be a small window, a very short time, before the lights moved on in search of other targets, and she and Bill would be back in the dark. If it had been a question of height and range and bearing, she could have turned a dial and fixed their positions, all efficiency, but now she wavered.

'Well, are you going round there?' her sister asked, just as the air-raid siren sounded. It was probably a false alarm, but she needed time to think.

'The only place I'm going tonight is down the shelter. Come on!'

May told no one but kept the paper with Bill's address in her bag, getting it out over the next few days, and several times almost making the journey to St James's Road, where his family now lived. One day, about a week later, her mother asked her to go to the fishmonger's in the Blue, as she'd heard there was mackerel to be had. May queued all morning, and then, when she got to the front, the fish had run out. She began walking back home, past boarded-up plate-glass windows and sandbagged shops. As she came to the corner of St James's Road, she found herself turning into it, but at St James's Tavern she stopped. She was within a few doors of Bill's house, yet her courage failed her and she turned away, hurrying into St James's church-yard, where the covered slide, normally echoing to the excited shouts of children, was all but deserted. It was a day of freezing fog, and only one hardy child was making the ascent, strug-gling with a coconut mat almost bigger than himself. His mother looked on as she bounced a baby gently in its pram.

'Teddy, you be careful on them stairs, they're slippery!' she called and then, catching May's eye, she said, 'He's a handful!'

May smiled and walked on, wondering if Harry's son were a handful, wondering if Bill's mum and dad regretted taking on a child at their age. Even now, May could remember the feel of that baby in her arms, as its little lungs expanded to let out those attention-grabbing screams, and even now, like some invisible magnet, he was drawing her.

Finally she gave up the struggle and abruptly turned round, walking back in the direction she'd come. The mother at the slide gave her a puzzled look.

'Forgot something!' May laughed.

The Gilbies' house was directly opposite the back entrance to the churchyard, and May dashed across the road before she could lose her courage. She descended stone steps, slick with foggy moisture, to the basement. It was a three-storey house, but Peggy had told her Bill's family lived on the lower two floors, with their front door in the airey. The tidy front door was painted green and a deep floodboard was fixed in front of it. Sandbags lined the airey and the windows were criss-crossed with tape. Her knock was answered by a fresh-faced woman in her forties.

'I'm sorry to disturb you. Is it Mrs Gilbie?'

'Yes.'

'I'm May Lloyd. I used to work with Bill . . . We lost touch . . .'

Mrs Gilbie's face brightened with recognition. 'Oh, May!' The woman smiled as if she knew her, as if she was genuinely pleased to see her. 'My Bill's told me so much about you! Come in, love, come in.'

She followed Mrs Gilbie through a tidy front parlour. There was a polished round oak table and a piano, ranged along the top of which were photos of Bill, in air-force uniform, and two other young men, one a sailor, the other a soldier. Mrs Gilbie noticed her looking and stopped.

'My three boys, one in each service,' she said proudly, 'and I'm worried sick about all of 'em.' She took a deep breath and shook her head, as if to banish the thoughts from her mind.

'Let's go through to the kitchen. I've got a fire going.'

She showed May to a chair by the fire. 'Let me get you a cup of tea,' she said.

Soon she came back with a tray and began pouring tea. 'You know, my Bill was ever so upset when he didn't hear from you.'

Was that a hint of steel she heard hidden behind those warm tones? But May thought it was more like protectiveness.

'I did write!' May protested. 'But the letter was returned. And I even went to Grange House, asked if anyone knew where you'd moved. I tried to find him. It was so silly of me . . . not to get his address . . .'

She trailed off, as Mrs Gilbie raised her eyes.

'Silly? My Bill's just as bad, silly as a sack load. Clever . . .' she said, tapping her head, '. . . but not much common sense.'

Perhaps the woman saw May's uncertain look at what felt like a scolding, for she gave another of her warm smiles.

'Still, you're both only young yet. These things never run smooth, love. Believe me, I know!'

May was quietly astonished at how at ease she felt with the woman, at how natural it felt to be sitting in her kitchen, talking about Bill, almost as if they'd been sweethearts for the past year, instead of just passing ships.

Suddenly Mrs Gilbie cocked her head to one side and put up a finger. 'Ah, he's awake!' She disappeared through the kitchen door and May heard her running up the stairs. The woman was probably about her mother's age, but looked a decade younger and was surprisingly swift, for in a few minutes May heard her coming back down to the kitchen.

She was holding a little boy in her arms. He looked about a year old, with soft blond curls and tightly bunched fists, which he twisted around in his eagerness to get down. But Mrs Gilbie hoisted him up into an even tighter embrace. The little boy stopped protesting and instead fixed May with alert, bright eyes. Then he thrust out the two clenched fists, opened them and leaned forward to May.

'He likes you, and it's no wonder!' Mrs Gilbie laughed.

May had no choice but to take the toddler.

'You do know who this is, don't you?'

'He's the baby me and Bill saved from the ruins. But I couldn't believe it when I found out from my sister that you were looking after him!'

The little boy was examining her face with a prodding finger.

'Hello . . .' she said, then, realizing she didn't know it, she asked his name.

'It's John . . . but we call him Jack.'

An unexpected emotion caught in May's throat. Her heart melted, as she held the trusting little boy, feeling somehow that he really did know her.

'I had a brother called Jack,' she said. 'We lost him last year, in the bombing.'

'Oh, I'm sorry, love, Bill did tell me about it. It must have been terrible for you.'

May nodded, holding back tears. But the little boy was beginning to tire of May and now wriggled to the floor, where he immediately made a grab for the fireguard. With a practised dive, Mrs Gilbie scooped him up and sat him inside a wooden playpen, which had enough building blocks and toys to amuse him.

'How did you come to be looking after Jack?' May asked.

'Well, his father, Harry, he kept in touch with Bill, and he wrote to say that he'd have to put little Jack into an orphanage. An aunt of Harry's, over in Camberwell, had taken the baby on, but she'd died, and there wasn't anyone else to look after him. Harry was being moved back to London, so he was looking to find a nice home for the baby, where he could visit. Well, my Bill volunteered us! Not a by your leave nor nothing!'

But May noticed that Mrs Gilbie had a way of pretending to be upset, when she was in fact quite the opposite.

'So, me and my husband Sam, we thought, how can we let that little baby go in an orphanage?

Here we are, nearly a year later, and he's like one of our own. Mind you, it was a bit of a shock at the beginning, being woken up all hours! But it keeps me young.'

And as if to prove it, Mrs Gilbie launched herself across the room to the playpen, where Jack was attempting to stick a good-sized brick down his throat. She held it up triumphantly. 'See! He keeps me on my toes!'

'I think it's lovely Jack's come to you, Mrs Gilbie. Do you mind if I come and visit him, when I'm on leave next?' May got up to go.

''Course I don't mind. You come and see him whenever you like, love – you're his guardian angel, after all!'

May liked the idea of that, but now came the hard part. 'And do you think I could have Bill's address?' She felt herself blush, but just then there was a knocking at the front door.

'Would you watch him for me while I go and answer that?'

'Of course!'

May heard Mrs Gilbie greet someone and there was a muffled short conversation, which May couldn't make out. When Mrs Gilbie returned, she was followed by a girl about May's age, with longish, dark hair, swept back into a roll. She had a pale face and heavy-lidded eyes.

'Hello,' she said, unsmiling. 'I hear you're the girl who found Jack with my Bill.'

Mrs Gilbie stood beside her; all her easy manner

had deserted her. There was an awkward silence and for a moment May was at a loss. Did Bill have a sister? He'd never mentioned one. Finally Mrs Gilbie spoke.

'May, this is Iris, Bill's fiancée.'

CHAPTER 18

CRYPT FOR A BED

Christmas 1941

'Oh . . . pleased to meet you.' May stood up uncertainly, a fixed smile on her face. She willed it to change to something a little less like horror, but there it was – frozen. And the corresponding expression on Iris's face announced that the girl had understood May's feelings, perhaps better than she had ever done herself.

Jack began to cry and May blessed him. The distraction gave her the chance to escape, and she excused herself. 'Well, thanks, Mrs Gilbie, I'd better be going.'

'I'll see you out.'

'No need!' May just wanted to run, to escape before any more pleasantries were required of her. But Mrs Gilbie followed, and at the front door, she reached into her apron pocket.

'Here you are, darlin',' she whispered, pressing a scrap of paper into her hand. 'It's Bill's RAF address. Write and tell him you've been looking for him. He'd like to know that. But do it soon.

He's getting a new posting and who knows where he'll be this time next month?'

Mrs Gilbie held May's hand. 'I told my Bill not to give up on you.' She sighed, glancing over her shoulder down the passage. 'It looks like he's burned his bridges, but . . . just make sure you write to him! Bye, love!' And, seemingly on impulse, the woman leaned forward to kiss May's cheek.

The night was already drawing in. With snow beginning to dust the pavements and no street lights to guide her, May walked hesitantly into the gloom, feeling transported to those dark days of her childhood blindness. But now she was grateful for the experience, for though hot stinging tears blurred the icy street ahead, she knew how to navigate her way by touch alone. Through this opaque night, she felt her way forward as she'd done when a child.

She was making her way along St James's Road when the sound of sirens split the night. She looked back at the cloaked bell tower of the church. It was probably another false alarm, but she'd rather not go home anyway. She wanted to hide herself in the depths of a cave somewhere, to lick her wounds and curse herself for failing to know her own heart.

She supposed she could go back to Mrs Gilbie – for some reason the woman seemed to be on her side, and if she'd been alone in the house, May might have. But the prospect of a night in an Anderson shelter with the unsmiling Iris was impossible. The nearest public shelter was in St James's Crypt, so she joined a group of people hurrying towards the church. They clattered down a small flight of stone stairs at the side of the old Waterloo church, and when May entered the musty, damp crypt, relief flooded her, not for safety's sake but because she had found her cave to hide away in.

She looked around at the wooden bunks built into the crypt bays. Most had already been claimed by families, who were piling bags and bedding on to them. She pushed her way to the very end of the crypt, next to an iron grating, which blocked off an even darker, danker set of bays full of ancient coffins. Even she couldn't go that far into the depths, so she settled for the nearest empty bunk, and curled up on it with her empty shopping bag. Would her mother be worrying about her? She must know that May would take shelter. She comforted herself by imagining Mrs Lloyd already tucked up in her blanket on a platform at London Bridge.

May was glad of the bustle around her. Some children were chattering excitedly as they strung paper chains around the bunks, mothers were scolding, and someone on the piano struck up 'Away in a Manger', so that soon people all around the crypt began joining in softly, singing along to the old tune. The background noise was thick and white as the fog outside, and on it she was able to write her future as though it were the blank leaf of a book. *Dear Bill, I hear you're engaged . . .*

By the time the vicar came into the shelter, to lead them in a prayer, May had begun to resign herself to the consequences of the first big mistake of her life.

'Oh Lord defend us, from all the perils and dangers of this night . . .' he prayed, and though she knew it was a temporary refuge, for tonight, she was glad of this crypt for her bed and accepted gratefully all its protection and its peace.

May was drinking Granny Byron's dark brown brew, as together they mulled over the state of her mother.

'She's a bit better, but she's still up London Bridge every night, even when it's not necessary any more. I'm just worried this business with Peggy's going to set her back. You know Mum's turned her back on her?'

Her grandmother shook her head sadly. 'Cutting off her nose to spite her face. She'll regret it. You can't pick and choose! She asked for a grandchild, and that's what she's bleedin' well getting.'

'I think she'll come round. Not so sure about Dad, though.' May had been shocked at the strength of her father's disapproval and she wondered, would he give her the same treatment, should she ever disappoint him?

Granny Byron sat in her round-backed wooden chair, sucking thoughtfully on the old clay pipe. 'I've told Peggy she can come to me, if she needs help.'

Her grandmother could always surprise her, and it warmed her heart to know that when she went back to the gun site after Christmas, Peggy would still have at least one friend in Bermondsey to help her through.

May had told her grandmother about Harry's child being looked after by Bill's parents. Peggy had enough troubles of her own, so May had poured out her heart to her Granny Byron.

'I wouldn't write off Bill Gilbie, love,' her grandmother advised. 'You can have all the fiancées in the world, but it's not 'apporth o' coppers if you don't love 'em. It can *all* change. Specially in wartime. I saw enough of it during the last one . . .'

'I think that's sort of what Bill's mum was hinting at . . .'

'She sounds like a sensible woman. But what about your mum? We should have got her right out of London.'

May shook her head. 'She won't leave Dad.'

In the end they decided it would be enough to take turns collecting her mother from London Bridge each morning. Mrs Lloyd wasn't about to give up her nightly pilgrimage, but once there for the night she wouldn't stray, and May could keep an eye on her during the daytime.

In the days before Christmas her mother seemed to improve. There was no more confusion about Jack coming home from the war and, most of the time, she seemed to know where she was. May began to relax, hoping that now they were over the anniversary of Jack's death, her mother would return to her old self.

It was the weekend before Christmas. Her father had a night off from ARP duties and May felt bad about leaving him alone, but she'd arranged to spend the evening with Emmy. She'd seen very little of her friend so far this leave, but tonight, with only a few days of freedom left, they were pushing the boat out. They were going dancing in the West End. Emmy's brother, Frank, was home on leave too, and had invited himself along. When they arrived at a pitch-black Tottenham Court Road, May was glad he'd come along as their escort. A trip 'over the other side' was a rare event, usually reserved for special occasions, and May had no idea which way they should go. The darkened West End streets were bursting with servicemen of all nationalities – free French soldiers, puffing on strong-smelling cigarettes, Polish airmen, with their slick hair and moustaches, big-boned Canadians and bronzed Aussies. The mix of uniforms and accents was dizzying. Parties of girls, with matching hairdos and painted-on stockings, walked in excited bunches along Oxford Street. Without street lamps or illuminated shop fronts to light their way, it seemed easier to bunch up and follow the crowd. Falling in with them, May and her friends headed towards what they hoped would be the Tottenham Court Road Ballroom.

When the crowd came to a halt, May assumed

they'd arrived. Once inside, they had barely checked in their coats when May was swept off her feet by a sailor. It was as if, by walking through the doors, she had declared herself willing to dance with any stranger. He guided her expertly into the circulating flow of dancers so that, try as she might to keep her eye on Emmy, she was soon borne away on an irresistible whirlpool of dancing and music. The sailor, a Scotsman named Donald who seemed to know all the latest dance moves, set about teaching her the jitterbug, and in the glitter of the ballroom lights she found herself hoisted over his shoulder and swung through his legs. She knew she was an adequate dancer, but he made her feel like a brilliant one. By some sort of magic he transformed her, so that for once she felt deserving of her nickname, Ginger. The exhilaration of the night was only heightened when the sirens sounded and the required invitation to leave the ballroom was simply booed down. The dancing went on through the raid and by the end of the night her feet were sore, but her heart was lighter than it had been all that leave. She was happy to give the Scottish sailor his goodnight kiss, and when she made it clear there'd be no more, he draped her coat over her shoulders, pecking her cheek.

'Merry Christmas, May,' he said. 'Sure would've liked to take you home to Mother!'

'Merry Christmas, Donald . . . and good luck!' she called after his retreating figure, looking around for her friends.

Emmy had to be disentangled from the arms of a tall RAF boy, and her brother Frank was nowhere to be found.

'Come on, May.' Emmy linked arms. 'He's big enough to look after himself.'

But when they were almost at the Underground he caught up with them, emerging like a smiling ghost out of the black night.

'Bloody good escort you are,' Emmy said. 'Look at you, with that smile on your face. Who is she?'

Frank pushed back his field cap and stuffed his hands into his trouser pockets. 'Love of me life, Em. Swear it,' he slurred. 'Got 'er address an' everything.' He held up a crumpled packet of Weights, with an address written on the back.

'Bet tomorrow you won't remember your own bleedin' address, let alone hers!'

He smiled bleary-eyed, swaying and bumping against a Canadian soldier, who told him to 'watch out, pal'. And Frank, who seemed in love with the whole world, thinking he really was the Canadian's pal, did an about face and walked along beside the soldier.

'Wrong way!' Emmy said, hauling Frank back and steering him between herself and May, so that they managed to keep him on track. By eleven-thirty their Tube train was pulling into London Bridge and they had to shake Frank awake.

'Do you want to go and see if your mum's all right?' Emmy asked.

But May didn't want to come down to reality just yet. 'No. She'll be fast 'oh by now.'

'Go an' shee yer mum, May – go on!' Frank said, with a serious, drunk face. 'Should go'n shee yer mum . . . May . . .' He prodded her. 'May . . .'

'Chrissake, Frank, she can hear you, leave her alone!' Emmy said.

He gave her a look of exaggerated hurt, which she ignored.

'Take no notice of him, May.'

'Well, I suppose I could do. I might even stay the night here with her. I'll only have to come back first thing tomorrow morning to turf her out. Seems silly.'

'All right, love, if you're sure,' Emmy said, yawning.

'Oh, Em, didn't we have a lovely night?'

'Yes, love, we did, apart from this big lump,' she said, hooking her arm through Frank's.

They were walking towards the stairs, carefully avoiding the feet of sleeping bodies ranged against the platform wall, when Frank found his voice and decided to lead their fellow passengers in a slurred version of 'Ding Dong Merrily on High'.

'Shut yer cake 'ole!' came an angry muffled shout from beneath a lone blanket rolled up against the platform wall. A head poked out and a white-haired woman said, 'I'm tryin' a sleep here!'

'He's not with me!' Emmy raised her eyes and the two friends laughed, parting as May turned off towards the Northbound platform.

She smiled as she watched Emmy, supporting her great, six-foot brother, winding their way towards the exit. It had been one of those rare nights when, in spite of being surrounded by evidence of the war, she had felt above it all. She knew it was an illusion, but for a few hours she'd been able to play at living a carefree life. She had tried hard to banish those feelings of regret at losing Bill and perhaps she had succeeded, if just for tonight. She walked to the end of the Northbound platform, feeling hopeful, feeling that this war could not last forever and that, soon, she could begin to live her life.

In the months following the Blitz fewer people had bothered to come down to shelter in the deep Tube lines. But her mother and a few other diehards still had their regular pitches, and she found her fast asleep, near the tunnel mouth, wrapped up in two grey blankets. May lifted a corner of the top blanket and slipped under it, curling round her mother, who stirred.

'It's only me, Mum,' she whispered. Her mother smiled sleepily and, without opening her eyes, said, 'Good girl, best place for you, safer.' And she fell immediately back to sleep. Lulled by her mother's soft snores, May was soon drifting off to sleep herself. Oblivious to the late-night passengers stepping off the trains and over their huddled figures, May felt only her mother's familiar presence. And she understood how this place, deep in the earth, could begin to seem like home.

Her mother was delighted to find May lying next to her in the morning, remembering nothing of the night before. She seemed to take her presence for granted and May was eager to get her mother moving early, the peace and hope of the night before replaced by a need to get back to her real home. On the bus, May kept her mother entertained with tales of her night out and it wasn't until they got off and began walking up Southwark Park Road that she noticed the light in the sky had changed. A lurid, false dawn lay ahead of them. May spotted flames, flicking up from several houses and she broke into a run, but her way was blocked by a team of firemen. Struggling with a bucking hose, they aimed a jet of water into flames leaping from a hole in a nearby roof. She came to a halt. Following the jets of water to their target, she realized to her horror that their house was on fire. But how? It looked as if they had taken a direct hit, but how was that possible when there had been no raid?

Mrs Lloyd came up beside her and May held her mother back, trying to shield her from the sight of her home burning. But she pushed May away, the hint of a smile on her face, ruddy in the glow of the fire. 'I knew we'd get it,' she said. 'See! You thought I'd lost me marbles, but I knew we'd get it.' And the woman started to walk away. May ran after her, holding her tight, like a squirming child. 'No, Mum, you've got to stay here.' Then, looking back to the house, she remembered – her father had stayed at home last night.

'Dad, Dad!' she screamed above the whooshing of the water jet and the crackling of the flames. The top floor of the house was alight, but the downstairs hadn't caught. Perhaps her father was still in the kitchen. She screamed again, and felt a hand on her shoulder.

Her mother pointed to the fire crew. There was her father at the front, helping to direct the hose. May gripped her mother tightly as they stood and watched their house burn.

When the last of the flames had flickered out and the smell of wet charred timber filled the air, her father finally came over to them.

'How's me girls?' he said, in a smoke-gruff voice. 'All right?'

He slumped to the kerb, arms on knees, head dipped. May sat beside him, pulling down her mother too, who, careless of the dirt, joined them on the kerbstone.

'Dad, what happened? We never heard any sirens!'

'Unexploded bomb, probably been sitting there since the summer. Went off, burst a gas main and the whole lot's gone up. It's a miracle I got out, to tell you the truth, love,' he said, gathering May into his arms.

'What now, Dad?' May whispered.

'Might be able to save some of the downstairs, but all the bedrooms are fire-damaged. It's the rest centre for you two.' Her exhausted father could barely speak. 'I'm staying here, make sure nothing gets nicked.'

'Not me! No, I'm not going in no rest centre!' her mother protested. 'It'll be Keeton's Road School all over again – you're not getting me in one of them!' Her mother was remembering the bombing of a nearby school rest centre, where many sheltering families had been killed. Mrs Lloyd struggled to her feet, but May held on to her.

'Well, you've *got* to bloody well go there, and that's that!' Her father's voice cracked and he put his head into his hands.

Mrs Lloyd's shocked face probably mirrored her own; it was so unusual for her father to raise his voice. She saw despair, even desperation, in his red-rimmed eyes. But May knew how hard it had been to get her mother out of the Underground station. She was certain she'd never persuade her into the rest centre.

An alternative occurred to May, yet she hesitated, fearing to upset her father even more. But, torn between her dissolving mother and her breaking father, May had no choice. She caught Mrs Lloyd's elbow.

'Come on, Mum, I know somewhere you'll be safe,' she said.

CHAPTER 19

BOMBED OUT

Christmas 1941–January 1942

Letting the green uniform frock fall to the floor, Peggy stepped out of it and stumbled in the darkness across the blacked-out room. The short walk across the passage to the bedroom seemed too far, her legs trembled with fatigue and she swayed drunkenly, her eyes closing even as she dropped on to the sofa. She had no memory of falling asleep, but at some point in the early hours she'd woken shivering and felt around on the floor for her WVS overcoat. She pulled it over her.

An insistent knocking dragged her from deep sleep.

'All right, all right, I'm coming!' With the overcoat around her shoulders and half-closed eyes, she felt her way to the front door. When she saw them, she didn't have to ask what had happened.

There was May, dressed for a night out in her new royal-blue dress, now charcoal-streaked and pitted with cinders, Atkinson's coral-pink lipstick fading, dried tears streaking her ash-powdered face, pleading eyes begging Peggy to let bygones be bygones, almost pushing their mother over the threshold. And Mum. Poor Mum, hardly there any more, bewildered, homeless. What else could she do, but take them in?

But once her mother was settled into bed in the spare room, Peggy asked May, 'How did Dad take it, your coming to me?'

May pulled a face. 'He didn't like it. Said you were no daughter of his, didn't want Mum coming here!' She cupped the hot tea and sipped the steaming liquid.

It was no more than her father had already said to Peggy's face, but it still stung.

'And you stood up to him? What did you say?'

'I told him this was no time to be falling out with his family and if he wanted to lose Mum altogether he was going the right way about it. I slept with her last night, Peg, down the Underground, and I swear if we don't do something soon, she'll wander off – right under a bloody Tube train. I thought she might be getting better, but this has knocked her for six.'

Her sister looked thoughtfully into the fire. Peggy had just got it burning nicely. Normally she didn't bother with a fire in the morning; she was always up and out before the cold hit her. But her family had been out all through the freezing night and May's lips were blue.

'He's surprised me the way he's treated you, Peg,' May said finally. 'I've never seen him so stubborn, have you?'

Peggy sighed deeply and shook her head. 'I've really disappointed him, haven't I?'

May nodded. 'And all those tricks he taught us, "never look forward to anything . . ."'

'". . . and you won't be disappointed!"' Peggy chimed in.

It was true. Her father had walled himself in from disappointment so strongly that when he'd least expected it, there it was, smashing through all his defences, and she was the cause. No wonder he couldn't stand the sight of her. Peggy knew how he felt. She'd always been one to put her head firmly in the sand; avoiding a problem seemed easier than solving it. But her 'problem' had just turned up on the doorstep, in the form of her bombed-out family, and there was no ignoring them.

'But what can I do, May? If he doesn't want to see me I can't force him. You don't think he'll try to carry on living in the house?'

May shrugged. 'Depends how bad it is. But if he swallowed his pride and came here, would you have him?'

'He's still me dad.'

May seemed satisfied. She stood up and went to get her coat.

'What are you doing?' Peggy asked. 'You've had no sleep. You're not going out again now?'

Her sister pulled on her coat over the ruined royal-blue Christmas dress.

'I slept a bit on the platform. Besides, you're

318

forgetting I'm a gunner girl now!' May grinned. 'We're up and out in three minutes, all weathers, with our dinkie curlers under the tin hats. Sleep's something you do standing up!'

Peggy laughed. Her sister's life sounded very much like her own.

'We hide our dinkie curlers under our turbans at Atkinson's. Who's got time for hairdressers? Talking of which, I've got to get ready myself. Do you think Mum will be all right on her own?'

'She'll have to be. I'm off to find Dad. See you later, love . . . and thanks.'

Peggy caught May in a tight hug. 'You're my family, May. Just because Mum and Dad's fallen out with me, don't mean I'm any less your sister, or their daughter . . .'

May hugged her back. 'I'll try to persuade him.'

But that evening, when Peggy got home from work, the flat was deserted. Obviously May had failed to persuade her father, and Mrs Lloyd must have already left for London Bridge. Peggy began unpacking groceries she'd picked up on the way home. When her father had run from the house, he'd followed the drill and grabbed the suitcase containing the policies and ration books, and May had brought it with her. Peggy had used some of their coupons to boost her own. She was looking at the tin of despised powdered egg, wondering how she could make an edible dinner with that and a few rashers of bacon, when a knock came at the door.

It was May, with Granny Byron in tow.

The old woman looked at the powdered egg with disdain. 'Your George had his uses. Don't suppose you've heard from him?'

Peggy shook her head. 'I don't expect to, Nan. He doesn't want anything to do with me.'

She pulled out a seat for her grandmother and looked enquiringly at May. It was unusual for Granny Byron to visit her grandchildren; they were expected to do the visiting. But as May sat down next to her, it was clear that the old woman had come with a purpose. She took out her snuffbox and Peggy saw May grimace.

'Nah then,' Granny Byron said, once she'd recovered from a volcanic sneeze, pointing to Peggy, 'your dad's like you. Head in the sand. While he's off fighting other people's fires, his own family goin' up in smoke. Useless! So, we'll have to be the ones to help your poor mother. It's my belief she just needs a bit of peace and quiet and she won't get none round here.' She slapped the table to emphasize the point.

Peggy hadn't liked her accusing finger, but she did agree with Granny Byron about her mother.

'I could speak to the billeting officer at the WVS. See if we could get Mum evacuated?' she suggested.

'No need!' May chipped in. 'I've had an idea. I know someone, back at the base, who might be able to find her a place. A girl in my gun team's got an old bachelor uncle, lives out in the sticks, with an empty cottage on his land. She told me

320

just before we went on leave that he lost his evacuees and he was so upset about it, he was fond of them. Only thing is . . . he's a bit eccentric, I think . . .'

'Well, it'll certainly be quicker than pissin' about waiting for them lot to fill in all the bleedin' forms,' Granny Byron said.

Peggy wasn't sure it was a good idea to pair a nervous breakdown with a dotty bachelor, but her grandmother had made her pronouncement and it appeared the war council was over. Granny Byron reached for her well-worn handbag.

'All we've got to do now is sort out yer father!'

And she left them to their powdered egg and bacon.

'What's going to happen about Christmas?' May asked when she'd gone, and Peggy wished she hadn't. There was nothing she wanted to do less than be responsible for supplying forced Christmas cheer and mock turkey. Besides, the part of her that was alive was a hundred odd miles away. The cruelty of not being able to see Harry one more time before he went overseas was more painful than at times she could bear. Yet there was someone she could see, who would bring him that little bit closer.

'May, I was thinking—'

'What? Oh God, Peg, this egg is vile, want mine?' Her sister was chewing on a rubbery lump of what was supposed to be omelette.

'No. Listen, I was thinking . . .' Why was it so

hard to ask? Yet she was blushing. 'Before you go back to Essex, would you take me to see little Jack?'

May swallowed the egg. 'Oh, love. I didn't know how you'd feel about him. But of course I'll take you.'

Peggy smiled. 'Well, you said Bill's mum seemed to be on your side. I'm hoping she'll be on mine too.'

'She seemed a live-and-let-live type of woman. Besides, she knows George's got a different side to him. Her brother's a friend of his. Freddie Clark, do you know him?'

'Freddie Clark's her brother? He's got a lorry firm, up Dockhead. But he's gone straight. George always said he's under the thumb, but he's a nice bloke. Anyway, thanks, love. I just want to be able to let Harry know I've seen his little boy . . .'

But it was more than that. Little Jack was part of Harry, and half-brother to her unborn child. He already felt like family.

As they cleared away the plates, Peggy asked, 'So what happened with Dad today?'

May looked embarrassed. 'He's not budging. You know what he's like, defending the place from looters . . . so he says.'

Peggy doubted that was the only reason he hadn't come to her with the family.

'He's camping out in the downstairs kitchen,' May went on. 'There's running water, but no gas. He's got himself a camp bed from the rest centre and some blankets. Says he had to put up with much worse in the last war. But he can't live like that forever.'

'Did he say anything about me? You did make sure he knows he can come here?'

'He knows that, Peg.'

'It don't make no sense to me, May. He's got more loyalty to George than to his own daughter . . .' Her sadness and sense of betrayal had now become tinged with anger. 'And George is not exactly snowy white himself, is he?'

'There's one rule for the men and another for us, that's what Granny Byron always says.'

'Well, she's right there. Sometimes I think she's the only one in this family that's got her head screwed on right.' Peggy sighed. 'Oh, May, I don't know what I'm going to do.'

Suddenly fatigue and fear caught her in a pincer-like grip. Once she'd seen her future, clearly mapped out, dull but safe. Now this war had set everything in motion, nothing was certain, nothing solid. Tomorrow the walls of Purbrook Estate could come crashing round her; the pavement she walked along could explode beneath her feet. Perhaps anxiety was the price she had to pay for passion, and today she wondered for the first time if it was worth it.

'You're not on your own, Peg,' her sister said, putting a hand over hers. 'You've got Nan, and me, and now even Mum . . .'

Peggy laughed bitterly. 'Yeah, but only because she doesn't know what day it is.'

'Perhaps.' May smiled. 'But now she's staying here, Dad will have to come round, sooner or later.'

Peggy wished she could believe that.

But by Christmas morning her father still hadn't relented, and May told Peggy he'd be spending the day on ARP duties. She couldn't feel guilty; it was his choice. But she wasn't free from guilt about George. There were days, and today was one of them, when he came vividly to her mind. Usually it was in the mornings, when she put on her clothes. Her hand would sometimes reach automatically for the dowdy, old-fashioned blouses or skirts he'd kept her buttoned up in. Or sometimes when she put on lipstick, she'd feel him looking over her shoulder. But today was Christmas Day, and she remembered him at his best. The life and soul of the party, everybody's friend – 'a lovely feller', her mum had always called him. But they hadn't had to live with him. Still, today, she imagined him eating his prison Christmas lunch, and it was she who felt like the criminal. She had debated visiting him, before Christmas, but an encounter with Ronnie Riley had changed her mind.

She'd been persuaded by some of the girls from Atkinson's to go for a Christmas drink in the Turk's Head. It was the first evening off from the canteen she'd had in weeks and she'd agreed. Only intending to stay an hour, the girls were in good voice, and after a couple of drinks so was she. When Ronnie

Riley came through the door he walked past their table as if he hadn't seen her. It was unfortunate that they were in the middle of singing 'Somebody Else Is Taking My Place', though Peggy wasn't about to stop singing for him. But he was obviously listening, and when they got to the lines '*You go around with a smile on your face, Little you care for the vows that you've made*', he smashed down the pint glass on to the bar and walked over to them. Leaning heavily on the table, he stuck his face close to hers.'You should keep yer mouth shut, you should, *and* yer fuckin' legs together an' all. Showin' up George with that fancy man of yours – and his bastard!'

There was a stunned silence at the table as the girls took in what had just been said. Peggy had told no one at work about Harry, nor about being pregnant. Her face burned with shame and she was about to run out of the pub, when she felt a restraining hand on hers. It was Hattie, her hatchet-faced forelady, who in a voice like a Thames foghorn boomed, 'Piss off an' pick on someone yer own size!' Then, turning to Peggy, she said, 'Ignore him, love, he's just the organ grinder's monkey! What y'avin?'

Ignored by the girls, Ronnie shrugged up the collar of his camel coat several times before banging out of the pub door, accompanied by their laughter. As the woman went to get the drinks, one of the other married girls, whose husband was in the forces, leaned forward to Peggy and said quietly,

'You're not the only one to have a bit of fun, love. I met a smashin' soldier up the West End. What the old man don't know can't hurt him, eh?'

Peggy was grateful that the girls asked no questions and gave her only sympathetic looks, but, for her, the evening had been ruined, and not long afterwards she'd made her escape.

Their Christmas Day was a sad one. They sat squashed into her little kitchen, trying to be cheerful, all the women in her fractured family. No Grandad, no Dad, no husband, but most painful of all no brother. And May, whatever she said to the contrary, was forlorn without Bill, the sweetheart who had never been. And she without her Harry, the sweetheart who never should have been. The war had robbed them of all their men, one way or another, and she was glad when the day was over.

Before May returned to her base she made good her promise to take Peggy to see Harry's child. There was no hint of condemnation in Mrs Gilbie's face, as she showed them through her front room, where paper chains draped the ceiling and in one corner stood a decorated Christmas tree. How they'd managed to get one of those, Peggy couldn't imagine, but the place certainly had more festive cheer about it than her own flat.

'Come into the kitchen. Jack's in the playpen, where I can keep an eye on him. Little terror's into everything now!'

She would have known he was Harry's son, just by the eyes. So bright and alert, he spotted her, curious about this stranger in the kitchen, and pulled himself up on the wooden bars. Mrs Gilbie lifted the toddler out of the playpen and he clung a little shyly to her.

'Get the present out, Peg,' May said, and Peggy brought out a toy car from her bag. Immediately the little boy wriggled down from Mrs Gilbie's arms and trotted over to Peggy. Sitting down heavily at her feet, he began playing with the toy and Peggy was happy to be ignored. She looked up, smiling, at Mrs Gilbie. 'He seems a happy little thing?'

'He's good as gold. Bright as a button. He's a bit shy at the moment, but wait till you hear him talk. You wouldn't believe he's never been here before.' She looked proudly at little Jack and Peggy liked the woman, if for no other reason than her devotion to Harry's son.

'Have you heard from his dad?' Mrs Gilbie asked

'Daddy a soldier.' Jack didn't look up from his car, and the woman shot her a look 'Earwigo!' she said, and they all laughed at the clever little boy.

When Mrs Gilbie went to make tea, Jack stayed happily with them and Peggy turned to May. 'Doesn't it make you think, looking at him, he wouldn't be here if it wasn't for you.'

'And for Bill . . .' May said.

'What about Bill?' Mrs Gilbie came in from the scullery with a tray of tea things.

'Oh, we were just talking about the day we found Jack. It's strange how things worked out . . .' May said, a little wistfully, Peggy thought.

'Well, they still have a lot more working out to do if you ask me.' Bill's mother sat back and looked from one sister to the other. 'You two have got yourselves into a right pickle, haven't you?'

Peggy found herself going hot. She had hoped Mrs Gilbie might simply ignore the reason she'd come to see Jack. There weren't many people of the woman's generation who wouldn't condemn her, so Peggy was surprised when her clear blue eyes flashed with amusement.

'My advice to you two is to take a leaf out of my husband's book. Persistence pays off, was always his motto. He knew we were made for each other, right from the start, but I didn't see it for a long while . . .' She was silent, a small smile on her face, as she remembered that long-distant version of herself.

'Ah well, it won't be easy for you, Peggy, but there's nothing more important than being with the right one. And that goes for you too . . .' She shot a look at May, who seemed startled to be caught in the penetrating gaze of Bill's mother. 'Did you write to my Bill?'

'I did, y-yes . . .' May seemed flustered. 'I told him I didn't mean to lose touch . . . and, of course, I told him I was pleased for him, you know, his engagement.'

'Of course you did,' Mrs Gilbie said, with an

inscrutable shake of her head. She paused to retrieve Jack who had wandered off and was now inspecting the knives in the cutlery drawer.

'Let's take him out in the yard,' Mrs Gilbie said, coaxing him away from the knives. 'I'll show you our crater!'

The Gilbie's backyard at first glance was like any other wartime garden: an Anderson shelter dominated, there was an outside lavatory, an iron mangle beneath a lean-to and a tin bath hanging on one wall. But as they stepped outside the scullery door Peggy gasped, for almost the entire area of the garden was taken up with a bomb crater.

'Uncle Sam!' Little Jack pointed a finger at the crater. But Mrs Gilbie quickly explained. 'My husband was running to the shelter when the bomb fell, two yards away from him! But he'd just dug over all the yard to plant veg, lovely lot of manure he'd forked in. Anyway, all that soft earth must've taken the blast, because when I looked out from the Anderson, there he is, head poking up out of the crater!'

'Was he all right?' May asked.

'Well, apart from being covered in horse shit, he was right as rain. I pulled him out and dragged him in the shelter. I think I was shaking more than him. Of course, the little one here didn't miss a trick. He got so upset. But my husband says, "Don't worry, son. I didn't come through the last war just to get blown up in my own backyard!"'

They circled the crater. 'Jack remembers everything, don't you?'

The little boy grinned up at her.

Just then Peggy noticed a bent wheel with mangled spokes, propped against the back wall, and next to it the frame of what appeared to be an old bicycle.

'What's that?' she asked. And taking charge, little Jack said, 'Penny-farving.'

Mrs Gilbie led them further round the edge of the crater. 'The old penny-farthing came off worse than Sam. I think my husband was more worried about the bike than himself, to be honest. It was his father's, and he's kept it all this time . . .'

Peggy watched May bend down to look at the old machine. She looked up sadly. 'Oh, what a shame! Bill told me all about this – he said you used to ride it as well!'

And Mrs Gilbie threw back her head and laughed. 'I did, and what a sight I looked on it too!'

Peggy left the Gilbies' house feeling that, in spite of bombs in the backyard, Jack could not be in a safer place and that, like Mr Gilbie, she herself would emerge from the bomb crater of her life one day, perhaps able even to laugh at the experience.

The next day May was travelling back to Essex and Peggy made sure she set the alarm for an hour earlier. She'd been finding it harder to drag herself out of sleep these days. Perhaps it was the pregnancy, but she thought it more likely just a result of the long months burning the candle at both ends. But she wanted to send off her sister with a good breakfast. With so many train cancellations and delays, who knew what time she'd arrive back at the base. She had just wrapped a packed lunch of fish-paste sandwiches when her sister walked into the kitchen.

'Look at you, late on parade! And them buttons could do with a bit of polishing,' she joked, as May came to inspect the sandwiches. Peggy thought she looked good in her uniform, but it still seemed unreal that her little sister was a soldier in charge of a gun team.

'Now sit down. I've made you porridge and a sausage sandwich for breakfast.'

'Oh thanks, love, but you need to be saving rations for yourself!'

Peggy put the porridge in front of May and went back to the frying pan. 'Got to feed the troops first.'

'Well, you are the troops too. You know what they say about war workers, the girl that makes the thingamabob and all that . . .'

'Oh yeah, I wish. They put me back on talcum powder last week!' Her war work was obscure, but Peggy liked the idea that a plane part would have her stamp upon it.

'Well, packing talcum powder for keeping soldier's feet dry is all part of the war effort, I suppose,' May said.

Peggy laughed, but the contrast with her sister's return to the guns was stark and she began to have that old dragging sense of uselessness she'd had when George was home. Sometimes she'd felt like one of those ginger ale bottles, with the glass stopper pulled down tight. When he was put away, the glass stopper had come off and she hadn't stopped fizzing since. She dreaded a return to that old life, which had never felt hers. But, whatever work she did, she had her independence and the WVS canteen, and she had Harry, however forbidden and far away he might be.

After May had left for Essex, Peggy felt the burden of family responsibilities as never before. She began to realize how shielded she'd been by her early marriage to George, and she appreciated for the first time, how much May had held things together at home while she had lived in her sheltered little palace on the Purbrook Estate. Now she was the one to jolly their mother along and keep her in the land of the living, but she could do nothing about her father's lonely vigil in the bombed-out house in Southwark Park Road.

She worried about his health. Half the house was uninhabitable. January had come in with a deep frost, so that Bermondsey's streets were six inches deep in snow. The house had only half a roof and he was living in the kitchen, with only a primus stove to cook on. When she went to catch the bus for work one morning, Tower Bridge stood like a white-laced web across the Thames and all the sky above it was grey, with swirling snow filling the space between the towers. She shivered as she got off the bus and hurried down the snow-choked alleyway leading to Atkinson's gates. She made her way to the plane parts department, but was met by Hattie, the forelady.

'Sorry, Peg, you're still on talc,' she said.

'But I thought it was temporary!' Peggy said, disappointed.

'Still short-staffed. We're not getting enough of the new conscripts – all seem to be going into the ATS!'

It was no use grumbling. She walked upstairs to the hoppers and began the first of her many trips, heaving buckets of talcum powder up the ladder.

'Make sure you keep it steady!' she called down to her partner Ada, who had never conquered her fear of heights. 'No, don't look up at me, you'll get a crick in your neck – you just concentrate on holding the bloody ladder!' she shouted down from the top, and began tipping in the first bucket. But she was caught by a coughing fit, and remembered the major drawback of this job, the fine powder invading nose, eyes and ears, so that at the end of the day her face would look ghost-like with its white mask. As she coughed, she felt the ladder wobble.

'Hold it, hold it!'

But Ada's hands had slipped and the ladder swayed. Peggy made a wild grab for the edge of the hopper, letting go of the half-empty bucket, which tumbled down towards Ada, banging against the side of the hopper and showering its snow-like contents all over the girl as it fell. Ada screamed, ducked out of the way and let go of the ladder altogether. As Peggy felt the rung slip from under her feet and fall away, she grasped the edge of the hopper with both hands, like a high-wire act on a trapeze.

'Oh my gawd! Get the ladder back!' she screamed down to Ada.

Legs swinging wildly, her feet looking for purchase somewhere, she daren't look down, but heard a great deal of scrabbling and banging as the girl struggled with the heavy ladder.

'Hold on, Peg!' one of the other women shouted. 'I wasn't thinking of bloody well letting go!' Peggy shouted. 'Hurry up!'

Her arms were pulling out of their sockets and she felt her palms slipping on the powdery wooden edge.

'Here it comes!'

The ladder thudded against the side of the hopper and she edged one foot out until she felt it. Gingerly resting her feet on the top rung, she tested it.

'Are you holding it?' she called down. When she was sure the ladder was rock-steady she put all her weight on it, coming down one rung at a time. But her legs were trembling so violently and her palms so sweaty that she lost her footing. She felt herself falling and, gripping the ladder so tightly that her hands burned, she tried to slow her descent. Five feet from the floor, she lost her grip and thudded to the ground, her legs twisting beneath her and her head thudding against the floor with a crack.

'Oh, I'm so sorry, Peggy!' Ada was covered head to toe in the white powder from Peggy's bucket.

But Peggy couldn't move her legs and she winced as a sharp pain shot up the side of her head.

'Are you all right, love?' One of the other women was trying to help her up. 'I don't know about munitions, but I reckon they should give us danger money! You nearly had your lot! That would've been a good 'un, the first war worker killed by talcum powder!'

From a long way off, Peggy heard laughter, a couple of other women chuckling with relief. Then the grating voice of the forelady broke through the fog.

'Oi, oi, oi! What's all the bleedin' noise about? It's not a soddin' beano you know, you're meant to be working!'

'Sorry, Hattie,' Peggy heard Ada say. 'It's my fault, I let go of the ladder.'

'What d'you do that for? It's all you've got to do! Don't think I ain't noticed it's that poor cow going up and down it all day. Now stop pissin' about.'

As Hattie bent down to help, Peggy saw two of her hatchet faces looming above her, before she slipped away into darkness.

* * *

335

Peggy reached up to pat her helper's cheek. She was lying somewhere soft and comfortable, not the hard factory floor she remembered tumbling on to.

'Dad!' she said, her mind still a fog of powder. 'Dad? What are you doing here?'

She knew he shouldn't be here, but for the moment she couldn't remember why.

'I've run all the way from Southwark Park Road,' he said, his chest heaving, and she could feel his heart thumping as he drew her in tightly. He smelled of burned ashes and snow. 'Ada came for me. You've cracked your head, love.'

He stood aside and she realized that he had been holding her, and she didn't want him to move away. She held him with her gaze.

'You're all right now, gel. Just let the nurse have a look at you.'

And she obediently opened her eyes wide, as the factory nurse shone a torch into them, before pronouncing her fit to leave.

'The ankle's sprained, but no broken bones.' The nurse addressed her father, as if Peggy were a child. 'Just take her to a doctor if she starts to get drowsy.'

Her father draped his jacket around her as Hattie came into the first-aid room.

'You keep her at home till she's feeling up to it, hear me?' Hattie ordered her father, and the woman gave her an unexpected hug.

'Come on, love,' her father said. 'Let's go home.'

So Peggy found herself back in Southwark Park Road, sitting in her father's little camp, as this was what he'd meant by 'home'. It was certainly nearer than the Purbrook, but had none of the comforts.

He put into her hands a steaming mug of tea, which he'd loaded with condensed milk and a drop of brandy. 'Get that down yer, gel,' he said, and turned to stoke up the fire which he'd got going, throwing on to it something that looked very like a piece of her mother's carved wardrobe door.

He had put her in a chair, so close to the fire that her legs began to mottle, and he hunkered down next to her on a little stool so that she could look down into his anxious face.

'You don't look well, Dad.'

'Oh, I'm rubbing along all right, don't worry about me.'

She looked around the room. It was filled with an assortment of furniture saved from the fire damage: a wash stand and a few drawers from her parent's bedroom, and a pile of clothing that looked to Peggy to be going mouldy.

'Do you want me to go through that stuff for you? It smells a bit, Dad.'

He shook his head sadly. 'I tried to save some of the home, for when your mother comes back, but I suppose it'll have to go.'

Her head was aching and the muscles across her shoulders seemed suddenly on fire.

'I'm sorry I wasn't here to help, Dad.'

He shook his head. 'You would've been, if

it weren't for me. Stupid, stupid – I realized that when I thought you might have got killed in that factory and I never had a chance to say – well, I was wrong. Whatever you've done, blood's thicker 'an water and . . . you're me daughter when all's said and done.'

He wiped his hands across his forehead, shielding his eyes. But soon she realized he was crying.

'Oh, don't do that, Dad, don't, there's no need.'

When Peggy felt strong enough, he took her home to her flat. He insisted that she lie down on the sofa as soon as they got in.

'Let's get you comfy,' he said, tucking a blanket around her, before laying a fire. He hadn't shown her such tenderness since before she was married.

'If you're sure you're all right on your own, I'd best be getting back to the house,' he said, picking up his cap. He stood in front of the sofa and suddenly bent to kiss her cheek.

'I'm sorry, love, I should never have let you marry George. I thought it was for the best, you know, that he'd give you everything I never could . . .' She had never seen her father so vulnerable.

'Oh, Dad, I made my own choices . . .'

But he interrupted her. 'No, I'm your father. I should've known, and there's a lot I've found out about George since he went inside that I didn't know before. Stories about him selling stuff from bombed-out houses, standing in for shirkers at the recruitment office. I was shocked.' There was always a call for someone with such ill health as

George, to stand in for recruits and get them signed off as 'unfit' for service. Peggy had suspected it was one of George's sources of income, but she hadn't been sure. Yet she had never wanted her father to hate her husband, just to forgive her.

'George is always going to be a villain, Dad, and I can't say he was a bad husband . . . I just felt . . . well, dead,' she finished weakly, exhausted from the day, and asked, 'Why don't you pack up Southwark Park Road, and stay with us here?'

He hesitated, holding his cap. 'I suppose I could do.'

And Peggy felt nothing but gratitude that after the gulf that had opened between them her father was here, and she was forgiven. As the door closed, she had to smile at how this morning she'd gone to work anticipating another dull day. She should have known that in this war, dullness and danger were never far from each other. It was as she turned over to sleep, that she felt a sharp pain shoot through her stomach. 'Oh God, no, not now,' she prayed. 'Not now.'

CHAPTER 20

GOLD AND PLEASANT LAND

January–Spring 1942

The water in the bucket was frozen over. May picked up the shovel propped outside the hut door and started hacking away at the ice. The pipes had frozen in the ablution block, so the only water they'd have for washing was in the fire bucket. After a couple of whacks she'd chipped a hole in the surface and eased off the crust of ice. It wasn't going to be a very thorough wash this morning. She poked her head back through the door of the hut. 'Come on, rise and shine and bring us your mugs!' She heard groans from inside and a 'Put some wood in the soddin' hole!' from the direction of Emmy's bed.

'Well, when the water's gone, it's gone!' she warned, dipping her mug into the bucket and splashing her face and hands with icy water. Her fingertips turned white, burned by the ice. She flapped her hands around to get the blood moving and decided a cat's lick was all she could stand today. It was the best she could do with a cup of icy water and, shivering, she pulled her greatcoat

340

closer round her, peering across the iron-hard ground towards frost-rimmed trees at the edge of the gun park. Today her team was on reserve, which meant fatigues. She was almost glad she'd been detailed to help out in the stores. At least she'd be warm. Even if the rest of the camp froze, there was never a shortage of coal for the stores' stove.

As she entered the stores building she was hit with a blast of heat from the cylindrical cast-iron stove. The pipes here hadn't frozen and May was set to cleaning floors with bucket and mop. Pat's transfer to stores had gone through with no quibbling from her superiors and though she might not be the bravest of soldiers, she was a hard worker. She came over at once to help May and they soon got up a rhythm, their mops synchronized like a pair of rowers.

'How was Christmas at your uncle's?' May asked. For Pat had told her she was expecting another dull leave, with just herself and the bachelor uncle at his horse farm in Gloucestershire. May had felt sorry for her, but after her own troubled Christmas she'd begun to envy Pat's uncomplicated home life. Now the girl surprised her with a slow spreading smile.

'Not so dull after all – I met a chap!'

May always had the impression that Pat was somehow impervious to men; she flirted a lot, but never seemed to take things further than that. So to see her now, her face softened by the memory of a man, was something novel.

'You?'

'Well, don't sound so surprised. I'm not that unattractive, am I?'

'No, I didn't mean that! I just thought that you weren't interested in settling down.'

Pat, with her glossy dark hair, almost-black eyes and high colouring, was certainly not plain. But May had discovered that her attractiveness grew with familiarity. Initially her features could seem hard, her expression suspicious, sometimes arrogant. But over the months, May had seen Pat's appearance increasingly soften as her trust grew. It had been like watching the sun behind a bank of clouds; first the gilded rim had appeared and gradually the shadows of her face had lightened.

They had finished mopping one section and went to refill their buckets with clean water.

'I've got nothing against settling down, just never met the right man, I suppose. But this one . . . he's just . . .'

'Right?'

Pat laughed. 'Well, I think so – but I'm not so sure my father would agree if he found out. Mark works for my uncle . . .'

'What's wrong with that?'

'Oh, because he's a stable lad – my father would think he wasn't good enough for me. I'm not sure if my uncle will approve either. My only hope is if I can get the major on my side – he's got a soft spot for me, probably more so than

342

my father.' The old hardness flashed in Pat's eyes as she spoke.

May was confused; she thought Pat's father was the military man.

'Who's the major?'

'My uncle! He retired from the army years ago, but everyone still calls him the major. He's nothing like my father, though – at least he cares about me being happy. With Dad, it's all about appearances.'

'Oh.'

This was more than Pat had ever let on about her soldier father; she'd always seemed so proud of him.

'Anyway, it doesn't really matter what I do. I'll always disappoint my father. I wasn't born a boy, was I?'

May shook her head ruefully as they carried back their full buckets. 'Don't talk to me about disappointed fathers. We had murders at home over Christmas. Dad's not talking to my sister, and you know we got bombed out? Well, he'd rather camp in a ruin than go to her place. I thought poor Mum was getting better, but now she's practically living down the Underground again . . .'

Pat gazed at her sympathetically. 'Oh, May, I'm really sorry, I didn't mean to go on about my troubles. It must be awful, to have your home destroyed . . . but as I've never had one myself, I don't suppose I can *really* understand what it's like.'

May had gleaned, from a few conversations with Pat, that the girl's shell had been fashioned by a childhood so different from her own as to seem no childhood at all. With a widowed father in the military, she'd never had a fixed home. Shipped off to boarding school at an early age, she seemed to have put down no roots at all. May, with her inexplicable love of smelly, crumbling, noisy Bermondsey, found it hard to imagine not being attached to anywhere. She'd once shared her nickname with Pat, who'd looked thoughtful for a moment before replying, 'If you're a homing pigeon then I must be that bird who never lands at all, a swift, I think it is.'

'Can't your home be repaired?' Pat asked, as the two of them sloshed their mops into the full buckets and started mopping again.

May shrugged. 'Maybe, but the repair crews are so busy it might not be for a while.'

May shuddered at the idea of her father still camping in the unheated Southwark Park house during the winter.

'I'm sorry, and there I was complaining about having to stay miles from anywhere. It's definitely got its advantages . . .'

'One of them being the stable lad!'

Again came the slow, secret smile, which robbed Pat's face of all its harshness.

'Oh, but what about your chap, whatever happened to him?'

'What chap? I haven't got one.'

'Yes, you have, the one you were with when you found the baby!' She'd told the tale, one night over cocoa, when they were all swapping bombing stories, but she didn't remember divulging any more information about her feelings for Bill.

'No, we were just friends,' she said, rewriting her history, as much for her own sake as to keep Pat quiet.

'Friends!' Pat swished the mop and shook her head. 'I don't buy it. You were always looking out for a letter.'

May couldn't think how Pat had come to know her secret. Perhaps she hadn't veiled her emotions as much as she'd thought, unless . . . ahh, of course, Emmy. Emmy was a good friend, but she loved to gossip. Not that May minded. What did it matter now?

'Oh well, it's never going to come to anything. I found out Bill's got himself engaged.'

Pat groaned. 'Oh, you poor thing. God, you did have an awful time at Christmas.'

'I suppose I did. But don't you think this war makes you see things differently? When I look back on that leave, you know what I think I'll remember? Going dancing in Tottenham Court Road and learning the jitterbug! And I'll remember meeting that little baby we saved, me and Bill, and then it'll be only good memories, as if the rest never really happened . . .'

Pat looked at her sceptically. 'Well, it might be

the war, or it might be you're just an insufferable optimist!'

'Maybe. But there's one thing I couldn't feel good about, and that's Mum. She can't take much more of London. Me and Peg think she'll go off her rocker completely if we don't get her away.' May hesitated. 'And actually, that's what I wanted to talk to you about.'

'Me?' Pat straightened up, leaning on her mop.

'I need to ask you a big favour.'

'If I owe anyone a favour, May, it's you,' Pat said, looking at her intently.

May explained something of her mother's plight, while they finished their cleaning duties and then walked briskly back across the frosty gun park to change out of their boiler suits. All the while, Pat listened without comment. They ducked their heads against the chill blast that caught them as they rounded the ablutions block, but once in the lea of their hut Pat stopped.

'Do you fancy coming into town for tea and cake? We can have a better chat there.'

May agreed, for in the hut or the NAAFI there was always someone listening or ready to chip into any conversation, and it was almost impossible to keep a secret, as she'd just found out. She made a mental note to give Emmy hell later on for sharing her heartbreak with the world.

Because May had been on fatigues all morning, she was entitled to a half-day pass out of camp, and that afternoon she found herself in a little tea room in Barkingside, seated opposite the one person in her new life she'd been sure she could never be friends with. But this Pat seemed a very different girl from the one who'd accompanied her on that disastrous train ride to Pontefract. And no doubt, she herself was different. Either way, it seemed an odd, topsy-turvy world, where the friends you wanted to keep disappeared and those you never wanted in the first place ended up being the ones who stuck around.

'So, I was thinking, if your uncle still wants evacuees for his cottage, do you think he'd consider taking Mum?'

Pat had taken a bite of her toasted teacake, and it was a while before she answered.

'Brilliant idea!' she said, her mouth still half full.

'Whoa there, Dobbin, make it last!' May said, using the girl's newly acquired nickname. It had turned out that Pat had a very sweet tooth and the war had been particularly hard on her taste buds. She took every opportunity to graze on sweetness when it was available, but when Bee had caught her crunching on sugar lumps from the NAAFI, she'd christened her Dobbin. The strange thing was that Pat hadn't objected at all, in fact she'd welcomed it, and May knew why, for in the ATS a nickname was more a badge of honour, and the proof Pat needed that she'd finally been accepted.

Pat chewed thoughtfully for a moment. 'I'm sure he'll go for it. The only thing is, you'll have to explain to your mum that he's got his funny little ways . . .'

'Oh, don't worry about that. My mum's got a few funny little ways of her own!'

When they arrived back in camp that evening, they stopped at the army post office. There was a letter waiting for May. The tissue-thin beige paper, and the flowing handwriting were enough to send a flush to her cheeks. She hoped that her face revealed nothing to Pat, but the girl pounced. 'It's from him, isn't it?'

And May cursed the transparency that undermined all her practised disguise. She nodded. 'I *think* it's from him.'

'I knew it! Don't worry, I won't say a word!'

And May found another reason to be grateful to Pat, her new friend.

It wasn't until just before lights-out that she had a few moments alone to read Bill's letter. She propped a novel on her knees, a strange little tale that Bill had once recommended while on one of their walks around the ruined streets of Bermondsey. It was called *The Hobbit*, a child's fantasy she wouldn't normally read, but Bill told her it had something to say about them and their war. And it hadn't been hard to see it, as it told of a ruined world, with good and evil lining up on each side, ready for a mighty battle. Yet her war had never felt as clear-cut. Every time she targeted a German bomber she had to remind herself that she was on the side of good, and though she celebrated with the others if there was a direct hit, there was also an insistent, self-questioning voice: 'How will this ever bring back Jack?'

But the book seemed a fitting screen as she propped it on her knees, with the letter open between the leaves. *Dear May,* he'd written

I was so pleased to get your letter and you mustn't apologize. It was my fault as much as yours that we lost touch. I was just so glad to know that you went looking for me! And it's quite a turn up that you've actually been to Mum's and seen Jack, our little war baby. He's a character, isn't he? I thank God every time I see him that you persuaded me it wasn't a cat mewing in the ruins!

To be honest, I thought you must have long forgotten all about me and our walks. I know what it's like, once you get BT over with and receive your posting. It's another world, and our old lives just seem to vanish, don't they? Thanks for the congrats on my engagement, by the way. It all happened in a bit of a rush, on one thirty-six-hour leave. In fact it wasn't long after we lost touch that I met up with Iris again. She's that old flame of mine I told you about. But I wanted to make sure you knew, May, that I really had finished with her long before I went to Garner's. I don't want you to think I was hiding anything. The truth is, the only thing I was hiding was how I really felt about you. I think it's probably wrong to tell you now, but I might die and you'd never know. Do you remember my favourite song? 'All my life I've waited for an angel, But no angel ever came along, Then one happy afternoon I met you, And my heart began to sing a song.' Well, I think I found my angel that first day we went walking through the ruins. I just wish I'd had the nerve to tell her.

But perhaps it wasn't meant to be, May, because Iris came back into my life, just when I thought you'd gone out of it. That's the trouble with this war. Nothing's stable or settled any more. You make these decisions, biggest of your life, and you do it in two minutes. But I've promised to marry Iris and I'll stick by that, so I don't think it would be fair to her if we carried on corresponding. But I just wanted to tell you, May, in case anything should happen to me, that our walks and our talks, well, they meant the world to me.

So, I'll sign off now, May, and wish you a safe war and every future happiness.

Bill

May closed the book, with the letter still inside it, and turned on her side. She pulled up the covers over her head. It was the only way she could hide her tears. This was even harder than the day she'd discovered his engagement, for then she hadn't known he'd returned her feelings. To have found and lost something so precious, in the same instant, was unbearable. It would have been better if he hadn't told her. But she understood why he'd wanted to. When a walk down any street in any town could end in oblivion, when any 'goodbye' could be a final farewell, it was important for a life to be in order. And perhaps there were some secrets that shouldn't be taken to the grave.

Her shoulders heaved with the sorrow of it. To have found the one love, for him to call her his angel, only to have that snatched away, before she'd even tasted its sweetness, seemed too cruel. She was shuddering with the effort of suppressing her sobs and, as the bugle sounded lights out, she felt a hand on her shoulder.

'I'm so sorry, May,' Pat whispered.

Pat arranged everything with her uncle and May's mother made the momentous move from Bermondsey to Gloucestershire towards the end of January. Mrs Lloyd left her Underground life far behind, exchanging musty, airless tunnels for country air, sharp and clean with winter's frost when she first moved in and sweet with meadow grass by the time May was due to visit in early spring. Mrs Lloyd was firmly settled into Pat's uncle's cottage, and now, with a full week's leave due to her, May was making the trip to see how country life suited her mother. It was impossible to tell from her letters, which were mostly filled with questions about May's welfare. What little she said about her new life revolved around the comparative abundance of food, compared to the shortages in London. But there were inklings that she was at least taking an interest in the goings-on at the farm, where the major trained and stabled horses. May had to admit that she was looking forward to the peace and quiet of the place herself. The early months of the year had been gruelling, with winter extending its icy fingers far into spring. She'd had quite enough of washing in mugs of water, and tipping out of the hut in the bitterly cold nights, with nothing but pyjamas under her teddy bear coat and a cold tin hat covering her dinkie curlers. These days, as a practised gun team, they were expected to be out of bed and on the gun field within three minutes of the alarm. Often, there was simply no time to slip on tunic and trousers. Her hands were raw, in spite of the Atkinson's moisturizer Peggy posted her way, her face chapped and her eyes bruised with tiredness. The idea of sleeping in a country cottage, waking to sun-dappled peace and birdsong, was a fantasy that had kept her going through the dark winter months and she could hardly contain her excitement that it was actually here.

But Emmy was disappointed. 'Are you sure you want to waste a whole week stuck in the middle of nowhere? Why don't you come back to Bermondsey with me for a few days, then visit your mum afterwards? We could go dancing. You need to get out and meet people, May – there's plenty more fish in the sea, love.'

It had been impossible to hide her sadness from her friend, but the last thing she wanted to think about now was meeting other men. Her heart was too raw, and however foolish she might seem, it still belonged to Bill. She simply wasn't interested in anyone else.

'No, Em, I've missed Mum so much, and I want to see for myself how she is. Besides, it means I won't have to do that train journey on my own.'

Pat was also taking her leave and they'd agreed to travel to her uncle's together. The newfound friendship had not gone unnoticed by her old workmate, and she knew there was a touch of jealousy in Emmy's request. But Gloucestershire was another in the long line of unknowns she'd had to face since the war began, and she'd rather not have to travel there alone.

As the train neared Moreton-in-Marsh, May knew she'd done the right thing. They passed through magical countryside that reminded her of the Shire, in that children's book Bill had recommended. It was a gilded land, with hamlets of stone cottages snuggling like golden nuggets in the green pockets of enfolding hills. Long low ridges, outlined by stands of trees, fell away to wide valleys, patched with fields of young wheat and burnt-toffee earth. Solid buildings of sun-aged stone dripped with light and radiated warmth. May was again struck by the many stones of England which she did not know. These Cotswold stones were as warm as the Pontefract stones were cold, but both were equally alien to her familiar London brick. Getting out at the station, she was struck too by the quietness of the town. After they'd presented their pass tickets, they crossed the footbridge of the little station and Pat waved to a young man standing by a small trap. He was holding tight to the pony's reins.

'It's Tom!' Pat said, and the young man waved back. She seemed pleased that her uncle had sent someone to collect them as the farm was near the little village of Bourton-on-the-Hill, a few miles away from Moreton. The young driver helped them up on to the seat and at the sound of the clip clop of the horse's hooves May smiled broadly at Pat.

'The last time I was this near a horse was a donkey ride on Ramsgate beach!' As they drove along the high street, May was surprised at how wide and spacious it was; she'd expected nothing more than a village. The honeycomb-and-butterscotch stone buildings on either side had a prosperous, solid air: they were all old, all of a piece, and she felt the very foundations must be made of gold as well. The high street split round a large market hall and they turned down a narrower, steadily rising road. Leaving the town behind, they bowled along hedgerows, frothing with white blossom, and as they passed through the impossibly pretty villages of dusty gold her impression of the place was confirmed. This was another England. As she looked down from her perch, at a chequerboard of peaceful fields and solid church towers, she could almost imagine that, here and now, there was no war waging and no bombs ravaging her home back in Bermondsey.

The wheels of the trap eventually crunched on gravel and they were on the sweeping drive up to the major's house. She'd expected a farmhouse, but this was almost the size of the Bermondsey Settlement! They passed between two stone pillars, and a carved sign on one of them proclaimed this to be 'Angelcote House'. Built of the same butterscotch stone as the villages they'd passed through, it nestled in a crease between two gentle slopes and was cushioned by a backdrop of fresh green trees. The long roof, broken by three protruding gables, topped a façade pierced by a number of irregular stone-mullioned windows. A short flight of steps led up to the front door, over which a pair of curious carved angel's wings spread protectively. The door was open and standing on the top step stood a lean man, with a long face and straight nose. He raised a brown trilby hat to reveal a full head of white hair, swept back from his forehead.

'Welcome, ladies!' he called as he descended to greet them. He wore a suit of checked tweed and a yellow waistcoat, and looked like May's idea of a country gentleman. She could see no trace of the 'eccentricities' that Pat had warned her about, but as they stepped down from the trap, May got a closer look at the major and noticed that on his feet were a pair of embroidered carpet slippers. Not the normal sturdy footwear for strolling around a country estate. But she pretended not to notice as he shook her hand and told her how happy he was that she'd been able to visit.

'Your dear mother. Courageous woman, marvellous! And you two, fine soldiers, both brave women!' he said, saluting them. 'I've been under fire myself, been under fire, and never let anyone tell you shell shock is malingering. Damned liars if they do! Your mother! Salt of the earth.'

May hadn't realized Mrs Lloyd had made such an impression on the major. But she smiled and thanked him, noticing that Pat had fixed her with a look that dared her to show surprise.

'I'll take May up to the cottage, Uncle,' Pat said, pulling her by the elbow. And the major turned with a vague wave, padding up the gravel path in the direction of the stables.

'Does he know he's still got his slippers on?' was all May said, as they continued along the drive and round the back of the house.

'Probably not,' Pat said.

And when May replied, 'My Granny Byron sometimes pops out in hers – old age must be hard on the feet!' they both giggled.

The cottage was set back from the path, hidden

behind a little hedge. As they rounded it, May gasped.

'Oh, Pat, it's so pretty.' The tiny cottage was chocolate-box perfect, with small, leaded windows, a pretty front garden and a view of a wide valley, spreading out to a distant, treelined ridge beyond. Suddenly she heard through an open downstairs window the sound of a woman's voice.

'Dear old pals, jolly old pals. Always together, whatever the weather!'

Pat was about to say something, when May put her finger to her lips and cocked her head to one side. It was her mother singing, and that was something she hadn't heard since before Jack's death.

The front door was unlocked and they came upon her in the kitchen, rinsing potatoes at the sink. At the sound of her name, Mrs Lloyd spun round, a delighted expression on her face. 'May!' She held out muddy hands to hug her daughter. 'Oh, your uniform!' and she managed to encircle May without brushing mud onto the pristine jacket. Quickly wiping her hands down her pinafore, she shook Pat's hand.

'Stay for a cup of tea!' her mother said, as Pat made her exit. But May was glad that the girl declined. She wanted to enjoy the sight of her mother, happy for once.

'Just let me put this stew on. I should have had it done by now, but I've been up at the big house.' Her mother lifted the pan on to the range.

357

'What have you been doing up there?' May asked, intrigued.

'Oh, I do a bit of cleaning for the major. He's been so good, it's the least I can do, and to be honest, love, when I arrived his place was a shithole. His cleaner was a bit of a girl that don't deserve the name. People take advantage of his good nature, you see. But the dust on the skirting board, that thick!' she said, indicating with finger and thumb a coating which, if it were true, must have taken fifty years to accumulate.

'So you're getting on all right with him then?'

May sat at the kitchen table with her tea, quietly marvelling that her mother was actually making sense. It was as if she'd left her damaged mind behind in the ruins of Bermondsey.

'He's a diamond. What I call a right old English gentleman, no side on him, straight as a die.'

May nodded. 'He's not dotty then?'

'Him? Nah, sane as I am!'

A few months ago that would have been no recommendation, but now May smiled and said, 'So, he was wearing his slippers outdoors.'

'Oh that! He's got terrible trouble with his plates. All that bloody square-bashing when he was younger.'

After changing into her civvies, May sat down to a plate of her mother's rabbit stew.

'The major catches 'em himself. And the veg is all from his garden,' her mother said. 'And wait till you see this!' She dived into a little pantry and carried out, like the blessed sacrament, a dish of butter.

'Mum! That must be a pound at least!'

'I tell you, love, they don't know they're born out here.'

Her mother put the dish on the table for them to gaze upon. May hadn't seen so much butter all in one place since 1939.

After their tea, they sat in the tiny downstairs parlour, while her mother sewed and asked about May's experiences on the guns. Though it was spring, the nights were still cold and they'd made a fire. The warmth in the little room and tiredness from her long journey soon caused May to nod off, and it was barely dark when she made her way through what looked like a cupboard and up the narrowest stairs she'd ever seen to the upper floor. She dropped on to the tiny bed and fell asleep to the sound of wind rustling through trees outside the window. At first she was restless, alert for the warning siren that normally dragged her out to the guns, but when she heard the faint whinny of a horse travelling over from the stables she allowed herself to relax and fall into the most peaceful sleep she'd had in a very long while.

She was woken abruptly early the next morning by the sound of a klaxon blaring. She leaped from the bed and ran in a little circle round the room. Feeling about for her tin hat, she hopped on one foot as she tried to pull up her trousers. It was a full minute before she realized something was amiss. It couldn't be the alert because she wasn't at the gun site. Her heart stopped thumping and she moved to the window. What the hell was that racket if not a klaxon? She shoved up the stiff casement and looked down into the front garden.

The major was standing by the hedge, blowing a hunting horn. He was dressed in pale yellow pyjamas beneath a tweed jacket, and had a gun crooked over one arm. 'Morning! Rabbits!' he called to May at the window.

Putting down the horn, he dug into a leather bag and lifted a pair of dead animals for her to see, before laying them on the front step. 'Tell your mother!' he ordered, before striding off down the path. He was still wearing the carpet slippers from yesterday and May smiled that she was already providing a very reasonable explanation for the pyjamas. After all, didn't she regularly run out to fire a gun, dressed in a similar fashion?

After a morning's shopping in Moreton-in-Marsh with Pat and her mother, May couldn't wait to get back to the farm. She was finding the mixture of pure air and peace addictive and after a slice of bread, spread with a guilty thickness of butter, she insisted her mother come on a walk in the surrounding countryside.

'There's not much to see here,' her mother said, as they set off down the lane leading away from the house and cottage.

'That's the point! It's never quiet on the base. Sometimes the noise hurts my ears. If we're on parade we get bawled at, and then there's the noise of the guns . . . well, you know what they're like from a distance, but imagine being yards away? It's like being stuffed inside a bass drum while someone's thumping on it! Quiet's a luxury and so is this.' She swept her hand across the vista of pastureland, dotted with sheep, and the clumps of trees, stretching towards a long, low escarpment.

'Ahhh, emptiness!' She smiled, but her sweeping gaze was checked. She had spotted the figure of a man on the ridge top, silhouetted against the clear blue sky. 'Spoke too soon,' she said, almost resenting his presence.

'What?'

'Can't you see him, up on the ridge, by those trees?'

Her mother shook her head and squinted. 'We ain't all got eagle eyes like you!'

But May had definitely seen someone up there. She scanned the hilltop and caught sight of him again, as sunlight glinted off something in his hands.

'Look, there, he's got binoculars!'

'Fifth column!' her mother whispered.

And May instantly wished she'd not pointed the man out. The last thing her mother needed was the spectre of fifth columnists entering her newfound haven.

'Don't be dozy, Mum, out here? There's nothing to spy on.'

'Well, you never know. The army's requisitioned the top floor of the major's house. It's all very hush-hush. We just see them coming and going; no one's even allowed upstairs. I think they're doing top-secret stuff . . .'

'Oooh, yeah, and the major's really a Nazi spy giving away all our secrets!' May said, her eyes exaggeratedly wide.

'Saucy cow. Don't you take the mick. We've got to be vigilant. Haven't you seen that film yet, where this little village gets taken over by Nazis?'

'No, I'm too busy fighting the Germans to watch films about them, Mum.'

Which wasn't strictly true as she and Emmy often spent their half-day leaves at the Gant's Hill Odeon, but she was eager to diffuse her mother's forebodings.

They continued on their walk and when May next looked up towards the ridge the man was gone. They came to a paddock full of horses and, as they leaned on the fence, she called to the nearest animal, a large white mare, which as it turned revealed a smaller version of itself, trailing behind.

'Oh, look at the white foal, Mum! It's so pretty! I'd love to be able to ride.'

Her mother scrutinized her. 'You, ride a horse? You're getting adventurous.'

May shrugged. 'It's the army, Mum. You get used to doing new things . . .'

'That lovely boy up at the stables, he might get

you a ride.' It was May's turn to be surprised. 'Who's that?'

'Young stable lad. I know 'em all. They don't get many home comforts, so I take 'em up cakes when I make a batch for the major. But he's my favourite.'

'What's his name? It's not Mark, is it?'

'No, I'm talking about Tom, the one who picked you up from the station. You must have noticed him – he's the spittin' image of our Jack.' May's mother stared at the white foal and gave a sad smile at the memory of Jack. Then, coming back to the present with a start, she said, 'Poor Mark got the sack!'

'Oh no, Pat said her uncle might not like her going out with him.'

'Well, Tom told me it was a shock and no one knew what he'd done wrong. But it wasn't the major sacked him.'

'No? Who then?'

'Arnold, the head lad, just sent him packing one morning, no reason. But he's a mean bastard to all the stable lads. I don't think the major had anything to do with it. He's good as gold, May, but he leaves most of the day-to-day running of the place to that Arnold.'

'Well, you make quite a good spy yourself, Mum! At least I can let Pat know what's been going on. It'd be terrible if she thought her uncle had got rid of Mark. But don't you say anything about it, will you? She might want to keep it to herself.'

With her mother sworn to secrecy, they turned and strolled back to the cottage, following a stream through a small wood. May was getting the lie of the land and tomorrow she thought she might like to walk up to the ridge herself, just to see what the man with the binoculars might have been looking at. She didn't for one minute believe he was a fifth columnist, but she was, after all, a soldier, and perhaps as her mother had said, they ought to be vigilant.

CHAPTER 21

INVASION

Spring 1942

The next day, May decided to walk to the village. The square church tower of buttery stone stood above all the surrounding trees, and she used it to navigate by. Pat had told her the village consisted of a pub, a post office and a parish hall, with a few pretty stone cottages strung along the street, finishing at the church. Her walk took her along the same stretch of road as yesterday, and she thought she would climb up, just to see what was visible from the ridge. The slope was steeper than it looked and even with all her ATS training, she was puffing halfway up, and forced to stop and rest. As she gained the top, her eye was caught by a bird, hovering high overhead. Wings stretched flat, with the tips furling in the wind, it was cushioned on a current of air, so that it appeared almost stationary. The hawk was watching, waiting to pounce, no doubt on an unsuspecting field mouse far below. It reminded her of the watcher on the ridge. Without warning, the bird dropped out of the sky and disappeared from view. Something had died somewhere and May felt a chill reach up her spine.

She descended to the little wood they had passed through yesterday, and as she neared the margin, there came a sharp crack. From the corner of her eye, she saw a figure disappearing beneath the tree canopy. He moved swiftly, ducking out of sight. She was sure it was the man with the binoculars, and all at once the peaceful countryside was shot through with menace, and her isolation no longer seemed so soothing. She hurried on, glad when she reached the sleepy village and the ordinary concerns of its chatty postmistress, who sold her stamps and a newspaper.

She decided not to tell Mrs Lloyd about her glimpse of the man. He was probably just a bird-watcher, the hovering hawk some rare species he was trying to spot. Still, May was annoyed that she'd let her fears spoil her excursion. But nothing could ruin her pleasure in seeing her mother so bright. Sometimes Mrs Lloyd would look up from her sewing or pause over the range, seemingly lost in thought, and then May feared the old vacancy and disorientation were returning. But they were only brief moments and May was sure that the country cure was working when her mother announced that she'd agreed to become the major's full-time housekeeper.

'Do you really want to, Mum?' she'd asked, fearing Mrs Lloyd might still be too fragile for the responsibility.

'Oh, I don't mind. It can get a bit boring out here. There's only myself to cook and clean for, and this place is so small I can go round it in an hour. And it'll do him a favour. He might look well off, but he's had to pull in his horns since the racing's been cut back. He can't afford much help – besides, the gardener's joined the navy and the cook's gone into the NAAFI. Gawd knows what he'd be eating if I didn't send him over a dinner now an' again – bread and jam probably.'

'Well, if you think you're up to it . . .'

Her mother looked at her. 'I do know I lost me marbles for a bit, love. And I was ashamed of meself, I was. But the dear old major says to me when he asked me to be his housekeeper, he says, "No disgrace, Mrs Lloyd, you've not been put out to pasture just yet, you only needed a bit of peace and quiet." And no truer a word's been spoken. I believe I'm better now.'

May took her mother's hand and squeezed it. 'He was right, Mum, you've nothing to be ashamed of.'

Later that night, after she had gone up to the tiny bedroom, which was little bigger than their coal-hole in Southwark Park Road, May pulled aside the blackout curtains. The night was so dark it was hard to make out the line of trees marking the wood. Whatever she'd seen earlier, there was nothing moving there now, and the inky sky was relieved only by smudges of indigo cloud. The moon was the merest fingernail. She yawned, sinking into the little bed, which was narrower but much softer than the 'biscuits' on the bunks back at camp. Whether it was the mattress or the fresh air, sleep here was delicious, unbroken as it was by the cacophony of war. She drifted off and dreamed of a hobbit, up on the ridge, watching with binoculars as a fire-breathing dragon hovered above the farm. The dragon's breath cast such a bright glow that it lit the bedroom, with flickering incandescence. But in her dream, she knew that couldn't be right. She sat up with a jerk, completely awake and aware now of light sweeping the room. This was no dream and the voices she could hear outside weren't hobbits', but neither did they sound English. She leaped out of bed.

Her eyes were still getting used to the dark, but the lights and the foreign voices could mean only one thing. They were Germans and this was the invasion!

She dashed to the little window and, clutching the sill, watched as pale mushroom-shaped parachutes filled the sky above them. Flashlights glimmered beyond the wood and from somewhere high above came the pulsing drone of an aeroplane. May spotted tiny black figures dropping in a seeming unending stream from the plane's bowels.

Oh, Mum, I should have listened to you! May thought. *That feller we saw was a spy after all!*

From the window she could see the surrounding fields where clusters of paratroopers were bundling up their chutes and shouting to each other in their foreign accents. It was impossible to make out what they were saying, but she had no doubt, their intentions were not friendly.

When she saw the first groups heading towards the cottage across the fields, she knew the time had come to act. They would have to make a run for it, now!

Trembling, she ran to the bedroom opposite to wake Mrs Lloyd. But as she did so, May heard sounds downstairs. She froze, putting her hand over her own mouth before she could scream.

They're in the house! May's breath came in short harsh gasps. She dashed back into the bedroom, picked up the iron poker lying next to the fireplace and crept down the stairs, her legs feeling like water. She had no idea how she would fight off German paratroopers with nothing but a poker, but she gripped it tightly and eased open the living-room door. She could see no activity and quickly moved to the kitchen. Holding the poker above her head like a sabre, she swallowed hard, threw open the door and charged.

'Don't kill me, don't kill me!' Her mother raised both hands.

'Mum? What the bloody hell are you doing?'

Carrie Lloyd, wearing a long coat over her night-dress, was pulling tins of food from the cupboard and stuffing them into her battered suitcase.

'If it's the invasion, we'll need these!' she said, continuing to throw in spam and soup, and whatever else came to hand.

'Don't be ridiculous, Mum, we can't carry all that – we've got to go now!'

Yet her mother, with shaking hands, managed to close the suitcase and attempted to drag it off the table. But it was far too heavy and May gently prised her hands away.

'Come on, Mum,' she said.

And leaving the suitcase behind, they hurried out into the night. May, instinctively stooping low, led them out through the front gate and on to the gravel path that swung round to the big house.

'This way!' she hissed, heading towards the wood. 'They'll be avoiding the trees – we can hide there for a bit.'

She grabbed her mother's hand and felt the rigid fear in Mrs Lloyd's body. The idea that the Germans had followed her poor mother, even into this seemingly safe haven, filled May with rage. It was fortunate that anger and indignation had displaced all her own terror, for they weren't five paces into the wood before she was brought up short by a pair of German jackboots dangling in front of her face. She came to a sharp halt, so that her mother collided with her beneath an old beech tree. The dangling boots suddenly began kicking and May dodged out of the way, pushing her mother into the undergrowth.

She still had the poker with her and now began bashing at the boots till they were still. She looked up into the tree to see a white face glaring down at her. His body twisted slowly, suspended from the tangled parachute cords entwined around the tree branches. May thought he looked like a broken puppet rather than the fierce invader she'd imagined. A strangulated voice came from high up.

'Help me!'

'Help you? Why should I help a bloody German?' She was betrayed by an undeniable trembling in her voice, but she steadied the poker and said as fiercely as she could, 'You're my prisoner!'

The parachutist laughed, and then choked.

'German? I'm sorry, ma'am, but this German was born in Kamloops, and last time I checked my birth certificate I was Canadian. Now, are you going to help me down or not?'

His laughter came again, and suddenly Mrs Lloyd was at her side. 'Don't believe him, May, they're trained to talk like us . . . He'll slit our throats if you help him down.'

The man in the tree started to sing the national anthem and May began to feel very foolish.

'Mum, can you go back and fetch me a chair and a knife from the kitchen.' As Mrs Lloyd began to protest, May turned to her and said firmly, 'Mum, listen to me, he's no more German than I am!'

She shouldn't really blame her mother. She'd been blindsided herself by the mysterious 'fifth columnist' on the hill and the presence in the major's house of supposed secret intelligence officers. The propaganda they'd been fed for so long about a German invasion had certainly sunk in deep. What she really regretted was the effect on her mother. May's training should have prepared her to be steady under fire but she'd panicked, and instead of reassuring Mrs Lloyd, she'd dragged her out into the middle of what appeared to be friendly action. She only hoped this hadn't returned her mother to the spiral of fear that had sent her running from London.

'My mother will be back in a minute.' She craned her neck, watching as the Canadian tried to hoist himself up on the parachute cords.

'Are you hurt?'

'Only my pride, honey,' he called back down, cheerful now that he knew he would be rescued. 'Captured by a girl with a poker – I'll never live it down.' He chuckled.

'I'm sorry, we didn't know you were the allies,' she called back up.

'You can make it up to me if you like.' She could see that he was grinning now, perfectly white teeth flashing in the dark shadows of the tree. 'Agree to come to the dance tomorrow night at the base and we'll say no more about it. What d'ya say?'

May thought he was very forward and was about to refuse when Mrs Lloyd came back with the chair and kitchen knife. While her mother held the chair steady May stood on it, and handed the knife to the airman. He sawed away at the cords, till May heard a ripping sound.

'Timber!' he called, falling with a thump on to the soft woodland carpet.

May rushed to help him up.

'Ankle's twisted,' he said, wincing as he put his weight on to one foot and tried to walk forward.

'Here, lean on me,' May said, putting his arm over her shoulder, which he seemed to enjoy. 'Mum, can you take his other side,' she said quickly.

Between them they helped him hobble back to the cottage, and on the way he explained that the whole thing had been a training exercise.

'Well, I wish someone had told us about it. My mum nearly had a heart attack, didn't you?'

Her mother grunted, obviously unimpressed by the Canadian, who'd introduced himself as Doug McKecknie. He looked a little sheepish. 'I'm sorry about that, but it's meant to be as realistic as we can make it.'

And our panic was real enough, May thought, feeling a flush of embarrassment. Back in the little cottage, May was surprised to see her mother begin calmly boiling a kettle.

'I should've known it was you Canadians from over the base,' she said matter-of-factly to the airman, as May helped ease him down on to a chair. 'But you did sound a bit like Germans. Didn't they, May?'

'A bit – well, they didn't sound English!' said May. But in truth their voices had been muffled on the wind.

Mrs Lloyd put a cup of tea in front of Doug, who was laughing at her again. He gulped it down.

'Well, ladies, I appreciate your help. But I gotta rejoin my company, or they'll be sending out a search party. Can't have them finding me drinking tea with the enemy!'

He got up gingerly and tried his weight. Seemingly satisfied, he looked at May.

'See me out?'

May followed him to the front gate. Light from the kitchen crept through the edges of the blackout curtains, but otherwise the inky night hung about them. While he was in the cottage, she'd seen that he was handsome, in a rugged, big-boned sort of way, and now those white teeth flashed again as he said goodnight. Leaning on the gate, he smiled. 'So, shall I pick you up around seven?' She had to think for a moment, what he meant.

'I'm not sure . . .'

What wasn't she sure of? It was silly, but she had wanted to say that she already had a sweetheart, but the truth was, she didn't. Perhaps it was time to let Bill, or rather the idea of him, go and get on with her life.

'You did say you wanted to make up for your treason . . . and it's just a dance, May, not a court martial!'

She laughed. It might be fun.

'Yes, all right,' she said. 'Pick me up at seven.'

And as he limped up the gravel path towards the drive of the big house, she called after him, 'Providing you can dance!'

'Oh, I'll be able to dance all right, if I have to keep this ankle on ice all night!'

He waved a hand and May watched him disappear

374

behind the hedge. She strolled back to the cottage, wondering at just how much had happened, here in this out-of-the-way place. And to think that Emmy had warned her she would be bored in the country!

Pat came over from the big house next morning to see if May had heard all the commotion of the night before, and when she heard the story of the 'German' invasion, she began laughing so hard that she was soon gasping for breath. She held her side and flapped her hands at May as if she could do nothing to stop it.

'Well, it wasn't funny at the time – we were terrified!' May said, straight-faced, and Pat squeezed her cheeks with both palms in an effort to curb her hilarity.

'I'm sorry, hang on a minute.' Pat looked away, but was wracked by a new fit of hilarity and May waited patiently, until she too was caught up in the giggling fit.

'If you'd only seen Mum trying to squash all them tins into the suitcase!'

They walked over to sit on the little bench at the end of the garden, with its wide view of the valley and far hills.

'At least you got a date out of it! Was he worth the terror?' Pat asked.

May thought for a moment. 'Ask me after the dance. What about your Mark – have you seen him since we arrived?'

Pat shook her head sadly. 'As soon as we got here I went up to the stables to find him and Arnold told me he'd gone! I couldn't believe it, just went off without a word . . .' she said, looking miserable. 'Just my luck, the first chap I really click with . . .'

May's hand flew to her mouth. 'Oh gawd, in all the excitement I forgot to tell you. He didn't just leave, Pat. He was sacked!'

'Sacked? Oh God, my uncle must have found out about us. I thought he might disapprove, but he didn't have to take it out on poor Mark. The stables are his life.'

'But it wasn't your uncle sacked him!'

'How do you know that?' Pat asked, looking confused.

'Mum heard from Tom that it was the head lad did it.'

Pat stood up. 'Arnold? That bloody man! He's always made Mark's life a misery, but I never thought he'd sack him. I bet he's told Mark a load of lies about my uncle ordering it.' She thought for a moment. 'Come up to the lads' barn with me? I've got to find out where Mark's gone and tell him it wasn't the major . . . He thinks the world of my uncle.'

May followed her to the old barn, which had been converted into a hostel for the stable lads. Her knock was answered by the short, wiry young man who'd collected them from the station in the pony and trap.

'Tom, do you know where Mark's gone?'

So this was her mother's favourite. May could see nothing of Jack in him, but if it gave her mother comfort, what did it matter? The boy looked round nervously and let the door click shut behind him against the curious looks of a couple of lads. The dormitory that May had glimpsed reminded her of the barracks hut in Barkingside.

'No, I've got no idea where he is. Sorry, Pat. But I do know Arnold's banned him from the place. If I hear anything from him I'll let you know, though.'

As they walked away Pat looked at May and said, 'Looks like we're in the same boat now, May, both lost our fellers. Well, you know what they say, misery loves company. Fancy a walk?'

She looked so cast-down, that May didn't like to leave her, and after all she would only go back and rattle around in the big old house on her own. As they passed the stables, Pat stopped at an open stall to feed sugar lumps to a beautiful chestnut horse with long eyelashes and dark liquid eyes. He seemed to May to be expecting the treat. She stood a little to one side, until Pat beckoned her and passed her a sugar cube.

'Dobbin, you must really love these animals to share your sugar!' May joked, putting the cube to the horse's surprisingly delicate lips.

'I do,' Pat said. 'I can be myself with the horses – no expectations, no judgements.' She gave the animal's neck a firm stroke. 'Mark felt the same. I suppose it's why we got on so well.'

They left the horse and followed a track round the stables, where they began climbing the hill. They said very little, as the way was steep and Pat seemed lost in her own thoughts. Soon they were high enough to see the wide vale, spread out beneath them, with a line of hills so far distant they looked blue.

'You can see four counties from here,' Pat said, breathing hard. The hilltop was flat and wide and, as they walked along it, Pat said she wanted to show May something special.

'It was Mark's favourite place,' she said.

When Pat stopped, May looked around, but there was nothing to be seen, only bright green turf, stretching away in front and behind them.

'Where is it then?' she asked and Pat beckoned. As May walked forward on to the turf she was aware of suddenly treading on what felt like a luxurious cushion; her feet seemed to bounce on the grass and she smiled at Pat.

'What is it?'

'This place is called the gallops! It's where they bring the horses to exercise,' Pat said, laughing. 'Uncle says it's like walking on the finest Wilton with four underlays!'

May bounced on the springy turf, and then dropped to her knees to press her hand down on it.

Pat looked on, smiling. 'The gallops have been

here two hundred years, always used for the same thing. And it's hard work keeping it like this. Mark used to tell me about his job, "treading in the gallops", they call it. See where it all gets churned up by the horses' hooves? The lads get sent in with pitchforks to turn it over and then they have to tread every inch of it down. Back-breaking, but Mark said it was worth the effort.'

May admired the spreading emerald carpet and said softly, 'Imagine jackboots walking all over this, Pat.'

'I suppose it's what makes me stick at the army. I know I've never had a home like you, but this is the nearest to one I'll ever get. Even though I can't be a gunner girl, at least I can do my bit to keep it safe.'

Wind whipped up over the top of the ridge as they sat side by side, silent for a while, May enjoying the peace of this landscape that had the power to charm and soothe and nurture.

'I'll always be grateful for this place, Pat. It's given me back my mum.'

And it was true. May was convinced that, as much as the major's kindness, it had been the countryside that had restored her mother. Here there was nothing extreme or challenging, no threatening mountains or raging torrents, just enfolding hills and winding streams, gentle balms for her mother's shattered soul.

But suddenly the peace was broken by a sharp shout echoing like a gunshot across the gallops.

Startled, she spun round to see a man emerge from a stand of trees. He began running towards them and she pulled Pat to her feet, urging her to run. For May had recognized him immediately. It was the watcher on the ridge.

May instinctively put herself in front of Pat. But she edged May out of the way, and as the man drew near, he ignored May and swept Pat up into his arms with undisguised delight.

'*You're* the German spy with the binoculars!' May blurted out as he set Pat down on her feet again.

'The only thing I've been spying on was this one!' he said, looking down lovingly at Pat.

Pat was laughing and crying all at once. 'May thought you were fifth column! But where have you been staying? I've asked all over.'

'I suppose I did look a bit suspicious, but I've been camping out in the wood and I had to talk to you before I left, Pat,' he said. 'I didn't want you thinking I'd just gone off and abandoned you!'

Pat was clinging to Mark's arm. 'But you're not going anywhere now!' she said. 'Uncle had nothing to do with it. It was Arnold's idea. Once the major knows, he'll take you back.'

'It's good to know the old major didn't get rid of me. I wouldn't mind a reference. But, Pat, I couldn't go back anyway. I've had my call-up papers.'

Pat's smile disappeared and May could see tears brimming. She was beginning to feel superfluous now.

'I'll leave you two together,' she said.

'You won't know your way,' Pat said, but her eyes were still on Mark.

'I'm a homing pigeon – I can always find my way.' May smiled and squeezed Pat's arm.

She walked back down the hill, thinking of the sad farewells being said on the gallops, right now, and she played out in her mind all the sorrowful partings of this war. At least Pat had the one consolation she'd never had with Jack, that of being able to say goodbye.

When she passed the stables, Tom was there. She explained where they'd found Mark, and who she'd mistaken him for.

'Wait till you tell Mrs Lloyd who the fifth columnist really was!' he said, laughing.

Later Pat came to the cottage. 'Come for a walk. I need to talk to you. I've got news!'

Grabbing her jacket from the hook behind the door, May called back to her mother in the kitchen.

'Just popping out with Pat!' She hurried the girl out.

'Hold on, I've got some cake for the major! She can take it up to him,' her mother called out.

May raised her eyes and whispered, 'She's gone baking mad now she can get hold of the butter. I didn't know there was a black market in the country!'

'It comes from the dairy farmer down the road.

Uncle's given over some of his land for the cows.' May's mind, formed in Bermondsey, had imagined some rustic version of George roaming the lanes.

Her mother came to the door with the cake tin. 'Did she tell you about us silly sods last night?' her mother said, laughing, and Pat nodded. May looked at her mother's face, flushed from the heat of the kitchen, and untroubled. That the woman could now laugh at her own fear flooded May's heart with gratitude, which spilled over to Pat. She put her arm round the girl as they walked away. 'What's happened, Dobbin? Has Mark gone?'

'Not yet, but he's asked me to marry him!'

'Blimey, that was quick work. Congratulations! But what about your uncle?'

'I made Mark come and see the major with me. As soon as I told him what had happened and that Mark was going into the army, he gave us his blessing! Oh, May, I've never been happier.'

May was genuinely pleased for her friend; there was only the merest sliver of pain lodging in her own heart, as she hugged her. It wasn't jealousy; it was regret.

'Oh, you two will have to come to the dance with us tonight, to celebrate!'

And when the time came for Doug to pick her up she was glad not to be alone. They were all ready and waiting for him at seven-thirty, and as he rounded the hedge, she saw disappointment briefly cloud his face. He obviously didn't appreciate the company. But he recovered enough to smile broadly as he took her arm. 'Your carriage awaits,' he said as he led her to the gravel drive where a jeep was parked.

'Your pals can come too. I think there'll be enough room, but it's a good job one of you two is on the short side!' He grinned at Pat and Mark.

'Where did you get this?' May hadn't expected transport.

Doug pointed to his sergeant's stripes. 'Commandeered it! We're always being told to keep the locals happy!'

They all clambered up into the jeep and Doug drove at breakneck speed down the hill, along winding narrow roads, till they reached the mercifully flatter country beyond Moreton-in-Marsh where the airfield was situated. Still, by the time they arrived at the RAF base, May was feeling sick and she was relieved when Doug brought the car to a screeching halt outside the NAAFI.

The dance was being held in the sparsely decorated canteen. Not that May had time to notice much, for as soon as they pushed through the door they were greeted by a stampede of eager fighter boys. Doug put a proprietorial arm round her and without asking whisked her away to the brash music, blaring out from the band on the stage. They danced to the jolly, jazzy tune of, 'Somebody Else Is Taking My Place', while a Peggy Lee lookalike girl in WAAF uniform sang the incongruous words of heartache and regret. The tune won out and, ignoring the words, May gave herself up to the whirlwind that was Doug McKecknie. He swung her round and negotiated the dance floor as if it were a sky filled with Messerschmitts, steering her in and out of the other couples until she felt like one of the Spitfires he piloted, and that they were in a dogfight, not a dance. She hoped he was a more skilful fighter boy than he was a dancer for by the interval, May was suffering. She made her excuses and hobbled with bruised feet to a chair, while Doug went to get them drinks. When the band started playing again, 'Apple Blossom Time', Doug took her hand. May had been praying for the respite of a slow dance, and she thought she could manage this one. Doug pulled her in close as the WAAF girl sang from the stage: *'One day in May, you'll come and say, happy the bride, that the sun shines on today.'* The singer's yearning voice was not happy at all. Jolly tunes to sad words and sad tunes to happy words – it seemed the whole world was confused, not just her. But glancing over at Mark and Pat in a close embrace, oblivious to the melancholy music, May had a glimpse of something certain and longed to know it for herself. Perhaps it was this longing that persuaded her to follow Doug out into the wide, dark night of stars, and let him kiss her.

Carrie Lloyd hadn't said a word against him, but the next morning, when she'd asked about the dance and May had mentioned Doug, the look on her mother's face had told her all she needed to know. It was the sort of look she'd have given to a piece of inferior butcher's meat, along with the words 'not much cop'. And although Doug called every day for the rest of that leave, and her mother gave him tea and cakes every time, that look on her face told May he wasn't truly welcome.

But May enjoyed his fast, strange ways and the offhand manner in which he spoke about the danger he faced daily. Perhaps if she'd cared more she wouldn't have wanted to see so much of him, for he made it clear there might be a day when he just didn't appear. Just the other night, a plane had crash-landed, when almost home, into one of those tranquil hills that May found so comforting. When he asked if he could visit her in Essex on his next leave, she agreed. But when she told her mother as they were packing up May's kitbag on the night before her return to Barkingside, she shot May that disapproving look again. Mrs Lloyd folded the last of May's civvie clothes then hung up the dress uniform, ready for the morning.

'What's the matter with Doug, Mum? Why don't you like him?' May asked, exasperated. 'I've waited long enough to find someone. I'd have thought you'd be pleased for me.'

Her mother shook her head. 'He won't make old bones,' she said, in tones reminiscent of Granny Byron.

'What do you mean? No one's safe in this war, are they?' She didn't want to hurt her mother with a reference to Jack, but the thought was there. Walking home from a party, or flying a Spitfire – both could be equally lethal.

'No, but you don't have to take chances and I've seen the way he drives, and I've seen the way he is with you. Careless with other people and careless with himself. I'm telling you, love, don't get attached. Besides, I'll bet a pound to a penny he's handy, ain't he?'

May blushed. Mrs Lloyd had guessed rightly, but this was a conversation she never wanted to have with her mother.

'Thought so. If he comes down to visit you at Barkingside, you be careful. You're a bloody innocent, you are!'

May didn't feel this was fair. 'That might have been true once, before I joined the ATS. But I've seen more life in the past year, than I ever have. It's the education I never had, Mum, and I'm not talking about Goldsmiths.'

Her mother seemed to relent. 'All right, love, I'm sorry. It's just you were always the soft one, happy to be in your home. I can't get used to you going out in the world, all on your own. Still, I suppose you had to grow up quick when you went away. Gawd knows I wasn't there to help, was I?'

'Don't say that.' May put her arms round her mother. 'I'm just glad to have you back. Promise not to worry about me, and I'll promise to be careful, all right?'

When her mother left her, May turned out the lights and pulled open the blackout curtains. Looking out towards the wood, she remembered the night of the 'invasion' and her first view of Doug, coiled around a tree, unconcerned at his plight and laughing at her. She wondered, what if it hadn't been an exercise, but a landing on enemy soil? And what if she'd been a German, not a frightened girl? How long would he have lasted? Perhaps her mother was right, and it would be better not to learn to care for such a careless person as Doug McKecknie.

CHAPTER 22

LOVE ON RATION

Early Summer 1942

After a week's bed rest the doctor had said Peggy could do most things, so long as she didn't spend hours on her feet. The terrifying thought that she might have lost her baby had convinced Peggy that her days of climbing ladders in the powder room were long over, and besides, she was happier to be doing war work, even if it meant sitting for dull hours at the stamping machine, marking anonymous plane parts with serial numbers. She could only hope they would mean something important, to someone, somewhere.

The hardest thing to give up had been the mobile canteen. But Harry had already nearly lost one child, and she certainly wasn't going to endanger this one by over-stretching herself. So she took on a job in the WVS clothes depot, where she could sit and sort out donated clothing. Much of it was for children, often from the colonies or from generous Americans in places like Florida, where the climate was reflected in the beautifully made, but thin, cotton shirts and skirts. Her job involved finding suitable clothes for children of bombed-out families. Little girls would eye with undisguised desire the pretty American dresses, and young boys would covet the cowboy-style checked shirts. It made Peggy smile when they looked at themselves in the mirror and saw reflected back a child of the colourful fantasy land of America, instead of their own ash-dusted black-and-white world.

Her supervisor had said she could choose a layette from the donations for her own baby. It would certainly be a help, for in spite of the extra clothing coupons she received for the coming baby, whatever clothes she bought would have to last a long time. But so far, she'd resisted the romper suits and bonnets coming through the depot. She knew it was foolish, but the scare back in January had unnerved her and revealed a seam of superstition that she'd obviously inherited from Granny Byron. She felt that it would be tempting fate to dress the child too soon. That is, until she saw the dress.

It came, tissue-wrapped in a pretty box along with a shipment of other exquisite clothes, from a small town in California that she'd never heard of. A handwritten tag declared it: *A gift from the folks of over here, to the kids over there.* As she held up the dress, extravagant folds of the softest white cotton fell from elaborate pink smocking on the bodice. At the neck was a delicate lace collar, the like of which could no longer be found in the plain utility ranges. The dress would be too large for a newborn, and there were other far more practical items she could have chosen, but at the end of the day she folded the tissue-wrapped dress back into its box and took it home. It wasn't until she was placing the box at the bottom of her wardrobe that she realized there'd been no doubt in her mind that the baby would be a girl. And there again she'd been influenced by Granny Byron, for her grandmother had begun referring to the baby as 'she' almost immediately, and Peggy had followed suit.

Nevertheless, it was hard making all these preparations for the baby, without Harry. He was in North Africa, which was about all she knew. His uninformative letters had been loving, but his passion did not translate well on to the page, and she dreaded forgetting why she had loved him, so instantaneously and so recklessly, in the first place. She pulled her mind away from visions of tanks rolling over desert sands and went to the kitchen to see what was left of this week's rations. Food was becoming an obsession, and her child obviously hadn't heard of austerity because Peggy's cravings never seemed to be on the ration list. At the moment it was cheese. She could have eaten a pound of the stuff at one sitting; instead her two ounces had gone in a minute. But whatever the privations or the difficulties, she still preferred the freedom of living with her own choices to the prison of submitting to George's.

It was undeniable that without George's regular restocking with brand-new furnishings, her little palace on the Purbrook had begun to look as shabby and down-at-heel as everywhere else did in this war, but that didn't bother her. As she debated whether to use the last of the cold meat, she heard a knock on the door. It was Granny Byron: she was holding a pot of stew, wrapped up in a towel.

'I've brought your tea. You haven't done nothing yet, have you?'

Peggy wanted to kiss her, but the pot was in the way. Instead she followed her grandmother into the kitchen, where she took off her broad-brimmed green-feathered hat and placed it carefully on a chair.

'You sit down and let me warm this up. Take the weight off them legs, look at 'em, swollen up like elephants!'

'Thanks, Nan!' Peggy laughed and gave in; it was comforting to have her grandmother's flamboyant figure bustling around in the kitchen.

'Where's your dad?'

'Oh, he's gone up Southwark Park Road. He's trying to get a repair crew to do the roof.'

Her grandmother nodded and grunted, ladling mutton stew into a bowl.

'Good luck to him. He's been glad to stay here with you, though, ain't he? Shame you had to break your neck before he come to his senses.'

The estrangement with her father had been painful, but what was the good in keeping it alive? She'd seen how he'd sobbed when he thought she might have been killed in the accident. But she'd made the mistake of telling Granny Byron that when she'd nearly lost the baby afterwards her father had said it might not be a bad thing after all.

Her grandmother had been incensed. 'That's men all over,' she'd said. 'Selfish! Just so long as they're not inconvenienced, they're all right. And that's all it is, love, that poor child you're carrying's been nothing but an inconvenience!'

Peggy hadn't argued. For Granny Byron had been her tower of strength since they'd shipped her mother off to Moreton-in-Marsh, and she didn't think she could have managed without her. In fact, her grandmother had seemed to come into her own during this war. She was the one person Peggy knew who would sit at home in an air raid without flinching, or stand in a queue for hours on end and keep everyone entertained with her stream of banter. She never complained and she never worried. Amongst the anxious, pinched faces, and the drab, beleaguered figures peopling the streets, her cheerful, bizarrely dressed, gold-bedecked grandmother was proof that, for a very few, life need not be defined by the war. She was an infusion of colour in a grey world. Her bright shawls and feathered hats were not just pre-war – they were pre-two world wars, a reminder, Peggy thought, that sooner or later, all wars end.

But it seemed George's war with Peggy hadn't, and the day following her grandmother's visit he sent her a message. She was no longer walking to work, and as she stepped heavily off the back board of the bus she tripped, falling to her knees, one arm instinctively wrapped around her stomach, protecting the baby, the other shooting out to break her fall. She cried out as pain burst up her arm and her knees grazed asphalt. She felt herself being hoisted up from behind by the conductor.

'You all right, love?' he said, as she rubbed at her bleeding knees.

'I'm fine,' Peggy said, grateful for his steadying hand, feeling foolish rather than hurt. At least, she thought, she hadn't been wearing nylons, otherwise they would have been ruined. But nylons, like so many other things, were fast becoming a memory. Once the conductor was reassured, he jumped back on to the running board, ringing the bell, and Peggy turned towards the alley leading to Atkinson's. She was examining her grazed wrist and so didn't notice Ronnie Riley until she'd almost bumped into him.

'You wanna be careful, gel,' he said, his face showing anything but concern.

She tried to walk round him, but he was a broad man and the alley was narrow. He side-stepped to block her way and she found herself pinned up against the wall. The scent of flowers from the factory mingled with Ronnie Riley's breath on her cheek. He still smelled of last night's beer and she instinctively pulled her head away. He had no neck to speak of, so his face above his tight collar turned deep red as he saw her revulsion. His hand tightened on her arm and he pulled her in closer. 'What, you think you're too good for me? I could have you, but I wouldn't do it to George. I'm *loyal*, see.'

Peggy finally managed to pull away. 'Just piss off, Ronnie, and leave me alone.'

'Hold up, I've got a message from your husband.'

'Well, I don't want to hear it. Now get out the way. I'm late for work.'

But as she began to walk towards the factory gate, her ankle gave way. Damn it, there'd been a weakness there since her fall from the ladder. Limping forward, she was determined not to show any vulnerability in front of Ronnie. With pain burning her ankle, she heard him call after her.

'George's getting released in a fortnight, and he wants you out of his flat by then! Hear me?'

She didn't turn round. She'd been frightened this might happen one day and now it had, a cold pit opened in her stomach. The nest that she'd imagined bringing her baby home to had just disappeared and there was little she could do about it. George was the tenant and nothing was in her name.

She had the bad luck to be clocking in late when Hattie was passing. The woman had shown surprising moments of concern towards her, but she was still a supervisor and could turn on the sour hatchet-face reserved for such misdemeanours when necessary. But now the woman stopped her.

'Gawd, Peg, you've been in the wars! What you done to yourself?'

Peggy was almost glad of her injuries; at least they would explain away her shaky voice. But as she described the trip from the bus, her trembling only increased. Suddenly she didn't feel up to her newfound independence and wished with all her heart she hadn't spent half her life letting the men make all the decisions for her. If she hadn't allowed herself to be so cosseted, she wouldn't be feeling helpless now and would know what to do. But it looked as if she would have to go cap in hand to her father, and ask him to take her and her child in. The thought of bringing the baby home to the half-ruin of her parents' house brought on a fit of anxiety. It gripped her throat with its dry, choking hand, and she was annoyed to feel a tear on her cheek.

'Come on, love, don't get yourself in a two and eight. Sit down here for a bit.' Hattie helped her over to a bench near the clocking-on machine and Peggy let out a small cry as she put weight on her ankle.

'Thanks, Hat, I don't think there's much damage. It's the old sprain . . . and me hormones!' But Peggy's forced laughter turned into a sob.

'You're taking the day off. I'll mark you off in the sick book.'

'I'll be all right—'

'No arguments!' Hattie switched to her severe expression. 'And I'm getting you a lift home!'

Peggy sat back, resigned. She had no more energy to resist, and she doubted she'd be much use at work today anyway. At least she'd have time to figure out what she was going to do.

When Hattie came back, she helped Peggy up and whispered, 'All sorted. You're going home in style, gel.'

She led her out to the yard and stopped in front of the office building, where the boss's uniformed chauffeur was standing.

'He's standing around all day with sod all to do till they want him. Might as well make yourself useful, eh, Charlie?' She seemed well acquainted with the chauffeur and from the wink he gave Hattie, Peggy suspected they might know each other very well indeed. She'd have never thought it of Hattie, who'd always seemed such a confirmed spinster.

Charlie jumped to Peggy's side as if she were the managing director, helping her gently to the car. 'Ever been in a roller before?' he asked.

'No!' she said, looking at the dark green Rolls Royce, so highly polished she could see her reflection in it. Her eyes travelled to the front grill and headlamps, which were a gleam of silver: she recognized the distinctive mascot, flying on the front.

'I can't!' she said. 'You'll get in trouble.'

'Let me worry about that, love, I'd rather be in trouble with the bosses than Hattie any day . . . wouldn't you?' He grinned at her and Peggy had to agree. She stepped up into the car and sank into padded, dark green leather seats. She might as well enjoy the ride.

Her arrival caused a stir on the Purbrook Estate. Even before the war, a Rolls Royce drawing up outside the entrance would have caused comment, but with petrol rationed for private cars, the sight was a rarity that couldn't be ignored. Peggy heard a boy shout, 'Roller!' to invisible friends and soon she was aware of heads peering out of windows. By the time Charlie had helped her out, the car was surrounded by a gang of boys, inspecting every inch of the bodywork.

'Aye, aye, here comes the Princess of Purbrook!' She looked up to see her neighbour, Sally, calling down from the balcony. 'Did George nick it for ya?' The woman's loud laughter rang round the courtyard. If only she knew, Peggy thought, that the princess was about to become a pauper.

Once inside the flat she went straight to the sink to wash the grit from her grazed hands and knees. Then, walking from room to room, she took stock of what she might take with her. But looking for evidence of herself in this place was futile, from the glass bowl light fitting in the living room to the bedroom furniture, the whole flat seemed to accuse her of absence. Everything in the place belonged to George – except herself and the child she was carrying.

She spent the day packing her few clothes into the large cardboard suitcase her parents had given them for a honeymoon present. She'd long since given away the majority of the drab wardrobe from her days with George. After the clothes, there were Harry's letters, a few photos and some pretty things she'd been given as presents, mainly from her sister May. There was a touching memento of Jack, a strange thing, a carved crocodile that he'd made in woodwork class and presented to her as a present. She remembered he'd been so proud of it and, at the time, she was sure she hadn't been appreciative enough. Perhaps that's why she loved it so much now. It was the thought of Jack that steeled her. She was determined to stop feeling sorry for herself. She might feel alone and inadequate; she might feel that she'd messed up her life. But at least she still had a life to live. As she looked at the few possessions she'd collected together in the suitcase, she remembered one other thing. And going to the wardrobe, she drew out the box containing the beautiful baby dress. She allowed herself a peek inside, before placing it on top of the suitcase. She was ready to go. Now all she had to do was tell her father.

She made Mr Lloyd a shepherd's pie, using a small tin of spam and a lot of potatoes. Since their reconciliation he'd got into the habit of staying for meals and sleeping over sometimes, while camping out at Southwark Park Road the rest of the time.

Waiting until he'd finished his meal, she broke the news. 'Dad, George's told me he wants me out of the flat when he's released.'

'I don't believe it!' he said, his cup of tea halfway to his lips. 'George? He wouldn't do that! Doesn't he know I've been stopping here too?'

'I should think Ronnie must have told him. I haven't seen him, since . . .'

'How long's he given you?

'Two weeks.'

'What? Well, blow me . . . what a mean git!'

Peggy suspected that her father was really more shocked that his beloved George could do this to him, than that he should do it to her.

'Drink your tea, Dad,' she said, her eyes fixed on the brimming hot liquid his shaking hand threatened to spill down his trousers.

He banged down the cup, slopping tea into the saucer, and got up, looking angrier than she'd ever seen him. Even his reaction to her pregnancy hadn't been as vehement.

'Well, this takes the cake. You think you know people . . .' He shook his head, pacing up and down in front of the fireplace, pulling at his braces. 'It takes a war to show you who your friends are, love. It takes a war.'

And he sat down to fill his pipe, vigorously picking at it and poking, yet never lighting it, till she almost felt sorrier for him than she did for herself.

'So can I come home then?' she asked, and the reality of her situation seemed to dawn on him.

'To Southwark Park Road? What, and bring the baby?'

'Yes, Dad, I'll be bringing my baby,' she said, wondering what else he thought she would do with it.

She moved out the following week. Peggy closed the door on her one-time palace without regret and posted the key to George in prison. He was welcome to the place, and it was better to leave like this. She would be well out of the way before he came home. She wouldn't give him the pleasure of turfing her out personally. But when she entered the half-ruined house in Southwark Park Road, her heart sank. She walked into the kitchen, where her father had his base camp. He'd managed to keep it relatively dry over the winter months and had got the gas back on, so at least the cooker was working. The chimney hadn't been damaged in the blast, so they would be able to keep a fire going until the weather warmed up. He had a camp bed, which at the moment was stored under the kitchen table. She supposed she should be grateful that he'd been vigilant enough to keep the looters out, so the kitchen at least was still well-stocked. But when he took her upstairs she could have cried. The rooms were unusable. There were no beds; they'd all been either burned or water damaged. The cosy bedroom she'd shared with her sister was now a mouldy, damp home for sparrows, which fluttered in alarm up into the attic through a hole in the corner of the ceiling. She looked up at a patch of pale sky, visible through the shattered roof above.

'I'll have another try at getting a repair crew this week,' her father said apologetically.

She nodded. 'I'll go to the WVS depot today and see about a bed for me. Dad, I never realized it was still so bad . . .' she said, with a fleeting regret for the Purbrook front-door key, now on its way to George. 'But we'll make it more homely.'

She had to be positive, but it was only now that she realized how impossible it was to think of bringing a tiny baby into this damp shell of a house. Even with a roof on, it would still take months to dry out and clean up. She could put up with it for herself, but not for her child. And besides, however much he'd mellowed, she knew that her father would find it hard to have the result of 'her disgrace' actually living with him, gurgling and screaming its presence into his life.

After her fall from the hopper, she'd feared she might have to give up work altogether. It wasn't an idea she relished. She wanted to carry on earning her own money, for more than anything she feared reverting to a previous self she had begun to despise. She decided to spend the rest of the day making the house as habitable as possible. Her father went back to work at the docks and she set off for the WVS depot.

The large storeroom was full of an odd assortment of donated furniture and salvage from bombed houses. One of the volunteers showed her a bed that would do for herself, and a cot for the baby. For a small charge, they would deliver them later that day, along with a bundle of bedding. Her job done, she made her way to the clothes exchange. It was time to throw off her superstitions and find clothes for her baby. Her friends at the exchange stuffed a large bag full of everything her child could need: bibs, booties and bonnets overflowed. While she was there she bumped into Babs, who was still driving the mobile canteen.

'Oh good, I'm glad I've seen you before the baby's born!' Babs greeted her with a smile. 'Hang on!' She disappeared into the cloakroom and came back with a parcel. 'Here, a present for the baby. We've no children in our family, and I'm not likely to have one.'

'Oh, Babs, it's beautiful!' Peggy exclaimed with delight as she drew out an ivory lace christening shawl.

'It's our family shawl, but the line ends with yours truly, so I thought it should go to a good home.'

'Are you sure?'

'Of course I'm sure, but I expect an invitation to the christening!' she said, returning to her clipped efficiency.

Peggy was moved by the woman's gesture. She was normally such a brusque, no-nonsense type that it was a surprise to discover this maternal side. Babs must have realized, along with all the other girls, that this baby was not her husband's, but people had surprised her. Perhaps it was the war, but she'd received far more sympathy than she'd expected. Wartime romances and the resultant war babies were no longer a rarity, and if the father was in uniform there was a reason to be indulgent.

When the brief spring ended, ushering in a dull and wet summer, they fitted up the front parlour as Peggy's bedroom. Sofa and chairs were moved aside to make room for the bed and cot, and a chest of drawers, salvaged from her parents' bedroom, was brought downstairs. They kept a fire going to dry the room out, but in spite of her best efforts the place was still a travesty of home. It was an unending task to keep the dust at bay, for it blew up from the hundreds of surrounding bomb sites, sifting down through the roof, blowing through ill-fitting casements and swirling in gritty eddies every time the front door was opened. The midwife had visited the place once and declared she couldn't possibly have the baby there, so she would go into Guy's Hospital for the birth.

The time came when she had to admit that her working days were over. Her stomach was so big that it was preventing her even reaching the stamping machine as she sat at her bench. She had left it till the last possible minute, but now she was sitting outside the office, waiting to give in her notice. She was gratefully easing her swollen feet out of her shoes, when the door opened and a young woman emerged. The dark hair, hooded lids and pale colouring looked familiar, but she couldn't place her, and it was only after the girl had disappeared down the corridor that it came to Peggy where she'd seen her before. She was sure it was at the Gilbies' house, one Sunday teatime; the girl had been there when Peggy was visiting Jack. It was Bill's fiancée!

Iris had walked past as if she didn't know her, and perhaps all she'd seen was a heavily pregnant woman in a turban. Peggy was aware that much of her accrued glamour had disappeared with the weight she'd gained. But as Iris walked away, Peggy felt a stab of envy for the svelte figure and the unsuitably high heels, and the nylons. Nylons! What she wouldn't give for a pair of those, and she wondered fleetingly how Iris had got her hands on them.

It wasn't until her last week at the factory that she found out the answer from Ada. Her young friend had been transferred to perfume after her near-fatal failure in the powder room, but Peggy couldn't blame the girl and remained friends with her. They met in the canteen most dinner times. Ada reminded her of May. Inexperienced and naïve, she came to Peggy for boyfriend advice, which although she was ready to give, sometimes made her feel a fraud. After all, she was hardly an advertisement for good judgement of men.

Peggy was already sitting at a table waiting for Ada. The canteen was packed today and she'd saved the girl a seat. As rationing intensified, eating in the canteen had become more popular. The prices were regulated now and the food, unrationed, was not bad. She could get a steak-and-kidney pie and a rice pudding, all for ninepence. The ramshackle kitchen in Southwark Park Road didn't allow her to do much cooking, and her father preferred to eat during the day at a British restaurant near the docks. Besides, he was still in camping-out mode. Always on high alert, never settled, he came home in the evenings, washed and changed into his ARP uniform, and went straight out on duty. Sometimes she felt he was avoiding her, and without her WVS evenings she'd begun to feel lonely in the old place. She would miss these lunchtimes in the canteen, with their packed life and chatter and the music of *Worker's Playtime* being piped through the tannoy. Vera Lynn was singing 'Tomorrow is a Lovely Day', which, in spite of its sad tune, always managed to lift her heart. As Vera reached the verse, '*If today your heart is weary, If ev'ry little thing looks grey, Just forget your troubles and learn to say, Tomorrow is a lovely day,*' Peggy saw Ada walking towards her, tray in hand. She waved the girl over to the seat she'd saved.

'You're late, where have you been?' Peggy asked.

Ada was all smiles and stuck out her shapely leg, showing off her nylon stockings.

'Where did you get those? I must be the only girl in the factory who can't get hold of any!' Peggy said. 'Not that they could improve my pins now, look at them.' She pointed to her own bare swollen ankles.

'They're not too bad,' Ada lied. 'I can get you some nylons, though, if you want. That new girl Iris has come in with handfuls of them this week!'

'Iris has?'

'Yes, she's livened things up a bit.' Ada lowered her voice. 'She can get anything apparently – chocolate, cigarettes. She comes in of a Monday with a new stock.'

Then Ada lowered her voice even further so that May had to lean forward to hear.

'She goes over the other side, gets the stuff from GIs.' The last initials were mouthed rather than spoken. 'She's brazen with it, though, don't mind letting you know what she has to do for it!'

Ada had obviously been getting an education in the perfume department. A few months ago she wouldn't have understood that there was any other payment method but hard cash. But Peggy was so shocked by what she'd heard, her face must have betrayed her, for Ada put her hand to her mouth.

'Have I put me foot in it? I didn't think you'd mind about black market, you know, what with your husband . . .'

Peggy shook her head. 'It's not the nylons I'm worried about, love, it's the GIs. I don't think her fiancé would be too happy about them.'

'Noo! She's not engaged! She never said.'

Peggy was about to join in with Ada's indignation, when she realized that however outraged she felt for Bill Gilbie, she had done exactly the same thing to George. And hadn't she been grateful for those people who could turn a blind eye to her indiscretions?

'Well, who am I to judge. Don't say anything, will you, Ada, it's her business.'

And as she drew her syrup pudding towards her, Ada nodded dutifully. 'No, won't say a word.'

But the encounter had left Peggy facing a dilemma. She knew that May had given up on Bill, but Peggy had made a friend of Nell Gilbie, and she hated the idea of keeping this secret. Surely the woman would want to know something that could affect her son's happiness. Bill's mother had made it clear Peggy was welcome to see Jack whenever she wished and it had become something she looked forward to. Today she'd been invited for Sunday tea, but once they were all seated round the table she found it difficult to look Mrs Gilbie in the eye. She'd asked herself over and over how she would have felt if someone had told George about Harry before she'd done it herself. She might well have been able to sit on her secret if Mrs Gilbie hadn't turned to the subject of May.

'How's your sister? She remembered Jack's

birthday, sent him a little present. I shouldn't think she gets five minutes to herself where she is.' Mrs Gilbie looked thoughtful. 'She's a lovely girl. I shouldn't say it, but I used to think her and my Bill . . . well, it wasn't to be, but I think they would have been happy. What, don't you agree?'

Peggy's guilty secret must have translated to an expression of doubt. 'No! No, I do agree . . . It's just that, well, I heard something about Iris, and I probably shouldn't say anything.'

But Nell Gilbie was not the sort of woman to be put off and as Peggy told her about Iris she listened quietly. Then she nodded and said, 'It's no more than I guessed. But leave it to me. Don't say anything to anyone else, will you?'

And Peggy promised, glad for the distraction of Jack who had become very voluble and began holding court, impressing them with his vocabulary as Mrs Gilbie looked on with delight every time he produced a new word.

'If your'n ends up with as much bunny as this one, you'd better make the most of it before she learns to talk. He's got more rabbit than the butcher's down the Blue!'

Mrs Gilbie jumped up to help Jack with a piece of bread and jam that had fallen face down on the clean tablecloth.

'Made mess!' he said proudly, drawing on the tablecloth with a jammy finger.

'You think it's a girl?' Peggy asked, unconsciously laying a hand on her stomach.

'Well, you're carrying high.'

'My nan thinks so too.'

Perhaps Peggy's face had revealed more anxiety than pleasure at the birth, which was now overdue, for when Mr Gilbie walked in his wife handed Jack to him. 'Sam, will you wash his hands and face for me, love?' she asked.

Mr Gilbie took the boy with a grimace. 'Who's a mucky pup, eh?'

He was nothing like her own father, whose role at home had been strictly defined. She couldn't ever remember him helping out with washing and dressing them as children. But Sam Gilbie was a quiet man, with a reticent warmth that Peggy appreciated. She expected to be shunned by many, but she knew that in this house at least, she was unjudged and welcome. It was just as well Mr Gilbie seemed to love children, for the Gilbies now had another two charges living with them. Sitting at the table were the copper-haired orphaned children of neighbours killed in a bombing raid. Stan, a boy of about eleven, now jumped down from his chair. 'I'll help Uncle Sam!' He seemed glad to be let off the leash and Sarah, the little girl, soon followed. Peggy thought perhaps this was her cue to go.

'Stay for another cup of tea!' Mrs Gilbie began pouring before she could answer. 'You haven't got to rush off anywhere, have you?'

'No, I gave up the clothes exchange two weeks ago. This baby doesn't want to come.'

'Well, she'll come when she's ready. But you look a bit weary, love. Is it your legs?'

There was no disguising the swelling of her ankles, but her hormones betrayed her, and she found herself tearfully unable to answer. Nell Gilbie stretched out her hand across the table. 'What is it, Peggy? What's worrying you, is it the birth?'

She shook her head, and waited till she had swallowed her tears.

'It's just that George's chucked me out of the flat. Wanted me gone by the time he gets released next month.'

'Oh, love, I'm sorry. Can you go and live with your nan?'

'No, there's barely enough room for her and her hats. I'm back with my dad at Southwark Park Road.'

'But you can't take a tiny baby into a bombed-out house!'

'I know. Me and Dad can manage there all right, but not a baby. The only thing I can think of doing is sending her to Moreton-in-Marsh. Mum seems a lot better, and I think she's well enough to cope. But the truth is, Mrs Gilbie, I don't want to send my baby away . . .' Now the sobs returned and Peggy's shoulders shook as she held her head in her hands. Mrs Gilbie came to her side, putting her arms round her till the shaking subsided.

'You let it out,' the woman said softly. 'It's not easy, making all the decisions on your own. I know what it's like. I had to bring up my brothers and sisters on me own, but you learn to cope – you have to.'

Peggy sniffed and sat up, knowing she would have to be stronger than this, once the child was here.

'I'm not on my own really. Nan's been so good and Dad . . . in his way.'

Nevertheless, it was true, she'd never felt so isolated. But the loneliness was specific. She wanted Harry. Yet he, like everything else in her life, was on ration, and no one else could appease that hunger.

'It's just I can't bear the thought of sending Harry's baby away. She's all I've got of him . . . and little Jack, of course. I'm just being selfish, I know. There's thousands of mothers had to let their children go . . .'

'Oh, love, I wish I could offer to look after your baby, but now I've taken on the other two . . .'

'I wasn't expecting that . . . you've got enough on your plate. No, I'll get used to the idea.'

'But if you can't bear to send her to your mum, what about a day nursery? They've opened a new one for working mothers up by Spa Road. They're taking all ages. Why don't you go there and put your name down?'

Peggy wished she hadn't made Mrs Gilbie feel guilty. She was the sort of woman who would have taken in the world if she had enough bedrooms. But she was right, there were nurseries

411

popping up everywhere, and only last week she'd seen a campaign poster to encourage married women back to work, proclaiming: *Nurseries for kids, war work for mothers.* If the baby could spend most of the time in a clean, warm nursery, perhaps she wouldn't feel so bad about keeping her in Bermondsey.

She relaxed and sank back into her chair, and only now realized how rigidly she'd been holding her body. She'd been so tensed for a future parting from her child that perhaps she'd fooled her body into not giving birth.

'Don't worry about the baby being late, love,' Mrs Gilbie said, reaching out to pat her hand. 'She'll come when she's ready.'

CHAPTER 23

THE LAND OF BEGIN AGAIN

Early Summer 1942

Mac put the box Brownie up to her eye for the last time. She, May, Ruby, Emmy and Pat were out on the field behind the Nissen hut. It was May's turn to face the camera, and she squinted a little against the glare of bright sunshine.

'Say cheese!' Mac said and Emmy, standing to one side with a cigarette hanging out of her mouth, said, 'What's that?'

Which had the desired effect of making May smile. Strictly speaking, the dress May was wearing belonged to Pat, but they had all taken turns being photographed in it. One by one they'd dashed into the hut to change out of uniform. The dress was a navy polka-dot print, utility regulation A-line, no pleats, a single row of buttons, belt, short sleeves and round collar. Its most appealing feature was that it was new, and due to the latest reduction in clothing coupons 'new' was a rarity. Though Pat was working in the stores, she was considered an honorary member of their gun team, and the team shared everything from dinkie curlers to soap. Today, they were sharing her dress. Too short for Mac and too loose for Bee, they didn't care. Ruby squeezed herself into it and though the buttons didn't quite do up, she folded her arms across her chest, turning side on to the camera. May was being photographed last because she wasn't taking the dress off. Pat, who was on night duty, was letting May wear it for tonight's dance at the RAF base.

This weekend Doug was travelling up from Moreton-in-Marsh on a forty-eight-hour leave, putting up in a local pub. He had proved an ardent suitor, spending every leave since they'd met with May. But whenever she saw Doug again, May was surprised. Somehow, between visits she managed to forget what he looked like. It didn't help that she hardly ever got a night's uninterrupted sleep, and time for daydreaming was limited. For though the intense bombing raids of the previous two years had eased off, they were still seeing action several times a week and her mind became a thing that focused with intense precision while she was on the predictor, and for the rest of the time turned to a dazed mush. Today she had a half-day pass and planned to meet Doug off the train at Barkingside Station. Afterwards they were going on to the Saturday night dance at the Chigwell RAF base.

When Doug strolled out of the station, kitbag slung over one shoulder, there it was, that shock of surprise. His hair was definitely ginger not red, his face paler and his freckles far more pronounced, his nose more prominent. She stood to one side of the station entrance, and as the passengers gradually dispersed, she watched him, waiting for him to notice her. He looked around and his gaze seemed to pass over her; perhaps it was the polka-dot dress, it wasn't really her style. When he finally saw her, his face creased into a broad smile. As he took her in his arms, she realized she felt smaller, enfolded in his big-boned frame. Doug simply took up more space in reality than he did in her mind.

He pulled back to look at her. 'Hello, gorgeous, you look serious. Aren't you pleased to see me?' He grinned and planted a kiss on her mouth before she had time to reply.

He put his arm round her waist as they walked to the pub where he would be staying. He chatted about his journey and the inevitable delays, wanting her to praise his resourcefulness in changing his route three times in order to arrive on time. She let him talk. The thing she found most attractive about him was his voice. His Canadian burr was, for her, exotic and strange. He was as unknown as the man in the moon, and seemed to have come from just as far away. She couldn't comprehend Kamloops, it was a town in the middle of a desert high up in the mountains. And when she'd accused him of having her on, he'd laughed and said, 'Well, honey, I'm not saying it's the Sahara, but it is dry, so we all sort of huddle around the river.' And that she could understand, for it sounded just like Bermondsey. It had been fun finding out about his life, but as they went into the pub she was forced to confront the thing about Doug that wasn't fun.

'Want to come and help me unpack?' he asked, with a look which she'd got used to and which had nothing to do with putting a couple of shirts into a chest of drawers.

She shook her head. 'No. You're not a baby! I'll wait here. Be quick and we can have a drink before the dance.'

Doug raised his eyes and gave her a mock salute. 'Yes, Lance Corporal!' And he bounded up the carpeted stairs to the bedrooms above the pub. She was used to these sorts of requests. At first she hadn't been sure what to do, and had thought it was expected of her to go to his room. But the last time she'd ended up fighting him off and they'd had their first row. The Canadians had a reputation amongst the gunner girls as being the most persistent when it came to expecting more than kisses and, though she hated to admit it, Doug was not proving to be any exception.

The Saturday night dance at the RAF base NAAFI was always popular. With a dance floor large enough to prevent too many collisions and always a live RAF band to play the latest hits, it drew WAAF and ATS girls from the surrounding Essex bases. Tonight, when May and Doug arrived, there was a crush at the door and she was grateful for his muscular arm to steer her through to the dance floor. She spotted her friends and dragged Doug over to say hello. Emmy had been furious when she first found out about May and Doug, insisting that it simply wasn't fair May had caught her Canadian dangling from a tree in the middle of nowhere, whereas she had spent her entire leave scouring the West End's dance halls and still hadn't found a sweetheart. But when she'd met him, Emmy had surprised her by being unimpressed by Doug, and May didn't think it was jealousy. When she'd pressed her friend about her dislike, Emmy had said, 'He's tight as a duck's arse – fancy making you pay for your own drinks! And I bet he gets paid a sight more than you do.' May had protested that this wasn't always true. Sometimes he was very generous, and then Emmy had let slip the real reason for her dislike.

'Yeah, and then he probably wants something for it!'

Now, as they approached the group of friends, Emmy smiled at Doug, and although May could see it wasn't sincere, he was oblivious, quickly whisking her off on to the dance floor. The band was playing 'There's a Land of Begin Again', but May couldn't see the stage beyond the mass of coupled heads surrounding her.

'That guy on the piano's good,' Doug said, as they glided in a slow foxtrot towards the band.

417

'They don't usually have a piano in the band. He must be new,' she said, having to raise her voice above the music as the band came into view. She craned her neck to get a look at the new musician as Doug steered her swiftly past the stage. In her shock she stumbled, nearly causing a pile-up of dancers behind them.

'Hey, watch your step. Are you OK, honey?' Doug clamped his hand into the small of her back and they swept on. But her legs had turned to water, for she was quite certain that the new piano player in the RAF band was Bill Gilbie and she was also quite certain that he had seen her in Doug's arms. Bill's thick dark hair was shorter, his face leaner, but the deep blue eyes were the same, and when they met hers for a brief instant what she had wanted to convey was an apology, which was ridiculous, for she had nothing to be sorry about.

'You tired already, had enough?' Doug asked. 'Let's sit down.'

His forehead was shiny with sweat and seamed with concern. She used the heat of the crowded dance hall as her excuse.

'I just need to get some fresh air, Doug, and I'll be fine.'

His big frame carved a path through the dancers, and she followed weakly. With Doug's arm round her, she allowed him to lead her to the back of the hut, where not a glimmer of light shone from the windows. In the darkened base, the only things visible were the stars and a crescent moon. From the direction of the airfield, she heard the rising pitch of an aeroplane taking off, then another, and soon the night sky was filled with the silver wings of bombers, glinting in the moonlight. She looked up.

'I wonder where they're going tonight?' she whispered.

'I can't say too much, but there's a big push on. We're sending in a thousand bombers a night. They're in for a hell of a pounding.'

She imagined how the docks of some German town would be suffering the same fate as Bermondsey tonight. But the idea of adding German ruins to the sum of London ruins didn't equal anything remotely comforting and she let herself be turned into Doug's arms, away from the arrows of destruction disappearing in the direction of the Channel.

The sight of Bill Gilbie had unnerved her. And besides, she felt mean, having her mind on one man while she was in the arms of another. She gave herself up to Doug's strong arms and his kisses were at least a distraction. She had come to like the grown-up feeling of being kissed and wooed by the handsome Canadian, and liked being seen on his arm. It was exciting to feel life opening out for her, but she disliked the insistent weight of his pursuit of something more than she was ready to give. And once again as he pressed her back against the wooden boards of the hut, she felt that dogged persistence. Sometimes his probing tongue made her feel as though he were drawing the very life out of her. She knew herself, how she liked to observe from the shadows, never wanting to be centre stage, especially not in another person's drama. But like some passionate gold miner, Doug was determined to uncover every hidden seam, and she found her hands were flat on his chest, pushing him away as his hand slid under the regulation utility A-line skirt of the polka-dot dress.

'Hey, don't shove me away,' he said, his hand grazing the suspender belt holding up the nylon stockings he'd given her. 'It's time you thought about what I need, May. I've paid my dues.'

'What!' She couldn't believe that he had classed her with those girls who paid for nylons with sex, and perhaps it didn't help that used condoms were scattered at their feet, sordid evidence of all the other girls who tonight had come behind the hut, only too willing to pay in kind for favours received, or to comfort their fighter boys before a night-time raid which might not see them return.

She tried to wriggle out of his grasp, but his other hand was flat on the hut wall, his arm a barrier. She felt caught in a cage of her own making and panicked.

'Get off me!' she gasped, which only spurred him on, so that his mouth closed over hers, stifling her cries. He pulled at the elasticated knicker leg under the parachute silk petticoat and she felt the elastic break as his other hand grasped the front of her dress. The meagre utility buttons popped easily off the dress and as she struggled, she heard the fabric tear. The part of her mind that focused with sharp intent to keep enemy aircraft within her sight told her she must act now to unbalance him. She gave one last shove but was astonished to feel no resistance, for out of the darkness a figure had charged at Doug and was now grasping his shoulder, spinning him round. The crack she heard was Bill Gilbie's fist connecting with Doug's jaw. She saw the Canadian crumple to the floor amongst used condoms and dog ends.

'You've broken my damn jaw, you idiot!' he cried out, holding on to his chin while struggling to his knees.

Bill ignored him and took May by the elbow. 'May, are you all right?'

'I think so.' She was shaking. 'Bill, what are you doing here?'

'I put in for a transfer to a fighter squadron. Not been here long. Shall I take you back to the base?' he asked and she nodded.

'Here, take this.'

She felt him drape his tunic over her shoulders. When had the night turned so cold, and why couldn't she stop shivering?

'I've just got to let the band know I won't be here for the second half.'

They walked into the lobby of the NAAFI. The light seemed brutally bright to May and she shaded her eyes. Conscious now of the ripped front of her dress, she hesitated. 'I don't want to go in there, Bill,' she said and he laid a reassuring hand on her arm.

'It won't take a minute.'

'It's all right, Bill, don't worry . . . I'll just go . . .'

'Just hang on, stay there!'

He hurried off, but once he'd disappeared into the crowd of dancers, she turned to leave, eager to be out of this glare and feeling only shame that Bill should have seen her in such a horrible situation. She would just get a bus and hide herself away and hopefully never have to see either Doug or Bill again. She hurried out of the NAAFI and began walking up the gravel drive. There was a bus stop just outside the base gates, but as she walked, she drew the coat around her and realized she was still wearing Bill's RAF tunic. She stopped in the middle of the drive, hugged herself beneath the jacket, and let the tears fall. Then she heard hurried footsteps crunching on gravel behind her. Doug! She broke into a run. Of course he would not be the type to give up. But the hand on her shoulder when it came was gentle.

'It's only me,' Bill said. 'Let me take you home, May,'

They walked in silence to the bus stop and to May's relief they didn't have long to wait before the squat, unlit single-decker bus came into view. Bill shone a torch on to the bus's number. 'This one's going to Barkingside,' he said, flagging it down with his torch.

It wasn't until they were seated in the back of the bus that he spoke.

'Do you know him well?'

May blushed. 'Yes, of course I do.' She was mortified that he even considered Doug might be a stranger. 'I met him in Moreton-in-Marsh, when I went to visit Mum. She's evacuated there now.'

'He's your chap then?' he said. 'Perhaps I shouldn't have interfered, but it looked to me like you needed some help . . . was I wrong?'

'Oh no, Bill, you weren't wrong. I don't know what got into him . . .' But that wasn't exactly true, and she didn't want to lie to Bill. 'Well, I do know. In fact he's been trying it on ever since we met. I feel so embarrassed. I'm sorry, Bill.'

'You're sorry? I just hope I'll get another chance to make *him* feel sorry!' His face flushed, and his normally full lips tightened to a thin white line.

'Will you be all right getting back to your hut?' he asked, when they arrived at her base.

'Oh yes, I'm all right now. It was just a bit of a shock. Don't worry, Bill.'

The guard on duty was watching them and May didn't feel like prolonging the conversation. She took off his RAF jacket and handed it to him.

'Well, you know where I am . . . if you need me.' And he bent to kiss her on the cheek.

'Thanks, Bill,' she said. And she watched him

walk away. She wanted to touch her cheek where he'd kissed it, but the guard was still watching. So instead, she folded her arms across the torn dress with a mock shiver as though against the cold and, ducking her head, hurried past the sentry box. The night had been vile and wonderful in equal measure. She had no reason to be happy that Bill was nearby, and yet he had said, 'you know where I am, if you need me'. And knowing that, somehow helped.

She got to the hut door and realized she wasn't ready to be alone. So she made her way across the base to the stores. Pat looked up from the counter, where she was filling in a ledger. 'May! What are you doing back so early?' A look of alarm was followed by a flash of anger. 'What's he done to you?' She held up a finger. 'Let me just tell Sarge.' She disappeared behind some storage racks and was back in a few minutes. 'It's OK, I can take an early break.'

'Oh, Dobbin, I'm so sorry about the dress, it's ruined!' May said, beginning to let the tears flow, that she'd stemmed so fiercely on the journey home.

'Don't worry about the dress. Let's get you a hot cuppa – you're shaking like a leaf.'

Pat led her to a little cubby-hole of an office at the back of the stores.

'This is our hidey-hole – our sarge likes a brew-up.'

The room held a small table and a couple of chairs, a primus and a kettle, which Pat filled from a large enamel jug. Miraculously, tea and condensed milk and a couple of old jam jars appeared, and soon May was drinking mahogany-brown, intensely sweet tea that made her tongue curl. But it did the trick and soon the jar in her hand stopped trembling and she could put it to her lips without spilling any. Gradually she was able to tell Pat what had happened.

'I feel such a little fool. I thought I was so grown-up, Dob. Doing my job on the guns, not even worrying when we got strafed. My hands never shake, you know, when I'm making adjustments on the predictor. I've had bombs falling round me and never moved. I thought I was brave. Look at me!' She held her hand out, for Pat to see. It was trembling.

'You are brave!' Pat said fiercely. 'I of all people should know that . . .' And May looked up sharply, regretting now what she'd said.

'And so are you, Pat. I just think we've all got one thing that frightens us so much, we go to jelly. And this is mine. He could have done whatever he liked. I couldn't protect myself at all.' May gave a bitter laugh, 'Talk about gunner girl! All it takes is a bit of muscle and I'm done for.'

'Doug's a big bloody Canadian moose, May – of course you'd have had no chance. Don't blame yourself you couldn't fight him off. If they'd give us our own bloody guns it might be a different story, but heaven forbid they should treat us like real soldiers.'

May was touched by Pat's rallying to her defence and it made her feel less like this was her fault. But she was still ashamed of her naivety. Emmy and her mother had both tried to warn her, but she'd thought she could handle anything that came her way. Facing the dangers of being a gunner girl and defending her country hadn't in the least prepared her to defend herself.

She saw Pat looking at the front of the dress and her hand flew to close it up. 'I'll get you a new one, Dobbin.'

'Don't be daft. It's not important. Just so long as you're all right.' Pat touched May's arm. 'Look what the bastard's done to you.'

And May noticed purple weals encircling her arm like bracelets, the imprints of Doug's broad fingers plain to see. She rubbed her palm over the marks, wishing she could make both them and the memory of Doug disappear completely.

It had taken all her courage to meet him this morning and Emmy had tried to persuade her not to come. But May knew that her hard-won confidence was leaching slowly away, Doug had robbed her of something, and it wasn't her virginity – it was the new self that had been slowly growing since she'd left home. Now, she knew the braver thing to do was to confront him. She wouldn't stay cowering in the hut, while her friends fended him off for her. Before last night, she and Doug had already agreed to meet up in Barkingside at the pub where he was staying. If the weather stayed fine, they'd planned a picnic near Hainault Forest.

He was waiting for her outside the pub, looking at his watch. So he was still expecting her. She hadn't bothered to change into civvies and when he spotted her he grinned. 'Why the uniform? Don't tell me your leave's cancelled.'

She stared at him, briefly grateful that her uniform didn't include a gun.

'I'm in uniform because you tore my dress, didn't you?'

He raised his eyes, 'Oh, for God's sake, May, I only wanted a bit of fun. I could be dead tomorrow. And who was that clown who knocked me out? Have you been seeing someone else?'

She had expected at least an apology, however insincere. She hadn't imagined his anger would be directed at her. And now her own anger, which had been absent all through the long wakeful night she'd spent imagining what she'd done to encourage him, burst forth.

'Don't you dare insult me with that one! That clown, as you call him, is someone from home and he's worth ten of you! And whether I'm seeing anyone is none of your business. I'm packing you in.'

'What do you mean? We're finished?'

Doug's freckles had disappeared in the red flush spreading up from his neck. 'All because of a little fumble round the back of the NAAFI? You need to grow up, May!'

'Oh, don't worry about me. I'm grown up enough to see what type of bloke you are.'

May turned abruptly and dashed across the road, leaping on to a bus going back to base. She didn't look back.

At dinner in the canteen the girls gathered round, eager to hear what had happened. They broke into a spontaneous cheer when she told them about Doug's demise.

'Well, darling, you're well rid of him,' Bee said, 'You deserve nothing less than a gentleman!'

'Oh, she had one of them and let him slip through her fingers,' Emmy said, and May shot her a warning look.

'Who's that, her gallant rescuer of last night? We're intrigued . . .' And Bee leaned forward, elbows on the table, pushing her plate to one side.

May felt their keen eyes on her and blushed.

'That was her Bill, but he's engaged,' Emmy added.

'I can speak for myself thanks! And he's not *my* Bill . . .'

'Not at the moment he's not, but I had a letter from my sister Ethel, the one that works at Atkinson's, and she reckons his fiancée's got a roving eye . . . GIs. It's all over the factory – if you want nylons, chocolate, cigarettes, Ethel says, you only have to go to Iris.'

428

May felt her heart tighten. She couldn't share Emmy's glee.

'Oh no, poor Bill. But are you sure you've got the right person?'

If it was all over the factory, surely Peggy would have heard? But Emmy gave her a long look and nodded slowly.

'I'd get in there quick, gel, she's getting ready to give Bill the elbow.'

'Well, darling, it sounds like the poor chap might need rescuing just as much as you did,' Bee said, and the others laughed, all except Pat, who mercifully changed the subject.

'Well, now I've got you lot together, let's talk about my wedding. I want you all to come and be my guard of honour!'

They strolled back, the six of them linking arms, heading for the field behind the hut where they'd posed for their photographs yesterday. May thought of the dress. It had felt strange to go out wearing another person's clothing, the fit and the style not quite right. And perhaps that was what she'd learned with Doug: with men, as with dresses, she would in future be sure that the fit and the style were hers. And so any talk of Bill would have to be quashed; a romance with him would surely be like wearing someone else's clothes.

They sat on the grass outside the hut, continuing their discussions about Pat's wedding. She was planning to have the ceremony at the village church on the hill above Moreton-in-Marsh.

'Has your mum finished the cake?' Pat wanted to know. For May's mother had spent weeks saving up the major's and her own rations of dried fruit and sugar.

'She's finished it, but there's only enough ingredients for one tier. Mum's hiring a cardboard cake from the bakers and hiding the fruit cake in the bottom!'

Pat seemed happy enough with the idea. These days nobody expected layers of icing, but at least there'd be a slice of cake for everyone.

'And what about the dress?' Ruby asked. 'Are you wearing a white one?'

Pat shook her head. 'Can't get hold of the material. I've got a suit.'

But May had other ideas. 'You've got to have a proper wedding dress! Our Peggy's still got hers – you can borrow that!'

'Well, she won't be wanting that back, will she?' Emmy said. 'No happy memories there, not after he's chucked her out.'

The girls' attention was immediately diverted from the wedding to Peggy's marital problems, and May could see they expected details.

'She's had to go and live with my dad in our old house.'

'But I thought it was a ruin? Surely there's somewhere else she could go? She's about to drop the kid, after all!' Bee said.

'There's nowhere else,' May answered. 'And you're right, Em, I don't suppose she will want

430

the wedding dress back, not even when Harry comes home from Africa.'

'If he comes home,' Mac said sadly, no doubt remembering her own brother who had died in North Africa, blown up along with his tank.

But their talk was interrupted as a bicycle slewed round the corner of the hut and came to a halt in front of them. The uniformed rider leaped off and wheeled the bike deliberately towards them.

'I've come to see May,' he said, as though this were the only explanation necessary, and waited, one hand gripping the handlebar.

May didn't think Bill noticed the appreciative looks that passed round the circle of seated girls, but she did. He looked good in his uniform.

'Hello, Bill.' May sprang to her feet.

'Introduce us then!' Ruby broke the silence and May introduced Bill to her friends as if they'd never heard of him, let alone been only five minutes ago in deep discussion about his love life. He let the bicycle fall to the ground and sat down on the grass next to May. If he'd been captured in enemy territory he couldn't have undergone a more thorough inquisition. The girls quizzed him on everything from his mother to his piano playing; it was of course Emmy who brought up the subject of his love life.

'Have you got a sweetheart?' she asked with a smile and May stiffened, her hands clenching tufts of grass, praying that nothing would be said to betray her.

Bill laughed good-naturedly at the question. 'I'm engaged to a girl back in Bermondsey. Her name's Iris.'

'Oh, Iris what?' Emmy said. 'I might know her. Where does she work?'

May was desperate to change the subject, but to jump in now would be too obvious.

'Iris Bostle, she's at Atkinson's.'

'Oh! I know her now, yes, our Ethel works with her?'

Bill seemed delighted at the coincidence and May was staring fixedly at Emmy, her heart thudding and her glare, she hoped, blistering. If she said anything to Bill, May would never forgive her. It was at this moment that Bill chose to share the gift he'd brought with him. He got up and drew from his saddlebag a carefully wrapped flat package.

'I brought this for May, but she won't mind sharing, will you?' He smiled as he peeled back the wrapping to reveal a large box of chocolates. There were gasps and the girls dived forward to inspect the contents, which might as well have contained gold bars, they were so precious.

'Oh thanks, Bill, but I can't take these! There's two months' rations worth there,' May said.

'No, he's got them from Iris,' Emmy said excitedly, and May saw Bill's face freeze.

'No,' he said uncertainly. 'They're out of my own points. What makes you think they're from Iris?'

The other girls had gone quiet and the box of chocolates sat untouched, until Emmy retrieved the situation. 'Oh, it's only that our Ethel said they had some going round the factory . . . under the counter. She said they was almost sick of the stuff, they got so much.'

May thought that was a detail too far as no one in the sweet-starved world could get too much chocolate, in her opinion.

Bill nodded his head, seemingly satisfied, and passed round the box. The girls took the chocolates with exaggerated delight, but May could see pity in their eyes and her heart went out to Bill. To be so open and generous-hearted and to be so in the dark – he didn't deserve to be in such a position. But the truth could not come from her.

She walked back to the gates with him when the time came for him to leave.

'Thanks for coming, Bill, it was kind,' she said, when her friends were out of earshot.

'I was worried about you. Have you heard from him?'

There was a moment's silence as she wondered how much to tell him. 'I saw him this morning, packed him in.'

'Thank God.' Bill let out a breath. 'You deserve better, May.'

May thought silently, *and so do you.*

CHAPTER 24

'I'M LOOKING FOR AN ANGEL'

Early Summer 1942

May began to live her life from one Saturday night to the next – not that she would admit to going to the dances for the sole purpose of seeing Bill. She went with her pals, danced with whoever asked her, and in the intervals she talked to Bill.

Most Saturdays he was there, playing the piano in the RAF band, unless he was on night duty, and on those occasions the world seemed leached of colour. It was the difference between watching a film in vibrant Technicolor or grainy black and white. Tonight the tones were definitely grey, the piano was empty and, though she would have a good time with the girls, her disappointment was too strong to conceal.

'Looks like he's on duty again,' Pat whispered, as they slipped out of their coats and circled the edges of the dancers.

'He wasn't due to be,' May said, scanning the room in case he'd arrived late. Then out of the corner of her eye she spotted him, hurrying in from backstage. Suddenly there was colour in the room, the WAAF singer was sheathed in emerald satin, the bunting around the room was sky blue and ivory, the stage curtains shimmering gold. The band was already in full swing and she saw the conductor raise his eyes as Bill took his seat at the piano. May thought he looked flustered, but he quickly picked up his place in the number – which didn't surprise her as it was his old favourite, 'I'll String Along With You'.

The WAAF in glamorous mufti sang along with the band:

You may not be an angel, 'cause angels are so few
But until the day that one comes along, I'll
string along with you
I'm looking for an angel, to sing my love song to
And until the day that one comes along, I'll sing
my song to you.

May sat out the song, preferring to listen, and just as it came to an end she caught Bill's eye. He attempted a smile, but something was wrong. He looked miserable. His eyes, normally a deep-sea blue, had turned cloudy, and when the interval came she was glad when he came straight to her.

'What's the matter?' she asked abruptly. It was the way she'd got used to talking to him, in their days at Garner's. Back then, with only a brief hour to spend together each day, they'd developed a shorthand way of communicating that seemed to suit them both.

'I had a phone call from Iris. I was going back home next week to see her, been saving my leave, and now she's cancelled. Says her mum's ill and she'll be busy with looking after her, so . . .'

'That's a shame, Bill, but it can't be helped. You'll just have to wait till her mum's better.' May tried to sound sympathetic, but there was no denying her heart had leaped at the idea he would be here, rather than in Bermondsey.

'Suppose so. Oh, I don't know . . . it's not the first time this has happened.' Bill rubbed at his forehead. 'Shall I get us a drink?'

May found a table and when he came back with a pint for himself and a gin and bitter lemon for her, she asked him, 'What did you mean, "it's happened before" – is her mum ill a lot?'

'No – I meant, Iris making excuses, putting me off. You know, May, I'm beginning to wonder if she's found another chap.'

May fought a powerful impulse to enlighten Bill. Perhaps knowing about his fiancée's GIs would free him from his sense of obligation, but what if he truly loved Iris? He did seem really cast down by not seeing her. Discovering the truth would devastate him. And if May truly loved him, how could she be the one to inflict such a blow?

'Well, you ought to talk to her about it.'

'How can I do that? I wouldn't insult her with the question.'

'Is asking any more of an insult than thinking it?'

Bill smiled at her over his pint glass. For the first time tonight, she could see the colour of his ocean-blue eyes. 'You never did let me get away with much, did you? I'll do it. I'll take my leave anyway, and I'll ask her straight out. Thanks for the advice, May.'

He reached across the table and squeezed her hand. May heard instruments tuning up and silently cursed them, for they signalled Bill's departure from her side. He drained his beer. 'Duty calls!' he said and she was left sitting at the table alone.

But her encounter hadn't gone unnoticed and she was immediately pulled up on to the dance floor. It was Emmy, who grabbed her hands.

'Come on, love, I'll lead. Who needs a feller?'

And before she could protest, Emmy had launched into a frenetic quickstep, punctuated with military-style orders, which left May breathless and giggling.

'Running eight!' Emmy shouted in her ear in a sergeant-major roar. 'Elevate, elevate!' she ordered, charging through the crowd of dancers, who parted, applauding in their wake. Emmy might have the ability to put her foot in her mouth on occasion, but on the dance floor her feet were like wings and by the end of the dance, May had to agree.

'You're right, Em!' she gasped, holding the stitch in her side. 'Who needs a feller?'

*　　*　　*

The next morning May was on maintenance duty at the gun site, dressed in dungarees, boots and leather jerkin, for it could be a messy job. As team leader it was her responsibility to make sure the predictor machine was ready for action, and after parade and breakfast her team assembled at the gun emplacements. They polished the black metal predictor till it shone, then, with each of the girls in their places round the machine, checked that the calibration of the dials was spot on. The accuracy of their calculations was all important, for it was the predictor that determined when the fuse on the big guns was to be lit, and a fraction of a second could be the difference between a miss and a direct hit. After they'd finished at the instrument bunker they walked thirty yards across the field to where the big guns stood in their concrete pits, pointing skyward. Here, their next job was to polish the shells and check the fuses were in working order. The guns were becoming, if not old friends, then at least tamed beasts, dangerous yet familiar. It was May and her battery's job to know their quirks and foibles, anticipate their oddities. Did they fire low or high? Were they slow to respond or quick? Each gun had its personality, likes and dislikes, and sometimes May wondered if she could ever explain to anyone not involved how much she'd learned to use her instinct in her work.

Granny Byron might understand, and would probably have been proud of her, for it was May's job to predict the future. Where would the plane be, supposing it carried on at the same height and speed, and taking into account the time it took to ram home the shells and set the fuse? When would the gun need to fire in order to hit the target? Her dial told her the exact spot, then she would shout to the gunnery sergeant: 'Fuse – one oh!' He would shout back: 'Fuse set – one oh! Target!' and she would shout: 'Fire!' But she had noticed there was always the smallest fraction of a second before she allowed herself to respond, when she would wait for an inner silence amidst the blaring gunfire. Only in that moment of still-ness would she shout: 'Fire!'

'Good work, Lance Corporal Lloyd,' the gunnery sergeant said after inspecting their work.

'Thank you, Sergeant. Permission to return to the hut.' Sometimes, if the job was done quickly and well, he would allow them time off.

'Not so quick, Lance Corporal. We've got a little surprise for you lot today.'

The words were hardly out of his mouth when the nerve-shredding screech of the klaxon alert echoed around the gun park. After a second's hesitation, she sprang forward, calling, 'A-team, action stations!' Grabbing the tin hat slung across her back, she clamped it on to her head, and hurtled back to the instrument bunker. She could hear Ruby puffing behind her, but long-legged Bee was already outstripping them.

'Bloody practices!' Emmy panted, catching her up. 'Don't we have enough of the real thing!'

They scooted to a halt at the bunker. May, leaping over the sandbags, shouted: 'Positions, everyone!' And in seconds their heads were down, peering through the eyepieces. May checked her screen, ready for the height-and-range-finder girls to call the approaching plane's position to them. Soon she heard the distinctive hum of a practice plane, trailing its billowing scarlet drogue across a cloudless sky. May always thought the pilots of these practice planes deserved a special medal, their lives in the hands of often novice ack-ack girls.

'All right, girls, let's not blow his tail off!' the sergeant ordered.

May knew her team didn't deserve the sergeant's warning, for in action they'd been responsible for more direct hits than any other in the battery.

'Bloody cheek of the man,' May heard Mac mutter. 'I'll blow *his* damn tail off.'

'Let's show him then,' May replied.

'Target!' The height and range were relayed to them as May concentrated on the moving fingers on the dial in front of her. Calculating wind speed and the plane speed, she set the fuse time.

'Fuse – three oh!' she shouted the settings to the gunnery sergeant, who relayed them to the guns. The clatter of shells being rammed home was followed by the rumble of the guns wheeling into position.

'Fuse – three oh! Set!' roared the sergeant.

And then came the instant of stillness, before

May shouted, 'Fire!' and the man between her and the guns echoed 'Fire!' too.

In unison the barrels spat flame and thunder into the air. All the girls' tin hats tilted back as they followed the shell's trajectory.

'Direct hit!' the sergeant called as the drogue disappeared from the skies.

'How's that, yer bugger!' Mac shouted, and winked at May.

After firing practice they were dismissed, but as they turned to go, the sergeant called May back.

'What was all that about?' He appeared furious. 'Have you got no respect for army property!'

Now she knew she was in for it. 'Sorry, Sarge.'

It was ironic really. May's instinct had been spot on, but in practice the idea was to approximate a direct hit without actually destroying the expensive drogue. But she was amazed to see the sergeant break into a broad smile.

'At ease, Lloyd, you've got a crack team there, smooth as knicker silk. I'm recommending you for another stripe.'

May flushed with pride. The hard-won recognition made up for all the cold nights on the gun site and all the early mornings on parade. 'Thanks, Sarge!' she said, and ran after her friends. But by the time she'd reached the edge of the field they had disappeared. Instead she came face to face with Bill, who was wheeling his bike towards her.

Her heart lurched. He looked as if someone had died. 'Have you had bad news?'

'I'm not sure,' he said. 'Can you borrow a bike?'

May gave him a puzzled look. 'Yes, I can get a bike.'

'Fancy a ride up to Hainault Forest?'

She had the afternoon off now and the day was warm. Besides, her team's triumph on the guns today, along with her promotion, had filled her with a rare and almost reckless excitement. Whether he was engaged or not, she was going cycling with Bill, and after a brief hesitation she said, 'Let's go to the depot. But I'll have to change first. I'm not going out in these dungarees!'

Back at the hut she changed quickly into slacks and a pretty blouse. After checking out a bike for herself, they were soon pedalling side by side along the straight road to Hainault Forest. It was good weather for a bicycle ride, with a strong wind behind them, which helped them up the ridge ahead, to where a line of trees edged the forest. She was enjoying the sensation of covering so much ground so effortlessly. Every now and then, as they cycled, Bill would point out a feature in the landscape, an old oak tree standing alone, or a pretty weatherboard cottage, but though she wondered what could have brought him to see her she didn't probe him about his news.

They finally stopped outside a small tea room, in a clearing deep in the forest. May's ears had been ringing from the noise of the guns this morning and, in spite of the earplugs, she sometimes wondered if she'd end up deaf. But now, in the silence of the clearing, the ringing faded and all she could hear was the rustling of leaves as the wind took hold of the trees in a swirling dance. Borne on the wind were the forest smells: leaves and bark warmed by the afternoon sun; sappy grass from a nearby meadow where ponies were grazing. The cordite stench that still clung to her hair was blown away and the world felt so fresh and clean she would have liked to join the ponies who'd decided to roll around in the grass.

They found a table outside the tea room, which was a popular one, and with tea and cake in front of them May finally asked Bill what was troubling him.

'I had a letter from Mum.' He took it from his tunic pocket. 'Here, read it.'

The letter was a short one, beginning with the usual motherly questions about his health, but quickly turning to the state of his heart. May read:

I'm sorry to be the one to tell you this, Bill, but somebody must. The fact is your Iris has been messing around with GIs over the West End. I wouldn't have mentioned it, love, if I didn't know full well it was true. It's all over Atkinson's, she's so brazen about it. I know you would have stuck by your promise to her, even though you've not seemed happy with her, son. But I'm not having you wasting your life on someone who'll do this to you. So, I'm sorry if I've spoken out of turn, but it's only because

I know your heart belongs to someone else anyway. It's not for me to say, but you only get one life, son, and it's my belief you may as well spend it with the right one.

All my love, Mum

May handed the letter back to Bill. Her mouth had gone dry and she took a gulp of tea before speaking.

'Oh, Bill, I'm sorry you've had to hear this. You must be so unhappy.'

He looked at her for a long moment. 'No, May, the strange thing is, I'm not unhappy at all. I'm relieved.'

His mother had said that Bill's heart belonged to someone else, and now the thought brought a flush to her face.

'Relieved?'

Bill caught her hand. 'Mum's always been able to see right through me, May. I showed you the letter because I wanted you to see what the person who knows me best thinks. It's the truth – all the time I've been with Iris, my heart's been some-where else . . .' His voice lowered to a whisper. 'It's been with you, May.'

May let his words sink in. Then, as if she were slowly unwrapping a longed-for present, she let him glimpse the edges of her joy. She smiled shyly. 'With me?'

His eyes alone, full of an anxious hope, were enough for her to abandon all her wary instincts, and with a surge of happiness, she leaned across the table and whispered, 'And my heart has been with you . . .'

'Oh, May, I'd kiss you right now, but . . .' Bill looked round at the other diners and May smiled at him. In spite of her overflowing heart, he knew her shy ways.

'Come on! There's something I want to show you.' He grabbed her hand and left money for the tea and cake on the table.

She asked where they were going, but he smiled and shook his head. 'It's a surprise,' he told her.

They retrieved their bikes and wheeled them further into the forest. When they were out of sight of the café, Bill stopped at a spreading tree. It was magically encircled by a perfect fairy ring of large, pale, flat-topped toadstools. She gasped. She'd never seen anything like it. The circle must have been at least twelve feet across and within it was a lawn of springy grass. Enchanted, she walked closer to examine the ring.

'Do you think the fairies live under these?' she whispered, bending down to look beneath one of the toadstools.

'I expect so,' he said, obviously pleased with her delighted reaction.

They dropped their bikes and as he led her into the charmed circle Bill caught her round the waist, and the woodland sounds were replaced by the pounding of her own heart beating against his chest. Then she looked up into his eyes, which in an instant became all the world for her.

'I've loved you for so long,' he said, and brushed her lips with his. It was the softest sensation, yet far more powerful than anything she'd experienced with Doug. It was as if every loving thought she'd ever had for Bill passed between them in that one, brief kiss. And he drew back from her, smiling. 'You love me too?' he asked. Tears of happiness caught in her throat, but he waited for her answer.

'Oh yes, Bill, always.'

Then he drew her down on to the sunlit patch of grass beneath the tree, and their kisses seemed to last forever, the only inhabitants in a magical kingdom of their own creating, where time and war had ceased to exist.

But what had seemed like an eternity lasted only an afternoon. And though she hated having to leave that charmed circle, May was the first to draw away.

'We'll have to go, Bill. I'm on duty tonight.'

He sighed. 'Me too.'

'I don't want to step outside, do you?' She stared out from the fairy ring into the wood as they sat side by side, he with his arm round her, she with her head leaning on his shoulder.

The sun was lower now, glancing through the leaf canopy, dancing its light over the flat tops of the toadstools, turning them golden.

'We don't have to leave it. We'll keep it here.' And he placed his palm first on her heart and then on his own.

That night, back at the gun emplacement, the long, fire-breathing snouts of the guns seemed like beasts of another world, massive and ponderous, having very little to do with the new world she'd entered that day, where everything felt as light and pure as angel's wings. But the dream of love confused her instinct. She miscalculated the fuse several times, and when the sergeant cursed her, she forced herself to suppress her distracting euphoria. She mentally left the forest behind. She couldn't live there forever, but tomorrow she would see Bill and, for now, that hope of heaven would have to get her through this hell of pounding guns and raining shrapnel.

In fact, the only thing that fell from the skies was their own shrapnel. They'd shot down no planes, and though it went against all her training, she was glad that no one had died at her hand that night. As they'd lain in each other's arms earlier, Bill had whispered to her that she was his angel, and she couldn't bear that those longed-for words should be overshadowed by death.

Their next meeting was at the slightly less magical Odeon in Gant's Hill. When she saw Bill waiting for her outside, handsome in his blue uniform and field cap, she wished they'd chosen a less public place for their first real date. They sat through a silly George Formby comedy, which made her laugh, but the flickering images were only the backdrop for the more compelling feeling of Bill's hand in hers. Then came a short film entitled *An Airman's Letter to His Mother*, which sent a chill through her. She hated the thought of ever receiving a last letter from Bill. Although he was ground crew – a gunner armourer not a pilot – an overseas posting with a fighter squadron was never a safe option. And she certainly didn't want to see fighter boys on the screen putting their lives in danger, however noble the intentions.

After the film, they walked through the blackout to a nearby pub. Sitting in a corner, their hands intertwined, she confessed to him how she longed to protect their love from the war. He brought her hand to his lips and smiled.

'You really do want to live in the fairy ring forever?'

And she loved him so much that she allowed herself to seem foolish in front of him, and nodded her head.

'We'll have to agree on a time and place, where we imagine ourselves both there, and no matter where we are, how far apart, we'll go there in our minds. It'll be our safe place, forever.'

May sighed, relieved that he had understood. 'All right, before we go to sleep, every night, let's meet each other there,' she said.

'And if I'm overseas, I'll have to work out the time difference. But don't worry about that – my maths is up to it!' And he laughed.

But May didn't laugh. 'You're not being posted

overseas, are you? I'm not having that, not now I've found you again!'

'I'm not going anywhere! I'm keeping my head down. I've got no stripes yet, not like a certain ATS corporal, and my sergeant always says the only sure way to get yourself a posting is by getting stripes or by getting married. And I'm not planning on getting any stripes . . . so I've got a fifty-fifty chance,' he said with a mischievous smile, which earned him a playful slap from May. 'But seriously, they need all the armourers they can get over here at the moment, so you're not to worry,' he added, squeezing her hand.

After extracting senseless promises, which she knew Bill might not be able to keep, he took her back to base, where the girls had a barrage of questions ready for her, along with the traditional mug of cocoa keeping warm for her on the potbellied stove.

In the following weeks, whenever Bill had a half-day's leave he cycled over from his base, and they would walk in whatever part of the countryside hadn't been commandeered by the army or the air force. They wandered the paths of Hainault Forest, seeking out their fairy ring and the nearby lake, where they spent the fleeting summer days cocooned in their own world. For them, the future was a country more real than the one they lived in, a place where the fields weren't zigzagged with new concrete runways, or tangled with barbed wire, and where the blue skies weren't scarred with the white trails of fighter planes or bombers.

Pat's wedding gave her a glimpse of that tomorrow. She was to be bridesmaid, and Bill was invited too. They all took the same train together to Moreton-in-Marsh and it felt like a holiday. But Bill was nervous about meeting her mother.

'What if she doesn't like me?' he asked, as the slow train chugged its way westward, stopping at stations thick with servicemen who tried to crowd into their compartment. Fortunately, all the girls had managed to get leave for the wedding, so their carriage was already full to bursting.

'Oh, I can tell you how to get on her good side!'

Bill leaned forward and was paying such close attention, she felt like one of his armourer instructors.

'Got a pen and paper, want to write it down?'

'I just want to make a good impression,' he said, his face very earnest. Then, laughing suddenly, he kissed her quickly on the cheek.

'Just give me a clue.'

'It's easy. When she gives you one of her fairy cakes – which she will – just make a bloody big fuss about how nice they are. It worked for Peggy's George every time.'

The swaying of the warm carriage made her sleepy and leaning her head on Bill's shoulder, she closed her eyes. Mention of George had set her thinking of her sister. Poor Peggy, ousted from her home, living with Dad in the ruin of the old

450

house and dreading having to send her baby to live with their mother in the country. Peggy had paid a high price for following her heart. But it was only now she had Bill that May realized what Peggy must have gone through, being married to a man she hadn't loved. And she realized that her sister had tried to warn her. She would always be grateful to Peggy, for urging her to keep looking for Bill. For as much as he had found his angel, May knew that she had now found hers.

CHAPTER 25

'ALWAYS TOGETHER, WHATEVER THE WEATHER'

Summer 1942

She had Jack's eyes, bright jewels that shone out of the darkness as Peggy leaned over the cot next to her bed.

'Are you hungry again?' she asked her daughter wearily, to be met by a small protest which Peggy knew would soon rival an air-raid siren if left unanswered. Pearl had already earned herself the same unflattering nickname of 'Moaning Minnie'. Peggy's worries about the house hadn't gone away, and she fought a constant battle to keep this little corner of the downstairs dry and warm. Though it was now summer, embers of last night's coals still burned in the grate, for they needed a fire to keep the chill damp from the walls. But with fuel getting scarcer, soon they simply wouldn't be able to keep a fire going all the time. She lifted Pearl to her breast and, as she nursed her, stroked the little cap of silky black hair she'd been born with. Harry had written that it was a family trait and that, like

452

little Jack's, soon the black hair would disappear to be replaced by pale blonde.

'I love your hair, whatever the colour,' Peggy crooned to her baby. 'And we'll have your photograph taken soon, to send to your daddy, so he can see just how beautiful you are.' The bright eyes opened wide for an instant. 'Yes, he'll be so proud of you.' She smiled at her daughter, who hiccupped loudly. Peggy patted her back till a little milky froth bubbled from her rosebud lips.

'Good girl.' She yawned, gently laying Pearl in her cot.

Tomorrow they were going to Moreton-in-Marsh. Though the constant hammering of the Blitz had passed, nothing on earth would induce her mother to return to Bermondsey. So, if Mrs Lloyd wouldn't come to see Peggy's baby, then the baby would just have to go to her. She'd even managed to persuade her father to leave guarding the house and come with them. These past months he'd protected the place like a battered guardian angel in an old tin ARP hat. But even with new windows in the downstairs rooms, the house had been open to the elements for so long that it was crumbling with damp. The upstairs floorboards were slowly rotting and if the roof wasn't repaired soon, she feared the place would be declared unfit. Then, like so many other Bermondsey families, they'd be traipsing from rest centres to temporary accommodation, with nowhere to call home.

She listened to the wind, snuffling around upstairs, wheezing its way down through cracked plaster into her room. She hated the sound, for it resembled George's laboured breathing and always managed to stir up her half-buried guilt. Sometimes, as now, the wind would bring down plaster in dusty trickles. She brushed away a gritty handful that had covered her face and turned over to check Pearl, who'd begun to cry. Peggy put out a hand to pat the baby back to sleep, but her palm closed instead over a jagged lump of ceiling plaster. She leaped up, fumbled for the lamp switch and froze. Blood stained the cot pillow, and there was a scarlet thread oozing from Pearl's forehead.

'Oh, my poor baby!' Peggy snatched Pearl from the cot. The child's face crumpled as she gulped in enough air to fuel a nerve-wrenching wail. Frantically brushing off the pinkish gravel from her baby's head, Peggy examined the cut just above her eye. She hastily dipped a handkerchief into the jug on the washstand, and dabbed at the cut. It didn't seem deep, but Pearl struggled and screamed until Peggy felt like crying herself. She was a bad mother; she'd always known she would be. Why else had it been so hard for her to have a child? It was nature's way of telling her she couldn't do it. She'd been selfish, thinking she could keep such a fragile little thing safe in a place like this. The house was a ruin, and as a mother, she was a disgrace.

Her attempts to soothe Pearl only seemed to agitate the baby more. She was standing by the washstand, hardly knowing why she had the wet cloth in her hand, aware it had something to do with the fact that her perfect child had been damaged and it was all her fault, when her pyjama-clad father burst into the room. He had taken the precaution of putting on his tin hat, though sometimes Peggy thought he might actually sleep in the thing.

'Nah then, what's all the fuss? What's the matter with Moaning Minnie now?'

Peggy held the child for him to see. 'The ceiling's come down on her!'

He peered at the baby's forehead. 'Good gawd, it's a scratch, Peg! What are you getting in such a two and eight for? Give her to me.'

Her father cradled the baby, and Peggy looked on in wonder. Her mother had told her he never picked them up as babies, in fact took no interest at all until they could speak. But now, by some magic, Pearl's screaming died away to be replaced by some small shuddering sobs. The child allowed his leathery hand to pat the wound clean, without further protest.

'There,' he said, 'right as rain now.' And planting a kiss on the child's forehead, he handed her back to Peggy.

'Babies are a lot tougher than you think, gel. I've seen 'em pulled out of the rubble after three days and they still give you a smile! I'm going back to me bed.'

Perhaps he was right, but Peggy was glad to be taking Pearl out of Bermondsey, and not just because of the dangerous old house. There was another more selfish reason for her eagerness to be going to the country: George was back. She'd heard he was frequenting his old haunts and the other day when she'd taken Pearl out in her pram he was standing outside the Raymouth Tavern, taking bets. She was on the opposite side of the road, but she knew he'd seen her and felt his hostile stare following her. She couldn't blame him. Though he might have deserved his time in prison, he didn't deserve the shame of his unfaithful wife parading another man's child in front of him.

She'd wanted to turn round, tell him she was sorry, that she hadn't meant to hurt him. But what good would that do, when the impulse was merely one of pity? It could only deepen his injured pride, so she looked straight ahead and kept on walking. But it had made her wonder about the future. With George out of her life, the early years of the war had widened her choices, and she'd found she was capable of so much more than he'd ever allowed. But now she had Pearl to consider and her life belonged to someone else again. Her choices had narrowed and if they should have to move out of the house, though she might be able to bear the gypsy life, she wouldn't want it for her child.

The tiny cottage in the grounds of the major's house was as pretty as her mother had described in her letters. Its cosy warmth was everything Southwark Park Road no longer was. She and her father looked out of place, her mother's sun-browned face contrasting starkly with their own city pallor. There was a pot of tea steaming on the table and Mrs Lloyd had just removed scones from the oven. The smell filled Peggy with a memory of coming home from school, comforted by the knowledge that her mother would always be there. When Mrs Lloyd had gone away into that grief-fuelled exile, Peggy had resigned herself to the loss. She could hardly believe it, but here was her mother again, risen from the ashes, smiling and reaching out floury hands for her grandchild. There wasn't a trace of her earlier vagueness, nor a sign of her disappointment in Peggy.

'Thank God, she's here safe and sound. Got all her toes and fingers?' Her mother counted. 'She's perfect!' And then she spotted the little gash on her forehead and had to be told the story.

She shook her head.

'You know I wouldn't mind having her here, Peg. That house is a death trap and I've told 'im.' She inclined her head towards Mr Lloyd. 'But he won't listen. I do believe he won't leave it till it's fallen down on top of him!'

Her mother looked sternly at her husband and Peggy shot a glance at her father. She knew that Mrs Lloyd was fighting a losing battle with him. But her mother's words had already stirred a creeping anxiety in herself.

'But, Mum, look at her.' Peggy leaned over the child. 'How can I leave her, she's still so tiny.'

'Well, you could stay here an'all!' her mother suggested.

'What about Dad? He'd be all on his own.'

Her father grunted. 'Don't trouble yourself about me. I'll rub along all right on me own.'

Peggy shook her head. 'You know I need to go back to work, Mum. Anyway, I'll put her in a nursery, once I've started earning a bit again.'

'A nursery? How can you shove the poor little thing into a place like that?'

'It's a nursery not a coal-hole, Mum!'

'All I'm saying is she'll be better off here, and she's got to come first now, hasn't she?'

Peggy's heart felt wrung in two, as her mother's words echoed her own self-doubt. But just then a voice came from the door.

'Who's got to come first?'

Peggy spun round. 'May!' It felt as if she'd been rescued – she'd never been more pleased to see her sister. 'Come and see your niece!'

'Oh, look at her, she's so beautiful – look at those blue eyes! Come and see her, Bill.'

Bill stood by the door of the crowded kitchen and he blushed as all eyes were turned on him.

'Let's have a hold,' May said, lifting Pearl out of Mrs Lloyd's arms.

'She looks just like little Jack! Apart from the dark hair,' Bill said innocently.

May's smile was unnaturally bright, and Peggy

saw her nudge him. But Peggy was almost relieved that the elephant in the room had made its first appearance.

'Well, I think she's the spitting image of Peggy,' May said and Bill looked puzzled.

'Harry says she'll lose that black hair, and it'll turn as fair as Jack's.' Peggy swallowed hard and waited. Mr Lloyd never talked about Pearl's father, but Peggy was determined Harry shouldn't be turned into a dirty secret. 'I've had a letter from him – he's in Africa now,' she added and there was a silence, before her mother jumped in.

'Let's go into the parlour. There's no room in here.'

As soon as they were all seated in the parlour, her mother turned to the subject of Pat's wedding, which was to take place on Saturday at the old church on the hill. After the baby was asleep, and Mr Lloyd had taken Bill off to the pub, Peggy and May walked up to the big house together, where May's ATS friends were being put up by the major. As soon as they were out of the cottage May slipped her arm through Peggy's.

'I'm sorry Bill put his foot in it about Harry, Peg! Tact's not his strong point.'

'Don't be sorry, May. It's a relief just to be able to say my Harry's name. Mum and Dad think they can ignore him. But I'm divorcing George – me and Harry's getting married when he comes home.'

Her sister's eyes widened with surprise. 'Have you told George?'

Peggy shook her head. 'Not yet, but it's going to happen, so Mum and Dad will just have to get used to it!'

'It's not been easy for them. I'm surprised they came round so quickly.'

'Well, it didn't seem quick to me!'

May squeezed her arm. 'I don't know if I could've been so brave as you.'

'Brave! Me? Don't forget I was the one under George's thumb all those years.'

'But that's what makes you brave! It's not like you was ever a rebel.'

'That's true, but you know what Nan says – sooner or later, the worm turns. And whatever people think of me, I don't care, I've got my little Pearl out of it and I would never want to be without her. But what about you and Bill? Looks like I'm not the only one's been brave!' Peggy laughed and nudged her sister, so that they teetered on the edge of the path.

'Oh, Peg, I thought I'd lost him, and when I got another chance I couldn't let him slip away again!'

'So tell me all about it. How did you get together?'

'He found out from his mum that his Iris was messing about!'

Peggy made a show of being surprised, but May it seemed wasn't fooled. 'You knew, didn't you! But why didn't you tell me?'

'Don't jaw me. I thought you'd given up on Bill and, anyway, he might not have thanked me. But in the end I did say something – to his mother.'

May nodded her head slowly. 'So that's how she knew. But you're not in trouble, Peg. Emmy heard it from her sister – it was all round Atkinson's – and she told me what was going on. But I wouldn't have breathed a word to Bill. Mrs Gilbie did it all for me.'

'Thank gawd for Mrs Gilbie! You and Bill are made for each other.'

'He's lovely,' her sister said dreamily, and Peggy recognized the faraway look in her eyes.

'Do you love him?'

May dipped her head. Her sister was quick to penetrate other people's secrets, but her own she preferred to keep safely hidden away. Peggy lifted her chin, looking into her clear eyes.

'I thought so.'

'I think he wants to get married,' May said, with a soft smile.

'Oh, May, that's wonderful. When?'

But a troubled look passed across her sister's face and she said, 'Oh, nothing's settled yet.'

As they rounded the corner, Peggy had her first sight of Angelcote House.

'Blimey, look at the size of that! Don't tell me Mum cleans it all on her own!'

'She does, but a lot of the rooms upstairs are used by the army, something hush hush. They come and go by the back entrance, so they're not much of a nuisance. Anyway, the poor old major's brassic – he can barely afford to keep the place going.'

'Don't look like it to me,' Peggy said, her gaze sweeping past the many-windowed front to the hills and fields spreading beyond the terrace wall.

'The war's not done him any favours, Peg. Since they've cut back on the racing, there's not so much call for trainers. He still keeps as many horses as he can but he's such an old softie, he'd rather feed them than himself. He'd starve if it wasn't for Mum's rabbit stew!'

Just then the owner of the house emerged, wearing his carpet slippers and a top hat. He stood on the top step, beckoning to May.

'What d'ye think, m'dear?'

Peggy wondered if he meant the hat or the slippers. But then he spotted her.

'Another gunner girl! Welcome to Angelcote House. Come in!'

He stood aside, allowing them to pass beneath the carved angel wings above the door and into the square, oak-panelled hall.

'Major, this is my sister, Peggy. She's staying with us at the cottage.'

The major shook Peggy's hand and pointed to his top hat. From behind his back he produced another. 'This one, or this?' He swapped them.

'We'll ask Pat,' May said, though Peggy couldn't see much difference.

As they followed him into the house, May whispered to Peggy, 'He likes his hats. Him and Granny Byron'd get on like a house on fire!'

Peggy laughed. He certainly had his peculiarities.

But it warmed her heart to see how at home her mother was in this new life, when that evening the major insisted they all come to dinner at the house and Mrs Lloyd took command in the basement kitchen, resurrecting the large brass cooking pans that hadn't been used in years. She commandeered the ATS girls to help, as if she were a born sergeant major. Peggy had been let off kitchen duties while she fed Pearl, but had now come in search of cutlery.

'Not in here!' her mother said, red in the face. 'In the dining room, big old oak sideboard next to the fireplace.'

Peggy looked around at the girls, who all seemed to be busy.

'You lot look organized,' she said to May, who snorted. 'That's 'cause we know how to follow bleedin' orders!' She nodded towards her mother.

'Look at me, the spud-bashing bride-to-be!' Pat laughed, turning the handle on an ancient piece of kit that May had unearthed. As she fed potatoes into the wide iron funnel, blades inside the machine magically peeled the potatoes.

'Wish we had one of those back at camp!' Mac said, as she chopped up the peeled potatoes.

'Too easy for the army!' Bee told her, carefully slicing carrots.

'Well, I'll leave you to it,' Peggy said, smiling.

She walked up the back stone stairs, trying to imagine living in a place like this. The old pile was draughtier than Southwark Park Road and probably almost as dilapidated. But the cottage was a different matter. Compared with the shattered streets of Bermondsey, it seemed the safest and cosiest of places for a child to grow up. Like a slow trickle of dust, she could feel her resistance giving way to resignation. Perhaps she would have to let Pearl go after all.

Sunshine gilded the square tower of the church and May glanced up at the clock for the third time in as many minutes. But just then she heard horses' hooves as the trap, decked out in ribbons and flowers for the occasion, came into view. Tom helped Pat down and May arranged her dress. Then, with May holding Pat's train, they passed between the gunner girls' guard of honour and into the church. Following Pat up the aisle, May had an unpleasant sense of déjà vue, for her friend was wearing Peggy's wedding dress and May the bridesmaid's dress she'd worn for her sister's wedding. Something borrowed, Pat certainly had that, but May could only hope she wouldn't inherit the same shaky marriage. May forced herself to smile. She was being ridiculous, as superstitious as her nan. She caught Bill's eye as he turned to look at her from his pew and quailed. Love had come like a sweet wave, washing away every other concern, but in the past weeks it had begun to be shot through by ripples of fear. He hadn't actually asked her yet, but she knew he wanted to marry her. His deep blue eyes on her were full of love, and she couldn't bear that one day soon they might be full of hurt and incomprehension.

The wedding party hadn't been at all what May expected. The war had broken down so many barriers, even here. She couldn't imagine such a mixed bag of people sharing in a wedding like this before the war. And no doubt it was their common cause that had cemented them. They were all, May reflected, just fighting to the death for their homes. And whether it was a brick terrace in Bermondsey, a manor house in Gloucestershire or a whole country, it was the same fight and it was always more than a matter of bricks and mortar. She knew that if Bermondsey ended up being flattened to the ground, and there was not one brick left upon another, to her it would still be home.

Outside the church, after the wedding service, Pat and Mark sat in the trap ready to be driven down to the house when, with a deliberate aim and a grin on her face, Pat threw her bouquet high in the air. May, eyesight and reflexes honed by months of predicting where a moving object would be in space if it travelled at a certain speed, automatically raised her hand, effortlessly intercepting the posy as it arced above her. Only as her fingers closed round the stems did she realize what she'd done. A cheer went up and shouts of 'Watch out, Bill, it'll be you next!' came from her friends. It was the one occasion when May couldn't rejoice at a direct hit. Bill came over to her side and kissed her, prompting another cheer. The trap jolted into motion as Pat called to her, 'Just let me know when you need Peggy's wedding dress back!'

Dear God, don't let him ask me now! May prayed, for Bill's look was one of pure adoration and if he'd got down on one knee and proposed at that moment, she doubted she would have had the strength to resist.

'Sorry, May, but can you take her?' Peggy, looking flustered, dumped the baby into her arms. 'I've got to hurry back to the big house. Mum needs help getting the grub ready.'

'I'll come!' May said hastily.

'No, you're more use looking after Minnie. Bill won't mind – you'll have to get used to all this!' Her sister smiled at Bill, and May gritted her teeth as Peggy hurried away to catch a lift back to the major's. The old boy had been beaming all day, and though he was the only member of Pat's family there, he made up for the lack with his enthusiasm. He had insisted on hosting a dinner for Pat's guests, so Mrs Lloyd's services were again needed in the kitchen.

'Looks like they've got us married off already!' Bill said, dropping into step beside her as they strolled down the hill with the other guests.

May shifted the baby in her arms. 'Oh, Bill,' she said, 'do you remember the last time we had to look after a baby?'

He laughed. 'Could I ever forget it?' He leaned in to whisper. 'It was the day I fell in love.'

'Shhh.' May shot a look behind her at the girls following them.

'They can't hear us!' Bill said, and it was true, for one of her friends, probably Emmy, had made a joke, and from the sound of the girls' hoots of laughter, echoing along the lane, it was a dirty one.

'I know you don't want to talk about it,' Bill said, suddenly serious.

'About what?'

'Us getting married.'

'Bill! I know I've never had a chap, but give me credit. A girl can't talk about *anything* till she's been asked . . .'

But the girls had caught up with them, and Ruby said, 'Emmy reckons the major's sweet on your mum! What d'ye think, May?'

May raised her eyes. 'They're too old for all that!'

But Emmy chimed in. 'I'm telling yer, we should be warning your old man! She's practically moved in.'

May smiled indulgently, letting the conversation take its course, leading her away from Bill's probing questions. At least for the moment she could avoid explaining the real reason she was reluctant to talk about marriage.

At the house the couple greeted everyone with glasses of champagne perry, made from pears gathered in the little orchard behind Angelcote House. Everyone gasped at the cake, a three-tier white froth, which they all knew was largely cardboard. But when Mrs Lloyd removed the small fruit cake from its hiding place in the lower tier, it really was a surprise.

'Is there booze in this?' Bee asked May, her mouth full.

'Mum used the last of the major's sherry to soak the dates! I don't think she asked him.'

Even though the wedding dinner contained every variant of rabbit, from potted to pie, it felt like a feast. The big dining room had been shut up for the duration and the long table covered in dust sheets, but today all the sheets were removed and the table polished till it shone. Now, standing at its head, the major struck his glass and called for order.

'Please raise your glasses. To my dearest niece, Patricia, and her new husband, Mark!'

Everyone cheered and the second toast required a top-up of the champagne perry.

'And to her good friends, the brave gunner girls of the ATS!'

This brought another resounding cheer from the rest of the guests. It wasn't long before the champagne perry was gone and May saw Mark and the other lads carrying in several crates of beer. No one asked where they'd come from, but soon the party moved to sit round the grand piano, where Bill began playing some Vera Lynn favourites. Peggy asked for 'Tomorrow is a Lovely Day'. And they all joined in the bitter-sweet song about that wonderful day, which was always coming and never seemed to arrive. But then May's mother, who'd begun to relax once she'd seen her food such a success, broke in. 'Give us some of the old songs, Bill – let's have "Poverty Street"!'

Her mother was soon leading them in a loud, rousing version. '*When you're living down in Poverty Street, nobody knocks on your door. When you're living down in Poverty Street, the folks all know you're poor.*'

Pat came over to May and sat on the arm of her chair, putting her arm round her friend. 'Never thought I'd see my uncle joining in a sing-song – listen to him!'

'*But when your bits of silver turn into gold, they'll drive away all your care. Then you'll find that everybody's knocking at your door, when you're living in Golden Square!*'

'We're slipping off now, May, dear. But I meant what I said about the wedding dress – don't keep Bill waiting too long! I'll be expecting an announcement when I get back!'

'Good luck,' May whispered. 'See you at camp next week!'

And as she watched her friend slip out, she saw a vision of herself wearing the same dress, looking as happy. But then it vanished, as Pat and Mark closed the door behind them.

Peggy spotted Pat and her new husband slipping away. Even though that wedding dress no longer had any happy associations for her, she remembered the hopes and dreams she'd had when she first married George. She'd felt so grand and grown-up, basking in her parents' approval and her friends' admiration. She'd thought she loved George and had she not met Harry she might never have known the difference. Harry had promised to marry her, but it felt as if they were married already. Sometimes, as she lay in bed at night, she thought she felt his arms round her, could feel his fingers stroking her face, could even hear him whispering her name. If the miles of separation were irrelevant, then what difference would a marriage certificate make? But she would marry, for Pearl's sake. May had told her she was brave, but it was only Harry that had made her so.

The insistent ringing of a telephone in the next room interrupted her musings. Bill had just started them on 'Dear Old Pals', when the major called him to the phone.

'For me?' Bill stood up, looking worriedly over at May, whose face clouded over.

Mrs Lloyd quickly carried on a capella. *'Dear old pals, jolly old pals, always together, whatever the weather . . .'*

Peggy tried to join in, but she could only imagine that this was bad news for Bill and the words of the song froze on her lips. Ambushed by fear, Peggy's throat constricted, for though the bombing had eased up, there were still plenty of tip-and-run raids and it only took one bomb to destroy a family. She felt herself clenching her fists, so that her nails cut into her palms. What if the Gilbies' house had been hit? The idea of little Jack under another ruin made her nauseous and, in that moment, she determined to leave Pearl here with her mother when she went home.

Bill came back after a few minutes and he went straight to May, whispering in her ear. Her sister's face went white and she looked at Peggy. '*Always together, whatever the weather . . .*' The singers grew gradually silent and Peggy's hope faded away as she saw her sister and Bill coming towards her. But it felt an agonizingly long time before they were at her side. Peggy got up.

'Is it your mum's house?' Peggy's voice rasped from her dry throat. She knew it, without being told.

'Peg, come outside a minute.'

Her sister's hand was on her elbow and the silence hung heavy in the room now. She let herself be led into the next room, her legs turning suddenly weak, so that she stumbled and Bill had to catch her other elbow. They sat her down in the major's chair near the fireplace and May got on her knees in front of Peggy. Her cheeks were wet.

'Has your mum's place been hit, Bill?' Peggy asked him again.

His face was grey and she saw the muscle on the side of his jaw clenching.

'It's little Jack, isn't it?'

May took hold of her hand as Bill drew a hand down his face.

'No, Peg, it's not Jack – it's Harry.'

'Harry? Did he come home on leave?' Peggy couldn't understand why he hadn't told her. 'What was he doing at Bill's mum's house?'

She felt May's hand grip hers more tightly. Her sister was crying and now the blood began to pound at her temples, till she thought her skull might split. 'Is it bad? Tell me!' She looked in terror, from May to Bill, who had turned away towards the fire.

'He's not come home, love. Bill's mum got a telegram today . . . Harry's been killed in action.'

Peggy heard her own scream, and then nothing. She felt herself expanding, leaving her heavy body behind her. As if made of light, she stretched herself halfway across the world, searching like a circling winged creature, looking from high up down on to the small figures far below, tanks and jeeps and streams of soldiers, but he wasn't there. Then with a jolt like an electric current she was back in her body, the pain slicing her like a knife, and the scream ripping through her brought her mother rushing to her side.

'I'm here, my darling, I'm here.' And her mother held her as tightly as she could bear, and still she wanted it to be tighter, to squeeze out the knowledge of her loss.

'Oh, Mum, oh, I can't bear it, I can't . . .'

'I know, love, I know how it hurts.' Her mother held Peggy against her breast, until she was stiff with holding herself rigid and every limb ached with grief. At one point May came in with a cup of tea and some tablets, which Peggy refused.

'They'll help you sleep, take them,' May had insisted, waiting till she swallowed the tablets.

Soon Peggy's eyelids began to close, though she fought to keep them open. She didn't want to go into the dark. But as her mother stroked her hair, she eventually gave in to the merciful blackness, where pain could no longer find her.

CHAPTER 26

'TOMORROW IS A LOVELY DAY'

Summer–Autumn 1942

The wedding party had broken up in sombre mood. May was grateful that Pat had left early enough to be spared the sad end of their day. The following morning they moved about the cottage softly, careful not to rob Peggy of any balm she might still find in sleep. Mrs Lloyd had insisted on sleeping with Peggy last night and May had helped almost carry her sister into the bedroom, where she'd allowed her mother to tuck her up like a small child.

In the early morning, as May was making breakfast for herself and Bill, her mother crept downstairs to see them off.

'How is she?' May whispered, handing her mother the cup of tea she'd just poured for Bill.

Mrs Lloyd looked hollow-eyed, all her newfound country lustre tarnished by her daughter's pain. 'Not good, love. She's broke her heart crying most of the night. It was getting light before she went back to sleep.'

'I feel so bad for her, Mum. She was so happy.

She told me she was having the baby's photo taken for Harry next week.'

Mrs Lloyd shook her head, rubbing at her face. 'I know I was against it, but she did love him, May, and now I wish I hadn't been so hard on her.'

Her mother tried to sip the tea, but instead her face creased into tears. She put the cup down and lowered her head. May, frightened that this new tragedy might send Mrs Lloyd back to her own dark place, hugged her and put her cheek against her mother's, saying firmly, 'Don't start blaming yourself, Mum. You've had your own battles, haven't you? Who better to help our Peggy get through this? Now's the time for you to be strong, for her sake. Blame's got nothing to do with it, hear me?'

Her mother patted May's cheek. 'When did you get to be the wise one? You sound like your Granny Byron. But you're right, love. I've shed my tears over Jack; now she's got to shed hers for Harry. And she won't be on her own, not if I can help it. But where's Bill? You two'd better be making a move.'

'I suppose so; don't know what the trains will be like. I'll go and make sure he's awake.'

May poured another cup of tea and sliced the bacon sandwich she'd been making for Bill. In the parlour, where he'd spent the night, he was packing his kitbag and stopped to take the tea.

'Thanks, May, I'm gasping.'

She smiled. 'You're a right old teapot, aren't you? I didn't realize it till this weekend. Well, you learn a lot about someone living in the same house, don't you?'

He leaned over the cup and kissed her. Then he went to sit on the edge of the sofa, which last night had been his bed. Finishing the sandwich, he asked softly, 'Have you seen her this morning?'

'Still asleep. I won't wake her to say goodbye.'

'Perhaps not.'

May noticed that they were both whispering, as though the tragedy of days like this could be alleviated by hushed tones and cups of tea.

'Poor Peggy. She seemed so happy yesterday, joining in with the sing-song. None of us know what tomorrow'll bring, do we?'

'No, love, nothing's certain.' She squeezed his shoulder. 'Least of all the bloody trains,' she said, trying to lighten his mood. 'Last time I was late back they put me on a charge.'

But Bill caught at her wrist and pulled her on to his lap. He kissed her, till she was gasping for breath. And when he gave into her half-hearted pleading to be let go, he said, 'I resent every minute that the army has you and I don't, do you know that? This war's stealing all our precious time together.'

'Well, darling, we'll just have to make every minute count for an hour. My sarge says I'm efficient like that.'

Normally her teasing could ease him out of any dark mood, but today he seemed immune and she had little energy for optimism herself. He tipped her off his lap and stood her on her feet. 'I love you,' he said, and shouldered his kitbag. 'Let's go then.'

Back at the base, May allowed the well-oiled machine that was her gun team to distract her. If her mind wandered to Peggy, a dark wave of sadness would engulf her and so she kept herself too busy to think. But she knew that half of her heart was still back at Moreton-in-Marsh with her sister, where Mrs Lloyd had insisted that Peggy stay, at least until she was stronger.

Not long after their subdued journey back to Essex, Bill cycled over from Chigwell to spend their half-day leave together. After a tea dance in Gant's Hill, they walked to a pub.

'They've got gin, so my mate tells me,' Bill said, knowing her weakness. 'Come on, let's go mad, all the pubs could go dry tomorrow!' They hurried along, through the damp late summer evening, splashing in puddles like schoolchildren. They hadn't had a chance to speak about Peggy so now, as May drank her gin and bitter lemon, she told him what little news she had.

'The major let Mum use his phone. She says Peggy wants to go home and take Pearl with her.'

'You don't sound sure about it.'

'Only she knows where she'll feel better, but Mum says she seems almost a bit too bright, you know what I mean?'

Bill nodded and May studied him. 'It's upset you too, hasn't it, Harry dying?'

'Yes, he was a nice bloke,' Bill said. 'It doesn't seem fair, poor sod, blown up in some god-forsaken Libyan desert, before he can even see his daughter.'

'It seems so strange, we saved his child and now he's gone and little Jack's an orphan; Pearl without a dad. It's almost like he was never here . . .'

'Except he left the children.'

'Yes, there's the children.'

Bill pulled aside the pub's blackout curtain.

'You'll get in trouble!' May warned, but he ignored her.

'I'm in the mood for breaking a few rules. Let's go for a walk. It's a nice night now – look at the moon through the clouds, there's a rainbow round it.'

May didn't believe him. But once outside, she saw he was right. Tilting her head back, she stared at a radiant moon, on a black disk of sky, fringed by gilt-edged turquoise and purple clouds.

'It's so beautiful,' she said. 'We'd have no trouble spotting a Heinkel tonight, would we?'

'Oh, May, it's all about the war, even the bloody moon,' Bill said morosely. He put his arm round her and kissed her head. 'Sorry.'

'Don't be. It's getting us all down, Bill.'

Normally he was so accepting of the way things were, the orders, the drills, the need to be far from home . . . He lumped them all under 'duty', so it was a shock to see this small vein of bitterness creeping in. They walked to a nearby park, where the railings had all been removed for salvage, and ignoring a notice which asked the public to respect opening times in spite of there being no gate in evidence, May followed Bill down to a small seat by the lake. The reflected moon, twice as bright as the real one, shone back up at them from the inky water, and May leaned against Bill as she compared the moon above to the moon below. The night smelled of damp leaves and wet grass, and it felt to May as though she couldn't take deep enough breaths to fill her lungs.

'Oh, Bill, my poor sister. I can't stop thinking about her. He was everything to her. If you'd only seen the way her face lit up when she talked about him. She risked everything for him, Bill, and now she's lost him. It's not fair.'

His arm was strong about her and he pulled her coat tight across her shoulders.

'You're getting cold, come here.' The warmth of his body, the strength of his arms, all felt like an accusation – this was everything her sister no longer had.

'I don't know how she'll get through this, and she's got the baby to look after . . .'

'She'll get through it *because* she's got the baby,' Bill said.

May nodded. 'You're right, as usual.'

Bill smiled down at her. 'I'll remember that. But, May, listen, it's made me think about us, and I know it's not the best time in the world, but you said I needed to ask you first. Well, I'm asking you now – May, will you marry me?'

She took in a deep breath. 'I want to keep you,' she whispered.

'So, is that your answer? Is it yes?'

'It's my answer.' Her voice trembled and she hugged herself against the chill and the shaking of her body. 'But it's not yes.'

'What? But why not?' He sprang away from her. 'I know you love me, May.'

His face was in shadow but his voice, trembling as much as her own, revealed his shock.

'Yes, I do love you, Bill, and that's why I won't marry you. You told me yourself that as soon as you apply to get married, you'll be flagged up on some list and get sent overseas!'

Bill had mentioned several pals landing overseas postings directly after marrying – it was like sticking your head above the parapet it seemed. This had been the root of her nagging unease about marrying Bill.

'But that could happen anyway, May – nothing's guaranteed!'

'Well, I think we should wait – till the war's over. I'd rather have a fiancé here, safe and sound, than a husband dead a thousand miles away! I don't want to end up with nothing but a telegram, like our Peggy. Can't you understand that, Bill?'

He stood up now and began pacing up and down in front of her.

'I understand, but it's precisely because of Harry that it's made me want to do this now. We're always talking about tomorrow, May. What were we singing the night Peggy found out? It's a lovely day tomorrow? Well, it's not. We're always singing about it, dreaming about it, making up stories about it. When the war is over, we say, we'll do this or that. But in this war, there *are* no tomorrows, don't you see, there's only today. Today!' His voice rose and suddenly he was on his knees in front of her. 'How many times have you said, you're so glad we found each other again? Well, how can you be sure today won't be the last time you see me? You say you don't want to lose me, but every day we're not together you're losing me, and I'm losing you. It's got to be now or never, May – it's the only way I can get through this bloody war.'

He took her hand in his and she could feel tremors of emotion passing through him to her. His expressions of love had always been so restrained, always as if he were half surprised at his own captivation, a willing but puzzled slave to his love for her. But now his passion was almost fierce and, taking her in his arms, his kisses were insistent, as if he wanted to distil all the essence of his love through normally gentle lips.

When he drew back, she saw tears shining in his eyes.

'Believe me, May, there *is* no tomorrow. Marry me now.'

And though she had promised herself she would not be dissuaded, love proved stronger than her fear and she had no strength left in her to deny him.

'Yes, Bill, I'll marry you,' she said and, enveloped in his arms, she let herself believe only in today.

Bill and May applied for permission to marry and told their friends and a few of the family their happy news. But there was one person in particular May couldn't bring herself to tell. The others were sworn to secrecy, until May felt the time was right to tell her sister. The leaves had just begun to turn gold, drifting about them like late butterflies, as they took their bike rides into the forest, snatching whatever time they could together in their time off. The tree above the fairy ring had shivered and begun to shake its golden coins into May's lap, before she decided she could put it off no longer. For though Peggy had continued her life with a brittle courage which had surprised them all, insisting on returning to Bermondsey with Pearl, May knew she was still as fragile as one of those dying leaves herself.

Even now May wondered if her sister would forgive her. Her mother had cocooned Peggy in the country for as long as she could, but within a month Peggy was back home, hardly time enough for Angelcote to work its magic. It was too soon, her mother said. But May had only had reports and she'd not seen Peggy for herself. Now she would have to, for she could only break the news face to face.

She set off on a cold autumnal morning and, with only a forty-eight-hour pass, she prayed that for once the trains would be running smoothly. It would be too cruel to turn up, tell her the good news, and then run away. But as she'd feared, a tip-and-run raid and a burst water main delayed her train, so that she didn't arrive until late afternoon when the light was already failing.

She always loved the feeling of coming home, however much it had changed. Trees still lined Southwark Park Road, planted almost two decades ago by their MP, Dr Salter, and his wife, Ada. They were familiar sentinels, now doubling up as signposts in the blackout, white rings painted round every trunk marking the way home. Their filigree of branches looked pretty tonight, she thought, as the dying sun caught their last leaves on fire. Repair crews had obviously been hard at work, for there were fields of razed rubble where jagged ruins had stood a year ago, and she noticed that some houses, once uninhabitable, had been reoccupied.

But as she approached her home, she realized something wasn't right. Flo's house was gone! So was the Harpins' house on the other side of the Lloyds. When had that happened? And how could her father have failed to tell her? Perhaps he'd got so used to bits of their world disappearing that the vanishing of their nearest neighbours no longer deserved a mention. Their house stood alone, its sides shorn up with timber and iron 's' frames bolted to Flo's bedroom walls. May could make out Flo's rose-patterned wallpaper and her fireplace, hanging precariously from the bedroom wall. It was as if a giant cheese-cutter had sliced the houses into neatly rationed pieces, leaving only their own unconsumed. May craned her neck as she walked along. At least their house had a new roof.

She felt ill at ease. Her life, so long bound up with this house, now felt set adrift. She *should* have known Flo's was gone! And she was rehearsing the scolding she would give her father, when she saw Peggy pushing Pearl's pram towards her. Her sister was leaning down over the pram handle, talking to Pearl as she walked.

'Peg!' she called, running to meet her.

But when Peggy looked up from the pram, May let out a gasp. 'Oh, Peg!' She threw her arms round her sister, who looked ten years older.

'May!' Peggy's smile creased, pale papery skin taut on her cheeks. But the over-large eyes in her shrunken face failed to smile. 'We were expecting you earlier!'

'Oh, the trains were all up the wall. Here, let me carry that.' She took a heavy shopping bag that Peggy was trying to lever out from the end of the pram. Her thin wrists looked as if they might snap under its weight.

They manoeuvred the pram into the passage and

only then did May allow herself to look under the pram hood, for the baby had looked near to tears at the sight of her.

'She's gone all shy!' Peggy explained. 'She'll get used to you again.'

'Oh, look at you, blondie! You've turned into a little angel!' May said, smiling at Pearl, who burrowed deeper into the pram.

Just then their father came into the passage. 'Hello, love! I was beginning to think I'd have to go out before you got here.' He kissed May, smiling broadly. He was already dressed in his warden's uniform. 'Here, giss me granddaughter.' He lifted Pearl, because it was clear Peggy couldn't, and gave a small shake of his head to May.

She was sad that she'd only have such a short time with her father, but there wasn't much that would prevent him from turning out every night to man the wardens' station.

He sat at the kitchen table with May, while Peggy went to feed Pearl. 'She's not eating,' he whispered.

'No one told me!'

'Well, we don't like to worry you. You've got enough to do on them guns all day and night.'

'And when were you going to tell me about Flo's? And the Harpins'?

He looked sheepish. 'Didn't like to upset you . . .'

'Well, it don't look safe, Dad.'

'Safe! 'Course it is, safe as houses!'

'Well, I hope it's safer than Flo's!'

'Did you see the new roof?' he asked.

'I did,' she said, raising her eyes. 'What's keeping it up?'

After her father had left, May went with Peggy to put her niece to bed in the newly repaired upstairs bedroom. The smoke-streaked wallpaper hadn't been changed, but there was a new ceiling and it was watertight. The only furniture was a second-hand double bed, cot and chest of drawers.

'It's better than sleeping in the front room. But I think Dad still prefers his camp bed in the kitchen. Sometimes I come down in the middle of the night and he's just collapsed on it.'

'Are you having trouble sleeping then?' May asked and Peggy gave a sharp laugh.

'Having trouble living, truth be told, love.'

May placed her hand over her sister's, which, she noticed, was trembling on the edge of the cot. Pearl gave May a wide-awake smile, lifting up her arms to be held.

'You want me now, don't you? Now it's time to go to sleep?'

Pearl blew a bubble at her and Peggy slipped a knitted bear into the cot.

'She'll be all right if we creep out.'

She switched off the light and once they were downstairs, May asked her, 'Don't you think you should have stayed with Mum?'

'No. It's too quiet there, too much time to think.

I don't need quiet, May, I need noise. Tell the truth, I can't wait to get back to work.'

'You sure you'll be strong enough? You're wasting away, love. If you're doing ten-hour days you'll need to start eating, won't you?'

Peggy brushed away the suggestion. 'Some women lose weight after a baby. I was never big. I'll be all right.'

'What about Pearl, though?'

'Oh, Nell Gilbie's offered to look after her for me. She's a good woman. I didn't ask – she just said she thought it'd be nice for Pearl to be with her brother. Don't you think that's kind of her?'

There was the same brittle smile, which showed too much bone beneath the skin, testament to every tear her sister had shed since Harry's death.

'Yes, she's a diamond,' May said, taking a deep breath. 'But, Peg, talking of the Gilbies, I've been wanting to tell you something . . . about me and Bill. We're getting married.'

'Oh, love, I'm so pleased for you!' Peggy hugged her and May's arms wrapped easily round her sister's thin frame.

'Are you pleased, really?' she asked.

But her sister's smile this time had reached her eyes, which were now shining.

'Oh yes, love, of course I am. Why? Didn't you think I would be?'

'It's early days, Peg. I wouldn't hurt you for the world.'

'I know what you're saying, but life can't come

to a stop, can it? Don't matter how much I miss him, don't matter how long you hold off getting married, you could stay a spinster all your life . . . but nothing's going to bring my Harry back.'

That night she and her sister slept in the same room they had as children, in that other life, when all they knew of war were the games of English and Germans they played in the street, re-enacting battles of a Great War, fast disappearing into history. Back then their house had felt as safe and solid as everything else in their lives. But now May lay awake, fretful, eager to get back to Bill and set a date, yet loath to leave her sister alone in her desperate bravery. Everything had a feeling of being stretched too far here: time, food, energy. Even grief had been a luxury her sister felt she couldn't afford, and it made May quail to think what might happen when Peggy could no longer hold back its rising waters.

But she had to leave, and after a brief stop at the Gilbies' to give Bill's mother a letter and a parcel of service-ration chocolate he'd been saving for them, there was just time enough for one more stop on the way to London Bridge. She got off the bus at Grange Road, and passed her old workplace, or what was left of it. The leather factory had stood with several other tanneries, corralled into a triangle of land reserved for the smelliest of Bermondsey's industries. But now they had been virtually bombed out of existence. All but one of the main buildings of Garner's had gone, and this stood on a blasted field of burned stones. From this single-storey building, business had carried gamely on, churning out thousands of military leather jerkins, perhaps one of which had kept her warm through all those cold nights on the gun park. But it was a sorry sight and, remembering how the place had once been all the life she knew, she wondered what had happened to the other hundreds of workers like herself, flung out of their predictable working lives by the bombs that had destroyed it. She felt oddly out of place and hurried on towards Dix's Place.

His scrawny wattle was bunched up over a spotless white cotton scarf and his flat, peaked cap bobbed atop a sea of foaming white hair. May stood at the door, with her mouth open.

'Hello, sprout!'

'Grandad! What are you doing here?'

'Well, blow me, not so much as a how are ya, kiss me arse, nor nothing.'

Her grandfather turned back towards the kitchen. 'Sal! Get the kittle on, we've got a visitor.'

'That's it with yer orders. If you think I'm running round after yer mates, you can go and axe my arse,' her grandmother called back.

From the passage May saw Granny Byron sitting by the fire, furiously sucking on her old clay pipe, while Troubles stood to attention wagging his tail just as furiously.

'Now don't be like that, Sal, it's yer grand-daughter.'

'Hello, Nan!'

Her grandmother's scowl turned to a smile and she jumped up, almost tripping over Troubles.

'Hello, love! I didn't know you was home. I'll put the kittle on.'

Her grandfather pulled at his choker. 'That's what I said.' Then, turning to May, he looked her up and down.

'You been out in the rain?'

May put a hand to her hair. 'What do you mean?'

'Well, you've shot up, you have. Almost as tall as me.'

'That's what happens when you don't come near nor by for years,' her grandmother said tartly.

Granny Byron had obviously not welcomed the return of her prodigal husband. She had often complained to May that there was no advantage in him at all.

'I've been busy,' he said, unperturbed by his wife's vinegary stare. 'Serving at His Majesty's pleasure . . . in the House of Lords!' He winked at May and picked up the cup his wife had slammed on the kitchen table.

'Yes, Lord Byron of Wormwood Scrubs, and I wish you'd piss off back there. But I'm not talking to you – I want to hear what me granddaughter's been up to.'

She deliberately turned her back on him, flashing her hooped earrings.

'I can't stay long – I'm only on a forty-eight. But I wanted to give you my good news. Me and Bill are getting married!'

'Oh, me darlin', come here!' Her grandmother enveloped her in a tobacco-scented hug and planted a kiss on her cheek. 'About time, now let me do your leaves.'

'Oh gawd, here comes the mumbo-jumbo. I'm off to see me bank manager.' Her grandfather pressed a ten shilling note into her hand. 'Congratulations, love, 'ere's a treat.'

Granny Byron didn't look impressed. 'I don't ask where it comes from no more.'

Her grandmother made May swish the dregs of her cup and then she bent to examine the damp brown leaves. She looked puzzled.

'I'm looking for the wedding.' She tipped the cup one way and then the other. 'Did you say you'd set a date?'

'Well, not yet. I was worried how our Peg would take it. It's so soon after Harry. That's why I came home to break it to her, but she was happy for me, Nan, really happy.'

Granny Byron sniffed and turned her sharp eyes on May. 'What have I told you about following your instincts! You shouldn't have waited, love, you've got to look after your own happiness in this world. And what harm does it do Peggy if you finds happiness? None! No harm at all. Now you get back over Essex and make your wedding plans!'

Whatever Granny Byron had seen in the leaves, it had left May with a sense of bubbling urgency and she rushed to catch the bus to the station. Someone, probably a bored child, had peeled away the edge of the green netting stuck over the bus window, which was a supposed safety measure against shattered glass. Through the little porthole she watched grey skies above Bermondsey's jagged skyline; the streets had such a battered, defeated look about them that she found herself unconsciously searching out colour. An advert for *In Which We Serve* was stuck on a hoarding erected round a flattened bomb site, and her eye was caught by the sailor giving his sweetheart a farewell kiss. Her finger scraped back a little more of the netting and, as she put her nose to the glass, she was shocked to see her grandfather standing in front of the hoarding. He was in animated conversation with George Flint. George, looking pastier than she'd ever seen him, appeared to be pinned against the poster by her grandfather's outstretched hand. George's trilby obscured the sailor, so that it looked as if he was the one being kissed. It was a ludicrous scene, yet her grandfather's face was deadly serious, and for all his years, he looked by far the more powerful of the two men. May knew that George and her grandfather had been involved in various joint ventures over the years. In fact, he'd been the one who'd introduced Peggy to George. But whether the conversation involved business or family, it was obvious George was frightened out of his wits. May sat back and sighed. Sometimes she thought Bermondsey was just too small. There was no escaping any connection and since her own exposure to the wider world, she'd come to understand that for all her love of the place there might be advantages in living somewhere else.

At London Bridge she was just in time to jump up on to the back of an army transport going to Liverpool Street, and she was back in Barkingside for teatime. In the NAAFI she found her friends eating bread pudding.

'We're playing hunt the raisin!' said Ruby. 'Here, we saved you this.'

She passed May a pale imitation of the dark, spicy bread pudding she was used to her mother making.

'Oh, May, Bill come over earlier. He told me to give you this.' Emmy handed her a bulky little envelope.

May took it and quickly tucked it into her tunic pocket.

'Ain't you opening it?' Emmy asked and May grinned.

'Nosey parker! I'm saving it.'

'Oh, all right, but I'll find out sooner or later! How was poor Peg about the wedding?'

May gave them the good news that they'd all be required to play honour guard again very soon, yet all she really wanted to do was to go somewhere quiet and read Bill's letter. But tonight was designated for kit cleaning, so it wasn't until her buttons were gleaming and her uniform pressed that she was able to turn to Bill's package. Mac had heated up a bucket of water and was making their cocoa, and May took herself off to her bunk while the others stood round the stove. Inside the packet was a sheet of the familiar RAF-issue beige paper, covered in Bill's careful handwriting. But something else was lodged in the bottom of the envelope. She shook it and a small object fell into her lap. It was a sweetheart brooch. Lots of the girls with service boyfriends had them; they had the insignia of the service and a photo of the young man in uniform. But this one was handcrafted. She held it up. It was a pair of wings, made out of clear Perspex, and inset into the middle was a heart-shaped colour photo of Bill, in RAF cap. With a half-smile on his serious face and his kind eyes, he looked nothing like a warrior. She supposed the wings must represent the RAF symbol but, on closer inspection, she saw that he had shaped them like a pair of angel's wings. For some reason, the secret gesture brought sudden stinging tears to her eyes. On the back he had inscribed: *To my angel. All my love, always, your Bill.*

She wished he was here, but the letter would have to do for now. She began reading. *Hello, darling, I hope you like your angel's wings! I got some ribbing from the boys about them, but you know what they mean, and that's all that matters . . .* There were questions about Peggy and whether she'd been able to see his parents, but May was alarmed to see she was reaching the end of the letter and his endearments had been far too few. Even though they saw each other every week, she'd got used to receiving long letters from him. Sometimes he would begin writing to her as soon as they'd said goodnight. She tried not to run ahead of herself, rolling each sentence around in her mind before moving on to the next, but a word caught her eye and a cold hand clutched at her heart. *Overseas* – someone else, please God, let him be talking about someone else. She skimmed ahead.

I'm afraid we left it too late, my darling. Someone flagged me up as A1, fit for overseas posting, and the orders have come through. It looks like we'll have to wait a while before we can marry, but believe me, May, I don't regret our decision and in my mind you're already my wife. I'm only sorry I couldn't kiss my angel goodbye. We're packing up today and I'll be on the train by the time you get back to camp tomorrow. I don't know where I'm going, May, and even if I did, couldn't tell you, but I'll write as soon as I can, darling.

She found it hard to breathe. She stared at the girls giggling over their cocoa and she wanted to shout at them to be quiet, they couldn't be happy, there was no place for laughter. Bill was gone, already on a train somewhere, he couldn't tell her where. She went back over the letter, searching for any details that would prove her wrong, searching for a mistake. How could he be already gone? They were getting married.

So, my darling May, keep your angel's wings with my picture close to your heart all the time I am away and remember our special place and time. I'll meet you in our fairy ring, every night, before you go to sleep. I'll reach out and kiss you, wherever I am, however far away, I promise . . .

And he had signed off with a row of kisses that filled the width of the page but left her heart empty and aching. She put the thin paper to her lips and smudged the crosses with her own kiss. When the bugle sounded lights out, she got into bed and imagined herself in the quiet clearing in the forest. She felt the golden leaves falling on her cheek and then Bill's lips on her own. She'd known he would come. 'Goodnight, my darling,' she whispered. 'I'll see you tomorrow.'

CHAPTER 27

LETTERS

Christmas 1942–1943

Rabbits! Here he was writing about rabbits and all she wanted were words of love. Could you bring a rabbit from Moreton-in-Marsh for my mum? he'd written. I know she'll appreciate it as she says meat is very short at the moment. May was going to Angelcote for a few days, before bringing her mother back to Bermondsey for the rest of her Christmas leave. The visit was an experiment, which if successful, May hoped would see her family reunited in Southwark Park Road once more. Her mother had been persuaded to leave her haven in the Cotswolds because Peggy needed her and Carrie Lloyd's fear of the bombs was paling in comparison to her fear of losing her daughter to the twilight world of grief.

But rabbits, how could he? It was hard, having to learn about the more annoying aspects of the man you loved through letters alone. You couldn't have a spat, pout and then make up deliciously afterwards. Bill's reserve on paper was infuriating.

But she smiled to herself as she realized they had never yet had a proper argument. Like so many other things, that would have to be postponed till he came home again. But for now, she was content to be mildly annoyed at him. She turned back to his letter: four sheets of paper covered in his blue looping handwriting. She tried not to, but was unable to resist skipping to the end. *All my love always, your own Bill,* followed by a satisfying row of crosses, covering the width of the page. It was something.

At least now she had his address and could write back to let him know how unsatisfying his letters were and what was required of him in future. He was in Morecombe, in civvie billets with a crowd of other unfortunates, all waiting for their overseas posting. And his days were spent killing time in the chilly, grey-skied seaside town. Since he'd been there he'd wandered the length of the prom countless times, roamed the town and found not much to delight him. He made light of it and she wondered how he could talk so normally, when all she could think of, day and night, was what hellhole of a foreign battlefield he was destined for. He'd never been to the flicks so often, he said, four times in as many days, and always the cheap seats of course, ha ha, and nothing like Leicester Square . . . But the NAAFI was good and the civvie billets even had sheets and . . . *Oh, Bill,* she thought, *why won't you tell me you love me? Are you too embarrassed by the censor?*

And it hurt to hear he was eager to be gone. The waiting was too hard, he said. If they had to go, best it was soon. But she thought the opposite, best if he stayed in Morecombe, best he be bored witless by the endless grey waves rippling towards the prom and the old flicks repeating in the Odeon. So when she replied, she told him that he must forget the censor, and speak to her as if it were just the two of them, in their special place, and though she loved to hear what he'd had for his dinner, he must tell her he loved her and say something sweet for every mention of rabbits for his mum.

Since Bill's departure life on the gun park had been frenetic. As corporal she'd been required to familiarize herself with the new radar system which they were putting into action on the heavy guns. It was a miracle of night-time tracking which, although it would make her job on the predictor much easier, kept them even busier on the gun emplacements through the deepening frosty nights. But at least the ceaseless activity helped to alleviate the worry of those sleet-filled days when she was getting used to being without Bill.

A letter a day, sometimes two, came with reassuring regularity and, with each one, she could feel Bill's deepening sense of loneliness matching her own. If she'd known he'd be kicking his heels in Morecombe all this time she could have asked for a day out of her upcoming

Christmas leave and gone to him. Even if it were only for an hour, at least they would have the chance of a proper goodbye. After a week of his absence she was thinking of doing just that, when a letter arrived with a different address on it. He was still in Morecombe, but not for long, he said, and any future letters must be sent to this new address. She looked at it blankly. It wasn't a place; it was a series of numbers and letters, denoting nowhere:

1429071 Ac/ GILBIE. W.
B.P.O.
ROYAL AIR FORCE
c/o A.P.O. 8250

Where was he? There was nowhere on earth or sea that she could place him and panic took her breath away, she breathed deeply and slowly, imagining the fairy ring beneath the tree, and his arms round her. She looked back to the letter and felt ashamed.

> *I know it's hard for you, my darling, but you must be a brave kid and know that all day, every day, my thoughts are with you. And I promise, wherever I am in the world, if it's at all possible I will write every day, until I am back home, God willing, in your arms again. All my love, always,*
> *Your Bill xxxxxxxxxxxxxxx*

The next day she woke to a leaden feeling around her heart. As corporal it was her duty this morning to muster the early parade and she couldn't get out of bed. Emmy came to her bedside. 'Rise and shine, Corp!' She pulled back the scratchy blanket that was covering May's head. 'Oh, love! What are you crying for?'

'I can't do it, Em, I can't be a bloody soldier today . . . Bill's on the ship, he's gone . . .' And she gulped back a sob.

She knew he'd be disappointed in her. He'd told her to be brave, and there were hundreds of women in the camp in worse situations. But today was her twenty-first birthday and she felt as old as Granny Byron this morning.

Emmy gave her a hug. 'Listen, don't come to parade. You stay there and I'll tell Sarge you've got your monthlies. All right?'

May nodded and flung the blanket back over her head. Since leaving Bermondsey, she'd only ever wanted to defend her home and help end the war. She'd never imagined that it would be love rather than the enemy that would lay her so low. In the darkness beneath the blanket she allowed hot tears to turn her face red and puffy, and even the threat of being on a charge couldn't stem the flow of her self-pity. From under her pillow she pulled out the birthday card Bill had sent her. In his letter he'd told her that the words of the card spoke his love far more eloquently than he ever could, but May disagreed. His own sweet words were always the best.

501

Soon she heard the other girls tramping back from breakfast, their boots thudding on the duckboards, Emmy's voice the loudest. 'Move your arse, Rube!' May heard her shout. 'It'll be stone bleedin' cold by the time you get there!'

A blast of cold air invaded the hut as the door banged open and her friends hurried in. They came over to her bed and Bee peeled back the covers, while the rest of them shouted 'Happy Birthday, Corp!'

May sat up, bewildered, as Ruby spread a towel over her lap and placed a covered plate on it. 'Breakfast in bed for the birthday girl!'

She removed the cover with a flourish to reveal sausage, bacon and beans, with a slice of fried bread and, most surprising of all, a real egg.

'Oh, you lot are amazing! How did you wangle this?'

'We bribed Enid in the NAAFI with Bee's chocolate ration,' Emmy said, handing May a knife and fork. 'Here's your irons. Tuck in before Sarge comes for hut inspection!'

They all sat on the bed, watching as May ate, and when Ruby's hand reached out for the fried bread, Mac slapped it away. 'Keep your paws off, greedy guts, it isn't you needs cheering up.'

'No, nor fattening up,' Bee drawled, raising an eyebrow.

'Thanks, girls, you're the best,' May said, after she'd cleaned the plate.

'And tonight you're coming with us to the dance in Barkingside, no arguments!' Emmy said.

And though she hadn't felt like living, let alone eating an hour ago, just knowing that she had friends like these, who simply wouldn't allow her to sink into despair, made it easier to face the future. She flung off the blanket, and set about barracking her bed, ready for inspection and a new day on the guns.

She caught the night train alone to Moreton-in-Marsh, Pat having travelled up earlier with Mark, who was on leave. She spent the night wrapped in her greatcoat, fur boots and grey sheepskin mittens, which she knew from their ingenious flapped design had come out of the Alaska fur factory opposite Garner's in Bermondsey. She wiggled her fingers into the fine sheepskin and blessed the girls in the factory, working treble shifts to keep the forces supplied with winter gear. There were no seats to be had, so she sat on her kitbag and jolted into an uncomfortable slumber in the unheated corridor. A pewter day was just dawning as she tumbled unsteadily off the train, but she was lucky enough to pick up an army lorry at the station, which dropped her at Bourton-on-the-Hill. Bare trees, rimed with a silent frost, lined the road and, as she mounted the hill to Angelcote House, silver steam rose from pale green fields. The silence was broken only by the scraping of her steel-tipped boots on the frosty road, and the cawing of some rooks in a black-branched tree. But then a sharp crack startled her. Gunfire! She knew the sound well, though her guns boomed rather than snapped. She peered over the hedge and saw the familiar trilby hat. The major was abroad and he already had six rabbits strung on a pole. He lifted his hat.

'For your ma!' the major said.

Bill would be pleased.

Later, that first night at the cottage, snow fell, and she woke to views of hills, piled up like white pillows on a feather bed. Ice had frozen on to the insides of the windows and she ran across the landing to Mrs Lloyd's room, jumping into bed with her.

'Are you awake?' she whispered.

'I am now.' Her mother groaned and pulled the blanket up over her shoulders.

'Mum, I was wondering, do you think you'll stay in Bermondsey?'

Her mother sighed. 'I don't know, love. Perhaps, if our Peggy's really bad.'

'Don't you want to go home?'

'It don't feel like home to me any more, May.'

But after two days in the snow-shrouded peace of the country, it was time to leave for Bermondsey. Stepping off the bus in Southwark Park Road, the contrast between the frost-encrusted, fairy-tale landscape of Angelcote and that of Bermondsey was stark. Snow had fallen on London too, but here the trees lining the streets were often truncated, broken by bombs and torn by shrapnel, their jagged snowladen arms pointed accusing fingers at the ashen sky. May led her mother in a halting progress along Southwark Park Road. She had the benefit of her army boots, but Mrs Lloyd's feet slipped continually on the packed snow and May could feel her trembling as she leaned heavily on her arm. Eventually they came in sight of their pathetically isolated house, its cracked walls buttressed with timber on either side, like some abandoned fortress. An involuntary gasp escaped her mother's lips.

'Oh, me neighbours have gone, we're all on our own!' she said, and May felt her grip tighten.

'It'll be all right, Mum, I promise.' She urged her forward. 'There's been no raids to speak of for ages, and inside the house is quite cosy again.'

This was stretching a point. The house had a roof and Peggy, before her bereavement, had taken trouble to make it more comfortable. But it wasn't the home her mother would remember.

'I just want to get in and see our Peggy.' Mrs Lloyd pulled herself upright and set her chin. 'Come on then.'

A couple of their neighbours, tottering along the icy street on their way to the shops, looked up in surprise at seeing her mother back home and, though they wanted to stop and talk, it seemed Mrs Lloyd had no energy for anything other than reaching her front door. May had already begun to wonder if it was a mistake for her to have left the haven of Angelcote.

But as soon as Mr Lloyd opened the front door

a change came over her mother. The family had gathered in the front room, including Granny Bryon and her grandfather. There was a fire in the grate and the best plush tablecloth covered the table, on which was laid what counted as a feast these days. Mr Lloyd fussed over his wife as if she were returning royalty. But as she was plied with tea and Granny Byron's mince pies, May could see her eyes darting towards the passage.

'Where's our Peg?' she asked eventually. 'Hasn't she heard us come in?'

'She's upstairs seeing to the baby,' Granny Byron explained.

'I'll go and fetch her.' May went upstairs, intending to volunteer to get Pearl to sleep, but when she crept into the bedroom her sister was standing at the window, looking down into the street, and Pearl was already slumbering peacefully in her cot.

'Hello, love, it's me. Mum's downstairs,' May said.

Peggy slowly turned to her and it was obvious she'd been crying.

May stood beside her at the window and took her hand. 'I know. You must miss him so much,' she said, thinking of her own separation from Bill. 'But Mum's really worried about you. She never would have left the major's otherwise. Come down, she's dying to see you, Peg.'

Her sister brushed a tear away. 'George offered to take me back, you know.'

'No! What did you say?'

She heard Peggy swallow. 'I told him I'd think about it.'

No wonder her sister had been crying. 'You did *what*? Surely you don't want that, do you, Peg?'

'Don't be stupid – of course I don't!' her sister snapped. 'But I haven't got much choice, have I? My wages don't keep me and Pearl, and I can't expect Dad to bail me out forever.'

'But what about Pearl?'

'He said he's willing to take her on.'

Peggy's willowy body sagged and she leaned her pale forehead against the windowpane. May tried to imagine her sister forcing herself back into that prison.

'Well, he's changed his tune. What's come over him?' May asked.

'I don't know what changed his mind.' Peggy spoke to the fat flakes of snow that had begun to fall. 'But just the thought of going back to him made me feel like I'd lost Harry all over again. Perhaps he was trying to rub my nose in it. He knows I've got nothing left.'

Her sister placed her palm against the steamy windowpane and the gesture reminded May of something. She saw her grandfather, placing the flat of his hand against George's chest, pushing him back into the Technicolor face of John Mills on that film poster.

'As a matter of fact I don't think it was George's

idea at all. I suspect someone might have leaned on him . . . literally'

'What are you talking about? Who?' Peggy stood up straight, suddenly alert.

'Grandad! Remember last time I was on leave? Well, I saw him giving George an earful. I reckon he was reminding him of his responsibilities.'

'That just makes it worse. I don't want George's pity, or Grandad's interference! I wish people'd just leave me alone.'

Peggy went to sit on the edge of the bed.

Her sister's bitterness had shocked May. 'You can't say that about everyone, Peg. You might not want to go cap in hand to George, but what would you do without Mrs Gilbie? You couldn't have gone back to work at all without her, could you?'

Peggy gave a weak smile. 'Nell Gilbie is different. She's the only one who doesn't look at me as if I'd lost me marbles. And she's good for Pearl. Sometimes I wish she was my mum.'

'Peg!'

'Well, it's true. Mum will just get into a state and we'll end up having to run round her. I bet she thinks I'm as doolally as she is herself.'

'Oh, Peg, don't say that. You of all people should know what it can do to you when you lose someone, but Mum's better now. She might not be as strong as Bill's mum, but at least she's come back to see how you are. And if you want her to go away again, then the best thing you can do is come down and put a brave face on it.'

508

May led her to the dressing table and powdered her sister's face with Atkinson's Black Tulip, then she took out a stub of red lipstick and made Peggy purse her lips, finally dabbing behind her ears with California Poppy.

'There. Atkinson's finest, you're like a walking advert. Come on, love.'

And when Peggy made her entrance, May had to give it to her: it was a star performance. Her sister looked so much the picture of groomed grit, it was like watching Greer Garson in *Mrs Miniver*.

Towards the end of the day, May took Granny Byron to the scullery on the pretext of washing up. Her grandfather had passed out on the sofa, cuddling a bottle of rum, and Mr Lloyd was playing the piano, keeping his wife entertained with some of her favourite songs.

'Did you know George offered to take Peggy back?' May whispered.

Granny Byron raised her eyes. 'I'm not surprised. It's Lord Byron in there, thinks he can turn up out the blue and put the world to rights. Frightened the life out of poor George he did, told him he'd end up tied to the bottom of a Thames barge if he didn't do the right thing and give her back her home.'

'It's made her even worse. Now she thinks she's got to go back to him!'

'Well, that's a load of old cods. She don't have

to do nothing she don't want to.' Her grandmother flicked the tea towel vigorously round the cup.

If only, May thought, *we were all so sure of ourselves as Granny Byron.*

But she said no more about it, deciding to make the most of her family being together this Christmas, simply glad to spend time with them until later that evening, when she decided she must make good her promise to Bill and visit his parents. Two rabbits and a chicken had made the journey with her from Moreton-in-Marsh and she retrieved them from the safe. The cold weather had kept them fresh, but they needed to be delivered today. Peggy looked as though her forced cheerfulness was beginning to slip, so May asked her to come too, and together they made their way through the blacked-out streets to St James's Road. Moonlight bounced off the banked snow on either side of the road, and the white hoops round the trees helped to guide their way. When they arrived at the Gilbies, there was a party in full swing. May was greeted by Bill's mum and dad as if she were already their daughter-in-law, and Peggy was enveloped in a warm embrace by Mrs Gilbie.

'You two must be frozen. Here.' Mr Gilbie handed them both a glass of sherry. 'That'll warm you up. Come and say hello to our Sammy and Albie. At least we've got two of our boys with us for Christmas.'

Poor Mr Gilbie looked mortified as he saw May's face fall. 'Sorry, love, foot-in-mouth disease, me.'

But it did May good to be around Bill's family. It made him seem closer, especially when Mrs Gilbie took her aside and they compared notes from his letters.

'My Sam's of the opinion Bill will be going to the Far East, just from reading between the lines. Our Bill's asked for some calamine lotion, and he's not very good in the sun, so he's heading for somewhere hot, we know that much.'

It was such a small thing to hold on to, and even if it was wrong, it was comforting to picture him going towards *somewhere*. Now she could at least fix him in space and time. Mrs Gilbie asked after her mother and then looked over her shoulder at Peggy, who was laughing at a story Mr Gilbie was telling about Jack.

'This business with George has really shook her. It's none of my business, but I don't think it'll do her 'apporth o' good.'

'I agree, Mrs Gilbie, but she's trying to think of the future.'

'I've told her I don't mind how long I have Pearl, she can work all the hours God sends to make up her money, and to be honest, I think it'll be the best thing she can do. Keep herself busy.'

May nodded, wishing with all her heart that hard work was enough to ease the pain of Peggy's broken heart.

'What's going to happen about Jack? Has anyone from Harry's family been in touch?'

'Only an old uncle in Camberwell, but he's got

no kids – he'd be no good looking after a toddler. Harry never talked about his wife's family. I don't think they ever got on. So, unless we hear otherwise, love, it looks like it's down to us.'

The woman smiled, as if it were the most natural thing in the world to take on the responsibility of another person's child. But May had grown to expect nothing less from the couple, whose house and hearts always seemed open to all.

May hadn't woken to a Christmas morning without a sense of loss since the first Christmas of the war, when their lives had seemed far removed from the conflict. Now it felt natural for her mind to fly straight to her brother Jack and Emmy's family and all the countless neighbours they'd lost. But most of all this Christmas, her thoughts were with Bill, who she was determined would never be on that roll call. He might be absent but he would never be lost.

Still, it was necessary to try for some festive feeling, for without it, what was the point of a Christmas at home? She might just as well have stayed on the gun site. Her father gave his customary toast to absent friends and they made a great fuss of Pearl's first Christmas. They listened to the King's Christmas broadcast on the wireless, and, when he talked about the family circle, May couldn't help feeling part of a family much bigger than their own, whose losses were every bit as poignant.

After Christmas May returned to camp. She left her mother and sister with their father, and could only hope that the New Year of 1943 would once again see them all living back together in Bermondsey for the first time in over two years. She saw the New Year in with her pals and lifted a glass at midnight to Bill, knowing that he would be doing the same, if only in his thoughts. But her hopes for her rebuilt home life were shattered when, after the long respite from attacks, an air raid shook the Surrey Docks. Peggy wrote that the thunder reached all the way to Southwark Park Road, and that the shock waves had travelled along the river so their house shook. It was all their mother needed to shatter her newfound courage, and the next day Mrs Lloyd packed up her bags and took the train back to Moreton-in-Marsh.

For May, the year was lived through letters, the things that seemed most real to her. Bill's letters came in bunches, five or six at a time, and then weeks of nothing. Sometimes they crossed and she would have to painstakingly piece them together, like a puzzle that her life depended on. It seemed imperative that she get all the small events of his largely dull daily routine in their correct order. The letter which told her that he was safely on board the troopship made her feel woozy, as if she was the one getting used to the rise and fall of the deck beneath her feet. He couldn't tell her much about the ship and nothing about its destination, the censor's signature at the bottom of the letter a discreet reminder that they were not alone. But she knew he now slept in a hammock, slung around the side of the mess deck. He sometimes had no room at a table to write and so leaned on his kitbag. He said the food was much better on board than in Morecombe. He could buy fruit and as many cheap cigarettes as he liked. And though he'd been flung out into the wide world, it seemed to May that his world had shrunk rather than expanded. Bounded by endless grey seas, his letters were a record of small domestic details, interspersed with a refrain of melancholy longing for her, which he always tried to end on a cheerful note. *I am missing you terribly, and wishing that we had married when we had the chance. But am making the best of it, at least I can write to you and I can imagine what you are doing* . . . He asked her endless questions, knowing he would not receive answers for weeks or even months, never using place names, or the words 'bombs' or 'guns', for fear of alerting the censor. *How are things with your mother, is she home yet? Are things bad at the base? Has your dad's house seen any more trouble?*, finishing off with *I will just have to trust that all is well with you* . . .

How could she possibly reply, except in kind? With as much forced good cheer as she could muster, she shot off her letters into the dark, like shells from an ack-ack gun, and there was no black box of a predictor that could tell her when or if they would reach their target. But sometimes a letter would come back, and she would smile secretly to herself for she knew she'd scored a direct hit.

My darling, he would write, *how strange, that though we are so far apart, you should have been thinking about the very thing that I have!*

What did it matter if those letters were as rare as the nights when her team downed a Heinkel bomber; it meant that she and Bill were still somehow connected and it was the deepest joy she could find.

CHAPTER 28

ABSENT

March–June 1944

Emmy burst through the hut door and slammed it shut behind her. May looked up from the service-dress jacket draped over her knees. It was kit-cleaning night and she was working polish into the tunic buttons, buffering them to a shine.

'What's the matter with you?' May asked.

'I'm right cheesed off. The buggers have gone and cancelled all our soddin' leave and I was due ten days!'

May carried on polishing. 'All leave? Are you sure?' Emmy had a habit of exaggerating.

Her friend dropped herself down on to May's bed with such a jolt that she dropped her button brush. Immediately Emmy scrabbled under the bed to retrieve it.

'Dust under here, Corp! We won't get no prizes for best-kept hut like this.' She handed May the brush. 'That's not like you.'

The truth was that May's normal obsession with smartness had waned a little over the past year.

The war had been going on far too long and she was desperate for it to be over. As the Luftwaffe stretched itself thin across the world's battlefields there had been fewer bombing raids, and the battery was as slick and well trained as it was ever going to be. With radar, their night-time successes had been phenomenal, and though the war was by no means over, she was beginning to relax in the hope that there was simply no more that the Germans could throw at her home. Sometimes she allowed herself to imagine it ended, with Bill back home, and a chance to finally begin their life. All those dreams that had faded from technicolour to grey, perhaps they could be revived again.

'I'm not kiddin' you, May. Sarge told me. All leave cancelled, in-fuckin-definitely!' Emmy bashed the iron bedstead and May dropped the button brush again.

'Oh, for gawd's sake, Em.'

'Sorry.'

May gave up on her buttons. 'I tell you what, though, Em. If that's right, then it might mean it's finally happening . . . what we've been waiting for.'

'The invasion?'

May nodded. 'And if it is, we shouldn't complain because once that happens, we might see the end of it . . . Just think, Em, what if it's over this year?'

May felt a tremor of excitement and she could see that she'd caught Emmy's imagination too. 'Oh, I'd love to see me brothers home safe . . .

and your Bill. No more food queues, no more clothes' rationing. No more raids . . .'

'No more worrying, no more missing people . . .'

Emmy smiled fondly. 'Ahh, you poor thing, you're still as love struck, ain't you? He'll come back.'

And when news about the cancelled leave got round to the rest of the girls they all agreed with May: it must mean the final push into Europe was imminent. But not long after, when a US army camp sprouted almost overnight in fields surrounding the gun site, they were certain of it. Lines of tents appeared and though well camouflaged under acres of netting, it was obvious that jeeps and tanks were massing. The other arrivals, which went some way to make up for Emmy's loss of leave, were the attendant GIs, who flocked into Barkingside and Ilford dance halls like exotic geese, laying the golden eggs of nylons, chocolates and cigarettes. Before the month was out Emmy had nabbed one of her own, Chester from Milwaukee.

It was frustrating not to be able to go home to London, to know something so huge was about to happen and not be able to share it with her family. She had always counted herself lucky with this posting, for at least when the trains were running well, she could be back in Bermondsey in a couple of hours. But now she felt as cut off as if she were back in Wales. On her last leave in Bermondsey, a few weeks before the clampdown, she'd seen for herself evidence of the invasion plans coming together, when a mysterious pall of smoke had appeared in the sky over the borough. It certainly wasn't from bombs or fires, for there'd been no raids. It had seemingly materialized out of the air itself, spewing into the sky above London Bridge and forming a persistent low hanging cloud all along the river. Her father had hinted that it was connected with his unusually long work days at the docks, though all he would say was that there had been a lot of 'extra' activity going on which had nothing to do with unloading tea chests. He was too much a stickler about careless talk to put it plainly, but May had read between the lines. He'd put his hand on the side of his nose and said, 'I think that smoke is friendly, if you see what I mean!' And then she was certain that the dark pall was a British conjuring trick, smoke and mirrors to hide the construction of the rumoured Mulberry harbours being built at the docks from the Luftwaffe spy planes.

One night in June Emmy came back from a dance in tears. Chester from Milwaukee had stood her up and the girls duly administered their tea and sympathy. But the next day May discovered the reason for Chester's desertion. She had a couple of hours off and decided to cycle up to the forest, intending to visit the fairy ring. As the tree line came into view, she passed the site of a temporary US army camp, but the fields, where rows of tents had been, were now full of empty brown square patches. She stopped: there were no ablution tents, no generators, no soldiers in evidence at all. There were no loud American voices, calling drill; instead only a blackbird's song broke the silence. The whole army camp had simply disappeared overnight and along with it all the jeeps and tanks. She got on her bike and was speeding towards Hainault Forest when she felt the tarmac begin to shake, and a deep rumbling noise caused her to brake and come skidding to a halt. Bearing down upon her was a thunderous convoy of tanks. She hopped off her bike and scooted on to the verge just as the behemoths rolled by. She felt puny beside them, but their power was palpable and filled her with hope. She couldn't tell how long she waited and watched, as the jeeps and armoured vehicles paraded in front of her, but the line seemed unending. From one open-top jeep a GI waved, then gave her the thumbs-up. Another even threw her a packet of cigarettes, which she plucked from the air, eliciting a whoop from the young soldier. She wondered if Chester was in the convoy, hoping she might catch a glimpse of him and be able to tell Emmy.

When finally all that was left of their presence was the dust rising from the edge of the road, she set off again. And in the peace of the circular clearing, beneath the freshly greened beech tree, she sent her thoughts to Bill. She knew that he was able to get news reports where he was, but she wanted him to know *now*, so in a ritual she'd confessed to no one, she sat in the clearing and whispered.

'It'll be over soon, darling. I've seen our invasion force leaving. They won't need me on the guns, they won't need you over there . . . We'll be together this Christmas, I promise.' Then she took pen and writing paper out from her saddlebag, and began to write him only the things that the censor would allow, which included neither disappearing US army tanks, nor smoke and mirrors over the Thames, nor indefinite cancelled leave.

After the jubilation of the D-Day landings had subsided, it seemed May had been right. They began to get used to the idea of the turning tide. Their talk was of nothing but what would happen to the battery now, and May wondered if they would even be needed in the ATS. Perhaps she would go back to Garner's, or what was left of it, and make shoe leather for the boys tramping all over Normandy. But then reports began to filter through that there would be reprisals for the invasion, and that a weapon which needed no eyes to steer it, no pilot to put himself in danger, and which travelled at four hundred miles an hour was coming their way.

She heard the first one, long before she saw it. Nothing like the undulating pulse of a plane engine, more like the grating cough of a motorcycle. Then she spotted it, caught in the darting searchlights that sliced the night sky, a small black torpedo shape, with a jet of flame spewing from its rear. She'd never been so frightened, not even in the Blitz. This eyeless, inhuman assailant looked like something from a Flash Gordon film. But as the searchlights foundered, and she and her team struggled to keep up with the readings being fed into the predictor, it dawned upon her. This weapon was flawed: its very inhumanity made it vulnerable. And later, after her team had been relieved and they came back to the NAAFI, trembling with fatigue and stinking of cordite, she explained to her teammates why they must not be afraid.

'It's our dream come true! I'm telling you, we can beat it!' she said, so excited she forgot to blow on the, for once, steaming cocoa and scalded her tongue.

'Tell that to the hundred that got away tonight!' Bee said, before she groaned and put her head on the table. 'Your optimism sometimes makes me tired, Corp.'

'No, listen, it stands to reason. These things are set to go at a constant speed, a constant height and on a constant target. Once we've got those fed in, we can't *help* but hit them!'

Once this had sunk in, it was as if a smile migrated round the table. Finally, all their training meant something. Now May understood why she had chosen the predictor for her speciality. It ran in her blood, for what else did Granny Byron do, when she read the leaves, but predict where in space and time a person would have to be in order to rendezvous with their fate? Now she felt she could harness all her grandmother's second sight and roll it into science. She would use it, just like any other instrument or weapon, in her efforts to defend her home. For the doodlebugs' set target was somewhere dear to her heart – they were being aimed at Tower Bridge. All of them, heading straight for Bermondsey. But first, a good few had to pass over Essex, and May was one homing pigeon who wasn't going to rest while she had a chance of knocking every last one of those merciless birds of prey out of the sky.

These were nights when May barely slept. Not since the height of the Blitz had she felt such purpose and camaraderie. Then one night, as they were tracking a doodlebug at two thousand feet, May heard the silence, deep and destructive, which always preceded their explosion. It was a sure sign that the doodlebug had run out of fuel and would even now be dropping like a stone. She couldn't understand why her team and the girls on the height finder weren't all diving for the shelter. The silence was ear-splitting; it would be scant seconds before the thing landed. She shouted a warning: 'Shelter!' And four pairs of eyes stared at her in incomprehension. 'Shelter!' she bawled again, then not waiting for them, she threw herself under the lea of the sandbags, quickly followed by the others. They had barely time to wedge themselves in before the blast hit them. These pilotless bombs would always explode above ground, sending shock waves across hundreds of yards, demolishing everything in their path, so that although the bags protected them from the full force of the blast, May and her team were upended like skittles in a bowling alley. She felt herself thrown over the concrete wall of the gun emplacement, rolling and bouncing till at last she came to rest on her back with a pain like liquid fire tearing through her arm. Screams and shouts reached her and then, through a lurid wall of flame, she saw the barrel of their gun come spinning through the air, as though it were light as matchwood. It seemed to be heading straight for her, but before it pounded into the place where her head was, a pair of hands grasped her ankles and she felt herself dragged out of its path.

When she came to, she was lying face down, her mouth full of wet clods of earth. With eyes stinging and watering from the smoke, at first she couldn't make out what or who had survived. But then she felt a stirring at her side and a voice groaned, 'You all right, May?' Emmy crawled forward on her elbows.

'Right as rain,' May croaked. 'So much for my predictor girl's dream. I didn't factor in the fuel running out . . .' Her own voice seemed to come from far away.

'Well, whatever you didn't factor in, you knew it was coming before the bleedin' thing cut out and that's what saved us. We'd have all been dead otherwise, May.'

May felt herself descending into the centre of a red mist, as she puzzled at what Emmy was saying. Surely they'd all heard the silence, hadn't they?

But it seemed they hadn't, and before she finally crawled into bed that night May earned another commendation. It was May's prompt action, the captain said, that had saved the lives of her team, and he would be recommending her for her sergeant's stripe. She drifted off to sleep, bruised but exultant, wondering if Bill would be proud of her. Tomorrow she would write and tell him all about it.

The phone call came through early next morning. She was up, mustering the parade, her bandaged burned arm not seen as serious enough to excuse her duties. With pounding heart, she raced to the duty officer's room. 'Dear God,' she prayed, 'don't let it be Bill.'

It was a voice she'd never expected: her grandfather's, broken by unhelpful tears. 'They've been blasted out. They're still under it all, gel. The side wall's fell in on 'em, they was in the kitchen.'

'Who? Who's under it all?'

A choking sigh obscured the name and she had to ask him to repeat it.

'I said it's your dad . . . and Peg. Thank gawd the baby was at Mrs Gilbie's. You'd better get yourself home.'

And though all leave was still cancelled, and

every possible body needed on the gun park, when the voice of her grandfather, cracked and broken, had said, 'You'd better get yourself home', the summons had rung more clearly than any call to arms. She ran to the captain's office and begged the clerk outside to get her in. The captain, the one who'd said she should have another stripe, listened intently as she gave her reasons for requesting compassionate leave.

Then he offered her his handkerchief.

'I'm sorry, Lloyd, but I can't grant you compassionate leave. If I did that, I'd have to give it to everyone. I've had women in this office who've lost husbands, lost parents, and I've had to say "no" to them. I simply can't make an exception for you. The order is still in force – no leave until further notice. I'm afraid this is a sacrifice you're being asked to make for your country, Corporal Lloyd. Just as important as the sacrifice of our boys in Normandy or Singapore, just as important . . .' He looked at her, not unsympathetically. 'You do know how much you're needed here, don't you?'

'But, sir, my gun took a direct hit last night. It's out of action. Surely . . .'

'You'll be needed to support the others and I don't have to remind you that every buzz bomb we stop here is one more that can't fall on innocent families like your own. Dismissed, Lloyd.'

The captain bent his head to his paperwork. She wanted to throw her extra stripe back into his understanding face; she didn't deserve it. For though she might have saved the lives of Bee, Mac, Ruby and Emmy last night, one of those doodle-bugs with Tower Bridge written on it had got through their defences and made its way unerringly to its target; the fuel had run out just before it passed over Southwark Park Road.

Knowing it was useless to plead further, she put the captain's handkerchief on the desk, saluted and marched determinedly towards the stores.

Pat ran to her from behind the counter. Taking both of May's hands in her own, she looked her fixedly in the eyes before speaking. 'Tell me what's happened.'

'Dad and Peggy – the house's been blasted and they're under it!'

'What do you need?'

'I need a pass and a travel warrant.'

It would be hours before anyone knew she was missing. She'd already been excused parade, and no one would notice her absence from breakfast. Bee was going to explain to the sergeant that she'd gone to first aid for her arm to be re-bandaged and that would take care of hut inspection. In the afternoon she was due to check fire buckets and stirrup pumps around what was left of their gun station and Emmy had promised to cover that.

She looked out of the train window at the early morning mist dispersing above the fields. Mentally urging the train to go faster, she patted the forged documents buttoned reassuringly in her top pocket. Pat hadn't faltered. She'd left May in the little brew-up room with a cup of hot sweet tea while she disappeared into the stores to find a blank book of passes and a travel warrant. She'd sat at the table beside May, carefully copying the captain's signature from an old pass of her own. Then she'd stamped it with a brand-new stamp from supplies.

'This'll get you through Barkingside and on to the train. But the MPs at Liverpool Street are mustard, so change or get off earlier, anywhere but a mainline station, all right?'

May nodded. It felt strange that for once it was Pat directing her, but as a stores woman she had access to all the documents May needed and being an army brat had picked up all the dodges for evading MPs. Pat was a ready-made escape committee, but May knew she was asking a lot of the girl.

'You'll get into trouble, Pat, once they find out.'

Pat shook her head. 'Once you get home, just destroy the passes. They won't have any evidence. But whatever you do, when you get to Bermondsey, don't stay with your family, or anywhere they can trace, because the MPs will be after you, May, as soon as they know you're missing.'

It had been Pat who'd come up with the plan for the girls to cover her absence.

'I'll fill them in, Corp, don't you worry. Just be sure it's what you want to do – it could be a court martial, you know . . .'

May's hands had trembled slightly as she took the papers from Pat. 'I'm not frightened of that, Dobbin. My place is at home now . . .'

So, thanks to Pat, she was on her way, squashed up against the window in a carriage full of RAF boys. May gave up her mental tricks; nothing could make this clattering old heap go any faster. She closed her eyes, pretending to be asleep. But persistent tears forced themselves under her lids and she had to keep brushing them away. She felt like a child, too young to understand hide-and-seek, who shuts their eyes tight, believing that alone will keep them hidden. She counted the stations until the one before Liverpool Street and then she opened her eyes. Like floodgates opening, the brimming tears fell freely and she had to blink several times to see the station sign. She hurried off the train. The plan was to change here on to the Tube and get out at Tower Bridge Station, which would be her back door into Bermondsey.

She prayed she'd only have to show the travel warrant to the ticket collector, but as soon as she stepped off the train she saw the tall figures of two MPs painstakingly checking each pass. She tried not to stare at them and tucked herself behind a huddle of rowdy sailors making their way to the barrier. They'd obviously made the most of their shore leave and though it was only nine o'clock in the morning, some still looked the worse for wear. She made sure she had the pass and travel warrant to hand, and was about to present it when one of the sailors came to her aid by vomiting over the polished boots of the first MP. As he hopped back, May skirted the groaning sailor, now doubled up and surrounded by his concerned shipmates.

She hurried out into the fresh June morning and darted straight as an arrow across the road, dodging traffic and late office workers to reach the Tower of London. This side of the river always brought back memories of a childhood trick Jack had played on her. One day her brother, seeking to test her homing pigeon instinct, had the idea of blindfolding her in Bermondsey, then leading her across Tower Bridge and removing the blindfold before running away, leaving her to get home on her own. As she was only five at the time Jack was in deep trouble when he returned home. Her parents were just about to go to the police when she arrived home herself, having navigated by a sense she couldn't name back over the bridge, keeping the Tower on her right, left down Tooley Street, following the smell of the river, the shape of roofs and the light in the sky until she fetched up at Cherry Garden Street, where they lived then. Her mother had been in tears and so had Jack, but it was the first time May knew that not everyone had this ability.

This morning the old fort looked battered but unbowed; it had taken a few hits and its soot-streaked stones were knocked about in places, but it hadn't sat there for eight hundred years to crumble for the Luftwaffe. May breathed deeply as she skirted the wide moat, now packed to the bastion walls with neat allotment squares. She looked down upon rows of fresh green leaves and tall bean sticks, with wispy tendrilled plants coiling up them. A few stooped-backed gardeners were tending the rows, in utter defiance it seemed to May of the doodlebugs, which, needing no cover of darkness, were arriving by the hundreds at all hours of the day. She hurried on round the back of the Tower, past Traitor's Gate, with the smell of salad and strawberries wafting up from the site of so many tragic entrances. To her right, the dank river smell curled up from the exposed foreshore of the river. Then, taking the steps two at a time, she mounted the stairs to the bridge, looking all the while downriver towards Southwark Park Road. In the middle of the bridge she halted, while office workers and servicemen skirted round her. Did they know, she wondered, that they were standing at the heart of the bullseye, that the Germans deliberately aimed all their venomous darts at this very spot where she was standing? She looked down through the gap between the bascules, the sun glinting off the rippling waters. Today the Thames looked gentle and suddenly she felt exposed. Though it was summer, she shivered and broke into a half trot. The sooner she was off this bridge, the better.

She pondered whether to make a detour to Guy's Hospital, for she preferred not to believe that her father and Peggy might still be covered by tons of rubble. But it wasn't certain they'd be at Guy's. No, the only place for her to go was home.

She hopped on a passing bus going up to Rotherhithe Tunnel, then ran the rest of the way to her house. She hadn't gone far before she came upon the blast destruction, which seemed to have spread out from a hit on a neighbouring street, its deadly ripple stripping trees bare of their bark, smashing through front rooms and kitchens, tossing a child's cot on to a rooftop, levelling a pub and school, flattening hundreds of houses and shops in its wake.

Ambulances and fire tenders clogged the cordoned-off road. Choking dust caught in her throat and she looked around for someone to let her through. Everyone seemed busy, so she took her place in the queue at an Incident Enquiry Point that had been set up in a caravan near the cordon. She gave her name and house number to one of the WVS volunteers, who shot her a worried look. 'Are you Peggy's sister?'

'Yes, I am.' Then May recognized the woman. 'Is it Babs? You were Peg's driver, weren't you? I remember you from the christening.'

'Yes, I gave Peggy the shawl.'

'Do you know what's happening, is it bad?'

'I'm so sorry, my dear, but your house is still cordoned off. The rescue crew's not finished, but . . .'

Bab's ashen face said more than words ever could and May swayed slightly. The woman caught her.

'I need to get down there.'

The woman turned to whisper something to the other WVS volunteer.

'Come with me, dear.'

She led May to the cordon and spoke to the Pioneer brigade sergeant who was manning it. Before she passed through, Babs hugged her. 'God bless, my dear, I'm sure you'll find her.'

Then May dashed forward into an area so thick with fine brick dust and ground glass that it seemed night had already fallen. But she could not find the spot where her house should be; there was nothing she recognized. This was impossible; she was the child who could *always* find her way home. She looked around frantically, ducking low as a small crane swung in an arc above her head.

'Miss, miss! You can't stay here, get back!' A dust-covered man paused in front of her. 'It's dangerous – that roof could go any minute.' He pointed to where a slate-pitched roof was balancing precariously on three walls of a house. One side wall had collapsed inward. The slates on the roof were new and May recognized them.

'That's my house!' she screamed at him. 'Have you got anyone out yet?'

He took her by the shoulders, pulling her away from the pile of rubble where two more of the rescue crew were tossing brick after brick over their shoulders in an attempt to uncover what was beneath.

'Not yet, love, but you're best to leave us to it . . .'

'No!' She shoved him away and ran to the side that would have been Flo's house, if it had still been standing. It was breakfast time and Dad and Peggy would have been in the back kitchen.

She called to the crew standing on the mound of debris. 'You're looking in the wrong place! Here, here's where they'll be!'

And getting on her hands and knees, she tore at bricks and hauled out bits of a splintered window frame. Coming across her mother's pewter soup ladle, tossing aside a saucepan, and digging her hands into a packet of flour, she was dimly aware of the crew joining her and she heard one man say, 'Leave her be, she knows where they are. Get the crane over here.'

She tore fingertips and fingernails, throwing the broken remnants of their home behind her like some tunnelling mole, until finally her fingers touched warmth, soft flesh instead of hard brick. She felt along the yielding shape, an arm, a shoulder. Then gently brushing away a thick covering of ashes, she revealed a face. Lashes, powdered with white dust, flickered and eyelids opened. Cloudy eyes searched her face and bloody lips parted.

'Who's that? I can't see you.' The voice was cracked and each word pronounced with great effort.

'It's me, Dad, May.'

He attempted a smile. 'Is it my May? I never expected you home . . .'

And cupping his battered face in her torn hands, she said, 'Where else would I be, Dad? What sort of bird am I?'

CHAPTER 29

MISSING

June–October 1944

The sound was annoying, a persistent drip, drip, drip. Dad really should have got round to fixing that blasted tap by now. It had been dripping like that ever since the awful Christmas in 1941. He didn't need a bloody repair crew for a tap, that was for sure. She'd better get up, but she was so tired. Some people complained about treble shifts, but she preferred it – night times were the worst. What was the point of staying awake all night tormenting herself, thinking about Harry? So she'd volunteered for another all-nighter at the factory. Thank God for Nell Gilbie, but the poor woman needed a respite. She ought to collect the baby, but oh, she was tired. Just another five minutes. No, sod it, she couldn't lie in this bed a moment longer. She tried to open her eyes, but they were stuck fast, heavy as lead. She pulled her slumbering consciousness to the surface, only to have it sink back again. The bed was so warm, so wet . . . Don't be stupid, Peggy. Now with a monumental effort, as though she were lifting a ton weight, she opened her eyes. Blackness surrounded her, not a chink of light sneaking in through the blackout curtains. That's having an ARP for a dad. She blinked and went to throw off the covers, but they were wet. The dripping of the tap resolved itself into a pulse. How strange, it was dripping in time with her heartbeat, and she could even feel her heart, throbbing against the eider-down. But the cover was heavy, pushing down on her chest, compelling a sleep she never wanted to leave. She clenched and then unclenched her fist, feeling it wet and sticky, and from her finger-tips came a steady drip, drip in time with the tap. And only now did she understand. It wasn't water at all, it was her own lifeblood, drop by drop, draining away. And it wasn't her quilt cover pressing against her heart, but a wooden board. The table? Yes, she hadn't been in bed at all, she'd been sitting at the kitchen table, pouring tea for Dad.

Had she left the gas on? It smelled like it. She'd better get up and check, but she couldn't move, not a muscle. And then she remembered what had happened and a scream ripped from Peggy's throat.

It was a muffled, strangulated cry, rising in strength and pitch, till it tore through May's heart.

'Over here!' she called to the nearest crew-member. 'I've found my dad!'

She stood up, and while two of the crew set

about uncovering her father she scrambled to the place where she'd heard the scream. It was a small mountain. Almost the whole side wall had tumbled into a cone on top of where the kitchen had been. She pulled aside another crewman. 'I think my sister's under this lot.'

The man wiped grit from his eyes and rubbed his blackened face. He pointed to Flo's old cast-iron fire surround, which was perched on top of the mound, and then the great beams which had been acting as props to keep the side wall up. 'This lot'll take some shifting. Hang on, love. Swing that crane over here!' he shouted, then scrambled back over the brick and stone-strewn ruin to direct the driver.

But she couldn't wait. She heaved at the fire surround. It moved an inch. 'Hang on, Peggy, I'm coming!' she screamed at the ruined stones of what had once been her home. 'Stay with me, Peggy! I'm here!'

Tears were blinding her as she strained at the black lead grate, then bracing her feet against the massive beam, she inched the fireplace down the slope, pausing only to brush the stinging tears away. With the grate out of the way, she began scrabbling at the hundreds of red bricks, shoving and tossing them till she had the beginnings of a tunnel. She was aware of more crewmen surrounding her and the crane being lowered, hooked around the beam, lifted up. But as the beam rose into the air, a pile of bricks trickled down like sand in a giant hourglass and another scream tore up from beneath her feet. May darted forward.

'No! Come away, love, you can't do any more here and your dad needs you,' the crewman said. 'Let the crane do the work here, eh?'

A light was making its way through the blackout curtains. 'Put that light out!' her dad would have said. They weren't curtains, Peggy knew that. But she had no words to describe them, hard, cold, crushing. Curtains of stone, brick and cement, they were letting in chinks of light. The dark was better. In the dark, she could cease to struggle. It was almost soothing to listen to the steady dripping of her lifeblood. There was no breaking out of this cocoon anyway; she had tried before. George had kept her bound and straitjacketed, just like this, and she'd thought to escape once, but no, it was useless. She closed her eyes and drifted back into the darkness.

'Peggy, stay with me! I'm here!' A voice woke her; she knew that voice.

'Harry!' She opened her eyes to the light and it blossomed out like a flower, petal by petal of radiance, and gazing from its luminous centre, a pair of bright eyes. Startling blue, just like Harry's. Then he was walking towards her, looking healthy and bronzed from the African sun, smiling, laughing, as if surprised to see her. 'What are you doing here?' he asked. 'Shouldn't you be at home, with our Pearl and Jack?'

'I know, I just wanted to see you before I go and fetch them. Will you be here when I get back?' she asked, and he took her by the shoulders, kissing her tenderly. 'I'm always here, Peggy.'

May stumbled to one side, her hands clasped in unconscious prayer, looking round to see the two crewmen easing her father out and lowering him on to the stretcher. She ran to him and grasped his hand. 'You'll be all right now, Dad.' And she felt a feeble squeeze from him in response. His eyes fluttered open. 'Peggy – is she all right?'

'Yes . . . she's fine, Dad.'

'Thank God. And what about me roof, is me new roof all right?'

'Yes, Dad, the roof's fine.'

'That's all right then. So long as you've all got a roof over your heads.'

Speaking seemed to exhaust him and he fell back on the stretcher. But as he was being put into the ambulance, he lifted his head again.

'I'm so proud of you, my little homing pigeon . . . the further you fly . . .'

But the driver had slammed the ambulance door and she never heard the rest.

'We'll take him to St Olave's, love,' the driver said, before speeding off.

She watched the ambulance weave its way, siren blaring, towards Jamaica Road and then she turned back to the house. She hadn't lied. The roof was miraculously intact. It was just everything else that

540

was ruined. The crane lifted beams and copings, the kitchen stove, as with agonizing slowness, each heavy obstacle came swinging overhead and the men formed a chain of grim efficiency, excavating, brick by brick, the tunnel to Peggy which May had begun.

'Gas!' a crewman shouted. 'Get all those people out of it!'

A Pioneer brigade sergeant plucked at her arm, pulling her further away from the house. It was only then that she noticed her grandparents. Babs must have got them through as well. Her grandfather looked ancient, and shrivelled somehow. But Granny Byron stood ramrod straight, two hands clutching her outsized handbag, holding it in front of her like Britannia's shield. Her feathered hat and black coat were dusted with ash. May went to stand between her grandparents.

'All right, love?' her grandmother asked.

'I don't know if they can reach her, Nan. She sounded so far away.'

'They'll get her out. She's got no choice but come back.' The old lady's stare was unwavering. 'It's not her time.'

May prayed her grandmother was right and silently followed every move of the repair crew, trying to interpret each shout or command.

'D'ye get away from camp all right? Did they give you compassionate?' Her grandfather's voice broke her focus.

'No, Granddad, they wouldn't give me leave.'

'You done a runner?'

She gave a brief nod and her grandfather gave a low whistle. 'Chip off the old block,' he said, putting his arm round her shoulders.

Just then a shout came from one of the rescue crew. 'Got her!'

The others gathered round, bending low, some on their knees, hands reaching out to support Peggy as she emerged, soft and vulnerable, from her chrysalis of stone.

Babs got them transport to St Olave's Hospital, where May tried to find news of her father, and after an hour's wait they were able to get the attention of a harassed-looking nurse. 'I'll take you to see him,' she said, after checking their names. The injured had been brought to a make-shift basement ward, where beds were packed together in rows of three. The nurse led them to a screened-off bed at the end of the ward, and as she pulled aside the curtain, May saw her father, lying quite still.

'I'm terribly sorry, my dear,' the nurse said.

'Oh no! Has he gone?'

'His injuries were too great, I'm afraid. He died on the way here. I'll leave you with him.'

May could feel Granny Byron holding her tightly, keeping her upright, leading her towards the bed.

'I'm sorry, Dad, I should've stayed home with you. You never wanted me to go away, did you?' She fell on to his chest, longing for one last word from him, wishing she had been at home with him and finding no comfort in her grandmother's words.

'You couldn't have done nothing if you'd been here, love. You'd have just been under the rubble with the two of them. He's at peace now,' Granny Byron said, and May wanted to shout that there was no peace for either the dead or the living, not while this war dragged on year after year, robbing them of all that was dear, all that made life worth living.

Eventually her grandparents took her arms and between the two of them half-dragged her from the ward.

Peggy had not woken up, they said. The doctor wouldn't let them see her; they would have to give it time.

As they were returning to her grandparents' flat, it struck May that her mother didn't know.

'What about Mum?' she asked her grandmother.

'Grandad'll telephone the major. You're not to worry.'

They turned the corner into Dix's Place and May saw the backs of two MPs disappearing towards the end of the buildings. May was so tired she could barely walk, let alone even think about running.

But her grandfather seemed unfazed. 'Ne' mind about them, gel. Your grandmother can deal with the police.'

'I've certainly done it often enough for you, you old villain.' She kissed May on the cheek. 'I'm sorry you can't stay with me tonight, darlin'. But you be brave and I'll see you tomorrow. He'll look after you.'

Her grandfather seemed suddenly energized. 'I might not be much of a grandad, but one thing I'm good at is keeping ten steps ahead of the Old Bill.'

'You've always been good at running and I've always been good at hiding, so we should do all right between us, eh, Grandad?'

He rubbed his thin-skinned hands together and said, 'We'll have them chasing after their arses for a few days at least. Come on.'

He steered her towards the Harris's flat. Emmy's mother took one look at them and swung the door wide open. Once inside, May let her grandfather explain.

''Course you can stay here, sweetheart. I'm so sorry to hear about your dad and Peggy. The bloody army, run you ragged and can't even give you a day off compassionate. I told you and my Emmy not to join up, didn't I?'

May didn't have the energy to argue. Her father's pale, statue-like face was all that she could see, her only consolation his last words, that he had been proud of her.

Before her grandfather left, she asked him to make sure Mrs Gilbie knew what had happened. 'And ask her if she wouldn't mind keeping Pearl, just till we know about Peggy. And do you think Mum will come home?'

'Don't you get yourself in a two and eight, me and your nan'll sort all that out. You just get yerself some kip.'

She hadn't been aware till now of her own injuries, but Mrs Harris insisted on cleaning up her ripped hands. She must have kneeled in glass, for her khaki stockings were caked with blood. Once her wounds were cleaned and bandaged, the woman put her in Emmy's bed, which she shared with Emmy's sister. In the night May woke briefly to the comfort of another body close by, though the girl snored worse than her father, making the thin walls tremble, with a noise like a coughing motorcycle – the sound of a doodlebug. As May drifted back to sleep, she heard the four-finned bomb tearing past the bed, a flash of flame spurting from its rear, and she wasn't sure if she were dreaming or if she'd simply woken to the nightmare of another day of Vengeance weapons.

This was only the first of her hiding places. In the following days her grandfather's string of boltholes was put to good use, as each night he moved her to what he called a 'fresh crib'. The first two MPs had indeed been dealt with by Granny Byron, who'd kept them talking for half an hour and then sent them off to May's Uncle Jim in Blackheath. The family saw very little of him, so May could only imagine his surprise when two MPs knocked on his door. But her grandfather assured her they would be back, so he moved her to a place she never thought to see again. Her second night was spent in the little palace on the Purbrook.

It seemed Grandad Byron had persuaded George Flint that the needs of his estranged wife's family came before his own, and though May did wonder where her brother-in-law was spending the night, she was glad to have the flat to herself. She could do without George's wheezy presence reminding her of Peggy's doomed bid for a new life.

But the little palace was looking the worse for wear since Peggy's eviction and, from the sparse, untended look of the place, George's fortunes must have taken a turn for the worse too. Next morning May realized why, when, hunting around for a clean cup in the kitchen, she came across a quantity of empty whiskey bottles. George was obviously drinking away his contraband instead of selling it on.

When a knock came on the front door, she froze. It could be George, or it could be the MPs, and she didn't want to see either. She squatted down under the sink, so that she couldn't be seen through the kitchen windows. She heard a tapping on the window. 'It's me, open up!'

She breathed a sigh of relief. It was Granny Byron and she had Mrs Lloyd with her. May put her arms round her mother, who smelled of train smoke and lavender; the hankie she was clutching must have been laid on a bag of it. As she pulled back, May saw that she had powdered her face to hide the bruised rings beneath her eyes.

'I'm so sorry, Mum.' She didn't feel she had strength to carry her mother through another swamp of grief. Her mother shook her head and said, 'He wanted to protect our home, that's why he stuck it out here. He died in the place he loved.'

Now May understood that her mother had discovered her own comfort and strength. She wouldn't fade away again.

'Oh my gawd, this is a shithole!' Granny Byron was pulling her finger across the greasy tabletop. 'And it stinks to high heaven of booze. George's gone to pieces since Peggy left him. I never could see why you liked him, Carrie,' she said to May's mother. 'He's a cold bastard. Anyway, I've brought you some civvies, May. Mrs Harris give me some of her daughter's. I think you'll be all right to come to the hospital today. I give them MPs so many addresses they don't know if they're coming or going.'

Her mother looked surprised. 'MPs?'

May took the clothes. 'Thanks, Nan. I'll get changed.'

She heard her grandmother's whispered explanation as she dressed and wondered how long she'd be able to evade capture. Long enough to bury her father? Long enough to see her sister come back to life? But her ability to predict the future seemed to have deserted her.

May had expected her mother to berate her for absconding, but there was an imperturbability about her that was quite new, as though she had surrendered to all the tides of life and now was floating wherever it took her. She had accepted everything.

'Your family comes first, May. What you fighting for if not that?' Was her mother's response when May emerged from the bedroom.

It was a shock to hear her meek mother say such a thing, and now she wondered if some of her grandparents' rebellious spirits had made their way into her conventional mother's blood after all.

But at the hospital, as the women kept vigil for hours at Peggy's bedside, Mrs Lloyd's strength finally gave way and, nearly fainting from weariness and hunger, she let Granny Byron whisk her off to a nearby café, leaving May to watch. She drew closer to the bed and took her sister's hand, willing her back into the world. And it was as if Peggy had waited to be alone with her sister, for at that moment her eyelids fluttered. She woke and smiled. 'I saw Harry, and he's all right.'

'Peggy! You saw Harry?'

Her sister nodded. 'He sent me back for the kids.' She winced and tried to sit up. 'I saw Dad too.'

May patted her hand, glad to feel its warmth and aliveness and not wanting to talk about her father.

'He told me to tell you . . . ow!' Her face creased with pain and she sank back.

'Don't try and speak, love, just rest.'

'No, he wants you to know something. He said, tell May the further you fly, the nearer you get to home.'

'Did he say that, love?' She let her tears fall on to the warm hands that she clasped in her own. 'That's so lovely, Peggy, but Dad . . .'

'I know,' Peggy said, before closing her eyes and falling into a calm sleep.

Once May had assured herself that Peggy was finally out of danger she set her mind to her own future. That night her grandfather found her another hiding place, a room above a pub in the Blue. But when he began discussing plans to get her out of London the next day, she stopped him. 'I'm going back tomorrow, Grandad.'

He stared at her incredulously. 'What d'ye want to do that for, you dozy mare?'

'Because I can't spend my life hiding away.

She walked back into the camp in Barkingside four days after leaving it and found her sergeant.

'Where the fuck have you been, Lloyd?' he said when she presented herself to him. He was in the NAAFI, enjoying a well-earned sausage sandwich and a jar of tea, the mugs having all run out.

'Home, Sarge.'

'Home, Sarge! I know you've been home – I mean where the fuck have you been?'

May realized she needed to put it another way. 'A V-1 buried my dad and sister. Dad died.'

'I'm sorry about your dad, Lloyd.' His broad flat face softened. 'Sit down.' His fat fingers pushed the jar of tea towards her. 'And drink that.'

She did as she was told. She felt calm, knowing that she had done what she needed to.

'Now listen to me, Lloyd. When I take you to the CO, you let me do the talking. You keep shtum. I need them fucking cat's eyes and that nose of yours sniffing out these bastard buzz bombs. And whatever you've got to say, the CO don't want to hear, right? Anything to do with my gunner girls, he hears from me!'

He led her first to the barrack hut to smarten herself up, then quick-marched her into the CO's office. After a minute's interview with the CO he came out, roaring at her, 'Quick march!' And as she stood before the CO, he announced: 'W271932. Acting Sergeant Lloyd. Absent without leave, sir!'

The CO turned his long face towards her. 'These charges are very serious, Lloyd. Very serious indeed. What have you to say for yourself?'

May saw the sergeant raise an eyebrow. 'Nothing, sir.'

'Exactly so, Lloyd. Nothing you can say to alleviate the gravity of the offence. I think I explained when you requested compassionate leave there were to be no exceptions and you directly disobeyed my order.'

He gave a swift look in the direction of the sergeant, who was staring over May's head.

'Your sergeant is of the opinion that you are needed in the defence against these latest weapons and so you are to be stripped of your stripes. You will forfeit two weeks' pay and in addition to your usual duties, you will be on ablution fatigues for one month. Needless to say, you will not be granted leave for the foreseeable future. Dismissed.'

'Quick march!' The sergeant hustled her out of the room before the words were out of the captain's mouth, and he didn't come to a halt until they were back at the barrack hut.

'Thanks, Sarge,' she said, wanting to hug his pigeon-chested frame, but standing to attention lest he change his mind and march her back to the CO.

'Don't thank me, Lloyd, not till after you've cleaned out the carseys. On the double!' he roared.

'Yes, Sarge!' she said, turning on her heel.

'And get yourself on post tonight, two hundred hours!'

When the girls found her she was on her knees, scrubbing the toilet-block floor, with tears streaming down her face. Emmy kneeled down and held her. She more than anyone knew that all the words in the world would make no difference to May now. But they each came and sat beside her, on the cold damp floor smelling of disinfectant and bleach, gradually coaxing the story from her, so that it was her own words that gave her the most comfort.

'At least I was there, to hear him say he was proud of me.'

In the coming months, as the V-bombs continued to roar over the south-east, those that got through the coastal barrage, through their fighter planes and through the barrage balloons had only one last hurdle between them and the civilian population: the heavy artillery batteries, like May's, that formed a ring round London. May's team, with Mac as their new Number One, would go to bed at seven in the evening, wake at one-thirty a.m. and be on post in minutes. The routine was punishing, but at least they were getting results and they had almost begun to feel hopeful that they had the doodlebugs beaten when a new threat filtered through. Some people were calling them flying gas mains because of the rash of supposed exploding gas mains all over London. The battery was told to prepare for a threat that no predictor could track and few guns could reach, weapons that travelled at the speed of sound and only announced their coming after they had arrived, so that at least you never heard the one that killed you.

Through all this, May had little news of Bill. She had not received a letter from him in months. Though she hated such long silences, she had grown used to them. Learning to love him at a distance was nothing new to her – it seemed to have been their way from the moment they met, and sometimes she wondered, if the day ever came when they could live together, would they even get along? But in the meantime she sent off her own letters, written sometimes in the early mornings, straight from the gun park, or in the evenings with a torch under the blankets, eating into her precious sleeping times. She tried to pour out all the forestalled emotion that their separation had forced upon them, wanting him to know how, if he were there, she would hold him, kiss him. Yet all she could really do was match the number of X's on the bottom of the letters to his own. Knowing Bill as she did, he would die of embarrassment to think the censor might ever read her most private thoughts about him. The delays in the mail were always explained eventually, usually caused by a move from one camp to another, or sometimes to a completely different country. The hiatus would be followed by a flurry of letters. But this had been the longest silence since he left and, because she was on constant duty except when asleep, it came as a surprise when she actually had time to count the weeks since his last letter and began to worry even more than she usually did.

Then one day in October she received a huge bundle. Seventy-six letters! They were jumbled up and she had to force herself to hold back from plunging midway into the treasure chest, so that she could arrange them in date order. Then she spent every spare minute reading them, quickly at first, then slowly, twice and three times. She never tired of reading them, embellishing each small detail in her imagination. The mention of prickly heat and the discomfort of sleeping beneath a mosquito net had her looking up remedies and issuing warnings about malaria in her next letter, which no doubt he was already only too aware of. Out of one letter slipped a small, fuzzy snapshot and at first she didn't recognize him. Although he'd told her to stop imagining him in RAF blues long ago, still the predominant image in her mind was always the dark wavy hair beneath his blue cap and belted air-force blue tunic, with its gunner armourer insignia. The young man in the photograph was so thin he hardly looked like Bill. Stripped to the waist in just a pair of khaki shorts, she could see that his skin had darkened in the baking sun. In front of a long, open-sided, palm-covered building, foot resting on an ammunition case and elbow on knee, he was leaning forward, looking intently into the camera. May knew that sometimes the fighter boys would use old film from the gun turrets in their cameras, and the resulting snaps were always grainy. Although half his face was shadowed by a tilted bush hat, he looked out at her with an expression designed, she knew, to show how much he loved her, but which revealed only a deep sadness. The face told her, more than all his words, how much he missed her.

It was still almost impossible to work out exactly where he was in the world, though there'd been long stationary periods where she could fix him. She knew that after the troopship, he'd arrived in India, with mention of rupees, annas, women in saris and char wallahs making that much obvious. He'd told her the story of the poor boy who sat on the ground outside their billet from seven in the morning till eleven at night, serving them tea and biscuits and how, one day, he'd asked the young chap what he felt about his job. *Imagine my surprise, May, when he answered me in perfect public-schoolboy English, 'Well, sir, I'm pretty browned off about it!' So I gave him a couple of rupees, poor little tyke. I tell you, May, some of the working conditions out here make Garner's seem like a picnic!*

At the Indian airfield, his daily routine seemed very like Morecombe, with long hours of boredom, waiting for orders, interspersed with trips to the nearby big town, eating in local cafés and going to the flicks, compared to which, he said, the Star in Abbey Street was a palace. Then followed a gap of many weeks, after which he wrote of a trip further into the jungle, and his most frightening experience to date. Stirrings and rustlings in the jungle had announced the appearance of a huge, dragon-like lizard, walking slowly towards him as he sat on the pole latrine. *I wasn't at my best, as you can imagine, and I couldn't have been more scared than if the enemy had come running out of the jungle at me, bayonets fixed!*

So he was near an enemy. And then she'd had to stop reading for a while, until she could trace on a map the most likely place near India he might be. With the information that there were Japs around every jungle path, and the help of another clue, the name of the local horse-drawn transport, which he'd said were gharries, she concluded that it must be on the border with Burma. The reports that had come back from there made her blood run so cold, she wished she'd never checked.

It was easier to think of the small events of his life. And she had helped herself in this at least by memorizing all his small, habitual mannerisms before he left. When he wrote his letters, he might be in a jungle hut, using an ammo box for a desk, but she knew he would be biting the end of his pen while he searched for a word, and though his tea might be served to him out of a bucket by a char wallah, he would still be blowing the surface absent-mindedly to cool it, whatever its temperature.

One of the hardest things was not having him there to talk to about her father. Of course she'd written and told him, but she would have given anything for one strong hug from Bill, to lay her head against his chest and cry for her poor brave father. But only an echo of her grief would ever reach Bill; it was just another of the precious times together that war had stolen from them.

But by now she had surfeited herself on his seventy-six letters and though the last of them had been dated three months earlier, she was content in the knowledge that at least then he'd been alive and well. So when she received more mail at the end of the week she was surprised. But the letter wasn't from Bill. It was from his father and he was sorry to tell her they'd been informed that Bill had been listed as missing.

CHAPTER 30

WINGS TO FLY

October 1944–March 1945

When Peggy had finally left St Olave's Hospital she'd felt reborn. There was nothing to harm her. She'd seen death and it had Harry's face; what was there left to fear? Though her mother begged her to go back to Moreton-in-Marsh, at least until her injuries healed, she refused to be chased out by the doodlebugs. But the truth was, she now had nowhere to live in Bermondsey. Dix's Place was barely big enough for her grandparents and Southwark Park Road had been left nothing but a roof on a shell. Nell Gilbie came to her rescue. Peggy and Pearl could take over her front room, she said, at least until somewhere more permanent could be found. Together, she and Mrs Gilbie had strained to move the woman's heavy oak table. Fashionable in the previous decade and her pride and joy, it must have contained more wood in its bulbous legs than an entire utility table. Peggy would sleep on the overstuffed sofa and Pearl had a cot bed from the Sally Army.

She was grateful for the temporary refuge, for it gave her the confidence to refuse George when he made another offer to take her back. She was walking the pram along the Blue, when he dodged out from behind the eel seller's stall. She took in a breath, shocked not only by his presence but also by his appearance. He stood in front of the eel sink, with its grey, wriggling tangle of bodies, and he seemed to be squirming himself.

'Hello, Peg.' His pallid face had a sheen of sweat on it, though it was a cold day.

'Hello, George.'

She tried to push the pram round him, but the crowd on the pavement prevented her. He stepped aside to let her through and began walking beside her. Wondering what he was up to, she was shocked when he blurted out, 'I'm sorry about your dad and the house . . . and, well, I think you should come back to me . . .' Peggy stopped the pram and looked at him. He licked his lips and wiped the sweat from his face. He looked worse than she'd ever seen him.

'Is this Grandad's idea?'

'No!' He smiled nervously and dug his hands deep into his overcoat, which she noticed was greasy around the collar. 'Why would it be his idea?'

She wasn't fooled. She'd found out what her grandfather had over him. Somehow he'd acquired George's book, the one listing dates, names and payments received from all those healthy young men who hadn't fancied fighting for King and country, the ones that George had stood in for at the draft office. It seemed the prospect of having Peggy back under his roof was far more appealing to George than a charge of treason.

'I just think we should put the past behind us,' he went on, 'and let's face it, Peg, you ain't got much going for you, not since that feller of your'n died, have you?'

'You don't look well, George,' she said, quickening her steps. He couldn't keep up with her. His breath came in painful gasps and she couldn't help herself; she looked back. He was leaning against a wall, taking in a long whistling breath. He'd been cashing in on his own ill health for so long, doing his deal with the devil, that now it seemed punishment was being exacted. His breath was shorter than ever, but the yellow pallor and trembling hands spoke of more than just lung disease and she remembered what May had said about the empty bottles in his flat.

'George, you need to take better care of yourself – look at you!'

'Well, I ain't got you to look after me any more, have I, princess?'

'I wasn't happy, George. I didn't want to be a princess. I just wanted to be me.'

'I did love you, princ . . . Peg, it's just I was too old for you. Probably come down too hard on you. I'll do it different.'

She shook her head and began walking back towards St James's Road. 'You can't be any different. I know you, George. I appreciate the offer, but I've already got somewhere to live.' She pointed vaguely towards the Gilbie house.

'I'll be straight, Peggy. Your granddad *did* suggest it, but it's not the reason I'm asking you to come back.'

George wasn't giving up and a familiar panic began to take hold of her. She felt her heart beating, like a butterfly in a web. She was after all virtually homeless, with no income and a child to bring up on her own. But at that moment Pearl woke up and looked at Peggy with Harry's eyes. It was as if Peggy had woken up herself.

'Thanks for the offer, George, but it wouldn't be the best for me or Pearl. But I wish you well, I really do.'

She walked away, feeling the tight band around her heart release. She filled her lungs and took in a deep breath, then leaned forward to tuck Pearl in. 'We'll be all right, won't we, darling?' she said as her daughter smiled at her, revealing tiny pearls of teeth. She had almost reached the Gilbie house when the klaxon sounded. The spotters on Pearce Duff's roof had obviously seen a doodlebug. She looked up. Not fifty feet above her and losing height was the terrifying finned shape, shooting flame and roaring. She stopped dead and watched as it passed over, fearing nothing.

When the doodlebugs were joined by rockets later that year, Peggy's fatalism seemed to become universal. People took again to the shelters at night, but during the day the V-2s could not be evaded. There was no prayer or charm that could protect you. Everyone said it either had your name on or it didn't. Even her sister May admitted that there was no warning system against them, unless the ATS spotters along the coast happened to catch the puff of smoke when they were launched from the French sites. Once the rockets were on their way, heading towards Tower Bridge at thousands of miles per hour, there was not much anybody could do.

After two explosions ripped apart the ill-fated John Bull Arch within a matter of days, everyone agreed it was too much of a coincidence to be put down to gas mains. One after another the two V-2s had ploughed down through the railway line, crushing the old John Bull pub and flattening buildings all along the Blue, and now the government was forced to admit that they were under attack from a new and terrible Vengeance weapon.

The day after the second V-2 destroyed the John Bull Arch, Peggy and Mrs Gilbie stood on the corner of Blue Anchor Lane, looking down the rain-slick street towards the collapsed railway line. The temporary bridge that had been hastily erected after the first attack ten days earlier had been blown clean away.

'The train tracks look a bit like the roller coaster at Margate, don't they?' Peggy said. The whole centre section of the arch had fallen in upon itself,

561

leaving the rails unsupported. They were bent down into a massive twisted loop, almost touching the road. The usual cranes and rescue vehicles were packed into the street, and though men in white tin hats still swarmed over a mound of bricks and timber, the clean-up operation was well under way.

Peggy shivered, thinking of those who'd lost their lives or their homes, and remembered the first bombing of the arch in those early days of the Blitz.

'That was where your brother Jack died, wasn't it?' Mrs Gilbie asked, while she gently jogged four-year-old Jack as he slumbered in the pushchair.

'He wasn't sheltering under it. They found him not far away. He used to ignore the warnings all the time. We think it was shrapnel or debris got him. The worst thing was that we didn't find him for days . . .'

'Makes you wonder why some places get hit over and over,' the woman said.

'My Granny Byron would tell you it's fate.'

'Well, she might be right, love, but it's my opinion if we'd had a few more proper shelters ready in nineteen-forty, we wouldn't have been under the arches in the first place, would we? Sometimes you can help out fate a bit, you know.'

'I'd like to put you and Granny Byron in a room one day, see who comes out on top!' Peggy smiled, leaning over the big pram to pull up the hood against the rain. Peggy loved Nell Gilbie for her

562

practicality. And she'd had reason to be grateful for it in the past couple of months, during which the Gilbies had made her and Pearl part of their family.

Since these latest attacks, Peggy really could count herself without a home, for their old shell of a house in Southwark Park Road had finally resolved itself into nothing but dust and ashes. The blast from the V-2s that had smashed into the John Bull Arch had brought every unstable building in the area crashing down, and their home had finally succumbed. She doubted that she could even find its position now, not that she wanted to see the sad remains. But she knew she couldn't impose on the Gilbies' generosity forever. She would have to find a place, and an income, of her own.

In the end, it was Harry who'd given her the way. One morning, during the same week they'd learned Bill was missing, the Gilbies received another letter. Nell came into the kitchen, holding it almost at arm's length. Peggy took one glance at the official-looking document and knew what Mrs Gilbie was thinking. It could only be more bad news. Peggy was holding Pearl, and with a tacit understanding the two women had exchanged their burdens. Nell took Pearl into her arms and Peggy took the letter. She'd had enough experience of receiving bad news, but she hadn't learned how to give it, and her fingers had fumbled opening the envelope. When a cry escaped her lips, Mrs Gilbie had lowered her head, drawing Pearl more tightly into her arms.

'Our Bill?' she'd asked in a small voice.

'No.' Peggy had shaken her head. 'It's about Harry.'

The letter was from a solicitor's in the City. And Mrs Gilbie had made her read it aloud twice. Did they know the whereabouts of a Mrs Margaret Flint, last known address the Purbrook Estate? They were trying to settle the estate of a Mr Harry Steadman. Letters addressed to Mrs Flint had been returned, not known at this address. But Mr Steadman had made provision for his son, John, known as Jack, and for the Gilbies and Mrs Flint. This was a shock, for Peggy had always assumed Harry wasn't a wealthy man. Army uniform could be a great leveller. And in fact, it turned out she'd been right, for Harry had very little to leave them – when he'd died. But after death, it seemed, he had saved one final gift for her.

Harry might not have been prosperous, but apparently his family was, and had owned property all over South London. Now, with the death of his remaining uncle, the estate had passed to Harry's children and to Peggy. She found herself the owner of properties in Dulwich and Camberwell, as well as in Bermondsey.

Over the past weeks the solicitor had helped her sell some, and others she planned to rent out. But on this particular morning she and Mrs Gilbie were going to see the house in Fort Road. It looked the best prospect for what she had in mind but she needed Mrs Gilbie with her, for the plan would involve both of them.

Turning away from the remains of the John Bull Arch, they made their way towards Thorburn Square, cutting through it as the rain came on again, slanting across the churchyard, which looked bare and exposed without its palisade of iron railings. But the lofty old London plane trees still stood like temple columns round its four sides, shielding the church in the centre. Broad red and gold leaves fell wetly about them, sticking to the pram wheels as they approached Fort Road. This part of the street had largely escaped bomb damage and soon they came to the empty terraced house that the solicitor had described. She fished out the key. It seemed strange to be a woman of property and, though undeserved, she intended to make the most of it.

They manoeuvred the prams inside and, with both children fast asleep, were free to explore the place. At the end of a long narrow passage was a kitchen scullery, where a side door led into the garden. Off the passage were two large rooms; the first, with its tall sash window, faced the street. Peggy paced out the floor and looked inside two cupboards built into alcoves on either side of the fireplace.

'It's plenty big enough. We could store toys and games in here. What do you think, toddlers in this room?'

Mrs Gilbie nodded. 'Babies in the back room – it'll be quieter.'

Peggy's plan was to use the house not only for her home, but as a nursery for women in war work. The government was still crying out for married women to return to work, but lack of childcare was a major drawback. Most mothers that Peggy knew of would be only too glad of a factory job to supplement their soldier husband's allowances, but nursery places were scarce. Peggy had spoken to the WVS childcare officer and had been accepted on their register, but she would need help, and Nell Gilbie was ideal. After all she had been taking waifs and strays into her home since she was a young woman.

The smaller back room looked out on to the backyard and had the advantage of being nearer the kitchen.

'It's a bit dull in here today with the rain, but on a sunny day it'll be a nice bright room, I think.' Peggy stroked the old-fashioned wallpaper with its dark red background and gold curlicues. 'We could put up some prettier wallpaper and repaint the doors. Why did they always paint everything dark brown and green? Uggh.' She stopped suddenly. 'What are you looking at?' she asked.

Mrs Gilbie stood at the door, a half smile on her face. 'I'm looking at you, Peggy. It's so good to see you happy again.'

Peggy smiled. Though she knew this wasn't happiness, she certainly felt lighter and more at peace than she had in a long while. 'Well, it's good to have something worthwhile to do.'

'You're right there, love. It's the best medicine.'

Taking Mrs Gilbie by the elbow, Peggy led her out into the garden. Of course, the woman needed to be busy herself – she had her own griefs and she had borne them so bravely. You wouldn't know that she was praying daily for news of her son, except that sometimes in the evenings as Peggy sat with the Gilbies, listening to Victor Sylvester on the wireless, she would see Nell drift away. Then suddenly the woman would come back to the room with a start and say something like, 'Oh, my Bill likes this song.' Her husband would look up with a worried expression, and Mrs Gilbie would say, quite fiercely, 'I'm not going to stop talking about him. So don't look at me like that, Sam. I never give up on you, did I? And I'm not giving up on him neither.'

So Peggy got into the habit of talking to her about Bill, and because she didn't want to forget Harry either, she was happy to speak of him, and of her father too. It was almost a conspiracy between them, for everyone else seemed vaguely embarrassed by the subject of their missing men.

The garden was small, a patch of grass with narrow beds. Peggy lifted a yellow dahlia, droopy with rain. It was like a sunburst in the grey day.

'What did you mean, the other night, Nell, when you said you never gave up on Mr Gilbie?'

The woman lifted her chin, and though her hair

was streaked with grey, Peggy could see a flash of the determined young woman she'd been, the one who'd had the gumption to get on that penny-farthing contraption and ride all over Bermondsey to make a few bob.

'In the last war, my Sam was posted missing and I could've gone to bits. But something told me not to give up and sure enough, he came home. If it can happen once – it can happen again!'

'There's always hope,' Peggy said, knowing from her own experience that although it might be dashed, hope was never wasted.

They went back in and mounted the stairs.

'Have you heard from May at all?' Mrs Gilbie asked as they came to the first landing, which opened on to a long back room.

'Not lately. I daresay there's no time to write – she's hardly ever off duty! She says her gun site is one of the last chances to stop these rockets getting through.' She paused, thinking of how her home-loving little sister had changed. Peggy owed her life to May's newfound nerve and courage, she was sure of that. She had heard how, standing atop the ruins, May refused to move until they searched the very spot she insisted on. Now it was Peggy's turn to help dig May out of whatever crater she had crawled into.

'I wish May could talk to you, Nell. I know deep down she's worried sick about Bill, but she doesn't say nothing.'

Mrs Gilbie shook her head. 'I've a good mind

to go down to Barkingside myself. If they won't let her have a day off, they can't stop me seeing her, can they? She shouldn't be just soldiering on all on her own.'

Peggy agreed, but the last time she'd spoken to her sister on the telephone, which was the day the news came through about Bill, she gathered that May had wanted to do just that: soldier on alone. And unlike Mrs Gilbie, she didn't want to talk about Bill.

As they mounted more stairs to view the rooms on the second landing, Peggy had an idea. 'Perhaps we'll both go down, take the kids!' she said.

'Why not! And you can tell her all about your plans for this place, let her see there's life outside that gun site.'

May did a double-take at the sight of them. Was that really her sister and Mrs Gilbie pushing prams towards the barrack huts? May had just come out of the NAAFI after dinner and was looking forward to catching up on a few hours' sleep that afternoon, when she spotted the pair. They were in front of her but, even from behind, Peggy's striking tall figure, with the fair hair and red hat, was unmistakable. But what was Nell Gilbie doing here? May immediately felt a stab of guilt. She should have written to Bill's mum. She wasn't the only one suffering. But no matter how many times she'd begun a letter, something had prevented her from finishing it. She knew he wasn't dead. She just didn't want to hear from anyone who suggested that he was. The words that Mrs Gilbie expected from her were simply not in her vocabulary. He was still, in her imagination, the young man who'd walked so close beside her into the wood and held her tightly in the charmed circle of the fairy ring. The one whose letters had shown that his love could endure long months of separation. She preferred to see this latest silence as a pause between letters. A day would come, she was convinced of it, when she would hear from him again. And though she knew everyone pitied her and made allowances, she didn't care.

She contemplated running away in the opposite direction. They'd come unannounced. She could be anywhere on camp, even on a route march. They weren't to know. She would do as she had when a child – find a hiding place and wait it out till they'd gone. But just then Peggy turned. She was wearing red lipstick and for a moment May was angry with her, for demonstrating that life was possible after loss. If the worst happened and Bill didn't come back, could she go on, live, wear lipstick and smile? But she was being harsh. Of course she was happy that her sister had found a way to go on.

'Peg!' she shouted, breaking into a jog. 'What are you two doing here?'

May kissed her and then Mrs Gilbie.

'We've come to see you!' Peggy hugged her.

'How the bloody hell did you get past the guard?'

'What guard?'

May put her hand to her forehead. Someone would be in trouble if her visitors were discovered. Pearl had woken up and was whimpering to find herself in this strange place, and Jack was shouting at May to pay attention to his wooden boat.

She bent to admire it. 'Come on, let's get you lot out of here before an officer notices! I'll take you into Barkingside for tea and cake.'

'No, you won't, it's my treat,' Mrs Gilbie insisted.

They caught the bus and went to the tea rooms that she and Bill had liked best. In the cosy warmth, over toasted teacakes, May found her muscles beginning to relax. Living on high alert did strange things to the body and most of the time she felt as though her very bones were on fire. Sometimes when she was called on to post in the middle of the night, she woke with an excruciating earache, where she'd clenched her teeth tightly in preparation for whatever unexpected attack the night might bring. But while eating teacake and talking about Peggy's plans for starting a nursery with Bill's mum, the world shifted back into a gentler focus. She was also pleased to discover that she'd been entirely wrong about Nell Gilbie. The woman never stopped talking about Bill. It seemed they were allies after all, both firmly on the side of Bill's sure survival.

The only time her good spirits failed her was when Peggy told her about the blast damage from the latest John Bull Arch bombings.

'I'm sorry to be the one to tell you, love, but that's the end of it for the old house,' she said, looking anxiously for May's reaction.

'I suppose it was stupid to think we'd ever go back there,' May said, despondent and vaguely disorientated. What good was a homing pigeon with nowhere to return to? She was like a compass without a magnetic North and the feeling was almost like sea sickness.

'But when you and Bill get married, you'll be looking around for your own place, won't you?' Mrs Gilbie said.

May was startled by her matter-of-factness. 'Yes, of course, you're right, Mrs Gilbie, we will,' May said and, leaning her elbows on the table, began to weep softly, covering her face with her hands in a vain attempt to conceal her sorrow.

There came a day in the New Year of 1945 when May noticed that there were fewer rockets flying overhead. Their numbers had decreased in proportion to the Allies' continued advance across France and Belgium. They were disabling rocket launchers as they went. May's predictor team finally found time to polish their kit and curl their hair. They even had evenings off, when they went to the occasional dance at the Chigwell RAF base. But this was one activity May found particularly hard. For the RAF band had found themselves a new piano player. He had all the latest songs in his repertoire, but sometimes May would be caught unawares and he would strike up one of Bill's favourites – 'I'll String Along With You' or 'Kiss Me Again' – and the yearning would be too hard to bear.

When in the springtime they heard the battery was to be broken up May went into Hainault Forest to see the blackthorns' frothy white blossom and the first bluebells. Wood anemones were scattered like stars over the emerald mossy floor of their fairy ring. Bluebell quills had pushed up, their bells already forming a hazy blue quilt. She lay in the silence, looking into the green light above her. Then, closing her eyes, she imagined other leaves, spiky palms and looping vines, outsized and alien. She felt on her face, not the cool freshness of English air, but the humid heaviness of a jungle, sweating all around her. The sharp sappy scent of grasses and the powdery sweetness of new bluebells were replaced by a dank, honeyed musk of exotic trumpet flowers. Somewhere he was. She extended her faith on wings, and sent it flying to a remote jungle half a world away.

'What shall I do, Bill?' she asked.

The question was one she'd asked herself many times since the news came through that her battery was to re-muster. No more bombs, no more doodlebugs, no more rockets would fall on Bermondsey. The war wasn't quite over, but everyone expected the good news to come through soon. All the mixed batteries were being disbanded, releasing the gunner girls for other duties. She had fought her fight, it seemed, and now they wanted her to sort mail. It felt wrong. Her war *wasn't* over. It couldn't be, not while Bill's was still raging.

'What shall I do, Bill?' she asked again, this time aloud.

There was a rustling sound overhead, branches bent and new leaves shivered. She caught sight of a movement somewhere above her, pale grey wings spread wide, flapped, and, with one sharp snap, the wood pigeon lifted itself skyward, its homely rounded body transformed by the grace and power of its flight. She had her answer.

CHAPTER 31

SHIPS THAT PASS

March–August 1945

'What do you mean, you're not coming with me?' Emmy was incredulous.

'I can't go and sort letters, Em.'

'But it won't be for long. The war'll be over in a few months. Everyone says so. And besides, what else are you going to do? It's that or cook officers' dinners!'

It was hard, having to say goodbye to all the girls. They'd been through so much together and they all agreed that, however much they wanted a return to normality, it felt as though much of the meaning had been sucked out of their lives. They had given everything, left home and family, worn themselves to the bone. Their lives hadn't been their own since becoming gunner girls yet however hard it had been, fighting to defend your home had a purpose to it, which sorting mail never could, however necessary a job it might be. They'd talked endlessly about what to do when the battery disbanded and May's team had taken for granted that they would all go together.

May shook her head. 'I won't be cooking dinners either. I've made up my mind. I want to retrain in signals, see if I can get a Far East posting.'

'What the bloody hell d'you want to do that for, you dozy mare?'

May had to laugh at her friend's face, which looked as though it might explode. 'Don't look at me as if I'm bonkers, Em. There's still a war on . . . over there.'

Emmy had to sit down on the bed. 'Well, I know that new sarge's been recruiting for the Far East, but I never thought you'd be the one to go. If any of us, I'd say Bee, or even Mac, but not you, May. You won't know your arse from your elbow in a foreign country.'

'I don't see why not. I never had a thought of leaving Bermondsey before the war, but I managed all right when it came to it. Besides, the new sarge's already said she'll recommend me. She's done a stint overseas herself; she says it's exciting.'

'Excitin' my arse.' Emmy looked at her intently. 'You don't fool me, May. You're not going for excitement, are you?'

May flushed. Emmy knew her too well.

'What is there left for me here, Em?' she said, dropping her forced brightness. 'Mum's still at the major's, and Peggy's got her own life with her kids and the nursery.'

'But don't you want to get back home to Bermondsey?'

'What home? It's gone.' *And what use is a homing*

pigeon without a home to fly back to? May thought. 'Anyway, you can call me crazy if you like, but I won't be able to rest if I stay here, not while Bill's still out there.'

'It ain't crazy, love. I suppose I can understand it. It's just . . . I'll miss you.'

May threw her arms round Emmy. 'I'll miss you too, Em.'

The two friends were still hugging, when they were interrupted by the rest of the team bursting into the hut.

'What's all this Sarge tells us about you applying for overseas?' Mac came and stood in front of May, crossing her arms. 'You can't! I thought we'd agreed. We're all going to Nottingham, mail sorting together!'

Bee sauntered over and slumped down on the bed beside May. She took a deep breath. 'Sorry, girls, I might as well admit it now May's made the first move, but I don't think I can bear postal duties either. I'm going with a battery to Belgium.'

Ruby burst into tears. 'That's it then. Nothing'll be the same again.'

'Oh, Rube, don't cry.' May tried to comfort her. 'We'll keep in touch, won't we, girls?'

And they all agreed they would, but looking round at their faces – Ruby, Mac, Bee and Emmy – she found herself trying to fix them in her mind, just in case she never did come home again.

Before the battery disbanded, they lined up for one last photo and May, with her oft-derided passion for neatness, insisted they all wore dress uniform. Pat was dragged over from the stores, for they still saw her as part of their team, though as a married woman she'd already been given her demob number.

'You'll be the first to go, Dobbin,' May said, lining them all up for inspection. 'If I don't get down to the major's before I go for training, can you give a copy of the photo to Mum?'

'But you'll come and see us before you go overseas?' Pat looked alarmed. 'Your mum will want to say goodbye properly!' The girl took her hand. 'We all will. You're like my family now, May. I've got precious few of my own, and I'm not letting you off the hook that easily.'

'Of course I'll get up to Moreton before I go!' But May knew that seeing her mother would be the hardest part of leaving, and she only prayed her resolve would hold when the time came to say goodbye to her.

'All right, come on, you lot, let's get into Ilford and get pissed as puddins!' Emmy said after the snap had been taken and the box Brownie put away for the last time. 'It's our last night, what they gonna do about it, put us on a charge?'

Emmy's throaty laugh was always infectious and they drew together, linking arms, on their way out of camp, singing at the tops of their voices. '*Round the corner, behind the tree, Sergeant Major, he says to me, would you like to marry me, I should like to know, because every time I look in his eye he makes me want to go . . . rrrround the corner, behind the tree!'*

And the final memory May took with her was of all her mates, creased with laughter, swaying back to camp well after midnight, giggling as they tripped over duckboards and stubbed their toes on their iron bedsteads, before falling on to the hard biscuits in deep alcohol-fuelled slumber. In the early morning light, May's last goodbyes were tempered by an almighty hangover, and on the train journey to the signals training camp at Guildford she let herself sleep and dream of the long journey still ahead of her.

Bermondsey was burning. And for the first time in six years May was glad of it. For they were the victory bonfires. Pyres and beacons were lit, tall as houses, constructed from the still plentiful bomb wreckage strewn all over the borough, and the flames crackled up into the air. Instead of the sirens' wail came a bellowed, delirious chorus of song, in which she joined until she was hoarse. For so long, the acrid stink of smoke and charred wood had conjured up defeat and loss, but today it was the sweet smell of victory. She had her arms round Peggy, but Mr and Mrs Gilbie had preferred to stay at home with a quiet drink, looking after the children. May knew why they didn't feel like celebrating: the war in the Far East was still coming to its tortuous end. They had two sons coming home, but there was still no word of their eldest. But though they'd heard nothing of Bill since he'd been reported missing six months earlier, May was still convinced she would know if he was dead.

Before she and Peggy left the Gilbies' house for the celebrations, Sam Gilbie had called May out into the backyard. The sun was low over the rooftops, an orange disk that only accentuated the jagged silhouettes of broken roofs and splintered trees beyond the garden fence.

'I want to show you something before you go, May,' he said, ducking under the lean-to where the mangle and washtub were kept. He emerged with the old penny-farthing bicycle. May gasped. What she saw brought a smile to her face.

'It looks brand new!'

The twisted wheels had been straightened and their spokes now shone, so that they caught the orange glow of the setting sun. The metal frame was newly painted and the saddle re-upholstered.

'It's beautiful, Mr Gilbie. I didn't even know you still had it.'

He smiled. 'Well, it's done my family proud over the years, and our Bill was always on at me to fix it up again. I'd hate to think it was still a wreck by the time he gets home.'

She looked into his brimming, dark eyes, and put her hand over his on the handlebars. 'He's told me so many stories about this bike, how you used to wheel him round and round the yard on it when he was little. I know he'd be pleased it's getting a new lease of life.'

Mr Gilbie gave a little smile. 'Jack's just the same, never gets tired of having a ride on it. But listen, May, I wanted to let you know how proud I am of you. It's hard, what you're doing, going off to a foreign country, and I dare say your mother'd rather you stayed home. But I know why you're doing it and if you need anything at all, you just say the word. And don't forget to let us know if . . .'

'You'll be the first to know if I hear anything about Bill, I promise.'

May had been touched that Bill's father wanted to show her the penny-farthing. She knew it had always been a sort of symbol of hope for the Gilbie family; that was why, though it had long outlived its usefulness, they still held on to it. Now she felt she'd been invited into their circle, and given a magic talisman to take with her on her journeying.

Tomorrow they were planning a victory street party, but May wouldn't be there, for this was her last night in Bermondsey. Victory in Europe! How long they'd waited, and the announcement came just as her signals training at Guildford was ending. But there was no turning back now. It seemed perverse, but after so many years longing for the war to end she was about to set off in search of the tail end of it, almost as if it had become such a part of her life she couldn't bear to let it go.

But tonight she had been content to spend with her sister, singing themselves hoarse and being kissed by far too many strange men before leaving the bonfires, which would certainly burn through the night. After collecting Pearl and Jack from the Gilbies, they were making their way back to Peggy's house in Fort Road, when May stopped.

'You go on, Peg. There's just one more goodbye I need to say.'

And though Peggy asked where she was going, she shook her head. 'Tell you later, don't wait up!'

When Peggy hesitated, May shooed her on. 'I'll be fine. I'm going halfway round the world on me own – you can't be worrying about me now!'

The blackout had already been lifted, and the skyline was ruddy with firelight, but even had it been pitch-black May would have been able to find her way there. She stood at the top of St James's Road, tilting her head back to look at the whirling stars, and listened to the distant shouts of revellers. Walking further along the Blue, she caught the strains of 'We'll Meet Again' drifting over from the Blue Anchor pub, and passed tipsy groups celebrating in the streets. One of the young men made a good-natured grab for her and though she evaded his clutching hands, she was grateful to pass under the repaired John Bull Arch in the little group's company. For even on a night like this, the arch had the power to sap her courage. Once through, she hastened along Southwark Park Road, till the particular bend in the street and the tilt of the stars overhead told her exactly where, in all that crushed rubble, her home had once been. When she found the spot, she bent down, took up a handful of ashes and poured them into her handkerchief. Making a little pouch, she stuffed it into her coat pocket.

'What sort of bird am I?' she asked the ruined ground.

They were going the wrong way. There were no signposts in the sea but she, of all people, knew west from east, and they were not sailing east. But they should be sailing east. Every evening since leaving Southampton she'd made her way up to the deck, so that she could watch the sunset. She never tired of the way the sea turned to molten gold, but they had been journeying into the setting sun for over three days. No one could work out why – unless the captain feared some rogue U-boat captains were still hanging about in the Atlantic, but there certainly weren't going to be any Japanese subs in the vicinity. The only explanation was that the orders hadn't yet been changed. Convoys headed for the Far East had always dog-legged into the Atlantic to avoid enemy shipping, and until the order came to desist, May could only assume the captain was sticking to the rules. But she wished they would just get a move on. The fact that she was losing patience with the voyage so soon after their departure didn't bode well. She had another five weeks at sea. If only she could have flown. But ATS signals girls weren't priority passengers and so she would have to make the best of it. She turned away from the setting sun and looked eastwards.

She surprised herself by being a good sailor. Some of her fellow passengers had started being sick an hour out from Southampton, but apart from a little nausea during a choppy spell on the second day, May quickly found her sea legs. She'd even begun to find sleeping in a hammock quite fun. When she and the other fifty-odd ATS signals girls had first boarded the grey bulk of the troopship they'd each been handed a ticket by an MP, showing which part of the ship they would be sleeping in. She was allocated a space on the lowest mess desk – just above the water line. It was uncomfortably cramped. They each had a space at the mess table, above which they were to sling their hammocks at night. She spent half the first night rolling out of the hammock and landing on the table with an uncomfortable thud. After a couple of sleepless nights she was so tired she simply gave herself up to the swinging cocoon and started sleeping like a baby. She couldn't help comparing her experiences to Bill's descriptions of the troopship he'd sailed on and could only conclude that she was having a better time of it. One of his letters described how he'd been detailed to work in the galley, which he said was hell, especially when the ship reached warmer climes and the temperature soared into the hundreds.

But May's only duties so far were to attend lectures on Indian culture and turn up for PT parades, which would have been a welcome change if it weren't for the fact that they formed the morning's entertainment for a ship full of a thousand men. Some of the girls took advantage of the scores of eager servicemen, but that was one distraction May simply wasn't interested in. In fact the high-light of her first week was when she noticed that she had to change her position on deck to view the setting sun. They were heading south now, but it was only when the ship was pointing due east and began steaming through the straits of Gibraltar that she felt she was really on her way.

In the Mediterranean, she was grateful for her tropical uniform of light khaki drill blouse and skirt. She would certainly have melted in her old woollen battledress. Soon her arms and legs turned golden, and one night, as they approached Port Said, though it was forbidden, she took her hammock on to the open top deck and slung it between two lifeboats. The night sky was an enveloping velvet quilt, a deeper black than she'd ever seen. Swinging gently in the hammock, she gazed up into the heart of the Milky Way, scarcely believing that she, May Lloyd, home bird, was actually here, with the deep sea beneath her and a million stars above. She was such a long way from home and yet she felt at peace, soothed by the distant engine thrum and the cool, salt-laden breeze.

When she woke next morning the sea's astringent saltiness had been replaced by an altogether more human smell. They had entered Port Said. She tipped out of the hammock and ran to the railing. The first sight that greeted her was the bare backside of an Egyptian fisherman, protruding over the stern of a passing dhow. He appeared to be taking his morning ablutions in full view of the entire harbour. May hadn't been the only one drawn to the side. A group of gunners were jeering at the dhow. One of them exaggeratedly wiped his eyes and shouted to his mates. 'Sod me, that one got me right in the face. Better duck, boys, I can see right up his jacksy and there's more on the way!'

The ship berthed overnight, but they were not allowed ashore, and May was content to experience the alien sounds and smells coming off the wharfside from the safety of the deck. Once through the canal, their destination was confirmed – after a stop at Bombay, they would disembark at Calcutta. This was the best posting she could have hoped for, as she knew from a letter that had evaded the censor, Bill's final posting had been an airfield not far from Calcutta. The sense that she was following in his footsteps was overwhelming. She hugged herself with secret joy, that in India she might find, if not Bill himself, then at least his last whereabouts.

After two days in Calcutta port, sitting below with kit ready, sheltering in their berths from the heavy monsoon rains which had just begun, they were finally allowed on to the wharfside, only to be ushered through crowds of curious dock workers to a waiting steamer. With uniforms soaked through, kitbags heavy with rain, they streamed up the gangplank to be packed like sardines on the deck of the steamer. There was a central awning which the girls jostled to get under. May couldn't see the point, she wasn't going to dry out any time soon, but after an hour of chugging down the coastline, the pelting of the rain on her head became painful and she found a small corner beneath the awning to sit under. She could see nothing of the coastline, it was veiled in chutes of rain, and it was impossible to chat to the other girls for the drumming on the awning was worse than sitting under the John Bull Arch with ten trains thundering overhead. It was the worst journey of May's life, and made even more uncomfortable because they had no idea where they were going.

A young girl from Liverpool sat shivering beside her. 'Oh, I do feel ill.' She looked up at May, pasty-faced, teeth chattering. They had been issued malaria tablets every day, but some girls didn't like taking them. May suspected the girl had a dose of malaria and hoped she wouldn't faint because there was nowhere for her to fall but on May.

'Can you hold out till we get there?' she asked the girl, who shook her head weakly.

'I don't think so.'

May squeezed herself upright. 'I'll go and look for Sarge. Hang on.'

She picked her way through damp bodies and finally spotted the sergeant through the cabin window, talking to the CO. She quickly ducked inside, letting in a bucketful of rain, just in time to hear the sergeant ask the CO: 'Couldn't we get these girls below deck, sir, or by the time we arrive in Chittagong tomorrow morning, they'll all be down with fevers!'

The blast of rain had caught the sergeant's attention and as May stood sucking in the raindrops still trickling over her lip, she turned impatiently. 'What is it, Private Lloyd?'

'Private Donnelly's sick, ma'am.'

A look passed between the CO and the sergeant. 'All right, Lloyd, get back to her and we'll send a first aider out.'

That night the sergeant got her way and they were squeezed below deck, with cold rations and no hope of sleep. For the first time since she'd left Southampton, May began to wish she was sorting letters in a warm depot in Nottingham.

When morning came, they emerged still damp so that May felt as wrung out and stiff as a shirt put through the mangle on washing day. The wharfside was a running stream. Lorries sloshed through it to take them through town to their billets. Though the town was hazy with pounding rain, a bright red building that looked like a temple caught May's eye. As the lorry jolted through muddy ruts, she wiped steam from the window and gasped. She'd seen that building before. But where? Then she remembered. A few months before Bill went missing she'd received a parcel, with some tiny, poor-quality snaps. And on the back of one Bill had written: *Me and my pal Bert outside the railway station*. He'd been dressed in bush hat and tropical uniform, lean, serious-looking and squinting into the sun. Of course, there must be a million buildings like it in India, but she called down to where the sergeant sat, 'Sarge, do you know what building that is?'

'I think it's the railway station, Lloyd. Why, you thinking of going on a trip?'

The other girls laughed, and the suffering Donnelly chimed in, 'Yeah, I'll join you, all the way to Liverpool Lime Street, eh?'

'Is there an airbase here, Sarge?' May asked, ignoring their laughter.

'Oh yes, quite a big one, you'll find Chittagong full of airmen, RAF and Commonwealth, Yanks too. They go on raids over the border into Burma all the time, and they're making airdrops for our troops, of course.'

At home, with the war in Europe over, it had been hard to imagine the war still going on out here, but now May realized just how close she had come to the fighting. Their lectures on the troopship had made it clear that although the allies had been pushing the Japs back from the north of

Burma all the way to Rangoon, the Indian border lands were still full of pockets of resistant Japanese troops. The war was certainly not ended, over here, and her job in communications would partly be to relay reports and orders to and from the ever-changing front line as the army tried to mop up the intransigent enemy forces.

It was stupid to go in the monsoon. Even though the old hands assured her that the rains would soon end, May couldn't wait. She had to get out. She was fed up of being stuck either in the thundering drum of their tin-roofed billet, or the steamy depths of the wireless room. So when a group of girls suggested a trip into town, May jumped at the chance.

'I think a trip to the flicks'll do you the world of good, want to come with us?' she said to Sadie Donnelly, the young private who'd been ill on the steamer. After leaving the sick bay she'd attached herself to May. It felt odd to be the experienced one, but May had happily taken her under her wing. Sadie confessed that she'd signed up well under age, fearing that the war would be over before she could see any of the excitement. She'd got her wish and hadn't been in the ATS for more than a few months before she'd landed an overseas posting. She was even more homesick, if it were possible, than May had been in her early days at Pontefract.

After being virtually confined to camp for two

months, a trip into town was like a holiday. But it wasn't just that she needed a change. May wanted to see more of this town, which she was sure Bill had been in, just to reassure herself that she'd not been imagining things. They went in on an army lorry and were dropped by the station in the afternoon, with orders to be back there for pickup before sunset. The town was like a swirling watercolour and immediately she recognized the same gaudily painted, hooded rickshaws that Bill had described, being pedalled around the flooded streets. At the station they were inundated with gharry and rickshaw drivers clamouring for trade.

'Shall we get one to the cinema?' May suggested and she and Sadie hopped aboard the nearest rickshaw. On the way she spotted other things she recognized from Bill's descriptions: the temple with its gilded rooftops, the children begging beside the road, the street traders carrying impossibly heavy loads on baskets slung on poles over their shoulders, the short-horned skinny cattle wandering along the middle of the road – it was all as he'd described it. And now she remembered seeing the sickle-shaped, sharp-prowed fishing boats lined up in the harbour when they'd first come into port, and how Bill had marvelled at the boatmen's skill in standing up to row the slender craft. As the rain beat upon the domed hood of the rickshaw, May looked out on a world that was totally alien and yet felt strangely familiar. It was odd to think that her connection with Bill had brought her to India a long time before she had actually set foot upon its shores, and she thought of their pact to meet every night in the fairy ring of Hainault Forest, a place where time zones and distance had no meaning.

Bill's description of the fleapit had, unfortunately, been as accurate as the rest of his accounts of the town. It was steaming, so much so that the condensation hanging in the air threatened to obscure the screen. The seats were sticky, the air thick with the food being cooked at the back of the cinema. They saw an odd film, which featured about as much rain as still pummelled the roof of the cinema. It was called *I Know Where I'm Going*, the story of a plucky young woman who travels to the Outer Hebrides to marry one man and ends up with another. Almost from the opening scene rain was falling in sheets, and the heroine, lashed by stormy weather, spent half the film in a sou'wester. It was a very watery film, which Sadie said she didn't quite get. But May had to admire the young heroine for sticking to her guns – at least for most of the film.

Emerging from the cinema, they sheltered in a doorway, deciding where to go next. They were about to make a dash for a café across the busy street when May bumped into a serviceman. He had his cap pulled down and his head ducked against the rain. They rebounded off each other before he lifted his chin. She knew him immediately, even after all this time.

'May! Strike me, it's May!' His face broke into a broad grin. 'Fancy meeting you here of all places, May, it's a miracle!'

May was conscious that her mouth was open, wide enough to catch raindrops. Bumping into Doug hardly seemed a miracle. It felt to May more like an unhappy accident.

CHAPTER 32

ASHES AND ANGELS

August–November 1945

Doug insisted they go for tea at the café together and May was glad of Sadie's presence. The young Canadian seemed to have forgotten the circumstances of their last meeting. He told her he was based at Chittagong airfield and was full of tales of his piloting exploits. He'd only just returned from a sortie across the border into Burma.

'I'm flying heavy fighters now – Thunderbolts, mostly strafing railway lines or Jap columns, but last trip out I was picking up casualties. It's tough going for the boys, fighting every inch of the way, and the poor guys that get injured have to rely on being lifted out. But tell me about your war, May.'

He dropped his gaze, as if he'd all at once remembered who he was talking to, and then May knew he hadn't forgotten what had happened that night at the dance when Bill had intervened.

'I've been a gunner girl for all of the war, on the predictor, made Corporal. Our battery chalked up the most direct hits in the south-east, even managed to get quite a few doodlebugs.'

Doug raised his eyes, impressed. 'Young May, who'd have thought it! So what brings you out here? Couldn't you have stayed home now it's over in Europe?'

He sounded genuinely interested, so May told him.

Doug whistled. 'Sounds like you've had a hard war. I'm sorry about your dad. Your poor mother must be heartbroken. I remember she made lovely little cakes . . . fairy cakes, she called them.'

May had to smile. 'Bill loved those too.'

'So your fiancé, Bill, is that the chap who . . .' Doug's freckled skin could not hide his blushes, and he glanced at Sadie.

'Yes,' May answered hastily. 'My knight in shining armour.'

The barb was not lost on Doug.

'Look, I never got a chance to say I was sorry about that . . . I was so ashamed of myself, I couldn't even say goodbye properly. I've been kicking myself ever since if I'm honest.'

Sadie looked awkwardly at May. 'I'll just pop out and see if the rain's stopped, shall I?'

Doug laughed. 'You'll be lucky. It's the damn monsoon – it never stops till it stops!'

Doug was obviously risking his life every day and if this was the last conversation May ever had with him, then she didn't want to let him go away unforgiven. So in spite of Sadie's presence she said, 'Doug, we've all done things we're ashamed of. It's all water under the bridge.'

At that moment a passing lorry piled high with caged chickens splashed a huge wave of rainwater against the café windows . . . and they laughed.

'All right, water under the bridge it is!' Doug said.

Before they went their separate ways May asked Doug if he could find out anything about Bill. 'I'm sure he was based here before he went missing. But the RAF's not told his mum and dad a thing about what happened. It's left us all up in the air . . . we just want to know.'

He seemed to hesitate. 'You shouldn't get your hopes up, May. The Japs are ruthless and anyone who goes missing in the jungle, well . . .'

May felt his words like a blow to the stomach and took in a gulping breath, before pulling herself upright. 'I *will* keep my hopes up, Doug – and not you, nor anyone else, will convince me to do any different!'

He chuckled. 'Same old May. What was the name of that film you just saw? *I Know Where I'm Going*? You always did, May.' He put his pilot's cap back on. 'I'll ask around at the base. Be seeing you.'

And before she had a chance to pull away, he bent to kiss her cheek, and so that she couldn't object, he kissed Sadie too.

When he'd gone the young girl widened her eyes. 'Oohh, he's a right charmer. You're a dark horse, May. Two fellers on the go?'

May shook her head; she didn't feel like explaining. 'Come on, let's make a dash for it or we'll be late for the pickup.'

She ran out into the rain-washed street, and was soaked to the skin in the few seconds it took for another eager rickshaw driver to pull up and hand them into its hooded shelter.

In the week that followed May put her meeting with Doug to the back of her mind. But he had obviously not forgotten her, for he tracked her down to her billet. He was waiting beneath the corrugated iron porch that jutted out from the hut. Opening up a large umbrella, he walked towards her, smiling, and May felt oddly guilty, almost as if she were being unfaithful to Bill.

'Fancy a trip over to the airbase – we've got a good servicemen's club, we could have a bite to eat?' he asked as he held the umbrella over the two of them.

'I don't think so, Doug.'

'Well, I've got news. And if you want to hear it, you'll have to come for lunch. Deal?' He tipped his head to one side in a gesture she knew he thought was charming. But she wanted to hear his news.

'All right then. Wait while I change into something a bit dryer.'

She put on a clean skirt and blouse, then sheltering awkwardly beneath Doug's umbrella, they made their way to the taxi rank. They rode in a rickety three-wheeled taxi and the driver seemed to have no notion of where the brakes were. May decided she much preferred the slower pace of the rickshaws. She tried to prise the news from Doug on the way, but he refused to give her a hint of it until they were seated in the servicemen's club with beers and a lunch far superior to anything she could get at her army base.

'Come on then, tell me. What's this news?' she asked impatiently. 'What did you find out?'

He half stood, peering above the heads of the other diners. 'Ah, here he comes.'

'Who?'

'Someone who knows something about your chap.'

She held her breath, putting her beer glass carefully on the table, steadying her voice as she said hello to the young aircraftman who sat down at their table. He'd brought a mug of tea with him.

'This is Colin, he's ground crew. Tell her what you know, Col.'

The young man smiled warmly. 'It's like we've already met, May. Bill had a photo of you, above his bunk . . .'

'You knew Bill!' A surge of hope rippled through May as she leaned across the table, hanging on to Colin's every word.

'Oh yes, we were mates. I'm a gunner armourer too – we worked together in the same fighter squadron. He was a good bloke, decent, you know.

And he thought the world of you, May, but I expect you know that.'

She did know it, but to hear it from a stranger made her feel strangely close to Bill, almost as if she were seeing him through a secret window. If only she could call through the window, get him to turn round, come out and find her . . . but Colin was talking now about the time Bill went missing.

'Well, there were a few nasty skirmishes over the border round about that time. Me and Bill, we were in a contingent of ground crew, sent over into Burma to set up a temporary airfield. We'd cleared the strip and were getting things operational when a troop of Japs made a lightning raid. Came out of the jungle, yelling bloody banzai, bayonets fixed.' He shivered. 'Enough to curdle your blood it is, when they come at you.'

Colin seemed to be talking in slow motion, for everything in the background – people seated at tables, eating, drinking, walking in and out – all melted into a swift blur, their chatter receding, and she listened as intently as when the orders were coming through on the wireless headphones. Only aware of Colin's voice, she waited for him to go on.

'It was a matter of minutes. They overran the whole airstrip, killed as many ground crew and pilots as they could. We had no warning, you see, no defences. It was slaughter.'

'Oh, Colin!' Cold fear grabbed at her heart and

she dug her nails into her palms. 'But not everyone. They didn't kill you all . . . you got out! What about Bill?'

Colin shook his head. 'I was lucky, but, May—'

'No, no, no.' She put her hands over her ears and shut her eyes, trying to hide from the impossible truth.

'Listen to him, May.' Doug grasped her hands, pulling them down from her ears, as Colin continued.

'Me and Bill, we just had time to grab our packs and run off into the jungle. Half a dozen of us ground crew escaped, but somehow we got separated. I'm not sure, May, but I think Bill might have got hit. He was lagging behind and when I looked back one time, he seemed to be limping, but that was the last I saw of Bill. By the time we'd stopped running, he wasn't with us.'

Now the young man gave her an anguished look. 'I'm so sorry we couldn't go back for him, May. It's our training. If you're separated you have to just keep going, hope you'll meet up at the rendezvous point. But he wasn't there either and we walked all the way back to India, took us days. We got back, half-starved, in a terrible state really.' He paused, looking down at his tightly clasped hands. 'I'm sorry not to have better news for you, May.'

She stared at Colin for a brief moment and had to shake herself back into the present. She had been in the jungle with Bill, living his terror, urging him to run, run faster, her heart thudding as though she'd been running for her own life.

'No, don't be sorry, Colin. I can't tell you how much of a relief it is.'

Doug looked puzzled, but May couldn't explain that though it wasn't the best news, it was good enough. If Colin had seen Bill killed she would have cause enough to mourn, but the last time anyone had seen him Bill was alive, and that was one more reason to hope.

'He could have been taken prisoner,' was the best she could do.

'May, if that happened, then I'm sorry, but you should know it might have been better if he'd died in the jungle,' Doug said.

Colin looked as if he disapproved of such bluntness, but May's hackles rose. 'Don't you dare say that!'

She hated Doug at that moment, but he looked at her with weary eyes. 'I just don't want you to have false hope,' he replied dully.

'There is no false hope,' she said.

As it was, the war ended before the monsoon did. May was in the communications centre with Sadie when she heard the news. The tin roof was exploding with the thundering downpour and the sergeant had to turn up the wireless and call for quiet. They gathered round the set, listening intently to the tinny voice which came through, announcing that the Americans had dropped an atomic bomb on Hiroshima in Japan and that the Japanese had surrendered.

'What's an atomic bomb?' Sadie asked.

And as the sergeant turned off the set, she replied, 'Imagine a million heavy explosives, land-mines, doodlebugs, V-2s, artillery shells, then times that by a million . . . get the idea?'

As the news sank in some people cheered and ran out into the compound, while Sadie and some of the other girls formed a Conga line, singing as they snaked out of the door. But May sat immobile as tears began to trickle down her cheeks. Others might take them for tears of happiness if they wanted to, but now that the long years of war were over, she found she could not rejoice at the destruction of someone's world. All May could think of were the homes – all those Japanese homes, flattened, crushed, reduced to ashes, just like her own.

The war might be over, but of course she wasn't going home. They were sending her to Singapore. Doug insisted that she come over to the airbase to say goodbye and she supposed she owed it to him. After all, he had helped give her that lifeline of hope, which had kept her going over the past weeks, but now she was leaving Chittagong, she felt it slipping through her fingers. Soon she would be adrift again, and she had to admit it had been a long way to come for such a slender promise.

She took one of the lethal three-wheeled taxis out to the base, where Doug met her at the gates.

As they made their way to the servicemen's club they passed rows of American bombers and British fighter planes. The camp was still full of airmen of all nationalities.

'It looks busy as ever. Why won't they just demob you?'

'The British Empire still has a lot of tidying up to do in Malaya before any of us get out! The only way you get a fast ticket home is if you're ex-POW or come down with malaria.'

After lunch Doug took her on a tour of the place and she saw the bamboo huts, with open sides, which she recognized from photos Bill had sent her. She saw the wooden bunks, swathed in mosquito nets.

'Oh, I recognize those huts. Bill used to hate the mozzie nets, couldn't sleep at all! Said as you turn over you get caught up in the bloody things and he'd rather get malaria!' she said, with a half-smile of reminiscence.

Doug looked at her for a long moment. 'You're still in love with him, aren't you, May?'

She blushed.

'You don't have to say anything, and I know I've got no chance. But, May, I want you to know there's been no one for me, not since I made a mess of things back in Essex. If you could ever forgive me . . . well, I'd like another go at it.'

Now it was his turn to blush. His eager big-boned face was deadly serious, though, and she felt a pang of utter hopelessness. She would rather stay in love with Bill, in this world or the next, than launch out into the unknown with Doug. Perhaps it was a decision she'd regret. Perhaps that was how life was supposed to be – you let go the dream in order to grasp the reality. But she couldn't do it.

'I'm sorry, Doug,' she said gently. 'I do forgive you. It's not because of what happened back then. I just can't let him go . . .'

Singapore was like a transit camp for the whole world. It was as if someone had shaken up all the military personnel in South East Asia and thrown them down in a heap on the island, where they were being shuffled around until they could find their rightful place again. Everyone seemed to be waiting. British and Commonwealth troops were in makeshift barracks and billets, waiting with their demob numbers until a ship became available to take them home. Australians and New Zealanders were flying out, as were the GIs. The wounded in Red Cross centres and hospitals were convalescing until they were declared fit. But it was the POWs fit enough to travel who were ushered out first. One leave day, May and a group of signals girls went to the harbour to see the allied fleet of ships that had amassed there. They stood back letting a pathetic line of POWs, liberated from the island's Changi Jail, troop past them. They were dressed in new uniforms, clean-shaven, trying to hold themselves erect and proud, but there was no disguising the gaunt skeletal frames beneath the khaki. They all looked so old to May and yet she knew that many of the wizened faces belonged to young men the same age as Bill. She searched every face for his and when the girls wanted to move on to a nearby café frequented by GIs, she made an excuse that she wasn't feeling well. When they were gone, she stood in the same spot, till the whole column of POWs had passed and she was absolutely certain that Bill was not amongst them.

Afterwards, her dreams were full of home. It was always summer in the Southwark Park Road house, as she dreamed of those hot childhood days when her mother would fill the grey tin bath with cold water and let them splash around in the backyard. She dreamed of the chicken run that her father had made and how she'd cried when she realized the connection between her feathered friends and Sunday dinner. Over and over, she dreamed of the kitchen, with the Ascot and boiler, the deal table, scrubbed white. But sometimes the dreams would take her where she didn't want to go. The table would be holding back a ton of rubble from crushing her sister; sometimes she would find herself trying to move a pile of crushed stone and slate with her mother's old soup ladle. She would wake in a cold sweat and find herself longing for the old familiar comfort of that place, which no longer existed. And then she would get up and look into a sky filled with foreign constellations, and wonder if there was anywhere on earth she could still call home.

She should have known the army's ways by now. Only two months after her posting to Singapore she was given her demob number and had joined the displaced souls all over the island in the long wait for a ship. Her sergeant pulled all sorts of strings to get the signals girls on the same troopship home, but some POWs had to be squeezed on board at the last moment and May had to wait for another berth. So it was she found herself, and a few other ATS stragglers, squeezed aboard a hospital ship taking home a large number of refugees and wounded. Rather than spend the entire voyage kicking her heels, she decided to volunteer to help out the Red Cross nurses. She made beds, emptied bedpans, and even learned how to change bandages after a little training.

She'd received a stack of letters just before embarking and tried to adjust to the idea of a world that was fast moving on from war in Europe. Peggy had decided to keep the nursery going and her mother had come back to Bermondsey to live in Fort Road with her. Pat had returned to Angelcote with Mark and they were now living with the major.

May was pleased for them all; they were already inhabiting a future she was frightened to imagine, because for her, it would be a future without Bill.

In Singapore she'd experienced a curious sort of loneliness. The place was full of people, yet sometimes she felt locked in a solitary prison of invisible, impenetrable walls. Sometimes she would go dancing with the girls, dance with young men, just for the illusion of not being alone, but always she'd come back to that prison. Like a street mime artist she'd once seen on Tower Hill, she put out her hand and touched those invisible walls and wondered how they could be so strong.

The ship made a stop at Ceylon, taking on fuel and a contingent of ex-prisoners from Singapore's Changi Jail. One of the Red Cross nurses explained to May that these were the prisoners who'd been too weak to make the journey home when they'd been released and had been sent first to a convalescent hospital in Ceylon. Two months of very careful feeding and supervised exercise had put on the required weight and muscle strength necessary to continue their journey.

'Mind you, they'll still be all skin and bone,' the nurse said to May. 'Some of them were only four stone when they got here! You can make yourself useful later on with the meals. They can't have the same as everyone else, they've got baby-sized stomachs and a roast dinner will kill them! So we'll go to the galleys and sort out their food, and then we'll have to serve them. Are you OK to help out with that?'

May nodded. 'Of course – you know I don't mind what I do.'

And the nurse patted her hand. 'You're a good girl, and you're right to keep busy. I lost someone myself – it's why I joined the Red Cross. You feel like you're helping the one you loved . . . don't you?'

May shouldn't have been surprised. She was a soldier in a different sort of army now, the legions of those who had lost someone. It doesn't take a genius to spot us, May thought ruefully, though the little sweetheart badge with the angel wings and photo of Bill that she still wore close to her heart might have given her nursing friend a clue.

After they had toiled in a corner of the stifling galley, they served tiny meals to the newly arrived men, who, whatever their depleted physical state, had carried aboard with them a universal brimming humour which seemed to proclaim how sweet life was when there were three certain, if small, meals a day and a lifetime of tomorrows ahead. May had never, not in any pub or dance hall, been in such jolly company as these poor emaciated men, with their malaria and fevers and all their painful memories. It made her feel ashamed of her own self-pity. So when the mess deck was cleared and someone suggested an impromptu concert, she was happy to join in. With two of the weaker men supported on either arm, they walked slowly along the corridor to the rec room. A little band had already been formed in the convalescent hospital in Ceylon and now the musicians found their places. While May was settling her two charges into some chairs near the door, the band struck up.

Why did they have to be playing that song? It was normal, she told herself, there would be all sorts of reminders of the life that might have been hers. But this was the one guaranteed to shake her foundations. The band's crooner reached the verse '*I'm looking for an angel, to sing my love song to, and until the day that one comes along, I'll sing my song to you.*'

And all May's hope seemed to melt away. She turned round and walked out of the room with tears stinging her eyes.

Next morning she dragged herself out of her hammock after a sleepless night. Her hand felt the damp canvas and she felt ashamed of the tears that had soaked it. She only had to walk up on to the decks to see hundreds worse off than her. These men had been robbed not only of years and youth, but dignity and humanity too. But they were alive, and she knew it was only hope that had kept these ones from dying, like so many of their fellow prisoners.

She told herself to buck up and after a morning spent answering letters, she went to see what the nursing sister had for her to do that afternoon.

'The weaker cases are taking the air up on deck. Could you go up and help give them a spin in their wheelchairs?'

The nurse gave her instructions where to find the invalids, and after walking the length of the ship she found them near the prow. A small area had been set aside for the convalescents, with an awning to shade them from the heat of the day. Some were lying in daybeds; others were in wheelchairs. As she came to the first daybed, the man raised a bony hand and gave her a toothless grin. May smiled at him. She couldn't imagine how thin he'd been when he arrived, if this was what he looked like after two months' feeding up.

'I'm looking for the men in wheelchairs,' she told him.

'Are you indeed, lucky beggars!' he said, and pointed with his thumb further along the deck.

The unruffled sea shone like a brass plate under a full sun. Almost blinded, she had to squint against its brightness, feeling her way along the handrail. Some Red Cross nurses had already set off with their charges on a perambulation of the top deck. A small welcome breeze lifted her hair and suddenly she felt the fine hairs along her arms rising. She stopped in front of a young man, who sat in his wheelchair, eyes closed, head tilted back to catch the sun. A stillness came over her, just as she'd felt on the predictor, before setting the fuse, or when she'd lain alone in the fairy ring, imagining herself outside of space and time.

The young man must have sensed her presence, for he opened his eyes. Looking into the sun and shielding them against the glare, he asked, 'Are you looking for someone?'

'I'm looking for you,' she whispered and kneeled down so that he could see her.

In the instant their eyes met, the past three years disappeared. She cupped his hollow-cheeked face with her hands, and he leaned forward, a look of wonder on his face.

'May? But how . . .'

She drew the sharp-boned, thin-skinned face towards her, and kissed him gently, almost fearful that he might break. The full lips she remembered were thinner now and as she closed her eyes, one hand moved to the back of his fragile neck, down his bony spine, across wing-like shoulder blades. There was so little left of him, he was barely here. But when she opened her eyes and looked again into his sea-blue eyes, brimming with tears, she saw him come back to her.

'Bill!' she whispered into his mouth and held him as tightly as she dared. 'I've been looking for you for so long.'

Drawing back, he lifted the little sweetheart brooch with the angel's wings, which she wore at her breast. 'And I've been looking for you forever – my angel.'

Then clinging to each other, like two castaways who had found each other in a wide, lonely ocean, they wept tears of joy.

She felt Bill's arms and legs trembling with the effort, as he tried to rise to his feet.

'You're too weak, Bill,' she said, with a hand on his chest.

'I've imagined this moment for so long, May, but I never saw myself in a wheelchair. I'm getting up.'

He leaned on her arm and walked beside her on stick-thin legs, keeping himself upright by willpower alone, until they had found some privacy in the lea of a lifeboat. There, with only the Indian Ocean to witness them, they held and kissed each other until the sun sank below the horizon and the night enfolded them in its star-filled brilliance.

CHAPTER 33

THE WORLD THAT WAS OURS

November 1945–January 1946

To find Bill again had been miracle enough, but now they had each other all to themselves in this floating bubble, with no demands upon them, other than that Bill should follow the Red Cross nurses' strict orders to rest and eat at the designated times. And so their days were filled with nothing other than falling in love again. The hospital ship became their new fairy ring.

Bill refused to return to his wheelchair and May walked with him, still leaning on her arm, every day a little further round the decks. As they walked, they talked themselves hoarse. May waited until the second day to ask how he'd come to be captured.

'Didn't the RAF tell you anything?'

'Not a thing, Bill, just sent a telegram, saying you were missing in action. We didn't even know if you were alive or . . .' Her voice broke, and he put his arm round her.

'But you still came looking for me.'

'I never gave up! But it was hard, not knowing. I didn't find out anything at all until I got posted to Chittagong. Then I met your pal, Colin.'

'Colin! Bloody hell, he got back? Oh my God, I thought he'd copped it in the jungle. But how did you find him?'

'Strangely enough that Canadian I used to know, Doug. He was based in Chittagong and he did some digging around for me . . .'

'Well, sod me if he didn't jump into my shoes as soon as I couldn't be there to give him a right-hander!'

She laughed. 'Don't be jealous – he was only trying to help . . . He felt guilty, to tell you the truth. I didn't see much of him at all. He was too busy flying sorties across the border.'

'Well, he was doing a good job, so I won't go on about him,' Bill said, chastened. 'And what did old Col have to say about the skirmish?'

May told him the little she knew. 'He said you were separated after the Japs attacked the airfield, and that he wanted to go back for you but your sergeant said they had to push on.'

'It was the right thing to do, probably saved their lives. I got nicked in the leg by a stray bullet – the Japs sprayed every inch of jungle and I was just the unlucky one. But I didn't give myself up, May. I tried to get back . . . for you.'

She drew him in closer to her. 'You must have been terrified, Bill.'

'It wasn't so bad in the day, but the jungle at

night . . .' He shuddered. 'On that first day, after I lost track of the lads, I pushed on through the jungle. I had my pack, a compass and a silk map, walked to where I thought the rendezvous point was and when I got there – nothing. The boys were long gone. So I spent the first night trying to sleep up a bloody tree. Tied myself in. On the second day I met a young Burmese boy on the track. He took me to his village. They were good to me, May. Put some poultice on the leg and fed me rice, though they had sod all to eat themselves. I thought I could make it to the Indian border on my own, but the headman said no, go to the next village and they'll give you more food. So the boy took me, but the Japs had got there first. It was full of 'em! So that was me, darling, shipped off to Changi Jail. Really, I should count myself lucky. It wasn't the worst place to be, not according to the stories I've heard about other camps.'

May stared incredulously at him. 'Bill! How can you say you're lucky? You were half dead when you came out!'

He shook his head. 'You think I was bad. Some of the blokes in that hospital had been up on the Burma railway, slave labour. Compared to that . . . well, at least we got rice every day, if only a sock full. But that, and dreaming about holding you again, kept me alive.'

'Did you get my letters?' she asked, realizing that she'd been asking most of the questions.

'Not after I went into Changi, no.' His voice

was sad. 'A letter from you . . . well, that would have been like every Christmas rolled into one. I drove myself mad wondering how you were.'

'Can you remember what my last letter said?'

'I got a bundle of them, would have been just before I went across to set up the airstrip in Burma. Took them with me to keep me going. May, I got the one about your dad. I'm so sorry I wasn't there, darling. That was the worst thing in Changi, not being able to let you know how much I was thinking of you.'

'I knew you were thinking of me, Bill. Sometimes I even thought I heard you, when I'd go to our fairy ring and write my letters to you.'

'It *was* me! Don't tell anyone, they'd think I was bonkers, but one day, about six months after I got captured, I woke up in the jail and I thought, it's spring in Hainault Forest! And I stared into the bamboo roof of the hut, and I could have sworn I was looking up into our tree, bright green leaves, English green, not jungle green, and there was a great big wood pigeon fluttering around in the branches. And I called out in my mind and I told you that I was still alive.'

'I *knew* it was you!' she said.

Then, for the thousandth time, he said, 'To think you're actually here!'

'Do you want to pinch me, see if I'm real?'

'I'd rather kiss you, then I'd really be certain.' But their kisses were mostly saved for the night time, when they'd sit near the ship's prow, watching the sun go down, telling each other stories and reclaiming the life that had been lost to the war.

It was almost as if they were courting again, though the venue was more exotic than Gant's Hill Odeon. A couple of times a week there was a film show; out-of-date films mostly, but that was half the fun for May and Bill, reliving their first shy kisses at the back of the cinema, while missing half the action in *Now Voyager*. There were dances and, as Bill grew stronger, they even got their first long-dreamed of waltz together.

They were allowed to disembark at Port Said, and May made Bill laugh with her story of the Egyptian fisherman's bare backside protruding over the dhow, her first introduction to Egypt. While the ship took on fuel, the POWs were sent to a depot on the quay to be fitted out with new winter uniforms. When he came out in his RAF blue, and took her arm, she felt as if she'd come home. They might be in Egypt but the feeling was as comforting and familiar as if they were in Southwark Park Road. It brought to mind the strange message which Peggy had sworn her dad sent her while she was beneath the ruins of their home: 'Tell May,' he'd said, 'the further you fly, the nearer you get to home.'

She'd certainly travelled far, but it was only now that she understood it. Bill was her home.

Though the war might have finished with May, life had not. For after they entered the Mediterranean, the elements rose up against them, as if to show her that war was not the only challenge she would face in her life. Rain spattered the grey-painted deck as they took their evening walk around the ship. Soon the pale bulkheads were black with rising sea spray and rain. The deck beneath their feet became slippery and the wind rose, so that Bill had to shout. 'Better go below, it's getting rough!'

But the storm broke just as they turned back. Up till now their voyage had seen nothing but calm seas and smooth sailing. Within minutes the waves began to run higher than she'd ever seen them and the wind stung May's face, as it came at them with a force that found her battling hard to stay upright.

Bill grabbed her round the waist and gripped a stanchion as the ship lunged into the trough of a massive wave. She knew that she should be terrified, but the roiling sea felt almost benign, compared to the high explosives and missiles she'd faced over the past six years. There was no evil intent behind this danger – it was just life, the elements, and May felt almost exhilarated. But Bill was not so strong as she, and lost his footing. His frame was still light enough to be sluiced along the deck and he grappled for a handhold while she made a grab for him, as another even higher wave crashed over the bow. Her wet hand clung to his for an instant, but then the boat heaved, sending her sprawling along with Bill, down the deck, which was now at an alarmingly steep angle. As they slid towards the deck edge she caught the tail of his RAF tunic and threw herself across him, rolling herself round him as if they were a magic carpet, until they reached the safety of the bulkhead. She braced her feet against a locker and they clasped each other, unable to get up, unable to escape the lashing of the storm.

'I'm not losing you again!' she shouted into his ear and the howling wind whipped away her words. But she knew he had heard them, for blue lips parted and he answered, 'Never!'

But as the boat took another dive into the heart of a wave, the jarring onslaught slammed her head back against the steel bulkhead and she felt her grip loosen. She began to slip away from him.

Pain. When she awoke, it was as if a red-hot darning needle had been inserted into her right temple and some unseen hand was patiently working it through to the other temple. An evil seamstress was sewing one side of her head to the other. But she knew that couldn't be right. More pain. She let out a yelp as she tried to uncurl a leg, which for some reason was twisted beneath her and bolted to the deck by an icicle. No. She shook her head to clear her mind and wished she hadn't as a thousand stars exploded behind her eyes. Everywhere else was pitch-black. It was better to stay perfectly still. Then she remembered Bill.

She ignored the burning gimlet and the freezing icicle, and forced herself to her knees. Whimpering with pain, she felt her way forward along the chill, hard surface, and, sweeping her hands in a double arc around her, edging into the blackness, she called his name.

'Bill! Bill! Are you there?'

Now she remembered. The storm. The two of them rolled together, clinging on for dear life, and she'd let him slip away. No! She wouldn't have it. She thought her leg must be broken, for it gave way as she tried to put weight on it. Instead, with the ridged metal of the deck grating her knees, she pulled herself inch by inch towards the dim light of a cabin window. A fine rain was still visible in the glow, but the wind had dropped. Now she called again.

'Help! Anybody, help me.'

She was alone. How could she have let him slip away again! He must have gone overboard, otherwise he would be here, by her side. She groaned and lay down, with her cheek crushed against the deck, giving into its cold kiss. Gradually she felt herself letting Bill go. 'We weren't meant to be,' she said softly to herself. 'Granny Byron knew it would come to this: she said I would cross water and she said there'd be two men in uniform . . .' And though May wracked her burning brain, she couldn't remember if her grandmother had ever promised she would marry either of them.

She didn't know how long she'd been lying

there. It might have been hours; it might have been days. But just as she felt ready to sleep forever, she suddenly felt herself being lifted up. Arms slipped beneath her and she felt the warmth of another body.

'I'm here, darling, I've got you.'

She wished she could remember what Granny Byron had predicted. Aware that her mind was fuzzy and her speech slurred, she said, 'Am I meant to marry you?' and she heard a laugh, close against her cheek, as he staggered with her towards the cabin light.

'You are definitely meant to marry me!'

Only later did May discover that Bill had nearly gone overboard with the last big wave, but, managing to grab a rope on a lifeboat cover, he had hauled himself back along the deck to her. How he had found the strength she would never know, but it seemed the risk of losing her again had helped him find an energy he didn't realize he had. After a week in the infirmary recovering from hypothermia, and a severe sprain for May, Bill pressed the point.

'May, I don't think we should wait,' he told her, as they left the infirmary together.

'Mum will go up the wall, you do know that, don't you?' she said.

'I'll take the blame,' Bill said. 'Besides, you told me there's nothing left of Dockhead Church, so we couldn't get married there anyway!'

'There's a hut in the convent grounds . . .'

Bill put his hand over hers, which was linked through his arm. 'We'll have a blessing in the hut then,' he said firmly. 'But I am not getting off this ship until we're married.' He hesitated an instant. 'That's if you're sure you want me.'

She looked up at him with a straight face. 'What do you think I came halfway round the world for?'

He threw back his head and laughed. His bronzed face had already filled out; he was almost her old Bill again.

Three days before Christmas 1945, within sight of the North African coast, May and Bill were married by the captain and spent their honeymoon cruising back to Liverpool. May made sure they were on deck to see the coast of England come into view. She would have to disembark with the ATS girls, and he with the RAF boys, but for now she was content to have him close by, his arm touching hers, leaning upon the ship's rail. As the distant docks came closer, she could see the waiting crowd lining the quayside, the bunting fluttering and strains of a military band striking up. She gripped his arm and, resting her head on his shoulder, felt that there couldn't be enough days ahead to contain her happiness.

But the procedure for getting out of the services wasn't as swift as May had hoped. Almost as soon as the vessel berthed, they were separated. Bill trooped down the gangplank with the other ex-POWs and the wounded, who were the first to leave the ship, and May watched anxiously to see where he was taken. Bill had been warned he'd have to undergo a medical to make sure he was fit enough to travel, then stay overnight in a transit camp. So they'd made arrangements to meet up the next morning at the train station. When May walked off the ship with the other ATS girls, she felt like royalty. Cheering crowds welcomed them and complete strangers clapped her on the back as they passed along the dockside. England smelled so different. She had grown used to fresh, salty air and before that the spice-rich thicker scent of the Far East. Now she drew in a deep breath of cold English December air. Moisture-laden fog, mixed with burnt coke and smoke from berthed vessels, stung her nostrils. She let herself be shepherded to a waiting lorry, and looked out at a misty Liverpool morning. The colours seemed muted, after the vibrant palette of Singapore and the Med. They drove through streets of dun brick and grey stone, and tracts of ruined ground, until they arrived at the army barracks. There was little ceremony to mark her nearly five years' service. A lance corporal stamped her paybook and doled out money owed from a tin on the counter. She was issued with a travel warrant and clothing coupons, then shown to the barracks in the transit camp. She could hardly believe that tonight would be her last as a soldier, and she had to admit that she felt more at sea today than she had on all the oceans she'd sailed through. How could Liverpool seem more alien to her than the Indian Ocean, the Red Sea or the storm-tossed Mediterranean?

'What do you mean, you're staying at the Gilbies? Peggy's made you up a bed in my room.'

She had barely extricated herself from her mother's welcoming embrace when the consequences of her impetuous seaboard marriage hit home to May. She and Bill went first to St James's Road to break the news to the Gilbies. They were overjoyed, not just to have their son back, but to be given the added bonus of a daughter. May doubted her own mother's reaction would be as easygoing.

'Well, Mum,' she said, looking to Bill for support and noting that he hung back at the kitchen door. She put out her hand and he took it, giving her an encouraging squeeze. 'We've got some good news!' She felt a flush rising to her cheeks. 'We're married!'

'You're what?'

'Married. We couldn't wait, could we, Bill?'

Bill seemed to have lost all his bravado. He'd been ridiculously proud of being a married man. He'd fought through a war, survived horrific privations at the hands of cruel captors, and yet the thing he felt most proud of was marrying May. She pulled him in closer.

'We did it on board ship . . .'

Her mother and Peggy had similar open-mouthed expressions on their faces.

624

'It's all legal,' she said.

'Well, sod me. You've gone and got married without me.'

Her mother sat back in the chair and crossed her arms in uncompromising disapproval. May glanced at Peggy. Surely her sister would come to her rescue.

'You could have waited – I wanted to be your bridesmaid!' Peggy said.

Considering she'd rescued her sister from ten tons of rubble, May thought she'd at least be on her side.

'We're having a blessing at Dockhead Church, though,' she added, looking from one to the other. 'So the family can celebrate.'

'You'll be lucky, it's flattened,' her mother said, straight-faced.

'I know that. We'll have it in the hut in the convent grounds.'

'Lovely. If it wasn't enough your sister's a divorced woman, I've got you coming home not married in the eyes of the Church.'

It was an odd fact, which May was beginning to realize since she'd been home, that the things which upset people nowadays seemed so trivial, compared to the trials of the past six years. Perhaps the old May would have swallowed it.

'Can't you just be glad I've got Bill back in one piece? And, in case you hadn't noticed, I've come home without a scratch too. After all we've been through, Mum, don't you think it's time to be grateful just to be *alive*. And if I can be happy, married to Bill by a captain instead of a priest, then I think you ought to be as well!'

Her mother was dumbstruck. Little home-bird May was showing the tips of her talons. But her retort had at least brought Peggy to her senses.

'May's right, Mum. I should know. What wouldn't I give to have my Harry walking back through that door.'

May looked at her sister's face, which wasn't that of a young woman any more. She wanted to weep. She had delayed her own marriage, waiting for Peggy to recover. But now May realized that though she would make a life for herself and Harry's children, Peggy would never recover. She went to her sister and held her tight.

'I'm sorry, Peg.'

Peggy wiped the corner of her eye. 'Shhh. Don't be. I'm happy you two found each other out there. Miracles really do happen, don't they?'

There was no more carping from Mrs Lloyd, who had joined in her daughters' embrace, and it was settled that until they had their own home, May and Bill would live at the Gilbies', sleeping in Bill's old bedroom, which Mrs Gilbie had made into a little bedsitting room for them.

After Peggy had seen them off, May said, 'I suppose the sooner we can find somewhere of our own the better.'

'It's not going to be easy – half the houses have gone!'

'And if they haven't gone they've got bomb damage.'

It was the one thing that had struck May on her return to Bermondsey. There simply wasn't an undamaged house, church, school or factory. On every street were whole tracts of cleared land, places that she'd grown up in, obliterated or damaged beyond repair.

'Shall we have a walk down to your old house?'

May was silent for a long moment. 'It's not there, Bill.'

'I know. I meant, well . . . Let's just walk along Southwark Park Road, see what's gone.'

It seemed a strange pilgrimage. 'How can you see what's gone?' She knew she was being awkward, but why was he making her face it? 'All right, darling, if you want to.'

They cut through Thorburn Square on their way to the Blue. The three-storey Victorian houses were largely undamaged, and the missing railings from the churchyard were the most it had suffered. May cheered up.

'At least there's one place in Bermondsey that hasn't changed much! Don't you think this would be a nice place to live, Bill?' she said as they rounded the square, looking over the area walls and down into basement flats. Most of the houses, which had once belonged to the more prosperous Victorian residents, were now occupied by two or three families, with the basements the cheapest to rent.

'Anywhere'd be nice to live, so long as you're there,' he said, slipping his arm round her waist.

They turned into Southwark Park Road and Bill pointed out a whole row of bombed-out houses.

'Wonder how long it'll take them to get all that cleared? I used to imagine, when I was in Changi, I'd come back and all this would be rebuilt! Stupid dreams you have, when you don't know what's going on back home.'

Half the shops in the Blue still had hoardings covering broken windows, and there were still empty, burned-out shells waiting to be demolished. Then they came to the remains of the John Bull pub, with the arch beyond, and May hung back.

'Don't you want to?' Bill asked.

'No, no, I'll be all right. I can't live in Bermondsey and never go under one arch or another.'

'No, but this one is the hardest, I know.'

Now she knew why he had insisted. This wasn't a walk down memory lane. He wanted to lay to rest all the demons that might come back to haunt her now that she was home.

She took in a deep breath and walked under the arch. Just then a train passed overhead, rumbling like a distant explosion. If this was a test, she was determined to pass it. She carried on walking, and once out the other side, quickened her pace. They passed Raymouth Road, half gone courtesy of a doodlebug, and before long they came to the flattened row of houses that had once been May's home. They stood silently, as evening came on. The cleared bomb site had been fenced about with hoardings. There was nothing to see.

'It's all right, Bill,' she said. 'It's going to be all right.'

And they turned and walked back to St James's Road.

But their final visit had to be to the oracle, her Granny Byron. Next day they went to Dix's Place.

'Do you think your nan will be surprised we're married?' Bill asked and May snorted.

'Nothing surprises that woman. I swear she foretold it all before I'd even signed up. Knew about you . . . and Doug! Knew I'd go overseas.'

'Do you really believe all that?'

'All I know is that she gets a lot right!'

As they walked arm in arm up Grange Road, they stopped outside what was left of Garner's, just a single storey.

'Well, at least they kept working all through the war,' May said, and Bill looked doubtful.

'It's not what it was, though, is it?'

Nothing was what it once was, May thought, and perhaps that was as it should be.

Her grandmother, however, was the one fixed point in the ever-changing world. She showed them into the smoke-yellow kitchen where Troubles the dog, still unburdened by any of his own, greeted them with wagging tail and bright eyes. After making them tea, Granny Byron sat puffing on the old clay pipe, while May told her about finding Bill and their marriage aboard ship.

'As God's my judge, didn't I tell you? Didn't I?' Granny Byron sucked in a lungful of smoke.

'Still not given that up?' May asked hopelessly.

'It's me comfort,' her grandmother said, 'and gawd knows I need it, what with him running up the stairs to see Jack Ketch!'

Bill looked at her for enlightenment but it took some deciphering, even for her. She took the 'he' to be her grandfather, and Jack Ketch she knew from childhood warnings was the hangman all naughty children were heading for.

'What's Granddad done now?' she asked, stirring the tea and adding more milk to the mahogany brew.

'They're *sayin'* he's had that Ronnie Riley topped. They found him floating in the river up by Cherry Garden Pier.'

May choked on her tea and poor Bill looked as if he was considering whether he'd married into the wrong family.

'No! He wouldn't do that, Nan. He's just a tea leaf, he's not a . . . anything worse!'

'I'm not saying he is. I think that Wide'oh knows something.'

'Peggy's George? What's he got to do with it?'

Her grandmother tapped the pipe on to the grate and sat back, arms folded.

'Granddad found out it was Ronnie Riley stole your poor brother's wallet and papers, while he was layin' in the street half dead. He went up the wall, May. To think Ronnie would let us go through all that heartache looking for our Jack. Three days of it . . . if he'd had his papers we'd have found 'im, wouldn't we? Well, your granddad walked out of here . . . I won't say he did it himself, but I looked at the leaves after he'd gone and I saw death, as God's my judge, I did.'

There was a long silence and May was aware of Bill pulling at his collar.

'You don't think George was in on it, that he knew about Ronnie . . . all the time we were looking for Jack?'

Granny Byron shook her head, so the gold earrings swung.

'Nah, he's got his faults, but Wide'oh wouldn't do that to one of his own. Not that he's blameless. Granddad found out why our Jack was out in that raid in the first place – doin' a favour for Wide'oh, got it all written down in his little book. Paid Jack ten bob to deliver a parcel . . .'

May felt suddenly sick, letting the truth of Jack's final hour sink in. All the times she'd puzzled over what had kept her brother out in that raid and the answer had been there all along. Wide'oh.

'Still, once your granddad told Wide'oh what Ronnie done . . .' She paused to tamp down the pipe and gave May a meaningful look.

'Sounds like it'll be George running up the stairs to Jack Ketch then . . .' she said.

Bill's eyes widened and she added quickly, 'Not that I think he'd have done anything like that . . . of course I don't.'

And Bill looked relieved.

⋆   ⋆   ⋆

After that, May and Bill took several more walks around Bermondsey, retracing their old haunts, taking inventory of the world that had once been theirs and was no longer. And on the day before their marriage blessing, coming back from talking with the priest in the makeshift chapel at Dockhead, they both, without even asking each other, turned towards the river. It was a bright January day, sparkling with frost. Snow had fallen the night before and their feet crunched as they walked along Shad Thames, towards the street where they had first found little Jack. Apart from the structural damage, another noticeable effect of the war years was that the streets of Bermondsey were half empty. Bill had read that a third of its population simply hadn't returned. Either dead or displaced, whatever the cause, the result was a sometimes ghostly, deserted air, especially in the back streets down by the river.

Now not a soul was there to witness as they searched out the site of the ancient narrow house where they'd found baby Jack in his dead mother's arms.

They walked the entire length of the street.

'I think it was here,' Bill said finally.

'But wasn't there a pub next door? And I'm sure there was a warehouse the other side?'

'Both gone,' Bill said, taking her hand.

The only memorial to their encounter would be the memory they carried with them. There was certainly nothing left in the physical world to remind them.